MAYAN CALENDAR GIRLS

By

Linton Robinson, Grayson Moran

and

Team 2012

MAYAN CALENDAR GIRLS

By

Linton Robinson, Grayson Moran

and

Team 2012

Copyright © 2011 Linton Robinson, Grayson Moran, and Team 2012

Library of Congress Cataloging-in-Publication Data

Robinson, Linton
Mayan Calendar Girls

p.cm

1. Literature – Mexico. 2. Mexico – Fiction.

ISBN 13: 978-1-936955-00-8

www.mayancalendargirls.com

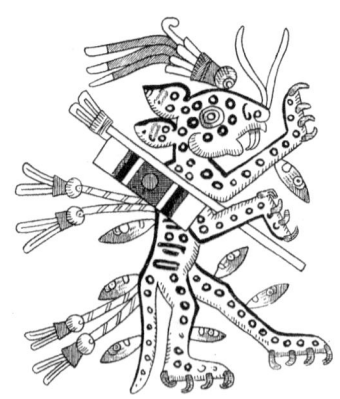

Bäuu Press
Winter Park, Colorado
http://www.bauuinstitute.com

CHAPTERS

1	Final Offering		178	Shout Outs
3	Stone Temple Harlot		182	Loose Ends
5	The Jetsam Set		185	Team Tranquility
9	Crystal Skullduggery		189	Minor Distinctions
12	Venus on the Half Soul		193	Teaching Tolerance
14	Mayan Lego		198	Ulama Rama Ding Dong
17	Tete a Tete		201	Bung Fu
19	End of Days Runner		206	House Call
22	Rivalry Revelry		210	Pique A Boo
25	Another Roadside Distraction		213	After You
28	Hocus P.O.T.U.S.		217	Inverse Proportions
32	Hospitality Sweet		221	Shop Talk
35	Zine Chat		225	Coaster Breaks
40	The On-Rock Cafe		229	Catching Her Drift
44	Pater Nostra		231	Halfway Measures
48	Sign: Sealed, Delivered		235	Secret Asian Man
51	Great Balls-Of Fire		239	Second Largest Dragstrip
53	Rapture of the Heights		242	Sins of the Fathers
58	Retroactive Privatization		246	Hair To Eternity
63	Nude Awakening		251	Parallel Curves
66	Can Soooo Do That		254	Highs in Mid-Forties
68	Rafter Dance		256	Means of Production
72	Doods, Junior Grade		260	Cherchez La Blonde
74	She Sleeps With The Fishes		266	Double Over Time
79	Sha Zama		269	Wide Tracking
83	Stand Up Guy		272	Medium is the Massage
86	One if by Land, Two if by Sea		275	Floating World
91	Getting Her Ass In Gear		281	Entourage
96	CosmiComics		284	Sins of the Mother
100	Strip The Light Fantastic		288	Cult Following
104	Helping Hand		291	Chopper Mama
107	Ennui on $360 a Day		294	Urge to Converge
111	Skeleton Crew		300	Lodge Brothers
115	Headhunter		302	Dream On
118	Telempathy		304	Les Folies Blancaneaux
122	Narrowing Gyre		308	Les Folies-Deux
125	Deeds of Doods		314	Les Folies-Trois
129	Flip Side		319	Rub A Dub Dub
131	Club Meds		324	Climatc of Climax
134	Divers Ed.		329	The Morning After Shill
138	The Come-Down		333	Transport From Paradise
142	After Math		337	The Road Again
145	Scattered Showers		341	Homecoming Queens
150	La Isla Bonita		345	Final Paperwork
155	Raiders of The Lost Chance		346	Latent Images
158	Close... But		349	Revolting Developments
162	Ms. the Boat		356	Don't Stoop to Concur
166	Badger Game		358	Lady Bee Good
168	Drumming Up Business		360	Call Waiting
171	Who Let the Dolphs Out?		361	The End of the Beginning
175	Rood Dood		362	Footnotes & Glossary

FINAL OFFERING

Her hair was a foreign banner on ancient Mesoamerican soil, waving long and lustrous under the late sun and flaring golden against the rough black stone. Her head lolled back over the edge of the Nohoc Mul pyramid,[1] giving Curtsy a superb upside-down view from atop the 140 foot structure. Though she was distracted to an extent by the series of powerful orgasms blitzing through her inverted skull and glorious, twisting body. Spread wide as an eagle and soaring as high, she gripped the corners of the stone slab and ground her groin upwards in frenzied response to the ministrations of Puch Pop, who she thought of as "Pooch" and of what he was doing to her as "screwing the brains out of a blonde, for Christ's sake".

Her legs came up, pointing skyward and quivering alarmingly as her hard, smooth athlete's muscles spasmed. If the tourists had still been down there, some Japanese *sariman* could have taken home photos of the Cobá[2] ruins featuring a vibrating victory sign on top of the tallest pyramid in the Yucatan. Or taped a sudden cry blasting out of her extended, relaxed throat; perhaps interpreting it as territorial monkey cries or the lust call of a jaguar. The sound triggered something very deep in Puch, and he collapsed on her as if shot by an ambusher's arrow. He lay on top of and between her, feeling the continued vibrations, his head pressed against her strong, lovely breasts. He shuddered in his own darkness, listening to the wild thrum of her heart.

"Some Mayan you are," she whispered to him in a slightly shaky voice after an indecent interval. "Aren't you supposed to tear it out while it's still beating? Offer it to the Gods?"

"That's what I've been trying to do," he mumbled into her hot flesh. "Only fair: it's what you do to me."

"Awwww." She spoke lightly, but was actually as moved as she could allow herself to be under the circumstances. She put her hand behind his head, wrapped her legs around him in a tight nether hug. "You're the sweetest guy ever, Pooch. But I just can't... you're going to have to settle for just a mindless blond sex machine."

1

"I can live with that." He lifted his head to smile at her, both of them fully aware it wasn't really true. "But I'd rather live with you."

"Then come with me."

Which they both knew wasn't going to happen. He was bound to the family "homestead" at CroCun, would never go far from it, though he couldn't have said why. It did fine under his parent's management and his little brothers, sisters, and cousins were much more fetching than he was at tossing food to the gators and selling souvenirs, which freed him up to work around the area, earning outside money by guiding tourists around the stone monuments of Cobá and the underwater tunnels of the *cenotes*. And meeting attractive foreign women, an important step in developing his manhood and identity.

Then he'd met the ultimate foreign blond: beautiful in face and feature, body a fine-tuned racing machine, as agile and delighted underwater as he was. The Maya had been the most resistant people in the Americas to the Spanish *conquista*, but the comely Señorita Kurtz had conquered him utterly without even trying. And now she was leaving. He responded to her invitation with silence, and by tightening his embrace.

"It's my dream, Pooch. I gotta go. You know that."

Oh, he knew. But had to give it a shot: would keep trying until he saw her walk off. "Look, I can stop working here at Cobá; we could spend more time diving the *cenotes*..."

"It's not the same and you know it."

"And Enrique said he'll take us out more, do some deeper reefs." That was where he really saw who she was, he thought, even more so than like this, straining her hard softness as he burrowed into her. She was still seriously interested in trying for freediving depth records: the two of them going a hundred yards and deeper, frolicking in the open ocean with their porpoise-tail monofins. Driving down the reef in a scatter of angelfish, blue tang and neon-striped wrasse.

"But I'd be working in tanks and BC's. You know I hate that whole SCUBA thing. Those jerks are all gear queer, want to be submarines. I don't want expeditions, I want to live down there."

"Me, too."

"I know. That's why I like you." She did a quick hip flutter, scrubbing her blonde pubic patch against his thin, black Indian gloss and feeling a little tumescence cranking back up. She smiled at him from inches away: shining glory on him. "But Dolphin Discovery... Come on, Pooch, you know."

He knew. She'd be working with marine mammals, her greatest passion. A passion he couldn't hope to supplant, is the way it was looking.

"I apologize for not being a dolphin or sea lion or something."

She made a sad face and put her hand over his lips. "You're the closest thing I've met, though." She ran her other hand into his lush, coarse hair and started to undulate against him. She'd been right about detecting resumed interest down there. And now he was moving, too. Things would be all right for a little while longer. "And you've got me right here. In your manly arms and on top of the world."

He looked at the stark, brutal architecture of the ruins, the scatter of lakes in the hot green jungle, the slash of road leading north. He kissed her long, deep and hot as he tried once again to move inside her to stay. He moved his lips to her ear and said, "For now."

"Now's all we've got," she said, her voice blurring as she responded to his urgency. "What else does anybody have?"

STONE TEMPLE HARLOT

"The fascinating part of the calendar is what nobody seems to care about. August 13, 3114. Before Christ. Like he had anything to do with it. How many peoples have an opening date?"

Winston was wound up, lolling crossways in his matrimonial-sized *henequen* hammock, tripping his brains out and just dying to share it all. As he usually did, he rocked back and forth in the hammock, each swing bringing the tip of his toe to a bamboo pillar where it could propel his next rock with a mere flick. Every swing slightly flexed the hammock's stanchions, which also supported most of the palm thatch *palapa* that provided shade and shelter on his handbuilt floating island. Seen from the lagoon, the sovereign islet of Winston Bacon pulsed slightly when he was in his hammock, the bamboo walls, palm thatch curtains, and various greenery growing on the roof of the slapdash shack of recycled detritus bouncing lightly on the plastic bottle floatation under its flooring, decks, sand "beach" and various potted shrubs and vines and trees.

"So let's look around the world of the times, where dates are a little sloppier, but more historically sanctified. The first Egyptian dynasty circa 3100, the first Mesopotamian city, Uruk, about the same time, though nobody claims to have found the cornerstone. Kali Yuga in India, 3102. It was a time of beginnings all over the world. And you can trace them through the ages of fire, earth, air and water. And now we're looking at the age of ether, the Fifth Sun, the Age of Center.

"Your people didn't just do things when it looked good. They timed it all out to the stars and Milky Way. Channel islands of the Pleiades, where they claim your people came from. Our system aligns with Alcyone in the Pleiades every fifty-two years, the exact length of the Calendar Round. You're a race of astronauts. Illegal aliens."

For once he wasn't raving to himself, though it's uncertain how often he knew the difference. He was taking this particular info-dump on the girl who squatted naked at the edge of the raft, gazing up into the shaky rafters that managed to hold up the roof mats as well as their festoons of mobiles, strange clothing items, garish souvenirs, drug paraphernalia, and outlandish sex toys. She was quite a sight for anyone who cared to stare instead of blathering about crypto-archeology: breasts as spherical as stone temple houris in India, Chinatown cheekbones, matte skin the color of cinnamon sugar, and sleek black hair so long it brushed the floor every time she shifted her delectable ass (which was the only time it ever got swept).

Her name was Xchab and she was as Mayan as they come: he'd found her selling cheap *Chilango*ware[3] shell jewelry on the beach dressed in a village *huipil*[4], tapestry sash tied around her hips, and about three kilos of braids piled up on her head. Which she considered her working outfit. She'd much rather have worn retro-slut black drag with Doc Martins and a buzzcut because she was a *ponk* at heart—a *ponkita*, actually, since she was emphatically female and drastically underage. But the only outbound ticket that had punched her so far was this old hippie, who liked her to wear her hair down and mostly nothing at all, which was fine with her. Anything to quit being Maya village people.

Although she was entertaining doubts about stranding herself on this crazy raft with this old *pendejo*. What her mother would call *me'ex káak*. What did he do all day? Smoked *mota*, which nobody did but low class losers, and get crazy on *hongos*, which nobody did

4

but psychos and gringos. Well, he was a gringo, more or less. So why did he like that jungle garbage instead of having some *coca* or better yet, "crack"? She had only heard of crack, but lusted for a taste because the name itself just sounded so very, very bad. Which is to say, of course, extremely good.

She stood up smoothly, though she'd been squatting on her heels for over an hour. She gazed at Winston Bacon, ranting on the bed, and shifted her weight just enough to give her pose a sexual tilt. She rocked her head forward, then shook it, her hair slithering around to hang in front of her the way he liked, her nipples staring out as round and black and beckoning as her eyes. She lowered her brow and stared at him from under her silken lashes, wetting her lips slightly. Under her breath, she said, "Winston, why don't you shut up with that nutty *Indio* shit?"

THE JETSAM SET

He wasn't really retarded. Not even a "savant" like some said because it was the only way they could explain somebody so talented in one field not having all the social skills and flashy acumen their own lives had led them to associate with intelligence. The best way to explain Ganzo might be to just realize he marched to a different drummer. A really slow, muted drum with wacko syncopation.

He waded ashore naked, the rip current tugging at his strong brown thighs. He stood stocky and firm, resisting the pull of each receding wave, moving forward as each new one flooded up from behind him. This ebb and flow was something he'd understood before anything he could remember, his ultimate measure.

He'd left his frayed white cotton manta cloth shirt and pants back on the other beach, the one just south of the postcard Tulum ruins where all the cabanas were. Clothes meant nothing to Ganzo. He'd learned you'd better have something over your hose when around other people, but the cabana crowd didn't seem to care. They ran around naked all the time, especially the women. Who Ganzo had learned not to stare at.

He had no way to evaluate these people who paid more for a night in waterfront shacks with no floor, mosquito screen, electricity or running water than he paid for a month in his shed on the restaurant roof. The phrase "pretty Eurotrash stoners with money" would have meant nothing to him. They laughed at him and bought him drinks. And bought his *obritas*. The women wore them. He'd see women so enchanting it stopped his breath and heart, splashing in the surf wearing nothing but a necklace, bracelet or anklet that he'd made at night in his shed, turning shells and coral and native wood and hennequen[5] fiber into something that brought him money, something that could touch that fascinating, forbidden flesh.

Once there was a blond girl with blue eyes who wore one of his necklaces around her waist. She would walk the entire beach every morning, completely naked, but with his necklace—a nice piece of coral with the tunnels bored out with a nail—dangling right in a little thicket of golden hair that shone in the sun. When he finished one of his *obras* now, he held it up and saw it nestled in fine gold threads, displayed on a bed of sunlight.

But they didn't come to this beach. It was a dangerous swim and offered nowhere to sit, no beachfront bars to sell them margaritas and dope. New arrivals would give him drugs when he walked through the bars selling his work. They wanted him to do something funny, say something weird. But they gave up when they learned that drugs had no effect on him. His drum beat on undisturbed, an ebb and flow in fifths and starts, diminished sevenths.

This was "his" beach, the realm where Ganzo was the King of Beachcombers, a fine-toothed comb over the sand and shallows where the waves built teacup beaches amid hollowed stone. He walked right to a little eddy between two shafts of limestone protruding out from the sand and reached down to scoop up a handful of tiny *caracoles*[6], mini-conchs less than a half inch long. Once the mobile homes of tiny mollusks, then of miniature hermit crabs, soon to be darling earrings to be taken back to Italy or Winnipeg and forgotten in a drawer. He sluiced the little calcium spirals in a wave and dropped them into the mesh bag hanging around his waist.

There wasn't much in the way of really useful coral today. He hadn't expected it. You got the best stuff after a big storm stirred the deeps and tossed its findings into the currents. Big blows brought in the real treasures, including *corazon de mono* seed pods, little pucks of hard wood that took on a deep polish when he buffed them with old pantyhose and rubbed them with a little oil from the side of his nose. They looked like a heart, in a rounded way, but even if he'd thought about it he would have had no idea why it would have been a monkey heart.

The storms last November had been fiercer than usual, flattening many of the cabanas and scaring away the hippies for a few weeks. But they had brought him the strangest treasures of all, his *coralcaturas*[7]. They had not been easy to swim over to the main beach, carry to a taxi, then tote up his shed, but they were precious in a way he couldn't fathom, held his attention as much as any naked beauty romping in front of Paraiso or Bocola. He had never shown them to anybody.

The weather had been fair this week, though, and he knew there would be no deep sea gleanings. But there would be other things. Perhaps the skull of a pelican or frigate bird. Boiled, exposed to the merciless tropical sun on his corrugated tarpaper roof, lovingly polished, lightly waxed and mounted in a hardwood shadowbox, they were beautiful mementos and some he'd made graced walls in Mediterranean villas and Heidelberg dormitories.

Or perhaps vertebrae from fish discarded by fishermen. Spinal bones from tarpon or marlin turned into wonderful adornments in Ganzo's instinctive hands. This beach was a sort of sargasso, a place where currents met and cancelled, cooperated to bring him things. If a dead bird fell into the water anywhere in a fan-shaped area of ocean extending out almost sixty miles, the Caribbean currents would beckon it to this beach and to Ganzo's sharp gaze. People marveled at the things the sea laid at his feet, but to Ganzo it was no more miraculous than sipping water or breathing air. He'd found everything from SCUBA gear to a boatful of huddled Cuban refugees on his beach. Nothing he could find here would be a miracle of any kind. Or so he believed before he walked around the last fingers of softened limestone before the beach gave way to the big cliff that tumbled straight into the waves.

Spectacular as his new find was, there was so much sand and seagrass piled up that a beachcomber less experienced and receptive than Ganzo might not even have noticed. But he spotted her foot and calf immediately and stopped to stand in a semi-religious shock. There was a woman washed up on his beach. He could see her leg sticking out from the pile of kelp, could see an outthrust hand rising from the wash of sand... could see a flow of long blonde hair.

He dropped to his knees beside this visitation and began the slow, tectonic shifts of mind that served him on those rare occasions that required thought. It was a naked blond woman with golden skin. White skin burned red in a stripe across her back and on the portion of buttock he could see without moving any sand or seaweed. She wasn't moving.

It took awhile for it to surface, but Ganzo faced the concept of death. This woman must surely be dead. And dead people were trouble. Deaths, even of beautiful women, were not unheard of on the hippie beach and they brought trouble by the carload. Ganzo reached out with glacial slowness, finally placing his hand on the woman's shoulder. It was warm. And beneath the surface, like the submarine currents that rolled and ground huge rocks beneath apparently calm seas, he could feel a throb: dim, muted, syncopated.

He moved then, all the thinking blessedly dealt with and leaving him a grateful slave to the innate movements of his hands. He tossed away seaweed, he moved sand, he splashed water. He excavated a beautiful woman in her mid twenties, muscular and shapely, with lovely proportion even in the slackness of her private sleep. Her hair was a twisting flow of cornsilk... and a curly delta of honeygold fiber. He reached out shyly and pried one eye open. It stared sightless at the sky, a pool of topaz blue. She was breathing, though barely. She was badly bruised and moderately burnt in the areas that most held Ganzo's attention. Her nipples were as pink as the inside of a shell.

He knelt with his head bowed, smitten silent and still by the presence of The Greatest Find Of All Time. Then it became mercifully clear what he would do. Again his hands moved unbidden. His right hand slid under her back, lifting her breasts up towards his face as her head lolled back, trailing gold glory. His left hand went to her thighs and sought the advantage he needed. Then he stood, his strong legs and shoulders hefting her slim frame effortlessly. He paused for a moment, holding her cradled, staring at her and breathing the briny musk of her. Then he walked into the water, clenching his toes for purchase against the pull of the receding waves. Simple enough for even Ganzo to grasp: Finders, keepers.

CRYSTAL SKULLDUGGERY

"**H**e's sitting right here." Blaster patted the round shape under the purple velvet shroud like a father doting on a real comer kid. "Man, I like, so hate to part company with this guy. He's like a member of the family. But you know how it goes?"

Oh, I know how it goes, Bannock thought, looking around the dingy motel room. Not even a Motel 6; more like a Motel 2.3. On a scale of a hundred. Cat smell, dope smell, hippie smell. And the gorgeous girlfriend dressed practically in rags. Yeah, if I was "Blaster", I might part with an incredibly valuable ancient treasure to scrape this lifestyle off my waffle stompers.

Loris was leaning back on the ratty couch, already cutting the cord. Which was a good thing. Sick transit Monday. But she had a few last words on the oXo deal.

"He changed our lives. Seriously." No need for that last word; her solemn brown eyes told all. "He showed us how to live, unsnarled our karma, opened us to The Love."

Wouldn't mind cracking a case of that myself; Bannock eyeing her just enough to let her know it was there if she wanted to nibble. But it's all about business, isn't it? He motioned towards the velvet lump, which somehow dominated a little clearing on top of the grungy, littered coffee table. "So, let's see what we've got here."

Blaster nodded, but Loris gave him a deadpan look and said, "Yeah, let's."

She didn't like anything about this, and this looming, soft-spoken heavy least of all. She couldn't decide if he looked more like a Mob soldier with his callused hands and callous expression, or some ex-military mercenary with his short brush of stiff, steel-gray hair.

Bannock hefted his black ballistic nylon messenger bag and tapped it significantly. "As agreed," he told her, not bothering to address Blaster anymore.

The shaggy dealer wiped his hands across the skidmarks on his hemp pants and reached for the velvet. "Good enough for me."

When he whisked the cloth away even as hard a case as Bannock stalled out for a moment, struck by the presence of oXo.

Criminy, he thought, lotta starglow for a piece of rock.

The quartz skull sat in the same gloom as the rest of the room, but seemed more luminous, as if touched by an overhead spotlight. "Aura" wouldn't be all that farfetched. There was silence for half a minute, oXo's usual effect. The toothy grin was enigmatic, but approachable: this was one skull that signified nothing of terror and death. The faint golden tone of the crystal seemed warm and wise, invited the touch. Enticed confidence.

Damn, maybe the whole crystal skull fetish has something to it, Bannock was thinking. At least he didn't have to go into some grungy old temple full of boobytraps for it. Though thinking of the cluttered, toxic motel room, he modified that to more like, Not totally, anyway. His hand surprised him no end by moving out unbidden to stroke the top of the quartz cranium. It felt slightly warm to the touch, smooth and caressable.

"You're going to take good care of oXo." Loris didn't make it a question, more of a kind of pointless threat.

"Sure I am. Some major people want to get in on his..." He glanced at her, the lovely young face now hard and the lissome body tense. "...guidance. His wisdom. There are lots of lives that need changing."

She relaxed a little, but still eyed him suspiciously. Hey, ol' oXo is sure as hell going to change my life, he thought. "How does anybody know his name?" he asked her.

"He tells you," Blaster blurted out. That's how we know it's 'Osho', not like 'ox-o' or something."

"There's a label on the bottom," Loris said.

The two men stared at her. Bannock picked oXo up with both hands, feeling a peculiar impulse to cradle the skull by his heart, wrap his arms around it. Carefully he rotated it, the crystal a dance of reflections and light shafts shattering down inner faultlines. And sure enough, there was a sticker: "Made in China".

That tensed Bannock up, but Blaster practically levitated. He jittered out of control, goggling at the others, staring at the label like it was an ace falling on the dealer's jack. The spasm passed over him and he fell back on the couch waving defensive hands towards Bannock and the quiescent oXo. "No way, Man. No fuckin' way. He's been... Look, I got him from Ginrick himself, he's... Ah, shit!"

Loris eased languidly forward and extended a natural colored but well-cared-for fingernail. She flicked the label off and leaned over to stick it on Blaster's forehead. It might as well have said "Vacancy" in that location. She smiled a beautiful little smile and said, "April fool, asshole. Just wanted to find out if you were really washing him every day like you're supposed to."

Blaster was *hors de combat*, Bannock thought he might be in love for the first time since his teens. Loris leaned forward, her loose hempen top falling open a little, revealing no evidence of support garments. She bored right into Bannock's eyes and said, "Now you show me yours."

Bannock could have used a little more eyeball time with her, but there was the business thing. He set oXo down beside him in the rickety plastic deck chair, lifted the shoulder bag onto his lap, and opened it. "There's good news and bad news about that, kids."

Blaster showed him a mild befuddlement he figured was his usual game face; Loris looked calm but reproachful.

"The good news is, I've got the money," he said, "The bad news is, you don't get any of it. Sorry."

Blaster jerked forward as if kicked in the balls. Loris slumped and looked around the room, then at Blaster, with a sad expression.

"More bad news," Bannock went on, sliding a very wicked-looking little .32 auto out of the bag. It was fitted with a dummy silencer he'd picked up; didn't work—and was therefore not illegal—but sure looked intimidating. Definitely slammed Blaster back onto the couch. "Good news, I never shoot anybody unless I absolutely have to."

Loris turned a very searching gaze on him and said, "You should consult with oXo before you do anything rash. He can help you work this out."

"I'll pencil him in for this evening, Sunshine." Bannock gently lowered oXo the bag, slung the strap over his head, slipped his gun hand inside it to continue vaguely covering them, and stood up. She stood up, too.

"Just ask him what you should do," she said in a neutral tone. "oXo knows about people, can get things done. Believe me, I've lived with him for three years."

"Maybe one of the things he got done was bringing me here to bust him out of this shithole."

He got a different look from her, then. He was unsure what it was, but willing to find out more. Slowly, thoughtfully, she said, "That's what I've been meditating with him about for the last few weeks."

Bannock backed towards the door, but kept his eyes on the girl. She shifted her posture almost imperceptibly, and just like that he knew where she was coming from. He looked her over head to toe, scanned her face with finality. Said, "You got a passport?"

She squatted quickly and dragged a big Mexican hippie bag out from under the coffee table. "Right in here."

Blaster stared at her but couldn't seem to settle on the right question. As she strode toward Bannock she said, "oXo told me I should get one."

VENUS ON THE HALF SOUL

One more thing pissed Aphra off—the gatekeepers and guardians you have to go through to talk to powerful people. And what pissed the pissiest was the way they always think they're the ones with the power. Always way more arrogant and self-important than the people they supposedly guard from whoever is supposed to be trying to crash their party.

She'd worked her way up to this jive-time turkey, Mr. Ivy League Don'twannabe trying to talk down to her and pretend not to be eye-fucking her in the process. Playing everything close to his tailored chest, trying to string her out. Carefully avoiding saying anything of substance, much less of interest. Not even, Get Lost. Only thing he'd made clear was that she wasn't talking to The Senator unless she told him exactly what she had to sell. And she'd been just as definite that she wasn't laying out the goods for anybody except The Man.

"A bit of a misconception, I'm afraid," he was droning on. "The whole idea that any Senator from the South, especially one who made the wise move to our party from the Democrats before..."

"Do people still say 'Dixiecrats'?" Aphra asked innocently.

"I suppose. Not around here, anyway." First smile out this stiff. About as sincere as his artlessly displayed PhiBate key.

"Oh, that's right, it's the *Republicans* who're the Jim Crow bloc these days, isn't it?" Aphra wrinkled her brow in thought, "I guess 'Dixicans' doesn't have that ring."

"Well, huh, huh…" Now was that the phoniest chuckle she'd heard, even here inside the Beltway? Tough competition, but it had the legs. "That's the sort of misconception I was talking about. Actually the Senator's record on issues relating to African Americans is…"

"I beg your pardon?" Aphra's first use of her Drop Dead Voice froze the aide in mid-sentence. "Do I seem deficient in English?"

"Your English? No, not at all."

"Perhaps I still haven't entirely shaken that nagging Ebonics accent?"

"Uh… why do you ask?"

"Well you seem to think I'm from Africa. I hope that isn't about the whole 'descended from apes' thing." He was starting to show that future-roadkill-in-the-highbeams stare she always liked to cultivate in a white man.

"And what makes you think I'm American? Rather than Canadian or Bahamian or something?"

"No, of course not. I meant, you know… your…"

"Oh my 'heritage'? Is that what you meant?"

"Well, look I just meant, Black people…"

Aphra stuck her arm close to his so aggressively he flinched. She said, "Your sleeve there is black. Am I that color?"

He got more flustered, then suddenly drew a breath and leaned back in his chair. "How about you tell me?" he said. "Make sure I got the right password for this week."

"Call a spade a spade?" That restored his fluster level in a hot minute. She shrugged. "I prefer to be referred to as a 'nigger', if you don't mind. Cut the BS, wipe out the cheapest shot in history"

He stared, giving her a chance for a chuckle or rimshot, but she sat there serious as a process server. He steepled his fingers and gazed over them. One more stunned victim of the N-attack. Whitey never realized he was forging us a weapon there. Anybody got the sense and gumption to pick it up and swing it.

"Appropriating the 'queer folk' model, are you?" the tout suit came up with, trying to regroup.

"They copped our licks, we're copping theirs."

"Well it sounds like a lot of fun, actually. I wish you luck on it. I'm dying to hear Diane Sawyer or Hillary Clinton drop that one on television."

She gave him a sly smile. Wouldn't mind seeing that, herself.

"Meanwhile," he said. "I assume you're just as prickly about your sex as your color. Have chicks retro-ed to wanting to be called 'bitches' as well?"

"If the shoe fits," she drawled, crossing her legs to dangle an Italian minimalist piece of footwear in his view. Mostly just luscious leather sole and the blatant hint of two straps. "I'll wear it."

Fifteen minutes later she was sitting across from The Man, pitching Her Plan. It's all in how you talk to honkies, she thought. Just speak slowly and enunciate clearly.

MAYAN LEGO

Keep turning the crank, May. Maybe you'll crank out an answer. Hit the right line-up and the past and future will fall out the bottom like a Vegas jackpot and you'll be PlayDate of the Month for History Channel. She grabbed the handle on the huge interlocking gears on the white wall, and turned them easily, watching the little glyphs on each cog come into new permutations.

There was something soothing in the clockwork reliability of the wheels turning within wheels, the little gears meshing solidly as they rolled each little Maya glyph in place to generate new combinations of human attempts to depict the silent sheets of time. She'd dialed up her birthday (12 Bakun, 18 Katun, 6 Tun, 3 Winal, 16 Kin, I Cib Tzolkin, 4Mol Haab), the day she got her doctorate(12 Baktun, 19 Katun, 11 Tun, 4 Winal, 99 Kin, 12 Muluc, 12 Uo, 8 Lord of the Night), the day she lost her virginity(12 Baktun, 19 Katun, 68 Tun, 5 Winal, 4 Kin, 8 Kan, 12 Zotz, 5 Lord of the Night-Edgewater Hotel, Seattle, Post-prom). And kept spinning it all the way forward, to where the glyphs stopped and the last three signified the winter solstice of 2012. 13.0.0.0.0. Otherwise known 13 Baktun, 0 Katun, 0 Tun, 0 Winal, 0 Kin, 4 Ahau, 3 Kankin, 9 Lord of the Night. Triple lemon. Locally noted as December 20, 2012 AD. 20/12/2012 does have a little more ring to it than 9/11/2001, huh?

She turned away from the huge calculator, the largest of its gearwheels stretching past the floor and ceiling of the museum hall. And wasn't that a lot of the problem, right there? It was in a museum!

Not exactly breaking news. It had been on TV, in U.S.A. Today (writhing in glee at the cool graphics to go with the over-simplified factoids), even the tabloids. A jillion psychics and psychos, mediums and medianauts, astrologists and asshologists, were all over it. There were seminars and conventions, like Star Trek. She'd been trying to come up with a "Trekkie" type name for Mayan Calendar groupies (Twelvies? Mayanistas? Baktunies? Tzolkin Heads?).

She walked over to the displays of Mayan buildings, highly accurate and spotless white models under the glass floor, and stared down at Palenque and Chichen and Uxmal like an astronaut god. They always reminded her of the little white buildings on the "Game Of Life" board. Probably built with Lego then customized, she thought. Wonder if they've put out a Mayan Set with snap-on blue warriors and feathered serpents.

But she had to admit, Burkhardt had been right. You take what's laying on the table and build on it, he'd told her, add the next layer. Forstemann[8] had cracked open the hieroglyphics with the Dresden Codex[9] two hundred years ago. And that lay on the table until Thompson[10], Lips, Deckert and L'huillier had layered on more interpretation on top of that, then that lay on the table until Vickie Bricker[11] came along and figured out the whole calendar system. The remarkable interlocking wheels of days that had suggested the cogwheel analogy she'd just been playing with, though the Mayans hadn't made any of those sidereal gearboxes. Wheels weren't their long suit: math and stargazing were. It was the stuff of public imagination, but nobody remembered Bricker now, did they? They talk about Arguelles[12] and McKenna[13], and the other New Age nutrolls.

Burkhardt had pushed her towards the next layer: beyond the Great Cycle. "The Day After Doomsday" was his idea of a killer book. With her meticulous scholarship and—as the old letch was always quick to toss in—her looks, she'd be a media star as well as an academic hero. The Sagan of archeology, the Lord Carnarvon of Mesoamerica. The Laura Croft of real life. But not if she couldn't figure out a way to turn this thing up to Eleven.

If she could only get past what she termed "materials failure". The realworld proof was not co-operating. She turned expectantly as Luis came up behind her. She was sure he'd struck out again. However much he desperately wanted to get on base. The museum staff had gone ballistic when she requested dismounting the Jade

Codex so she could examine the back of it. But Luis had been ecstatic to help: convincing the stuffy old politically-appointed staff at the Museum of Mayan Culture to honor her impressive credentials, doing the physical job and paperwork himself. To end up with nothing.

When she'd first come down to Chetumal[14], Luis had been highly apologetic that most of the relics in the state trophy museum[15] were replicas, especially the big impressive stones. She'd soothed his embarrassment on that issue with her genuine opinion that it was better that way. The reproductions were excellent, sufficient for study, perfect castings taken from molecular polymer molds. People could see the evidence, feel the impact of their own past, in which they were glorious lords of existence, not marginalized aborigines. Greatly preferable, she'd said, to looting the original stones and hauling them in like captives. Leave them where they belonged, not kidnapped like the Elgin Marbles.

Luis, a fresh-scrubbed INAH[16] rookie aided by his political activities while studying in Mexico City and a powerful uncle with PRI[17] connections, was extremely happy to hear such an opinion. He fit in well with the current National History Institute concept of creating cashflow Disneylands rather than boring digs. And he'd been extremely excited when she showed up talking about the obverse of the Jade Codex.

It was improper to call it a Codex, of course: it was more like a tablet. A pocket calendar, if you like. A slab of very dark jade the size of a legal pad and a half inch thick, intricately carved in a medium that had held the detail better than the limestone steles and friezes. Obsessively copied, lovingly displayed. And now revealed as inadequate. Maybe.

She'd shown him the citations to make him believe the probability that there was more on the back of the jade tablet, and that it was highly significant. "Just having an obverse is really unique," she had told him. "It's like the U.S. Great Seal."

"What, the *escudo* of the United States?"

"Yes. The only national seal with an obverse side. You must have known that. It's famous."

"Oh, wait, the pyramid and eye."

"Exactly." Find me an archeologist who hasn't been blown away by that image, and spent a career denying it, she'd thought. "The occult side of the official story."

"So the *Estados Unidos* has a Dark Side." He asked with playful innocence. Like most Latin Americans with college education he pretty much assumed it was all dark.

"Not dark: just out back," she had chuckled. Then struck a movie pose and wickedly croaked out, "Come over to the Back Side, Luke."

Her backside was something Luis was dying to come over, but the other side of the ersatz jade slab had come up smooth and empty; mounting studs cast right into it.

But now he stood there grinning, ready to play his trump. It had been like pulling hen's teeth to get it and she'd know that. There was some deep departmental embarrassment about the Jade Codex. But he'd gotten the lead to the original artifact. He held up a printout in front of her, but couldn't wait for her to read it. He said, "At Cobá."

Her gratitude was marvelous to behold. Licking his mental lips, Luis offered to drive her up to the Cobá site himself. She was just so damned hot. Quite beyond the firm curves on the delicate bone structure and the graceful fluting of her face and throat and calves, she was "*china*". The Yucatan borrows a lot from Cuba, including music and food, and one bit of slang was the term *china* or *chinita* to describe the highest and most erotic style of female. And if there was ever a girl who was *chinisima*, it was the lovely archeologist, Doctor MeiMei Chiang.

TETE A TETE

Bannock gave Loris a glance and smile when she came out of the bathroom, wrapped in a fluffy white Sheraton robe and toweling off her long mahogany hair. And looking very, very good. No rush. For a professional thief, extortionist, asskicker, and kneecapper, Bannock was far from brutal or crass with women. He knew quality when he saw it and he knew the hippie girl was a class act who'd made her call. He couldn't completely discount the idea that she had tagged onto him to try to get the skull back, but he figured she'd be around and patience would pay nice dividends. He liked the real thing.

So he turned his attention back to oXo, regarding him from the dresser as he crouched on the foot of the bed trying to look into those transparent eyes. He had a feeling there was something going on there, but was clueless about how to get a grip on it.

Loris swiveled past him and stepped out on the dinky harbor view lanai. Southern California is best seen from at least twelve stories up, was his theory. She sank into a lounge chair and busied herself with her hair. "You have to formulate a question," she said. "Not a demand, though. Try to be unselfish: you get more benefit that way."

Pretty much what he'd just been thinking, wasn't it? He stared into the gleaming nothingness of oXo. "Clue me in on how it works? I don't mean aliens or ancient kings or that crap. I mean, where is this dude coming from?"

"Crystals absorb and resonate vibrations," she said. "On a cruder level, that's how a radio works."

Ah shit, he thought. Why did I expect anything other than mystical spiels?

"Wherever he came from, he's been on Earth thousands of years and passed through many hands. Kings, murderers, courtesans. And he's absorbed vibrations from all of them. He's a repository of human wisdom. He knows the future and your fate."

Hmm. Not as flaky as much he'd read since starting his search for the skull, and no way to prove or disprove. He had a gut feeling that she might be right. And actually, she was.

However, for the last fifty years oXo had been in America, most of it in the Los Angeles basin. He'd moved from hand to hand, but they were all criminal hands and almost entirely—except for some movie people and one rich Arab—hands that chiefly handled drugs. He had been a sensation among top-level coke dealers, the ultimate status symbol and better poonbait than a Ferrari or yacht.

He'd been traded for staggering amounts of dope, gotten raked off by biker gangs, presided over grower communes, accepted animal sacrifices by Santeria-crazed smackers, wreaked havoc on the fragile psyches of tweakers. And most recently snatched up as Blaster ran towards the back door of a mansion whose owner was on the front porch being handcuffed by DEA agents.

And now he sat staring into Bannock.

"So I just ask him a question? Out loud?"

"Seems to work better out loud. Or write it and slip it under him."

"And he replies by email?"

"You just know. You sorta know something in your head. Once

18

you identify his voice you can't miss it."

Great, Bannock thought, feeling foolish. You get around these people and they always want to clean your aura, give you a coffee enema, make you listen for inner voices. He regarded oXo a moment, then spoke conversationally, "So, can I get you anything?"

Immediately he was aware of a thought, like one of those memos you do to yourself sometimes. Remember to pick up the laundry. Don't forget Mom's birthday again, asshole. Next time bring the shotgun. Except this one said, "How about a bong hit?"

Bannock stared for a moment more, then slowly turned to Loris, who was watching him intently, her hands poised on top of her head. He said, "You got a bong in your bag?"

She lowered her hands and shook her hair, stood and walked inside. She looked at him, then at oXo. "He likes you," she said, laying her hand lightly on his shoulder.

Bannock had a feeling she might not require quite as much patience as he'd thought. Little oXo was already growing on him. He gave the skull a pat on top and told it, "Hang in, little buddy. I'm taking you home."

END OF DAYS RUNNER

"Now mind, I can stare at a graph and look owlish as well as the next peanut down the road, but damned if I see what you're drivin' at, honey."

Yeah, sure you can't, Aphra was thinking. And if you weren't a Senator who can make me richer than Jesus, I'd "honey" your fat cornpone patooty for you. I'm slinging some major 'tel your way and you're thinking I look like a tasty poke chop. You know... for a lil Nigra gal. What she said was, "Over at the right side, there."

While he was pretending to puzzle it out, she checked out the only Senate office she'd ever invited herself into: the maze of flags and talismans on the wall, the pictures of Hizhonor hamming it up with a half-century's worth of Rich and Infamous, the Dogpatch bric-a-brac, the incredible clutter. Place could use some maid service, she thought. Another minute he'll be wanting me to tie a Jemima bandana around my nappies and grab a feather duster.

"You mean where all these different cycles sort of bottom out at once? Minds me some of my ex-wife's checking account?"

"Hyper-cycles, really. Composites of all that crop yield, stock values, incidence of conflict, major indicator kind of thang."

He leaned his considerable bulk back in the sturdy old walnut swivel chair that looked like it should be hauled up to a checkers barrel in some general store in Hootin' Holler, and regarded Aphra Alisander. Mighty fine for a colored gal, he was thinking. And just sashayed right on in here with her little printout of dyn-o-mite. Sometimes life's just a bowl of chocolate-covered dog dookie.

"Now if I was playing the market I'd be out there getting short right now." Instead of getting right long from looking at them Hershey Kiss titties there. "But being a simple Ways and Means senator..."

"Who just happens to head up the Committee to Steal the Presidency Back From The Jigaboo."

She thought his laugh was going to blow all her data off the cluttered old walnut clerk's desk. His wattles shook like the old bowlful and he threw back his head to give a cheap tour of the thicket of silver nostril fur inside his julepblossom nose.

"For a smart, educated gal you got a bit of mouth on you." Lord help us all, she does. Big, soft and red as the Harlot of Babylon. Damn. "But yeah, we could call it that, here among us people of color."

She stared at him, then caught the hidden smile. "Black face and red neck, huh? We could be an anarchy vaudeville team."

He let the smile out, almost charming with his good-ole-boy manner and white TV preacher pompadour. And moved on in. "So you've run your pretty little head over the... you know... implications here? Ramifications and whatall?"

"Know what? That's kind of why I came up here. I've got a plenty good job with Oracon, and could get fifteen minutes of media buzz with this, but here I am bringing it to Massa. Cause yeah, I think there's more play in predicting history's biggest economic collapse than just selling you short."

Damn, she did have a mouth, no two ways aboutin' it. He had a fleeting vision of lying around in bed on Sunday afternoon with some sippin' whiskey, his newspapers, and this gorgeous, overbuilt Afamercan, and being more interested in the conversation than crawlin' her too-tall frame. "The printout runs too long to make out the time frame too close. Down at the business end over here. In the, omigosh, election year. Think it might make a nice October sprize for somebody?"

She shook her head, the retro-Angela 'fro wiping the air like a brillo eraser. "Sorry. December. December 20, actually."

"Whuthehell, you got it nailed right down to the day? Got financial armaggedon zeroed right to Eastern Standard Time? Think I'd kinda like to pencil that into my DayRunner."

"It's bigger than that, by the way." That wiped the chitlins grin off him for a second.

He leaned back and stared for a full minute. "Bigger than what looks from here like the entire world economy going down like a hungry whore? I'm too long in the tooth to think that far out of the crokersack, sugar."

Yet you manage to spend your dotage as one of the dozen most powerful men in Washington. "A lot bigger, maybe. And I think I can find out what it's all about. Maybe how to cope with it."

"Given the right motivation? Am I peekin' up the right skirt there?"

"If you'll just turn your attention to that other document."

He picked up her proposed compensation package with two fingers like it was long-dead bigmouth bass. "Well now, that kind of money sort of holds my attention despite distractions like the Bear Buggerin' the Bull to Perdition. Not to mention the below-the-line stuff. Are you just trying to be paid more than that chimp over in the Formerly White House, or get proof you've got bigger balls than Hillary?"

"Well, everybody seems to think you Republicans have more money and business sense than the Dim-ocrats. But I haven't tried them yet."

He gave her a long scan that might do a nerve number on anybody less of a stone-cold Holdem player than Aphra, then reached for his old rotary-dial phone. "Hey, it's Lijah."

He held the black bakelite receiver out and stared at it in incredulous scorn then treated it to a brimstone thunder, "Elijah whompin' Weatherwax, Senior Senator From Crackertown, you dumbass hebe! How many Lijahs got this number?"

He rolled his eyes at Aphra, momentary inducting her into the tiny in-group of people with a clue amid the sea of struggling nitwits, then toned down to his karo syrup drawl. "I'm sending this little girl over there. Right this minute. BetsyAnn'll send you the paperwork. What there is of it on this one, if you catch my drift."

He awaited confirmation that the drift had been caught. Wow, I'm crypto-funded, Aphra was thinking. Took a redneck Dixieland pol to finally put me in a black bag.

"Give her a place to sit, one a them Ain'tMeBabe Visa cards, whatever she needs. Hear that? Any lil ole thing she needs." He paused, smiled, and ran a lascivious leer over Aphra. "Oh, definitely. But just wait'll you lay eyes on her."

He hung up and heaved himself out of his chair. He leaned forward with hands on the desk that suddenly turned back into one of the longest-surviving power consoles in the Free World. He gave her a look nothing like the Senator Fogbound clown show she'd been treated to so far.

Whoo, gettin' face from Stone Mountain, Georgia, she thought. Cold-assed ofay, will-be-done, face. She stood up to face him, but he turned to stare out the window at the Mall.

"All done," he muttered over his shoulder. "Now get your succulent black ass out there and earn it."

RIVALRY REVELRY

The Monsoon swizzled his watery drink in time with the oomp and pah of the chubby—but game—dishwater blonde's aftermarket boobs, idling wondering if it was a sign of decline that he found cheesy strip clubs relaxing these days, rather than stimulating. Probably. Among so many others. The jackals of The Hill were probably savoring the spoor of his decay out there in the darkness, the Beltway Buzzards circling too high to yet be seen. He tipped a unilateral toast to hungry predators everywhere, siphoned up a moderate snort, and he trolled for a receptive G-string with a folded bill.

"If I can tell from here that's only a one, she sure as hell can," Jerome Weistler scoffed. "Think she can't smell a Reno banknote from down the block?" He nodded acceptance of Munson's lightly flipped finger. He also found this misnomered "Gentleman's Club" relaxing. And one relaxing thing about it, it was unlikely that anybody of any importance would see him with Munson in a hole like this. Even if there was enough light. And if they did, they'd think twice about mentioning it.

Monsoon was on his wave length, as so frequently. "How come the Senators can reach across the aisle, but if guys like us, the real power, even shake hands it's godawful corruption?"

"Forget the aisle. I'm happy when they don't reach across the bathroom stall."

It seemed ironic and contra-instinctual, but it also stood to reason: Jerry and Monsoon were the only two guys in Washington, if not the world, who really knew what the other one did and thought. Each saw his opponent as his only real peer in a world of peerlessly moronic muggers, shysters and shitforbrains. Monsoon had once suggested that they just switch jobs. Both resign on the condition that the GOP National pick up Monsoon and the Committee to ReElect hire Jerry. His Republican counterpart had laughed, then furrowed his brow. "But wouldn't there be issues of trust?"

Which had cracked them both up so bad the Atlantic City tarts they were tag-teaming had been afraid they'd have to flee the scene of a double coronary.

They'd been friends since Sixty Eight when Jerry canvassed for Bobby and Monsoon was an under-assistant junior intern flackster for what he now called "SpiroDick". Back when they actually could switch jerseys between games. By now, of course, they were too powerful to have much say over their own lives. But they could sure as hell monkeypuppet other lives around.

Monsoon shifted his florid bulk and eyed the scrawny Weistler. Who gazed back unflustered through his scuffed horn rims that seemed constructed to announce: What, you never saw a skinny Jewish geek from NYU before? And who wasn't overly empathizing with Monsoon's bitching about running Obama's re-election campaign. They guy had all the incumbent advantages and did nothing but whine. Like now.

"The guy played on a state champ hoops team. Played in college for crissakes. But did I get to use that in the campaign? Nooooooo. Running against Minnie the Mooser, who's playing up her state championship for MukTuk High every time she turns around."

"Yeah, it's so unfair for white females to have a basketball advantage over black males," Weistler "commiserated".

"Natural order of things, there'd have been hours on ESPN comparing their roundball careers," Monsoon ranted. "The campaign could have been *about* basketball. But I couldn't touch it."

"So we run Palin again next time and maybe we can have a Network Sports Celebrity Half Court Shootout."

"You're on. But I'm just saying. What if McCain had a black grandfather but you couldn't bring it up?"

"I'd have leaked it and pretended we didn't want the press to go with it. But we're Republicans. Think we hire people of uncertain racial extraction?"

The Monsoon jiggled his slushy drink and gave Jerry the aggressively bland smile that let him know he was about to pop one of those no-man's-land things that came up now and then among the other nut-cutting, log-spiking and barn-razing. Didn't bother with a question mark, "Aphra Alisander."

Jerry smiled coyly, delighted to be caught out. "You're already on to those credit cards?"

"We've been waiting for them to light up, and one went off like a twenty dollar slot machine yesterday."

"But there's something you don't know?" Jerry secretly loved it when Munson was snotty/smug like that.

"Oh, you know... what, why, who. We already got the where and when. Or won't she be alone down in Cancun? Is Aphra short for Aphrodite?"

"Well, I'd say so. But that's just because I know what she looks like."

"If she looks like her mama I'd say you're right."

"Oh, you remember Debra Alisander? Good trivia points."

"I remember her better after she become Debra Fathiya. Kind of like, who remembers Lou Alcindor or Cassius Clay? Just another 'whatever happened to' episode these days, but I remember who she was. Talked like Huey Newton, looked like Cleopatra Jones."

"Well, standing by her daughter she'd look like a boy."

"Whoa. So what hold has she got on you guys' nuts?"

"You tell me. Betcha can't figure it out in thirty days."

"You're on. Hundred bucks?"

"Covered. Who'll hold the money?" Both their eyes turned to the blonde stripper, who had sniffed out the wagered C-note and was indicating total approval.

ANOTHER ROADSIDE DISTRACTION

There are problems with having your consciousness come adrift in time, but also advantages. Or at least novelties. Yaxche had grown a bit jaded from savoring moments standing on high thrones in various centuries and even of presiding, thus enthroned, over the end of all time and works, but she never lacked perspective. And just as she could stare down from the peaks of stone pedestals, she could appreciate the much humbler layout represented by CroCun, even seeing it when it was no more than another roadside zoo.

With a mere glance, or whatever you would term the ability to cast one's point of view down through the helical process of time, she could see the site as it will become, as it stands at whatever locus you want to consider "now", and as it once was. And how it became.

She could see the sinkhole itself over thousands of years, but it didn't really get interesting until people showed up. With the usual complications and transactions. The temporal point that made her curious was how the scruffy little patch of scrub jungle had remained in the hands of a Mayan family when the highway from Cancun to Tulum went through. The first anomaly, first clue to a miracle. Yaxche could see it happening, but not interpret or understand.

Under the stewardship of the Pop family the sinkhole had become a water source for *milpas*, providing subsistence corn along with the secondary plants woven among the corn hills in the ancient fashion: beans, chiles, hedges of prickly *nopal*. The Pops had even managed to grow enough maize to trade. Then came a fortuitous stroke from an alien and catastrophic source: the Europeans who had infiltrated the area would pay money for *chicle*, and bubble gum created a bubble economy for the Pop clan.

It was at about the same time that the Pop homestead was operating as a *chiclero* camp that it also became a Rebel Base. The sinkhole, created because an odd concentration of *cenotes* had eroded into one unstable hollow and collapsed, was close enough to the coast, but deep enough in untracked jungle to avoid scrutiny during the Caste Wars[18], as the Spaniards had called them. A waterhole with food supply owned by a family deeply committed to the rebellion against the Spanish, the Pop property was a major focus of the combat with civilization that the Maya never really lost. And a thorn in the side of colonists frustrated with their inability to put down the last nexus of resistance in all of the Americas. A period of interest when her gaze popped into those times, borne by a fierce young woman who'd taken the *nom du guerre* Kisin, a bloody earthquake of violence against the big, pale men who had abused and defiled her. Yaxche sometimes thought that the unquiet spirit of her fiery young avatar might have been responsible for setting her afloat on the circling currents of time.

After the wars were abandoned and the price of chicle reduced to nothing by the introduction of synthetics, time was a low, somnolent eddy at the Pop place, as flat and uneventful as the boring green carpet of jungle that overlays the flat slab of limestone riddled with *cenotes* that is the Yucatan. Then came the highway.

Once again, unpredictable foreign presence forged into the ancient jungles bearing mixed gifts. The road became the backbone of a bustling, destructive, construction-addled entity known as the "Riviera Maya" and strewed the stretch with tractors, condominiums, cities, hotels, restaurants, airstrips, churches to foreign non-entities... and tourist traps. And the Pop clan, suddenly located a short distance from the right-of-way, inevitably decided they should trap a few tourists themselves.

Their first venture had been, predictably, a humble restaurant that tourists ignored because it looked too shabby to be sanitary yet too modern to be "touristic", but frequented by locals and drivers because of the merited reputation of Kaax Pop, matriarch of that time slice, and mother of Puch Pop, who would capture more attention in later slices of years.

Señora Kaax supervised a kitchen crowded with Pop children, emitting fragrant steam like a volcano in Eden. And flowing with key lime soup, tamales tinted green from the plantain leaves they steamed in, *salbutes* with flaky tortilla shells, *papadzules* in spicy pumpkinseed paste, *poc chuc* with the pork practically dissolving in its sour orange sauce... timeless, lip-smacking feasts laid out daily within a few yards of the plummeting tourism buses and trucks full of spare parts for the re-invention of local civilization.

But not a particularly brilliant use of prime frontage location, according to Puch and his older brother, who went by Juanito because he thought Mayan names were bush and wanted to get his hands on the new world and new wealth that flowed past their little mom and Pop operation. He worked with tourists at the Cobá ruins and saw how money would flow out of people who were offered a reason to stop blasting around and pause a minute in the world they'd come to look at. He was hot to blow the Pop stand.

Puch, as befitted a youngster whose first exposure to a Mayan deity had been the Diving God[19], chief deity at the nearby ruins of Tulum, had always worked as a diver; first plunging down the reef on sheer lung power with a cane and re-bar spear powered by inner tube straps, then a guide for foreign tourists, most recently a PADI-certified Cave Diver shepherding goggle-eyed visitors through the underwater caves and rivers that connected the *cenotes.*

Their exposure to foreigners led them to conclude that the *gringos* and *europeos* and *japoneses* wanted to see wild life in a wild, but controlled, setting. They captured a large portion of the local surviving caiman population, trapped a dozen spider monkeys from deeper jungle far remote from the villages and westernization, and opened the Mark I version of CroCun, a reptile farm with Mayan trappings, idiotic spiels that were absorbed as if valid, a T-shirt and curio shop and, of course, a killer restaurant/bar.

At some point Juanito was feeding the little gators and gazing around the eroded limestone walls of the sinkhole, ticked off that Puch had beaten his time with the cute Barcelona girl on their last tour. As he reflected on the irony that the foreign babes he kissed up to so shamelessly were more interested in his brother because he played that whole Maya thing, an inspired instant fell around him—a concept that would twist the Pop estate into its final manifestation. They wanted Mayan, he would give it to them. He left the little lizards struggling over their grisly feed and jogged up the hundred yards to the main buildings, calculating rapidly. The first thing he'd need would be stucco. And lots of cement.

Eyeing him from her bailiwick of millennia, Yaxche exulted again at her continuous witness of the Beginning of the End.

HOCUS P.O.T.U.S.

Monsoon leaned over the monitor shaking his head like a bulldog confronting a marzipan bone. His whole dejected posture mimed the word, Why????? What he said out loud was a variation, "He must be out of his ever-loving mind."

Rodney, his AV guy, was careful not to touch any controls and piss off the suit from the network again, but pointed to the monitor, drew a nod, and watched deft fingers on the sliders remove the offending dazzle from the host microphone. With a commiserating glance at Monsoon he said, "Could have been way worse. He actually wanted to film live from the real Oval Office."

"Why am I not surprised?" Monsoon muttered. "Aghast, but hardly surprised."

"It's not easy working for a guy who thinks being out of the envelope is a winning virtue in itself." He caught a glare from Monsoon and hastened to say, "Hey, I'm telling you, right? We have envelopes for a purpose."

"So you built him a fake Oval Office set." Monsoon eyed the set with obvious loathing. There was an arch of lights overhead, but the camera showed only a reproduction of the Presidential office; complete with mockup of the desk, authentic seal, national colors behind the chair, even the window with a fake outside view. Except there was a couch next to the desk for guests and his second banana. Disgusting.

"Which was a pain in the butt to do here in the studio, considering there must be a dozen copies and replicas of the Oval around town. Not to mention back sets at Warner Brothers and such. We could have picked up the old West Wing flats for peanuts, I'll bet."

"They'd have made you take Martin Sheen in the deal."

"Careful, you're talking about a rainmaker and contributor."

Monsoon snorted. "I heard they're going to start that series back up with Will Smith playing the President."

Rodney smiled, "That must be why he changed his name to Akbar."

"Okaaaay, readddddy..." the network guy said into his headset mike. "And... cue."

"Here it goes," Rodney said, excitement of an historic moment replacing his cynical pose.

"Fucking bloody wonderful," Monsoon groaned, "The Presidency's finest hour."

The theme music blasted out, instantly igniting feverish applause in the studio audience. Live studio audience, Monsoon winced. Great idea. We should charge extra for assassins. I thought Stevie Wonder wrote the theme, he was thinking. This sounds like the Pointer Sisters meet K-Mart ad. But then an announcer's voice rode over the whole works. "And now... Give it up for..."

He actually said "give it up", Monsoon grumped silently.

"The hardest-running Chief of State in show biz today..."

Oh. My. GAWD! Monsoon thought. Or perhaps screamed unheard.

"Numero Uno... THE man... Heeeeere's Barack!"

The music jounced into a very jazzy version of "Hail To The Chief" before coming down under the wild applause. And the President of the United States stepped into a spotlight, holding a microphone, and smiling while awaiting relative calm before beginning his first monologue in the first ever television show hosted by a President. The audience was going out of their minds. The network people were floating on their own brand of weird event adrenaline. Barack Obama was smiling serenely and giving a sort of crypto-black-power salute. Monsoon was about to be sick.

"Thank you, thank you, America," the President said. And the applause rose another notch.

"Thanks so much, for so much," he went on after a pause. "This is really humbling."

Oh sure it is, Monsoon thought darkly. But The Man was a step ahead of him once again.

"And I'm not a guy who normally does humble," Obama said to a blitzkrieg of laughter. He turned and pointed into the darkness to the right of the set, where Stevie Wonder sat at a piano in front of a cheap boombox on a stool. "Now lemme have one for my band leader... Stevie Wonder!"

Stevie reached to turn a knob on the ghetto blaster and the theme faded out. He beamed in his sunglasses, tinkling a few notes of the "Hail to the Chief" variation.

"That's 'Hail to the Chief', right, Stevie? Not 'Inhale to the Chief'?"

The applause drowned out Monsoon, who stared, chanting, "No, no, no, oh sweet Jesus freakin' Christ almighty, no."

Stevie smiled wider and leaned to his mike, "It's all good, Barry. All good."

"I was going to sing the National Anthem," Obama went on. "But as soon as I said, 'Oh, say, can you see?' Stevie took a break. What was it you said, Stevie?"

"I said, 'If I could see, I'd know you cheap suckahs didn't really hire me a band, wouldn't I?"

"Pretty hard to pull the wool over Stevie's eyes," Obama went on. "Those budget cuts have to start somewhere."

He squinted out into the house, shading his eyes. "Great crowd tonight. Not a single vacant seat."

He gave a beat, then said. "And too bad, because Rod Blagojevich could use the money."

Monsoon staggered back from the console and collapsed into a metal folding chair, shaking his head in horror. He had to get this guy re-elected in less than three years. The horror, he thought, Oh, the horror.

On stage, though, the Prez had them in the palm of his hand. "It's nice being in the presidential 'honeymoon' period, so far."

On the couch, Joe Biden, who had slipped in quietly to take the Ed McMahon spot, piped up.

"Is it like a real honeymoon, Barry?"

"Not really. They don't screw you until the honeymoon's over."

There was an intake of breath in the audience, then a slam of laughter. The Prez gave it the perfect timing pause, then said. "And you don't suck until later."

"Maybe we can just call it a 'transitional period'," Biden said from the couch.

"Exactly. I'm still getting on top of it. Like for one thing, the term 'White House' is going to be pretty passé as soon as I can get any non-union painters to return my calls."

There was a brief shock on that one, too, but shorter. They're figuring out he's not your parent's prexy, Monsoon thought.

Obama moved around the spot like a pro. "Oh, they're giving me a new Cadillac, by the way." He gave a veiled look and said, "No stereotypes around here."

This time there was no pause, just laughter.

"The good news is, it's bulletproof, bomb proof, completely invulnerable. A creampuff, one-owner car."

The waited out his beat, expectantly. He said, "The bad news is, the one owner was Tupac Shakur."

Monsoon watched the monologue in fascinated repulsion.

—"Looks like I have to get some Foreign Affairs experience. Hope Michelle doesn't find about it. She told me I may be the Black Kennedy, but only up to a point."

—"Seems there are all these nuclear weapons out there in the wrong hands: Iran, Korea, Pakistan. Well, I think I've proved I can get nukes out of the hands of insane dictators. Three months ago the Republicans had The Bomb."

"Good luck getting bombs away from Bill Ayers," Biden quipped and the POTUS cringed playfully, bombarded with laughter.

—"We've got some good guests for you tonight, folks. And it wasn't easy. We tried to have Hillary and John Edwards, but they got in a big fight over who had to prettiest hair. Then we lined up Evangelical pastor Ted Haggard, but he said he couldn't make it. Although a dozen teenaged hustlers in Colorado said he can make it, but only if you chew gum and talk dirty."

—"But seriously people, we're proud to welcome a very special guest tonight: Camelot Carpetbagger Caroline Kennedy!"

Monsoon lurched out of the chair and dashed into the wings, scattering Democrat hotshots and television techs as he plowed for the door, fresh air, and a really stiff drink.

HOSPITALITY SWEET

The Irish girl would do just fine, was Aphra's size-up. Cute, not all that bright, but doing a great job filling out her Erin Go Bra. And flying a few flags she probably wasn't aware of, batting those Auld Sod green eyes and crinkling the famous cream complexion above them: "Ah, I thought I'd seen you. Wasn't I the stewardess on your flight?"

Been wack if you weren't, girl, Aphra thought. Since I stalked you out here all the way from the gate. "Yeah, you were. So I thought maybe you could help me a little. I never been here before, but y'all know the hotels and all..."

"Actually, the only one we know is the Radisson because that's where they always put us." She fell in beside Aphra, pulling her little luggagebarrow along the aisles wide and narrow. They passed by all the transportation and time-share pimps without a glance, then a big glass door shuddered aside and they were out in the brutal, sopping heat of Cancun.

"Must be okay, then. Should be vacancies this time of year?" Yeah, July had to be about as Low Season as tropical resorts get.

"Oh, I'm sure there are. And a nice beach and pool I barely get to use because I'm always back out the next day."

"They got a shuttle or something?" Something about the girl's wide, ingenuous green gaze and loose, blowsy stride told Aphra—to whom quick appraisal was a way of life—that she was striking the lode here.

"Sure. Just come along with me. It's five dollars and they bring us right to the lobby."

As so many hotel shuttles do. Aphra's next line was well-rehearsed and smooth. "Thanks, I think I will. I'm picky about rooms, though. Think I could have a peek at yours before I register, make sure?"

"Of course." The colleen had no objections to more chat with this sleek, elegant black passenger. Obviously a model or executive or something, the kind of woman you learned things from. Like how she'd gotten that slight hooked look to her nails or that supple yellow leather purse, for openers.

"That's really nice of you, hon. Tell you what, I'll buy you a drink, show my appreciation."

"I'm dying for a margarita or two."

"Two works for me." See if it works for you, girlfriend.

"Well, now, 'Spy' is such a loaded word, don't you think? I basically collect. Hunter/gatherer type. Poke around corporations and such, see if there's anything somebody might pay to hear."

Little Miss Fly United was all ears by then, couple of drinks in her and changed into a pretty nicely-filled bikini to grab the last sun on the balcony. And all rapt up in Aphra. Wow, Catwoman turned out to be some sort of spy! Bugger and begorrah and all that. She wasn't even thinking about dinner, just hanging on every word this swank negress had to say.

"Oh, I got some craft and all," Aphra went on, sitting in the other porch chair, sipping a strawberry daiquiri, and pretending to take in the blue water view she'd seen a dozen times from better hotels. "Like, you know, how to scan cellular frequencies, record conversations off vibrations of suite windows, read keystrokes from convention center suites. But it's mostly just keeping your eyes and ears open."

"You can scan cell phones?" Figured that a flight attendant would be interested in the whole giz/gadget, Agent Q, end of things.

"Not legally."

"Ah. So how do you find out secrets and... you know, that lot?"

"Oh, it's not rocket science or anything. Funny thing is, I run into these guys, bigshots at companies, who just walk over and buy me dinner and tell me stuff. Sometimes they like invite me to their house, even; let me poke around after they pass out. I don't understand it."

The United girl laughed prettily at that one. "Oh, you don't then? Well, there's a full-length mirror right there in the bathroom that might give you some clues."

"Oh, I know what they want, all right. In spades." She gave the girl one of her guarded race card smiles. "As it were. I just don't understand it, you see what I'm saying?"

"Uh, not really." She was trying to, though, you could tell by the furrowed brow.

"Well, maybe I will take a peek at that mirror. Show me to it, will you?" Aphra stood up lazily, grinning, "Gotta pee, anyway."

The girl walked in and pointed to the mirror, put her hands on her slim hips to await more laughs with her new pal. Who made a sinuous shrugging move that somehow released her shift to slither down in a pile at her feet.

She gawked as Aphra, naked except for a red Brazilian tanga that could justly be called "naked, but more so", did a turn, checking herself out. Slapping her own ass, which gave the tuned-up report of a ripe watermelon, then lifting her breasts and peering at them. Then up into the eyes of the flight girl, who suddenly felt like the small bathroom was very tight and warm.

"So you think you know what they're after, huh?" She turned and moved a little closer, a sheeny black presence amid all the white ceramic and linen. "Maybe you can explain it to me?"

"Explain what men want?" The attendant had stepped back, her bare thigh touching the top of the toilet tank. Suddenly in rabbit mode, wary but captivated.

"Nope." Aphra stepped closer yet. "What I want."

"Well, I'm starting to get a glimmer." There was something very fierce about the black woman's face, but her body was a shiny, plush invitation to stroke. She was confused, wanted to go get another drink. Wanted something, for certain.

"A glimmer, huh? That something in the neighborhood of a gleam in the eye?"

"Well, I wouldn't say that..."

"Know what I'd say?" Aphra was standing with her plumped purple nipples only inches from the white girl's tits, feet placed outside hers; a control pose. "I'm standing here naked and I'm sweating; all this Mexico heat. And you got clothes on and shit, must be sweltering. Look ahere, sweat kind of running along that soft gingery down on your neck there. See can I do something about that."

She inclined forward to place her hands against the wall on either side of the white girl's head, leaning in to erase those last few inches between their stiff nipples, her long tongue already extended. She could feel the quiver as she slid it up the soft, pale neck, lapping the salty dew, and ending up with a little fillip around the earlobe.

"You got any more excess moisture anywhere," she whispered, "I think I can take care of it for you."

Aphra sat in the breeze on the balcony, idly watching the rise and fall of the sleeping white chick's breasts while listening to her cell phone. "I'm here, but not checked in. No record of nothing."

She listened, chuckled, said, "Shit, it's almost midnight here and I ain't even got dinner. Just had a nice snack, though."

She listened again and gave a throaty laugh before replying and snapping the phone shut. "Just a little Irish stew."

ZINE CHAT

Whatever else you might say about it, Townsend was thinking, this is some set of wheels. Supposed to be able to take anything less than a nuclear hit, totally soundproof, electronics consoles an AWACS plane would envy, and a top-flight bar. He lounged on leather soft as a baby's butt, his lean frame composed with an athlete's grace as he looked around the somber dusk the black windows lent the back seat, trying to figure out what to say to these two Committee To ReElect The Incumbent guys. Always a safe bet, "Nice set of wheels."

Monsoon sprawled across the rear-facing jump seats, continuing to give him the blank eyeball-vetting he'd gotten since he'd been ushered into the Caddy, finally spoke. "It didn't really belong to that Tupac asshole."

"I sort of figured that."

"One way to look at it, it's a job perk. Not just his job... my job, too."

"Beats the shit out of a bus pass."

Weistler, the skinny Jewish guy, chuckled, but not a flicker from Monsoon's big, florid Kilarney mug. "What I'm trying to get across to you, a D.C. kind of perk. All mental."

"That's my impression."

Monsoon threw an exasperated look at Weistler. "Lord love us, he's a sarky as his old man." To Townsend he spelled out, "What I mean is this, hotshot. Michelle doesn't get to blast around in this car, do her shopping or whatever. Biden doesn't get to take it out for a spin, drop by his implant doc. But I do. See what I'm saying?"

"You're saying white guys have finally discovered the symbolic value of Cadillacs?"

"Hit him, will you Weasler? You're closer. Have him audited or something."

"Look, I'm already impressed. You made sure of that before you did this 'pick you up in a black limo long as the Mall' thing."

"No point in slugging him. He's as bombproof as ..."

Townsend cut in sharply. "My old man. Yeah, yeah. Can we move past that a little? Get to me?"

Monsoon gave him another searching glare, then nodded to himself. "That might be a sort of theme in your life, huh, sonny? Well, sure. This is your show, all the way."

"Rather, it's our show," Weistler came in. "But you've been cast in a plum role."

"I'd just like to thank all the little people who made it possible."

Weistler laughed and Monsoon made a disgusted noise like clearing his throat with a toilet brush. "Okay, sure. You're young, dumb and full of cum and all over this thing. Think we're a couple of superannuated pus-guts dwelling on the past. Fine. Thing is, everything in the brief is up to date, the priorities your chief mentioned are iron-clad. Deny knowing if you're captured or catch the clap; all that crap. Here's why you're here: for questions. Got any of those in there with the snappy answers?"

"None came to mind. If I ever figure out what the hell I'm after, I'll call you up."

"There you go. We very decidedly expect you to keep in touch. There's a bag of Dirty Tricks waiting for you in your townhouse: bugs, sweeps, sponders, creepy-crawlies, cams, all that shit you guys do."

"I don't suppose there's a lighter that can kill forty-three different ways or a briefcase full of gold sovereigns that turns into a helicopter?"

"Ya never know. Take a look in the package," Weistler smirked. "It'll be like Christmas morning for junior grade spooks."

"Cool. All I ever got at home was switches and hickory charcoal." He looked at both of these merry tricksters and took a more respectful tone. "Look. I'm on this and I plan on you guys getting you money's worth, or whatever you run on. I appreciate you picking me, I'll keep you posted to the max."

"There, see," Weistler said sweetly, "I told you he could kiss ass if he felt like it."

"Well, pucker yours up, honey," the Monsoon snarled. "I'm all about seeing results."

Weistler turned Townsend a glance, clucking sympathetically. "Not all Harps are jolly old elves. But listen, kid. I know you've heard this until you're sick of it, but in fact, I did have the privilege of working with your father at one time."

"Wait, I know this one." Townsend snapped back into his defensiveness about what he would probably hear again and again until a generation of monkeywrenchers died off or faded away. "Great soldier and patriot, intrepid crime-fighter, bulwark of the American way? He screwed your wife and gave her a dose? Or a variation on those themes."

"My wife hated him."

Okay, so she probably did screw him, Townsend thought. Legion of Lost Lambs with Fig Leaf Cluster.

"But what I was going to say was, that son of a bitch really knew how to party."

Hmm, more dossier on The Dads. "He's a man of many parts."

"So say 'Hi' if you see him."

"I'll certainly pass on your regards." In the unlikely event, Townsend was thinking.

Munson leaned forward and suddenly the fat-assed bottomfeeder slipped away and there was this force sitting in front of him, an unquestionable wind of will. He spoke softly, but with a palpable intention behind it. "Think you might see him soon?"

"Hard to say with the Pop." Understatement of the decade, but better than "fat chance".

"You should. In fact, I recommend it."

"I'll look him up as soon as I get back. Promise."

"How about before you go?" Only grammatically a question: in real time, a flat-out command.

"Okay. I'll do that. Pass on your compliments."

Monsoon gave an ostensible smile. "Good. Don't show him that picture of the spade bitch. He'd be on the plane with you."

Townsend replied with a non-smile of his own. "She's hot as an inside tip, all right. I'm so glad your bosses are equal-opportunity exploiters."

"I think we're on the same page," Weistler said smoothly.

Monsoon nodded. "Ready to rock."

A silence of finality and mutual lack of camaraderie settled into the back of the most expensive General Motors car ever and Townsend looked around, checking it out. And sort of wondering where they were going and why. "We should take this juggernaut over to Accokeek," he said brightly. "Pick some street drags."

"The attention span of the young," Weistler nodded with mock sadness. "How about we watch the rest of that tape?"

"Fuck that," Monsoon groused. "I sat through the real thing."

"Aw, it was just getting good." Weistler pushed some hidden button and the plasma screen lit up, showing the set of the POTUS Show, the Prez leaning forward towards his guest sofa, where Caroline Kennedy basked in the phosphor light.

Obama grabbed even Monsoon's disaffected attention by saying, "Being a designated New Yorker doesn't confuse your self-image a little?"

"Not that much. I've always been a fan of the, whatchacallem, Yorkies. I just forgot and left the little cap in the limo."

Weistler whinnied in glee and turned up the volume while Monsoon shook his head. "Can you believe that, kid? Chief Executive as Arsenio retread."

"I prefer Jimmy Kimmel, frankly."

Onscreen, Obama smiled ebulliently. "Doesn't sound like you have much problem with trading on unearned cachet from your family name in order to run for Senator of a state you never lived in and actually despise."

"Well, like I said, Barry, Hillary has always been a major inspiration to me."

Weistler howled with laughter and even Monsoon cracked a jaded smile. "I gotta admit, that was almost worth it."

Obama hid his reaction. "I'm surprised you didn't make a bid on my old seat in Illinois."

"Oh, I shopped around. But I got turned off by his whole, 'What would you pay to be a Senator? Don't answer now, because you also get...' approach. You don't treat a trusted public office like a blue light special. Plus I found out some of the bribe was earmarked for alcohol treatment centers in Chicago."

"You have a problem with rehab, Caroline?"

"It's a waste of time. My uncle's been drinking like a fish for decades and he holds down a job. So what's the point?"

"This has got to be scripted," Weistler said between guffaws. "She's not smart enough to come up with that."

"How about stupid enough?" Townsend tossed in, but was ignored.

"You're looking at reality TV there," Monsoon told him. "God help us."

"So, anyway, that's behind you for now," Obama continued onscreen. "Any future plans we should know about?"

"Well, it looks to me like the Secretary of State is easy to snag. I'm thinking of marrying some famous guy and going to secretary school."

Townsend thought Weistler might wet his pants over that one, but the show clicked off as "Cadillac One" coasted to a regal stop. He couldn't see much outside the one-way windows, but motioned the older men to proceed him. Both gave him canny smiles and big *apres vous* waves. He stepped out of the limo right into a clot of Secret Service men surrounding Barak Hussein Obama.

Townsend was cool as they come, practically from birth, but got taken dramatically aback to find himself standing in the presence of his Boss In Chief. He froze up, staring as Monsoon and The Weasler exited the other door and walked around, grinning. He was impressed in spite of himself. Had to admit there was more to the guy in person. Much less reminiscent of that little stuffed sock monkey he'd had as a kid. But still, a lawyer.

He could see an expectant look on the prexy's face, so he cautiously extended his hand, wishing there was photographer around. Start a collection of presidential flesh-pressing shots to rival his father's.

Obama smiled, did a sort of yuppified black fist salute.

Townsend shrugged, flashed a peace sign that he quickly lowered to waist level.

"Rock breaks scissors," he told the President. "You win."

He nodded and moved quickly away from the clump of prezbiz.

Obama glanced after him, shaking his head, then entered the car. The door was promptly closed by guys who made it look like hermetically sealing the fate of the world, but the window whispered down. He shot a quick eye at his re-election honchos.

Weistler was laughing. "Stone, paper, scissors. I like him."

"Pain in the butt," Monsoon groused. "Like his old man."

Obama nodded. "Who used to get it done, right?"

The window hummed back up as the Cad ghosted out of the building like a mafia sting ray.

"Fucking brat," Monsoon muttered, but Weistler didn't ask who he meant.

THE ON-ROCK CAFE

Monica had given him a long look as she poured his last latté, and neglected the dollop of Rompope he was known to favor, so Seagull gathered it was about time to do his trick. He picked up his battered old fake Gibson covered with forged signatures of great pickers and nodded to Congón, who was doing a little nodding himself. Four straight Americanos and the guy was ready to go to sleep, but he'd perk up quick when his hands touched skin. The two derelicts lurched up, Congón's sleek Latino hustler look clashing with Seagull's scuffed gringo *jipi* getup, sea urchin hair, and hornrims that so utterly stated "Long Island Jewish geek" that nobody even had to guess where his nickname came from. They hoisted their respective axes (the Cuban-made drum also scrawled with bogus *saludos* from famed congeros) and mosied over to a partially cleared area under the fresco of Kukulkan giving Quetzacoatl the finger and started thinking seriously about playing some music.

Thing was, Café Cueva wasn't the only coffeehouse on Isla Mujeres anymore. It had been the first, cranked up by Delmonica when the locals idea of classy coffee service was a non-plastic cup of lukewarm water and a clean jar of freeze-dried *"No-es-café"*. And was still the best and most favored by eurohostlers, springbreakers, and serious local javaheads. Partly because of the excellent beans selected in the highlands of Yucatan and custom-roasted by Italian craftsmen in Cancún. And being right between the Cosmicolas international abused book store and the superlatively tasty Cool Ice Cream didn't hurt. And the big thing was that the owners—laidback, daft cockney Del and his lovely, allegedly gypsy wife, Monica—were so popular that the new Italian and Israeli cafés weren't that much competition.

But enough competition that they'd found it helpful to provide some sort of music, especially during off-season. And since ComoNo had swiped Chucho, the resident pianist on Isla, they tried to scrape up talent of Seagull's caliber and pay off in coffee and snacks. Plus, Seagull's somewhat meager vocal abilities were offset by the fact that he was a known collaborator to the Blasé Sojourner, making him a sort of obscure star in the hospitality industry, like one of those suns going dark because it's collapsing in on itself due to excess gravity.

The BS, as it's generally known for a variety of reasons, is frequently compared (usually sneeringly) to the fictional "Hitchhiker's Guide To The Galaxy", a similar, seminal, user-written guide for international vagabonds and wastrels. And it's just possible that Seagull majored in Wastrelism in college. He had written up most of the downside locations on Isla for the current distro in typical BS fashion: going deeper in than most guides (Seagull and other BS contributors were smug in comparing it to scorned books they referred to as "Let's Go Spend Daddy's Money", "LoanMe Planet", "The Butch Guide" and "Fuddors") but in ways mostly of interest to the more disjointed and deshabille of movers and fakers. His section on Café Cueva, for instance, dealt with seamier side-events of a sexual encounter with a previous waitress and a photograph of a pyramid constructed of marijuana seeds adhered with the dark rich Mayan honey Monica insisted on providing.

The Blasé Sojourner is not, of course, an ordinary book, and doggedly post-Web2. It's actually considered a "distro" like Ubuntu, available as a DVD, SD Memory card or download from the Distro Duck website and distributed by means not so much "viral" as metastatic. Passed hand to hand like a foxy ingénue, shared on sites like Napster, Dumpster and Pirate Bay, bootlegged around on little USB flash drives and re-invented as podcasts. And the salient line from Seagull's rave (if not raving) review was undeniable: everybody on Isla will come through Café Cueva sooner or later if you just sit there long enough. Wait and see if they don't.

But it was time to sing for his sustenance, so he gave the glance to Congón, actually a very talented pro hand drummer who could have been contender if not such a dissolute alcoholic, and aided by the driving Afro/Caribe beat, launched into an original song that had caused him to get sacked from every tourist bar he'd ever sung it, but was a favorite at La Cueva. Because La Cueva, though very international (and anybody who wanted to examine the coins glued on the tip jar at the counter would have an extremely hard time coming up with a country that hadn't chipped in) was resolutely a local dive. He strummed, hit Congón's groove, then sang.

All you damn tourists are ruining this place
Raising the prices and jumping the pace
That's why I'm leaving. Cause I'm no tourist. I'm a traveler.
I've been traveling for years
I'll probably never get there
I'll probably never go home
Except for money. To keep traveling.

I'm staying in a cheaper place than you'll ever go
I shop in the market, not the places you know
I see that tourist jive as a rip
And I don't ever tip
Or if I do it's just some rubles or yen
'Cause I'm a traveler: not a tourist!
Hey, do I look like I live overseas?

I wear tribal clothing and some kind of robe
From Tibet!
The kind you haven't seen yet.
I wear huaraches and have a didgeridoo
Nothing made in Western factories
Well, just some sweatshirts of Marley and Che
Cause I'm a rebel, man! I'm not a tourist!
Hey, do I look like I own Nikes and T's?

I've seen every ancient ruin that you've ever seen
And more!
And I saw them before they got ruined. By tourists
And I never, never ever take no pictures
Well, if I do I use a big Nikon lens
'Cause I'm an artist! Not a tourist!
Hey, do I look like some damn Japanese?

Hey don't even talk about schedules and maps
I don't need any of that tourism crap
I speak the language. I live off the land
I can score!
And I can always get more.
Cause I'm hip. I'm not a tourist. I'm a freakin traveler!
Hey, do I look like I pay retail for ki's?

This land ain't your land, all lands are my land
From slums in Europe to a beach in Thailand.
I know the people, man. I'm part of the scene.
Which you've never seen.
Cause you're a tourist. And I'm a traveler.
Hey do I look like I pay taxes or fees?
No I'm a traveler. Not a tourist.
I'm just a traveler, out traveling, doing travel.
It's a lonely, lonely planet.
When you're a traveler.

PATER NOSTRA

The old man didn't seem as haywire these day, less surrounded by the reckless atmosphere he remembered from his boyhood. And if he didn't remember, there was always the flock of diplomats and cops and spooks and pranksters to tell him all about it.

Townsend had seen a new Dodge Viper as he came in, garaged beside the beloved '72 Stingray. And there was the unmistakable spoor of *nouveau bimbeau* around the place. Probably why they weren't out by the pool: sports pushing sixty so often don't like competition from handsome young jocks under thirty. Especially their only confirmed begotten.

But he was mellower all around, lounging barefoot on the comfy leather couch, the Classic Edition of Town's own tall, lean, blonde good looks. He almost felt he could talk to the guy. Almost. His father had just said, "First mission outcountry, right?"

"Yeah, my first." He felt the unaccustomed resentment of being patronized and head-patted. Great. Move through life as a sports hero, a powerful super-cop respected by all and feared by many, then get around the Original Davis Hardley for two minutes and I'm little Opie. All you have to do is mention the fucker around DC and it's: Hey, I knew your Dad. About fifty percent, "So I'm cool like he was", and fifty percent, "Hiya, Sonny". He asked, "Why would I be anything other than domestic?"

"Domestic," Davis snorted, "What are the FBI and NSA? Chambermaids? You realize they've got this underground office in a bunker under the East Wing, four guys cranking out stupid words to use instead of ones that might mean anything?"

"I've had my suspicions." He didn't agree with his old man much, but some things were just so pat.

"So where were your suspicions when they roped you into this horseshit? Temporarily detached? I spent half my so-called career TDY'd to some clusterfucked alphabet soup or another. Why would you go play fetch for freakin' Democrats?"

"What, you were on leave during Clinton and out taking a piss during Carter?"

"Not what I'm talking about." Davis shook his head vehemently. A head still covered with dark blonde ringlets, Townsend was pleased to note. No thinning, good teeth, but not so good as to be remods. Nice peek at his own future. But his dad continued to disown the Dems, "I worked for the country, for freedom and bullroar, the mission, whatever. Not a damned political party. Not direct with re-elect assholes. That's where Liddy and those guys got screwed: you go partisan and you're working with numbnuts and when the shit hits the fan you can't take cover behind national interest."

"Well, so glad you kept your skirts free of donkey doo. But they came to me with this stuff, heavy guys with a letter from the white house about fifteen minutes after a call from my section chief. If I'd known you wouldn't approve, I'd have turned them down cold."

"No need for the attitude." Davis swung up to a seated position with a limber motion, not spilling a drop of his brandy and soda. "I guess it's just my way of warning you. Is that okay?"

Townsend was a little embarrassed how grateful he was for that concession and sentiment. He shot his father his winning pressbox smile, but of course he was immune. "I appreciate that," he said. "It's why I wanted to talk with you before I went. And they wanted me to talk to you, too. Go figure."

"Who wanted?"

"Munson and Weistler."

"Ah, shit, Monsoon and The Weasler? Together at last? Didn't take you long to get in over your head up there, did it? Well, that's what generally breaks you or pops you up a level, being in over your head with heavier assholes than yourself. And that little comedy team is about the deepest shit I can think of, offhand."

"Deeper doodoo than the Republicans?"

"Look, whatever they say about the GOP, they don't have slimeballs quite that slimy."

"Yeah, the Pope's considering Carville and Ginrich for sainthood, I understand."

Davis sipped his brandy, flopped a hand. "You gotta point. But I'd put your pair of one-eyed jacks up against them for sheer scumosity any day. What'd they bring you?"

"Hauled me in, a few grins, handed me a file, bought me a ticket, looked at their watches."

"A ticket to Cancun. Not bad. There's kids your age going to Iraq, Afghanistan, Israel, Korea, real bungholes. You get Spring Break."

"Yeah, but in off-season." He caught the look and was secretly pleased, but added, "I'm kidding. It's great. I'm looking forward to it. I'm also looking forward to finding out what it's all about."

"Uh, oh. You're the ass on line and got no need to know?"

"About the size of it. No NTKFS."

"So what are you supposed to do? If you're at liberty to say."

"Of course. It's why I came. Thing is, I haven't got a clue."

"Got a handler?"

"Don't seem to."

"Ground contact?"

"That's what's weird, more of an anti-contact. I'm supposed to touch up with the competition."

"The Competition? Huh." He pondered a minute, staring off and scratching his still-flat belly. Then shrugged. "I guess I'm just too much the old Cold Warrior, because I don't even know who the competition would be anymore. No Soviets. Al Queda? Chinese? The Massad, maybe. For my money we're going to have to sort those Israelite fuckers out sooner or later."

"Another rare agreement."

Davis smiled, as winningly and fruitlessly as his son had. "Well watch out. You're already more of a Nazi than I ever was. Don't kids grow beards and smoke a few bowls and find themselves anymore?"

"We've got video and MySpace for that now. But anyway, I don't even know what the mission is. But there's some woman down there who's looking for something because GOP is paying her to."

"Some political capital in Mexico, maybe? Or not."

"Whatever it is she's looking for I'm supposed to find out and then, I guess, get it. If it's something that can be got."

"And if it isn't, kill it?"

"Hard to say. I don't know whether I'm supposed to instinctively know what to do when I see it or call them up for instructions. They gave me a wide-open directive."

"That's excellent. You're coming along well. This is the sort of stuff you build a career on. Of course, it's also the best way to fuck a donut and wind up in Anchorage guarding icemakers."

"So if it's a Castro agent trying to buy a nuke or something, what do I do?"

"Just don't do it until the little red numbers flash down to less than 5."

"Of course not. I told you we have video. Why do you think I got into this work?"

"I did everything I could to steer you into something useful instead."

"Oh, I don't know. You could have made me wear dresses and lipstick."

"Hell, I couldn't even make your mother wear dresses and lipstick."

Townsend nodded affably. Okay. Passengers please note that the Don't Go There sign is now lit.

Fortunately Davis didn't go there. "So she's a Mexican woman?"

"Not even close. She's Black, actually. Wears an afro, even."

"A retfro? Hilarious. I knew they'd come back. Shaving your head is too much trouble. People laugh at the Mod Squad naturals, but they sure beat Jheri Curl."

"People laugh at that, too, Pop."

"I laughed the first time I ever saw one. So what's with her? Works for? Age?"

"My age. Her file looks pretty freelance: NGO's, non-profits, think tanks."

"Hmm, mid-twenties, old school negritude, carrying paper for the Committee To Un-Elect Bonzo. Is she hot?"

"Not sure that's really germane in this case."

"Then make it germane, that's my fatherly advice. They didn't put you on this because of your weapons ratings."

"Say what?"

"Let me tell you something you might find useful."

"I'd appreciate it."

"Energy moving through a system acts to organize that system."

Townsend sat without moving, looking at him waiting, but that was it. He said, "So did they tell you that at an academy?"

"Not in so many words."

"Huge help. So is there anything I should watch out for in Mexico?"

"Yep." Davis was nodding sagely. "*Hongos.*"

"Ongos? How should I look out for them?"

"Don't worry about it. If you're ready for them, they'll find you."

SIGN: SEALED, DELIVERED

It was their third night at sea and they had started to hate the others in the boat as fiercely as they clung together in one sodden mass of fear and exhaustion.

They had moved too far south, the currents stronger than the two-by-fours and broken plywood the men rowed with, but had no real idea where they were. The movements of the sky showed them only which way was east—the direction they'd fled—and which was west, where they'd once hoped life would be better for them. Now they only hoped they wouldn't die of drowning or thirst. The children had stopped crying, perhaps knowing they couldn't spare the water.

The first night they had rejoiced. It was a miracle they'd avoided the spies on the roads and the patrols around the peninsula at Cuba's western tip. They'd taken their departure from La Fe as a sign, but by now their faith was eroded by the endless rocking of their flimsy and ungainly boat, the constant bailing necessary when there are only inches of freeboard on the high sea, the squirm of six adults and five children in cramped quarters, the lack of food, the empty beer bottles that had once held their idiotically small supply of drinking water, the unrelenting sun all day, the damp chill all night. The fear.

By now the fact that they seemed to be eluding the patrols of the Mexican Navy didn't seem so miraculous or wonderful. Capture would mean a few weeks of water and food in the *Federales* holding cells at the Cancun airport. They would eat better than they had in years. Then a flight back to Havana. Then the trouble would start. But they would not be killed or tortured. Others had come back after failed attempts, and their stories ran around the oral grapevines, and the underground computer networks or memory sticks passed hand to hand to avoid the internet censors. A few prayed that they would be captured by the despised Mexicans. Rather than...

Even Mama Corabán, the most devout among them, a staunch Catholic despite the decades of Communist intolerance, even she was losing her hope. Perhaps this was the ultimate destiny and lesson, she thought, sitting in the unwelcome moonlight and trying not to lick her lips: perhaps we are doomed to this baptism into death because we despaired, abandoned our place in life to do illegal things.

She was as superstitious and ignorant as any given Black/Indian mixed Catholic in Latin America, but had a reserve in spiritual matters. Too much pride to beg, she thought, even from the Virgin, whose mercy is boundless, whose son has the right ear of God himself. Her very reluctance to cry out for divine help was in itself a sin, she realized.

She stood up shakily in ankle-deep water fouled by eleven people. She felt hands on her, supporting her supplication as she threw her head back, lifted her arms to the sacred face that lies beyond the moon, beyond all our hopes and dreams and deaths, and called out in a parched voice. "¡Ay, *Madre de Dios!*" The cry was snatched by the steady Caribbean wind, left her voice raw and sore. But she called out once again, "Please give your children some sign that you have not forgotten us."

That was really all she could manage. She sank back down, leaning against the thin, flexing sides of their pitiful excuse for a boat. She saw nothing but a half moon in a dark sky, heard nothing but the maddening slap of the waves. Her head bowed forward onto her withered old chest.

It was Tomas' boat. He was the man of the sea among them. He had the eyes, no doubt about it. So he saw it first. But didn't immediately give voice to his vision, because he was sure he was seeing things. Not unusual after days on the sea without water. But it looked so real, even though it was impossible.

She moved right across the blinking bar of moonlight on the water, backlit clearly by the summer moon. A beautiful, naked young woman standing on the water, her hands spread out at her sides like wings, golden hair flying out behind her from the wind of her velocity as she skimmed across the surface as if on invisible water skis. Without meaning to, he yelled some incoherent syllable and she turned towards him. And waved.

His guttural ejaculation caused the entire boatload to stare towards this moonlit vision of miraculous beauty. They sat motionless and silent as the ephemeral vision disappeared into the dark and distance. They had unmistakably been in a supernatural presence, and the sheer innocent beauty of it, the resonant concept of walking on water made it clear what force beyond nature was responsible. And she was heading West, towards Mexico.

Mama started croaking out a prayer, droning on her *gracias* to the *Madrecita* for this vision, this renewal of their shaken faith. Thank you, Mother, for this sign. Little Dario started bailing energetically: they mustn't sink now. The men, already pushed far beyond even the limits they had learned from lives of physical hardship, now put a renewed energy into their rowing. Somewhere ahead was the dry land of the Yucatan and now they knew they were meant to touch that land.

With only a gesture to our tired eyes, Mama Corabán thought, the Virgin has saved our lives, drawn our souls back from the sins of fear and despair.

And she had lived, by the grace of God, to see a true vision, a miracle.

Slightly less than an hour later, two hours before the damn boatload of Cuban *idiotas* showed up and he had to save their stupid lives, Venucio Mengano had been cursing the wayward treachery of fish while taking deep nips off his bottle of Vengadores. He had just lowered the bottle and squinted out at the damnably empty nets drifting in his wake when he saw her. His reception was much more Mexican, much less spiritual.

She flashed by within fifty meters of where he sat staring. Moving along surfing a swell in the water. He drank in the fine breasts pointing forward into the wind, marveled at the tossing gold mane trailing behind her, felt his pants tighten as he watched her luscious white buttocks disappear into the night. Raised a hand towards her as she zoomed away, and was rewarded when she turned, smiled, and blew him a kiss.

He sat for a long time, staring at the night, imagining a glowing hole in the darkness where she had disappeared. Then he cast a long look at the bottle of tequila, shuddered, and tossed it overboard.

GREAT BALLS - OF FIRE

Copper walked out of the jungle into the circle of firelight and rhythm: an emergence that echoed the story of her life. She stood at the edge of the pounding drummers and girls swirling around the bonfire, holding her hands behind her back but weaving to the deep tattoo of congas and djembes. Steven looked up from trying to keep his crisp Senegalese djembe rhythm aloof from the chaotic hippy "dope beats" and saw her standing there, head tilted forward to strafe him with that seductive half-smile from under the spillgate gush of flame-colored hair. And thought; Uh, oh.

She wove her way through the circle of dancers: post-Deadhead hippies swirling dreamy in clouds of white gauze, Euro clubbers pogo-ing in tubetops and mini-wraps, two athletic Oz chicks joyously stomping with their colorful sarongs twirling like petals. She came right up to the wall of drums, leaned in over his sunfishing hands, and yelled, "You think of Palenque[21], what do you think of?"

"Ticks? Leeches?"

Paco, whamming away on a set of three congas, yelled, "Cockfights!"

Disgusting. After all she'd gone through to find these things. She held out her hands, heaped with fresh-picked Psilocybe Cubensis, then screamed, "Shrooms, you moron!"

She dumped the sacred mushrooms into the fanny pack riding low across her tight belly and slammed her hands onto the two closest drumheads, popping out a pattern of contra-rhythmic dissonance she'd picked up from a Kenyan drum master she'd had a fling with in Santa Cruz. The dancers faltered, the drummers stuttered and stopped, confused as to why their beats weren't working out.

Livid, her coppery mane seething with fireglow, she screamed at Steven in the impactive silence. "We're here in Palenque, you putz! In the shadows of Mayan wonders. We're surrounded by shroom vibe and you don't get a clue."

She sneered at the long-suffering Steven and spun around on the dancers and assorted flautists and didgeridudes. "You should be swarmed over with *hongos* here, for shit sakes. The people who built these temples were shroom-heads: you can feel that in a second. Just look at those carvings and murals: stone cartoons for stoners. Zap Comix for Mayaholics. Get with the program, you... drones."

She turned back to Steven, washed over with the realization: What am I doing, hanging with this eunuch? She strode over to her pack and grabbed her chains, then flashed back to the circle of drummers and embarrassment. She stepped up to lean on his drum, right in his face. "By the way. I'm out of here, you clueless dork."

Steven shrugged, "How you gonna dance with no drummer?"

She held out her hands again, but this time each held a charred ball of Kevlar cuffed to her wrists with two feet of chain. "I don't dance to music, dickhead. I dance to fire."

She stepped back, brushing through the dancers, almost into the flames. She extended her hands over them and leaned her head back, eyes closed. Invoking the closest thing she had to a religion, the cosmic circles of blaze. Then she turned her hands over and the balls fell into the fire, the soaked-in white gas immediately turning them to crackling comets. She turned and her fireballs swung around her: Deimos and Phobos sizzling out tight orbits of streaking light. Blurring into arcs around her as she danced, sheltering and exalting her in a red-orange sphere of hot light.

The drummers started up again, as if on command, and she moved smoothly into the shifting polyrhythms. Several of the drummers grinned at her. You go, girl. The dancers also swung back into motion, but outside the hot circle her dance carved around her.

She stalked out of the thatch lean-to wearing her road warrior drag: Doc Martins and jeans, big old backpack slung over both shoulders, liter bottle of gasoline dangling behind. Ah, shit, Steven thought, standing up and brushing off the remains of the green tamales he'd just had for breakfast. Another one rides the bus.

"Yo, Coptop," he called out, moving to intercept her as she moved out of the encampment and towards the village and highway. "Hey, thought we were going to do some shrooms."

"Wasted on you," she snapped, obviously in no sort of kiss and make up mode. "I'm going *sola*, asshola."

"Where?"

"The coast. Make some money for a change. Meet a better class of drummer."

"Meet the class of veterinarian who'll sell you enough Ketamine to veg you out again."

She nodded grimly, continuing to stride up the path. "Vitamin

K deficiency; you bet. But also need a cash transfusion. And a man who can keep a beat and swing his meat."

"Oh, dick is a big priority for you now?"

She stopped and turned on him, her simmer breaking into open fire. "No, but a man is! You know; human male? I've been carrying our busking, and I've been carrying the whole relationship. Making all the decisions, dealing with all the crises while you space out. I'm sick of having to be the macho around here. Now get out of my way before I slap you and make you cry."

That pretty well did it. He recoiled and slunk off, bitterly aware that he was proving her point. She turned back towards the highway and ran into Paco, a hammy sad look on his broad *indio* face. "Coper!" he said as if deeply wounded, "Where do you go?"

She leaned in for a quick peck on her cheek, avoiding any further contact he might have in mind. He was another one who'd seen her as being essentially bereft of proper male company and had offered to remedy that lack, do his part to serve her pale flesh, fiery crest, and tigrish moves. "To a Caribbean island," she said brightly.

"You having much money?" Paco asked with more than passing interest.

"No need," she called over her shoulder as she hit the dusty trail. "I know the guy who built it."

RAPTURE OF THE HEIGHTS

Bannock got the feeling oXo dug the vibrations of the big jet, but couldn't have said where he got that impression. Like last night: he'd wanted to leave the skull in the hotel safe, but he just somehow knew that oXo hated being locked up like that. A distaste he strongly shared.

But he'd wanted to hide the skull because he'd gotten a feeling that he and the girl were going to let the second double bed in the suite go to waste. And had no macho vanity to con him into thinking a woman like that couldn't leave him way too stunned and exhausted to wake up when she slipped out of the room with Mr. Muerte Under Glass. So he'd sent her down to the lobby for whatever personal items she didn't have stashed in her monster bag from Oaxaca and slipped the ever-grinning oXo into the toilet tank. And had immediately gotten a strong vibe that he'd picked the perfect spot to suit oXo.

He touched his foot to the carry-on bag that currently held the skull, snugly tucked under the seat in front of him like the cute Aeromexico stew had told him. Plenty of room for his mystic aura here in First Class. Which he didn't usually spring for, but there was Loris. You didn't cram a beauty like her into steerage seats any more than you'd put an orchid in a jelly jar. Or let her run around in those Little Annie Amphetamine rags she'd come with. They'd lunched and shopped on Rodeo Drive, but she'd headed into way different shops than he had expected, came out looking like Congo Harem Queen meets Old Testament: soft, unstructured wraps in slubby weaves and warm autumns. He picked her Porsche Carrera sunglasses himself. He'd felt she was something he had to step up to, frame her right, choose the perfect setting for an unflawed stone: he'd wanted her to get the incognito movie star treatment the flight staff was lavishing on her. And yeah, to grace his life. He had it coming.

She leaned forward slightly to peer out the window he'd graciously granted her and he admired the way the russet raw silk wrap slid around her slim frame. Reminiscent of the way her hard peach-sized breasts had ridden around on the noble arch of her ribcage last night, the way her supple body had skated all over him, cloyed and burnished him like a fine coat of fragrant oil. Definitely, absolutely a keeper. First one he'd met, actually. And he had no idea how you handle the keeping. But he was going to figure it out. And had a strong indication that the key to it was a blob of yellowish quartz currently adding the airframe thrum of a 747 to his library of vibrations. She turned from the window and touched his hand happily, the perfect blend of pat and caress. Finder's keeper.

"So where'd you get a name like that?" First time he'd bothered to ask a hippie why people called them Rainbow or Ganja or Snot or whatever.

"I made it up for myself."

"So I'm guessing his folks didn't christen him Blaster, either?"

Blaster was no longer a citizen of her universe. She said, "I did a quest for a spirit animal. The one that found me is called a Slow Loris."

"Sounds like a Brit truck."

"It's kind of like a sloth."

54

He gave her admiring glance. "Amazing. Anybody I ever heard who had an animal vision, it was always an eagle or wolf or cougar or something cool you'd name a car or NFL team after."

"I didn't choose it, it chose me."

"You don't seem particularly slow, to me."

She smiled and rubbed the back of her hand down the side of his neck. And held up her boarding pass, with her still-uncolored fingernail on the destination. "If you were telling the truth about taking oXo home, Cancun's certainly the right direction."

"I'm pretty good with directions. And I'm doing this risky social experiment: telling the truth to a woman I'm sleeping with."

"Then maybe I can get away with the kind of question I don't usually bother asking men." There was play in the gold flecks in her brown eyes, but backed up with a heavy dose of No Shit. "Snatching oXo wasn't your idea, was it?"

"Luckily, I'm not one of insecure macho guys you hear so much about."

"Yeah, I noticed the gun you brandished was kind of small. Good sign, I figured. Bet you drive a cheap compact, too."

"Some people knew about it and sent me after it. That's one of the things I do. Go get stuff and bring it back. And I get a decent amount of jobs. Know why?"

"Because you always bring the stuff back."

"You got it."

"No, you do. And you're going to take him to these people, right? Criminals, probably. Certainly people with money."

"I work for people with money. It just seems to work out best."

"So people who knew about oXo, sent you to steal something they could have just bought?"

"Well, oXo hadn't really kept in touch. They didn't know he was slumming around with some raggedy-assed hippie. Last they heard he was hanging out in a coke mansion."

"And..."

"I mentioned you're not very slow for a Loris. They said they'd go high as a quarter million."

"He's changed hands for much more than that in his time here. I know of at least two where he brought more money. Well, merchandise, anyway."

"More wholesale money or street value?"

"You only offered Blaster a hundred thousand."

"That what he told you?"

"Blaster quit trying to lie to me. So don't you start."

"Not a chance. Hey, I got the nine millimeter discount."

"Your clients are going to be so pleased they saved so much."

"I'm pretty ethical, actually. But not stupid."

"An ethical strongarm thief. Interesting." She leaned to touch her lips to his ear and whispered, "Especially the strong arms."

He gave her the nicest smile she gotten out of him yet but seemed to want to make his point.

"Let me ask you this: did I really take anything of personal value away from Blaster?"

"No chance. He hasn't got a clue. Any benefits he got from oXo were second-hand from me."

"Hmmm. Was your boyfriend once removed, by any chance, a previous happy oXo owner?"

"Matter of fact, he was." Her look challenged him to make something of it.

"Hey, there are shabbier things to be than a skull groupie. But how did that doofus get something that so many heavier people want?"

"He was there doing a buy when Ginrick's house got busted. I made him grab oXo on our way out the back." She shrugged, doing nice things to the drapey fabric. "Otherwise he'd have ended up in an evidence locker or something."

"And he doesn't like being locked in."

She nodded, probably understanding why he knew that. "Neither do I."

"So you tagged along with Blaster."

"No, I offered him a ride. In my Mercedes."

Boy, could he ever go head over heels for this kid. "So why didn't he just sell it?"

"I didn't want him to."

"Now that I can understand. But why did he offer to sell it to me?"

"His brain is starting to go Swiss cheesy. Also, you scared the shit out of him. Go figure."

"*Moi*? But what I'm saying, am I really taking anything from Blaster? Other than you?"

"He could have gotten money from other people."

"So you think there are other people with money who would pay Blaster for something instead of just taking it?"

"Okay, probably not. So who you took oXo from was me."

"That worked out, though, didn't it?"

She leaned back against the leather cushion and evaluated him with a sidelong gaze past her fall of rich brown hair with a slight bouquet of Indian soap. She said, "So far, so good."

Smiling and feeling as good as he ever remembered, Bannock looked past her to the window, a frothy cloudscape over the Sierra Madre. On a cloud just about covers it, he thought.

Then she said, "But now you're going to give him to these rich assholes."

"They're looking for business advice."

She laughed, a hearty male sort of laugh. "Then they're in for a rough ride. Because it's really hard to get advice from oXo without being greedy. And greedy questions turn out to be self-destructive."

"Really?"

"Yes," she said in the self-obvious tone we use to instruct slow children. "Because greed is self-destructive. So is violence."

He paused, staring out at the cloud-frosted blue. She waited without fidgeting or losing interest. "Know what?" he said casually. "I'm hoping you stick around. And not just because you're gorgeous and sensational in bed. I think you're good for me. I realize that's not a romance novel declaration."

"A violent thief wants somebody to be good for him?" Her eyes came back out to play.

"I'll admit that moral reform exposes me to certain professional hazard. On the other hand, I'm about to come into a couple of hundred grand and can swing a little risk."

"By turning over oXo."

"Hmmm. So maybe you'd go with him?"

"Hard to say. Understand, I have a long, rewarding relationship with oXo and I don't know you that well yet."

He lolled back in his seat and smiled up at the comfort controls on the overhead panel. "Know what, honey? You've said a lot of interesting stuff since I knew you but so far my favorite word was that 'yet'."

"My favorite was 'good for me'."

That seemed like a good place to shut up for awhile. He raised his right hand, palm upwards and spread. Her long, fine fingers slipped in and entwined. For a hundred miles they sat like that, seated in the clouds, rocketing towards the Yucatan through clean skies. Then he spoke to her in an easy tone that she immediately recognized as the voice a man uses with his mate, not somebody exciting he's trying to win. "By the way, the buyers here aren't exactly big CEO types looking for stock tips."

"Lucky for them, then, because I could tell you about a few guys who tried that. They were asking so many questions about how fast things would go up they never got past that part of it. They're talking to a genuine oracle and don't want to know the whole future, can you believe it?"

"Oh, I believe it. Half the jobs I do are because some smart, rich, powerful jerk did something incredibly stupid."

"I don't think they were the only people like that who went down the dumper with Enron."

"This is different. These guys aren't your common greedy, crazy, short-sighted egomaniac assholes. They're movie producers."

RETROACTIVE PRIVATIZATION

Things had been going really well until Luis told the local INAH guys why they were there. Then the whole bonhomie and "enchanted to meet the esteemed Doctora Chiang" thing frosted over and crashed. Luis shriveled as he discussed her quest with them, gesturing around the little Cobá museum. He glanced at her twice and all the come-on had evaporated. She knew the signs of a bureaucrat getting more bad news while hastily clabbering up a salvage plan.

It was so painful to watch Luis' deflation that she slipped outside. She got a chilled Coke from a machine, and just held it to her temples while watching a sodden group of camera-draped Japanese, obviously completing a tour that involved scaling these daunting stairs. Of more interest was the guide, a very well set-up, athletic-looking guy about her age, probably Mayan himself. She watched him move, loose and unbothered by the sopping heat, his manner obviously ingratiating the tourists. Not too shabby, she was thinking as he waved good bye, pocketed his tips, and walked straight toward her.

His sudden turn and approach took her slightly aback, more so because she'd been fairly seriously checking out his shoulders and chiseled calves. He seemed to have homed in on her, striding across the parking lot with no hint of misdirection. Then she realized she was standing between a working man and the Coke machine. She moved aside as he glided up to it, grabbed a can from the slot, then pressed it to his temple like she had. And smiled. Hubba, hubba, some kinda smile, was MeiMei's overall impression of Puch Pop.

The guide nodded a *permiso*? and moved by her, popping open the can as he entered the INAH office.

She drank half of her own Coke before he came back out and stood looking at her, a man obviously deciding whether or not to say anything. MeiMei was always in favor of men speaking their minds and tried to appear receptive and generally Yin. He walked by within a foot of her, using nothing but a glance into her face and subtle shift of his shoulders to suggest that she walk with him as he headed towards a thatch shelter obviously placed for the comfort of tour bus drivers. She followed him, thinking, Boy, this guy knows how to guide.

In the shade of the *palapa* he turned to face her, shot a glance back at the office to let her in on the idea that he probably shouldn't be doing this, and spoke in a calm, soothing baritone. "You're interested in the jade, aren't you? Not its value; what it says?"

"Yes!" MeiMei blurted without attempting to disguise her excitement. "You know something about it?"

He tossed another signal glance, at the INAH seal on the door of Luis' VW. "I can tell you," he said, "But only if it's private words. Just you."

"I understand. And yes, this is for me, not the history institute."

Luis stepped out of the office, flanked by two of the local functionaries and visibly unhappy to see MeiMei over there under a leafy bower with a handsome young stud. But trapped into what the two guys in white *guayaberas* were saying to him so insistently. MeiMei turned her full attention to Puch, great-looking Native whose name had yet to be dropped. And heard him say, "You want to know about the Oracle? The Talking Skull?"

Hey, wait a minute, did we flash over into Indiana Jones that fast? Archaeologists have to be careful of that, you know. "Excuse me? Talking skull?"

"Ah, then you haven't seen it."

"No, and that's why I'm here. And it's pretty mysterious that there's pictures on the back side, don't you think?"

"It's a skull. Not like these here, more the old Palenque style."

"Okay. Like the Temple of Inscriptions[21]? So it's giving some news? 'Talking'?"

"Yes, exactly. A big block of symbols small and close together."

"Yes, jade because it holds more detail... wait, so you know what it says?"

He nodded but paused slightly, which she read as embarrassment. "I speak Mayan, but I can't read that old writing." He smiled again. "Only foreigners can read my own language. And slick *chilangos* from the Institute."

MeiMei always had an odd feeling around actual Mayans. Not awe, exactly, but a hushed respect like you feel in museums: they are artifacts, vestiges, remains of the day. It's like meeting a Carthaginian or Cro-Magnon in the flesh.

The guide-muffin seemed to anticipate her thought. "We're still here. Nobody ever managed to get rid of us. And we do have a legend about that jade skull. It's like the calendar... you know, the Sun, the Tzolkin?"

"It's my specialty, actually."

He nodded solemnly. "That's wonderful. Anyway, it orders our days. It's why there is order, how our lives move through time, you understand? But outside that circle of order there is chaos, like a jungle or wilderness where things came from, and go back to when they're no longer in time. I hope I'm making sense. And the skull on the jade is telling about that disorder, about the life outside of time. Telling the living about the world of the dead, of the unborn."

MeiMei almost whispered. "Do you know where it is?"

He lowered his voice as well, leaned in close to her. "I am trusting you now. Please don't mention what I'm telling you to anybody else. Especially not that guy you came here with."

"I promise."

"It's in private hands."

Puch saw the dark squall that blew across the face of the pretty Chinita and knew why. Even so, he was surprised at the hardness that barged into her serene face and mild voice as she said, "Oh, man! Same story everywhere. Grabbed off..."

She spun around and looked at the unlikely little local museum with narrowed eyes. "Probably why it was brought here? Easy place to lose something, am I right?"

She must have transferred some of her anger when she turned back to him because he made placating gestures. "Not me. I grew up around these ruins. If I wanted to steal artifacts..." He surprised her with a sharp, clear laugh. "Actually, I have stolen them."

She didn't even manage to shift gears to deal with that confession before he went on. "We used to pick up things from the old buildings, then sell them out at the highway."

Raggedy little Mayan kids flogging broken carvings and potshards to tourists, she thought. Well, it was their stuff, wasn't it? "I wasn't thinking of you. But maybe you know who has it?"

"Of course not." But he was speaking from a too-straight face, so she waited. "It would be crazy to know that, you understand? Dangerous. What if was some rich, powerful *chilango* collector, kind of guy who runs Mexico, does whatever he wants?"

She thought it over a moment, watching Luis run through the elaborate leave-taking process. Better cut to the chase here. "That would be a bummer. Some guy up in Mexico City, you're saying."

"Probably not. His headquarters has been Cancun almost since they built the place. The word is that he bought a big yacht and is outfitting it like a palace, plans to live on it, traveling around the world."

"And where is it now?"

"The lagoon on Isla Mujeres. Last week they installed a helicopter platform. I know some Navy guys who worked on it."

"Omigod... so he's leaving the country?"

"Impossible to know. This guy is... well, he's not really a person like you or me. More like a government."

"He works for the government?"

"The government works for him."

"Uh oh."

"This is Mexico, *Chinita.*"

Luis was heading towards them now, so she spoke fast. "Would this non-person who didn't do what we weren't talking about have a name?"

"Julio Cesar Ronchel del Cumbre."

"Thank you...?"

"My name is Puch."

"I'm May. Thanks so much. Listen..." She could sense Luis approaching and blurted without really believing she was doing it, "How can I get to Isla Mujeres? Right now?"

He shook his head mockingly, but she could see fun and admiration in his look. "From Tulum. Local buses pass on the highway."

She was already moving past him, towards the road. And people say I'm never impulsive, she thought. She turned her head without stopping as he called to her. She saw Luis standing and staring, the Mayan guy effortlessly catching up.

"Look, if you're going to Isla Mujeres," he said quickly, "There's this girl there. She works at that "swim with dolphins" place. Blonde. Her name is Curtsy."

"And if I see her?"

"Well, I guess..." it was cute seeing a guy as self-possessed as him flustered and unsure of himself. "Could you tell her...?"

"That you think about her a lot?"

"Yes! Thank you."

"Oh, no," she said firmly as she quickened her pace along the access road, her shirt already plastered to her skin. "Thank you."

"If you plan on trying to take on Ronchel, you don't want to thank me. You should stay away from him. He can turn everything against you: police, government, heaven, earth, hell. You know?"

"Only in a really vague way. But I have to see that skull. It's like the summit of my work, my life."

"That's exactly what it is."

NUDE AWAKENING

The guy just stared, totally fascinated but not in a way that alarmed her. Which was a good thing, considering she seemed to be lying on the only bed in his weird little hovel, naked under a huge beach towel printed with faded jaguars and parrots peering out of a jungle. She didn't see any of her clothes and couldn't remember showing up here. The lack of a hangover led her to think it wasn't another one of *those* deals, though. She just didn't have a lot of recall at the moment. No big.

He brought her bottled water, then just sat staring at her. She sat up clutching the towel to her chest, smiled prettily, swept a handful of gold hair back from her face, and accepted the water. She sipped, then guzzled greedily, realizing she was very dry, perhaps borderline dehydrated. Might have something to do with her brain not hitting on all cylinders. He sat watching her drink, seemed to be working something out in his head. And must have finally figured out what it was because he suddenly said, "What your name?" in heavily flawed English.

"Let me get back to you on that," she told him seriously. "But how about you?"

It only took three re-wordings of the question to understand that the guy was named Ganzo. Good start. The rest would come back pretty soon. It always did, like it or not. Meanwhile, she scoped Ganzo out. Obviously local, but taller than the normal Mayan and pretty easy on the eyes. Nicely muscled, maybe a swimmer. What she was really wondering was whether or not the guy's looks and her nude presence in his bed were connected and if that was going to complicate her life. She kind of doubted it.

For one thing, she was getting the feeling this Ganzo guy was beyond uncomplicated: was more like not all there. Not so much because of his blank stare and limited conversational tools, or even the fact that he had a great-looking naked blonde in stock and didn't seem interested in much more than staring like a little kid: there was just a blankness to him, like a big dog or draft horse. Exactly the kind of animals she was very comfortable around. More so than good-looking men, actually. Legacy of her rodeo farmgirl childhood. Hey, now there was backstory right there. She lay back to think that over, but when her head hit the ball of T-shirts that served as a pillow she yelped in pain. Apparently her head had been beaten pretty badly. Hmm, head trauma, can't remember anything: just like the cartoons.

Her gingerly explorations of her lacerated scalp indicated that her wounds had been treated with iodine and a band-aid here and there. But no matted blood in her hair. Had he washed her hair for her? She palmed a handful over her nose and sniffed. It smelled of cheap hand soap. Like the big yellow cake sitting over there on the rickety table by the plastic paint bucket.

She raised the towel and took a peek: yep, her golden gorgeosity was marred into a camouflage pattern of suburn, scrapes and bruises. She thought about that a little as she drained the last of the liter of *Agua Pura*, but came up with zip. Ganzo came up with another bottle of water. This time she patted his hand before taking the bottle and chugging another few pints. "You rescued me, didn't you?"

He cocked his head at her like a dog, and with as much comprehension. Not much of a talker. She rather liked that in a guy, sometimes. Apparently. She toasted him with the bottle and slugged down some more.

And no, Ganzo never talked much. For one thing, he didn't have much to say. A physical type, you could call him. But also there was a sort of reticence inside him. When he worked the beach he held up his wares for examination, dickered with the foreigners using his fingers, stared at the women when they tried to draw him out—all the time conflicted over whether he wasn't worthy to talk to them or they didn't belong in his world. Or something. Concepts swirled in his head like clouds. Sometimes the clouds came together and massed to form shapes. He could express those shapes, adroitly carving them onto shell, coconuts, coral, driftwood, fruit pits. But the clouds almost never formed words.

Meanwhile, she figured her dehydration was responding well to treatment because she had to pee. She looked around the cluttered little palm frond shack but didn't see any sign of a bidet or vanity. She looked at Ganzo, who was still squatting on his heels, regarding her with his calm fascination. First word in *Español* a girl picks up around Mexico: "*Baño?*" He pointed at the door without breaking his stare. Okay, the towel was big, but not really up to a Dorothy Lamour shot. She tried another major word in Chick Spanish: "*Ropa?* My clothes? Nice fluffy guest bathrobe?"

He stood up smoothly and stepped over to some sort of workbench, snagged a bright red rayon sarong off the plastic armchair. Very nice hibiscus pattern. A Barcelona girl had given it to Ganzo two days ago. He'd looked a complete *espectaculo*, striding up out of the surf bronzed and naked, a blond goddess hanging off his hands. She wouldn't have been completely comfortable with the idea of a guy just carrying off a naked unconscious woman like that, but one thing Tulum beachniks figured out was that Ganzo was harmless. She'd made a bit of a play for him, like some of the other little sluts in the *cabañas*, but he just didn't seem to swing that way. He'd just stare at some topless Euro-hotty modeling his jewelry salaciously in front of him, his inner drum wacking out.

So she'd draped the red sarong over the comatose blonde and waved them off into the dusk before turning back to the bar swing for another cup of black espresso, shot of mescal, and line of toot.

When she stepped out of what amounted to an outhouse with a fall pipe located on top of a two story cement building in some tacky little village, she'd figured a few things out. Or remembered them, anyway. This was Mexico, the blue shine she saw to the east was the Caribbean, she was American, details to follow. Another thing she figured out: she could just walk down those risky-looking wood stairs, head up that dusty street and be free of this situation. She wasn't exactly kidnapped here.

On second thought, though, walking around wounded, wearing only a wrap, with no money or clues, wouldn't be the best plan of action available. So she turned back to Ganzo's hovel, seeing it now as a *palapa*, a wedge of woven palm thatch sitting up here on somebody's roof. She pushed aside the plush acrylic blanket with washed-out Mayan calendar print, stepped back into the dusky, gold-shot light of the *palapa*, and almost ran into Ganzo. He extended his hands toward her, running them into her hair and around her throat.

CAN SOOOO DO THAT

Now, what should have been the piece of proverbial cake was getting hold of Dr. MeiMei Chiang. Nee May Flower Chiang, how's that for precious? The woman had an office in a government building in Chetumal. And Aphra had actually had an appointment with her. What could be simpler than that? The hard part was supposed to come later, figuring out what it all meant.

Because Miss Mayflower is what it all came down to. All that McKenna "Time Wave Zero[24]" stuff boils down to Year of Our Bygracious Lawd 2012, couple shopping days til Christmas and every single crypto-cycle she could parse hit barebottom zero on the same date a bunch of Indians decided to end their 5000-year calendar. So you go to the guy who wrote the book, right? Who turns out to be dead, possibly from brainrot due to conspicuous consumption of every rainjungle mind-melter he could lay hand to.

So you find the next book, which it turns out got wrote up by cute little MeiMeiFlower, who turns out suddenly got gone and ain't nobody round the office wants to talk about where she mighta decamped to. Conspicuous by their non-knowledge, you know? Horny Mexican geeks got no idea there was this fine-assed China doll working in the next playstation. Make you go "Hmmmm" sometimes.

So here Aphra sat, cooling her sculptural buns in this weird park and getting her head around the whole depth of this Three Cultures mural. Conquistador daddy on the right, hot Mayan mama on the left, li'l mixed up kiddo in the middle. Easy art to interpret. One thing you gotta hand to those Spaniards, they were efficient. Instead of killing off all the Indians, then shipping in slaves from Africa, causing untold problems for all concerned, they just cut out the middleman and slaved the Indians. Out there building forts on the West Coast while the Anglos were mucking around with Dan'l Boone. Best give it up for know-how and firepower. Which had kind of been the idea all along.

So she's waiting for this Luis character to walk by for his coffee and yucky little cake stuff over there in the swank coffeehouse, serves freeze-dried coffee. Like he does every day this time, which she couldn't help but notice since she's had the whole place staked out while waiting for a turnover and failing to get back to the Cracker in Chief who's paying the freight for this little clusterfuck. Whiling away the time in this garden spot figuring out which way'd be best to wring out Sr. Luis' snippy little ass. When who should fall by but the shy cutie from the office there, closet violet shrinking among the male hotshots. Didn't even get her name.

Which turns out to be Lluvia. The picture there seems to be; she's a bit hot on Luis. Also quite impressed by the elusive Doctor Chiang. Who she likes and appreciates and would prefer not to see sullied and debased by Luis, her immediate superior. Presumably because if there's any sullying to be done on the Luis issue, she'd prefer being sole source.

So here she is, telling tales out of school. First whisking her off to this little... what the hell is this place, anyway? Internet café with candy and some really disturbing little comic books for school kids and beer for whoever, but also a taco shop with goofy tables made out of PVC barrels. Telling her all that soap opera shit between the lines, no idea what she's broadcasting. Typical government employee, really. But also telling the tale on this roadtrip thing. Luis hauls MeiMei up to something called Cobá and comes back without. Not happy about it, either. And not the least bit talkative. But what we got; last seen.

Little Lluvia's pretty adorable, by the way, especially all conflicted up on her loyalties and nice Mexican girl complications. Aphra wouldn't have minded browsing more of what she could see in that typical low-cut, pushmepullyou bra there, but it would have been too much like jacklighting Bambi. That Catholic guilt trip stuff all over her, dribbling a crucifix in that peekaboo cleavage like she means it: keeping us black-hearted vamp types at bay.

What it's worth, drop a few heavy hints that she could do much worse than shitcanning Luis, to include any and all fondest dreams in that general direction. He hasn't hit on her by now, he's too stupid to fool with. And FYI, honey, guys who take girls on rides out of town and don't bring them back aren't your best bet, anyway. But hey, can she give directions to this Cobá place? Which it turns out is an ex-place, really: big old Indian temples out in the bullrushes, near Tulum, which Aphra happened to recall is like another ruin that spawned a strip development along a wretched stretch of highway.

But snap... on her way up to Tulum in a shuttle van she'd just bought all the seats in, guess who rings her up? The Senator's jewboy logistics wonk, that's who. Telling her that lil MeiMei called home from a public long distance booth. Nobody home, left no message. But bottom line: from another local tourist ghetto called Isla Mujeres. Aphra gave a wolfish laugh that caught the driver's eye and said, "Island of Women? I can *so* do that."

Then she clapped her phone shut before Whosistein could ask what she'd turned up at her end. I'm a fourth quarter player, she thought. Best not be boring me with progress reports.

RAFTER DANCE

The deep wells of inner discontent that fed Xchab's struggle to be anything else but what she was born to be were roiling in conflict as she watched the redheaded newcomer strut around the floating island. On the one hand, Copper presented the most exciting template she'd seen yet for her thwarted will to become. Her skin was white as bleached clamshells, her hair as red and toxic as fire coral. She had the whole offhand post-punk, alt.worldly thing nailed: the biker boots, the jeans turned into artless sex lace by tears and burns, jewelry that blurred pre-Columbian with urban slasher in a puzzling but unmistakable manner...and total self-assurance in her every movement and glance.

On the other hand, she was obviously a bitch from some sleazy suburb of hell and patently bad news for the shaky domestic situation Xchab dreamed of dumping but suddenly felt the urge to defend against feline predators slinking in from the night.

Winston had greeted the hussy in an affectionate and familiar manner to say the very least. He'd yowled with pleasure and run halfway across their rickety bridge to embrace her, laughing and spinning her around. She'd responded like a veteran whore, turning the embrace into something laughably lascivious: wrapping her foot around behind his hips and feigning moans of ecstasy. When she glimpsed Xchab over his shoulder—standing flatfooted, topless, and stunned on the bamboo catwalk beside the eco-flimsy Gilligan shack—she'd done a little fake embarrassed "oh" with her lips and winked.

Winston finally pried himself loose from the arms and loins of this cocksure bitch and led her off the bridge to the "beach", scuffing through the sand painstakingly ferried over and spread on campaign signs supported by hundreds of thousands of old soft drink bottles. He was spieling his improvements in the home-made jungle madhouse, but when they came to Xchab he waved a hand and proclaimed, "Meet Xchab, my main squeeze."

The slut smiled with what had to be professionally dissembled friendliness and leaned forward to offer her hand. "Hi, I'm Copper." No response of any kind whatsoever.

She smiled wider and said, "*Hola, me llama Copper.*" That completely fried Xchab, who turned and fled, unable to put words to the sardonic irony of the doubtless false name the red ruiner had tried to hand her.

As she headed for some other part of the tiny islet, Copper noted admiringly that her buttocks were as firm and round as her tits. Winston said, "Typical *indita*, shy and mulish. I'm sure she hates your guts from go."

"Well, I'd hate for that to be a problem for you. Or her."

""She'll get over it when she gets to know you." Winston, longtime squaw man and hippie chick fancier, was philosophical and unattached. Copper shot him a wry grin and he amended, "Or not. Hey, lemme show you the papayas I grew right here. This place is really coming together."

"Wasn't the other one down in Playa coming together really good before the hurricane made it come apart?"

"Well, yeah. That's what hurricanes do. But since you didn't notice, this one's in a lagoon. Nicely protected. Rode out Dean."

"Which diverted down south, didn't it?"

"Yeah, went into Chetumal and trashed a bunch of Maya villages instead of their cash farm up here. This guy told me God had saved us from damage. I asked him what God had against the villagers who died down there, but he didn't get it."

"It's fabulous, Win. I could retire here. Let me know when you have condos and are selling citizenships."

"We're already citizens of the same country, Coppertop."

"You know it, *pedo viejo*, ambassadors of the rainbow."

"Potentates of the Horizon."

The tour of the island had drawn Copper's oooh's and ahh's; some complimentary, some genuine. This was Winston, all over.

Scrounging up garbage and turning it into floating unreal estate. Living on air and vibes, and always some young, baffled honey living it with him until she either came to her senses or took total leave of them. There was no sign of the little Maya chick during the tour. It wouldn't be easy to hide on this nutso raft, but she managed.

And continued hiding, freaked-out and broody, while Copper stowed her gear and strung a hammock up out over the catwalk. Xchab, regarding them silently through chinks in the palm thatch, was grudgingly pleased that she hadn't installed herself in the big hammock/trampoline/playpen she shared with Winston. But still. No idea what to make of the intruder, or how to get rid of her.

She listened to what she could make out of the pair's past together as they slugged down wine and passed a bong back and forth. Vagabonds. Sexual outlaws. Drug-soaked pirates. They kept talking about burning a man in a place called Nevada. She had a vision of a corpse aflame on a snowy field, Winston and *puta roja* dancing naked around him in a savage ritual. Her loathing for the woman was growing, but so was her treacherous admiration. She moved self-confidently, laughed and touched and snorted like a man. Then the bitch opened her big, sinister pack and pulled out two chains with cuffs at one end... And charred balls at the other! Xchab found herself charting her easiest path for a hasty retreat.

"You'll love this," she was telling Winston. "My new number. Like nothing you've seen."

"Hey, now," he said, expressing his doubts without a trace of worry or tension. "Let's keep in mind you're in a grass shack on a flammable island here."

"I'm a professional, Winston," she told him solemnly. "Do I go around burning down my performance venues?"

"I can think of three."

"Well..." As Xchab watched warily for any movement that smacked of arson or imprisonment or kinkiness, she unclipped the black balls of carbon and clipped on two small plastic devices. Then glanced at Winston. "If you're so concerned about fire hazards, why don't you blow out that lantern?"

He chuckled and raised the glass chimney to whuff out the mantle's flame and plunge the grass shack into darkness. Xchab had known it would come to something like this. She readied herself for God knew what.

Suddenly two dots of red light appeared in the darkened shanty. Like eyes of demons straight out of Xibalba or the Christian hell, was Xchab's impression. Moving wickedly in the darkness, dropping down almost to the floor, where they stared: seeking her out with their hot red glare.

"LEDs?" Winston asked calmly.

"High tech pocket flashlights for yuppie scum. Check this out."

Suddenly the two red motes swung into motion. They streaked through an arc a meter wide, trailing threads of red blaze in the black air. There were two whizzing red wheels in the room, turning together like the drive train of some satanic chariot. Then the wheels tilted and merged, spinning through each other. Xchab, who'd been ready to bolt, was frozen, staring at the ruddy gyres in the night.

The arcs spun overhead, carving out glowing disks just under the cane rafters that supported the thatch. Then turned into figures of eight zipping and winding. Then they sped up, spinning more and more solid circles as they began a complex, hypnotic interaction. Without willing it, Xchab parted the fronds that made up the "wall" in front of her and shuffled into the room.

The arcs were so fast now they seemed solid, red balls spun out by the two sizzling red dots. She could see faint flickers of Copper's hair, lit by the glow as she spun: a nucleus effortlessly weaving electron orbits around her. Atomic city. A living alien generating in front of her eyes. Xchab realized she'd never really seen the light, reached out her hand as unconsciously as a child. She wanted to touch the surface of the red spheres, stroke the light. Suddenly a chain whipped around her finger, a little plastic cylinder slapped into her palm, glowing red like a trapped firefly. Copper's face was right in front of her, bottom-lit into creepy, lurid angles. She was laughing. Winston was applauding. She turned and ran, this time to dive into the bed and burrow into the cotton blankets. She was aware that her embarrassment was tinged with wonder, less so that her disgust and distrust of the redhead was now sprinkled with sparkles of awe.

DOODS, JUNIOR GRADE

They'd named themselves Lords; the only cool way to claim such honors, really. But were having trouble making it stick. They circled the marina petulantly, gunning their SkiDoos and JetSkis into little jetés over self-created wakes, simmering. Those hippies and gas jockeys would rue the day they belittled the Lords of Xibalba[25].

Their mounts were as expensive and up-to-date as the overstoked, Mamon-fellating consumisimo culture of Cancun would allow. And that *juniors*[26] could use to establish that they might be out here in the sticks instead of running amok in the *Distrito Federál*[27] with the other sons of Mexico's ruling class: but they were every bygod bit as badass, corrupt, spoiled, rich, and full of crap as any swinging *pinga* among them.

The Xibalba name came not from scholarly respect for the Mayan past, but because they thought it was cool so they took it. They were the latest generation of the European conquest of these *indios* and that's how things were done. Glorying in an imagined past of the people they scorned, also par for the course.

They'd all gravitated to JetSkis and SkiDoos as naturally as they'd all been enrolled in the same snotty, post-modern *collegio* with its own stadium and helicopter pad. The Yucatan was Yacht World, and everybody they knew had at least a thirty meter Hatteras to anchor off Isla on Sundays and drink, or a Donzi to blast around showing their trash and scaring fishermen. They were the dream market for "personal watercraft".

They'd seen themselves as pirates, then as a trou-sagging, tattooed, crip-slouching urban gang riding expensive toys. Then they saw the film "Wild Hogs" and everything fell into place. They quickly backtracked through DVD's, gobbling up the Easy Rider, the Wild One, the dozens of loner dirtbikers kicking Hell's Angel's dorks in the dirt. They were a marine bike gang now, proud to sport the dimly understood name "Lords of Xibalba". Then they come in here for gas and some ancient gringo hippy dickhead laughs at them. And his fuckable but snot-nosed sidekick, the built redhead buying gas in a liter bottle, calls them "SkiDoods."

WE ARE NOT "DOODS"! was their general mood and they thrashed the oily water around the gas dock into a froth trying to figure out how to make that point. But by then the old grunger and Srta. Smackdown Bitch had split. She even waved back at them! "Toasted" them with her bottle of gas!

Finally Chimi, as his *cuates* called him, rather than Agosto Cesar Ronchel del Cumbre, stood up on his waterbike and rallied them with a sharp cry. He dropped to his seat, pointed out to the limpid turquoise of the Bay and dialed on RPM's so suddenly his JetSki rared up almost vertical before blasting out in the point position of a skimming diamond of Doods. Later for that pair of *babosos*, was in his mind as he skipped along over submerged coral and tarpon.

The formation flashed by their usual haunts on Isla—Rolandi's, O's, Tiburon, any place with a dock and liquor license—and rounded to Playa Norte. Spanking across the shallows, they dived into Buhos, scattering swimmers and sunbathers as they drove their slim hulls up onto the beach in direct violation of the kinds of laws that sons of powerful Mexicans observe only by omission.

Chimi smoldered over a Cuba Libre. moving sideways in the little rope swing that served Buho's beach bar instead of stools. He paid no attention to his droogitos prancing and jiveassing in the circle cleared for them by wary patrons. He had a score to settle.

Chango (known to others as Aquiles Tomaso Dominquero y Vasca) used the elaborate faux street dialect adapted by his wealthy peers to rag on Rambón, who was flaunting a new high-tech system that allowed him to blast out sounds even while doing the most hair-brained and waterlogged stunts. Drenching the peaceful beach with the raggedest in rap and reggaetón that money and obsession could acquire.

"It's nothing to do with reggae," Chango sneered. "It's rap in Spanish. What, don't you understand English?" A deep insult among educated, arriviste young Mexicans, for whom familiarity with U.S. culture is a badge of hipness.

"*Eso*," Corcho chimed in, "What's that all about? It's like Japanese mariachi or something."

"You are talking about Jap Mexicans, *pendejo*?" Rambón scoffed. "You've got some Chink word tattooed on your ass."

Chango laughed, touching his eye in the signal for having seen through a secret. "Oh, so you've studied his naked ass?"

"*No hay pedo*," Rambón replied languidly. "I saw it bouncing around on top of that Norwegian girl with the..."

"So that's what happened to her."

"What happened to his *verga*, too," Corcho snickered. "That's why he's not drinking any beer."

Chimi suddenly cut through the jabber. "So are we "Doods"?"

"Are we not men?" Corcho joked, but caught on that Chimi was in no mood.

"Fucking hippie, fucking redhead bitch," was Chimi's summation of it all.

The SkiDoods agreed wholeheartedly. "Fuck those gringo *mamones*," and such sentiments were echoed around the bar.

"So why didn't you do anything about it?" Rambón dropped out like a lead fart.

Chimi glared at him without a quick reply. But was saved from a lame one by Chango. Who up and spoke, "Well, we know where they hang out."

He drew eyes from the whole pack, waited a beat, then shrugged, "He's the *puto* who built that floating island in the Lagoon."

Chimi nodded gravely. Of course he'd known that. What he didn't yet know was, "So what are we going to do about it?"

"Something *chingón*!" Chango blurted, part of a chorus.

"*Algo tremendo!*"

"*Barbaro!*"

"*Chidisimo!*"

Damn right, Chimi mused. Fuckin A right we will.

SHE SLEEPS WITH THE FISHES

In two weeks she'd learned the ropes, picked up the drill, gotten to know the guys. Who had shown her around extravagantly and indicated their inclinations to extend the show and tell as far as she'd care to follow. Highly hetero, the dudes here at Dolphin Discovery. Probably why she got the job in the first place? But Curtsy didn't care. Dolphin groupies can't be picky over how they get to their inner tabernacle: access to living cetaceans.

She'd also gotten to know the various dolphins in the park, differing from her acquaintanceship with the male "guides" in that she actually gave a damn about the bottlenosed, grinning gray torpedoes that frisked around inside the basin closed off from the Bay by a double chain-link fence. A fence that Curtsy was now inversely "climbing" down in the dark; grabbing the squares of wire and pulling herself towards the dent in the bottom she'd seen her third day on the job and snuck in at night to enlarge and enable.

She'd come all the way out from the beach underwater; using her seven minute breath-hold not for depth, but to cruise without surfacing or trailing bubbles, driven by her powerful full body flex/ripple pushing water off her Russian-built, carbon fiber Glide Model 1 monofin.

The monofin was wonderful: not only the fastest way a human can travel in water, but mimicking dolphins in look and function. She felt most like a marine mammal when undulating deep, shivering through the water with the skulling of the rounded black "tail fin". She was saving up for a Lunocet, less cetacean-looking than the Glide, but faster, sleeker, more powerful with its outer space tex/flex. But for the moment, as she approached her personal grail and obsession, she had slipped her feet out of the twin footcups and secured the fin to the outer fence. This situation was not one where she wanted her feet bound together.

She had also peeled off the sleek black rubber cap and leaned back to shake out her hair, a blonde eddy around her head as she scanned the catwalks and landings of the delfinario. She'd tugged off the strings of her black bikini and stuffed both pieces into the foot cups of the fins, then taken her careful, measured "packet breaths" and slid silently down the wall.

The hole was easy to find, groping in the total black of underwater night; too narrow for even the smallest delphine female to slip out, but enough to squirm her slim torso through. She patted down the sand beneath the bulge in the fence and checked for any shifting or filling, feeling for traces of monofilament fishline, the true nightmare of a gunkholing freediver like herself and the real point of her omnipresent quick-release, hook-bladed knife. She kipped under and in, twisting and tucking her tight tummy to turn the corner up from the silt towards her goal. And oxygen. She was actually trapped beneath the fence for a few seconds, wriggling her butt in the oozy sand. Nothing to alarm a tuned athlete with her kind of downtime. She surfaced slowly and cautiously, sipping air as she scanned the walkways and buildings for night watchmen she was pretty sure would be in Alfredo's office watching the Toluca game. She looked up to make sure her chalk mark was where she'd surreptitiously placed it to mark her exit, on the planks of the catwalk where tourists stood to gawk at marine mammals performing in what they no doubt thought of as a natural habitat.

Before she even came under the inside fence she'd sensed them, "felt" their sonic scans with her skin. An alpha male brushed her as she paddled up towards the surface. But as soon as she moved away from the fence, they were all around her. Twenty three healthy bottle-nosed dolphins. Already her friends. Over half of them males that she knew by name, sight and touch. Already her lovers. But now she'd come to consummate that reality.

She felt more bodies sliding against hers, smooth muscles under skin as taut and slick as a wet marble. She heard their short, flutey breathing, reached out to stroke their moving forms. The beauty of it, the power, the sensual overload. Her breathing quickened and fluttered.

She felt stubby noses nudging the soles of her bare feet, the signal for her to spread her legs and let them bear her up and "noseride" her across the pool. Not tonight: she'd have to be quiet. One more love that dare not show its face in sunlight. But she kept her legs spread anyway, holding her face above water with helical movements of her hands. She felt Bruto brush by in front of her and threw her arms around his torso, thrilling in his sleek, wet glide through her embrace. This was the way to discover dolphins, by God.

A flank slid under her left foot, slick and insinuating. Something about the way it flexed told her it was Mayab, her favorite female. Then Caruso cruised between her legs, a smooth force on her inner thighs. She clamped onto him and he waggled salaciously. At the last moment of his transit he flipped on his side and the tip of his right fluke brushed her pubic hairs. She caught her breath, felt a hot flush in the cool water. No wet suit needed, she thought, I can get plenty wet as is.

Then she felt a blunt nose, the size of soup can, smooth as a wet dildo, bumping against her mons. Tap, tap, sniff, sniff. Yes, Chito, you can come in. Her pherenomes must be sifting through the water by now, browsed by the entire clan. She reached down to place her hands on Chito's head and hunched against his nose. He drove up in a powerful lunge, hoisting her upper body out of the water and tailwalking her twenty feet before letting her slip back down into the water. She dove, heading all the way to the bottom, handstanding in the sand, legs spread like a "Y". Cisco surged down and slid between them, pushing her downward, his big thick body thundering across her widening slit. She came to the surface with a gasp that was not all about accessing air.

Pinoccio moved up under her from behind, bearing her up on his back like a bronco queen, sliding under her, rippling more than necessary. She leaned forward, onto his back as it slid under her, then his dorsal fin slipped between her butt cheeks, dragged along her trough, and bore up against her until the last second, when it slipped out, kissing her slit with a little fillip. She was crying now, lost in sensation and emotion, beloved union at long last achieved.

Two of the males moved alongside her hips, mimicking a move from the show. She laid her hands on them, rising up on their support even as they slickered along and vanished into the night water. Then Pinoccio was back, sliding under her again. She spread her legs as wide as she could as he cruised under her saddle, curving upwards as he slowly finned forward. She fell against him, feeling his pale belly skin slipstream along her tight nipples. She shuddered and moaned, getting off on riding their bodies, giving full rein to what she'd always felt around dolphins.

She rolled and dived, grasping Pinoccio to her, lying on top of his belly with her legs moving up and down along his upper body.

Pinoccio was obviously aroused. And so were other males, zipping in to smoothe along her flanks as she slid her lips down the alpha male's sleek throat. He fell away, looping downward, and she floated face down, shaking. Her heartbeat, normally as slow as any athlete's, was racing, pumping heat and pinkness all over her. Her eyes fluttered and she turned her head to breathe and moan. Then he was back, a long traverse of her, his fin moving between her legs, then throbbing along her pussy. She coughed, stifled a yell, rolled onto her back as her first orgasm shook her like small craft in a squall. She lay her head back, her hands stoking dreamily below her. And Pinoccio surged up onto her, the way he blasted out of the water onto the platform to splash and delight the damned tourists.

She took a deep inhale as he skidded along her, his flippers caressing her arms, his belly slicking up along her breasts. She almost blacked out as he bore her down under the sea.

She had figured out early on that a dolphin in the grip of sex could easily bear a woman right down to the bottom, even her own exceptional strength and flexibility as nothing compared to his. Could drown her there, maybe thinking her death throes were a faked orgasm. But she felt no risk: dolphins know about life and death in people and have been observed saving human lives, but never taking them. Unlike the way we treat them.

And in fact she did feel her shoulders touch the bottom as he plunged against her. She just threw her arms around him, fondling the tender spots behind his eyes. And had the biggest orgasm of her life: the culmination of a lifetime love, combined with the dangerous rapture of apnea. She was dying, her life shaking itself apart from within, the lights flickering down while colored dazzle wove and flashed across a black expanse of velvet ending. Then he was gone and she floated, rather than swam, to the surface.

She broke the water face first, still rumbling with the orgasm, hot tears trailing off into cold water, her heart stopped, then re-started in a new world, inner muscles tussling and sunfishing, eyes closed to watch the play of light.

Light which suddenly smashed into her eyes on a wave of raucous noise and squawking. She popped them open and nearly came out of the water in sheer shock. A powerful flashlight was on her face, others playing over her pale body, naked under inches of water. Torches held by the night crew and a dozen of their work buddies, screaming with delight at having caught that stuck-up *gringa* bitch naked and fucking the fish!

Caught *flagrante delicto* and still dazed from the peak experience of her love/sex life, Curtsy just gaped for a long moment. A moment richly enjoyed by her male fellow employees, swigging their beers and joints. Only Alfredo wasn't laughing. He was totally pissed off, like supervisors get. Besides, Toluca had lost.

The *futbol* fans whooped it up over this unexpected double-header treat, howling with laughter as Curtsy finally reacted. She snapped into a racer's turn, took two butterfly strokes towards the chalk mark and went down. Sickness and shame flooding all over the rapture she'd felt just seconds before, she drove down to find the notch, twisted out through it and angled up towards the top of the outer fence with a strong breast stroke, trungeon kick. She drove upwards with hands extended, and when she hit the top of the fence she surged over it in a sort of modified Fosbury flop. Halogen lanterns highlighted her golden puss as she went over; cheers, jeers and catcalls impelled her. She ignored the suit and cap, just crammed her feet into the monofin and powered off, deep enough to block the light and hateful sound. She was at the beach in three minutes, fin already off as her feet found the chalky bottom, running bareassed to the palm copse where she'd left shorts, shirt and shoes in the basket of her rented motorscooter.

Alfredo's voice echoed over the water, "You are so fired, Kurtz. Don't even show your fishfucking face here again, ever."

Román yelled, "No, no, come back *Güera*. I'll put on a fin and squeak while I bone you. Just feed me some fish."

SHA ZAMA

Scanning the map of Isla Mujeres gave MeiMei the impression of a medial view of the human hand: long and narrow with fingers pointing north and the "thumb" creating a narrow inland lagoon. The thumb area was apparently called "Sac Bajo", a typical local mixture of Spanish and Mayan. So here she was right here, at the first knuckle on that thumb, identified on the map by a little number "9"; a lovely spa/restaurant named Zama. But none of the other numbers referred to "Evil Artifact Thief's Yacht/Lair", leaving her a bit stumped. She realized that the lagoon would be the location of any yacht swagers or whatever they called them: sheltered water like Lake Union back in Seattle. But that didn't narrow it down and she couldn't find anywhere to scope the lagoon out since it was ringed by thick mangroves. Bothersome.

She'd found Dolphin Discovery and asked about "Curtsy", partly out of courtesy to the helpful Puch, but also because it was the only name she knew on the island. At the desk of what was a startlingly large pleasure park for, apparently, human contact with penned dolphins, the receptionist had snickered when she asked and two male employees couldn't keep straight faces long enough to give her a straight answer. So she'd stumbled on this Zama place nearby, a really nice beachfront retreat with freshwater pools, a killer view across the bay at the white underbelly of the Cancun hotel zone, a huge conical *palapa* over marble floors and hardwood tables, and so many breeze-stirred white gauze hangings it looked like Maxville Parrish's washday. Especially since that breeze was starting to whip up into a freshet or gust or whatever you'd call it.

There was a long dock, which made her wonder if yachties hung out there sometimes, but at the moment it was empty except for a college couple who looked like they'd forgotten to go home after spring break, smooching graphically in one of the tiered pools. And this haughty black woman who showed up later in a bright red caftan, sort of cruising the place like a runway model before deciding it met her Iman-class standards and settled in to sip some see-through drink and intimidate the waiters. Oh, and the short, vaguely Asian guy who wandered up off the beach barefoot, sipping a margarita. She glanced at him: not many Asians around this area, but Isla Mujeres was apparently a worldwide destination. He looked kind of academic: exactly the kind of guy she got tired of as an undergrad.

She continued regarding the numbers on the map, looking for something that might provide a boatish clientele or observation tower. He startled her when he spoke from just behind her.

"Not fair, you've complicated the whole issue."

It was the little Asian guy, of course, lurking just inside the shadow of her cream canvas umbrella. Or whatever he was. Definitely some sort of geek with no gift for icebreakers. Kind of appealing in itself. She said, "Well, I'm always in favor of simple issues."

He pointed at her arm, eyes unseen behind the big glasses that gave him sort of a Ferdinand Marcos look. Oh, of course: Filipino. And yeah, some sort of academic because he came off like a gradschool lecturer with, "We residents learn to judge how long visitors have been here by their skin tone. You learn to practically read a travel itinerary off bronzed and peeling shoulders."

Well, points for originality at least. Big fat zero in finesse. "So I'm cheating by being Asian? Or by this farmer tan?"

"Exactly. You don't live here, but you're not a tourist trying to flash melanin back home."

"Are you making a study?" Just saying that made the guy seem a little familiar. Wait a minute...

"Well, I'm a bit of a generalist."

That's it! Tuan DeTomaso! Wow! "A bit? Didn't they call you

'the last generalist'? What was it, Newsweek?"

"News and World, actually. And actually I did not utter the 'beyond this point in time nobody can really know it all' quote. That's crazy. What would be the point of knowing everything? Do you really think even DaVinci really knew it all?"

"But if you're not over-specialized, then you must be..."

"A generalist. Who was it they called the Generalisimo?"

"Now see, a true generalist would know that. Chiang Kai Shek. The Taiwanese dictator. My parents were Taiwanese. And also named Chiang."

"So do you have a Taipei personality?"

She laughed. This guy was sure more fun than he looked. "No, I'm more a relaxed Type B. I wouldn't even get uptight if you had a seat. Generally speaking."

He sat and removed the glasses. Nice eyes: intelligent and gentle but not overly soft. He said, "My friends call me O.B."

"So you didn't generalize enough to get into GYN as well?"

He chuckled and waved his empty glass to an attentive waiter. "I live in San Diego. Actually a sort of anomaly called Ocean Beach."

"They have an ocean right there at the beach? Convenient."

"Lots of Filipinos reside in Sandy Eggo. So there was another Tuan in the department at UCSD. That was back when I was in physics. He lived in Pacific Beach, so he was P.B. Tuan. We were trying to recruit another Flipino physicist from Imperial Beach to complete the set."

"I.B. Tuan?"

"No, I bc Tuan. I thought we'd established that."

"I be May. Nice to meet you. So you live here? Cool."

"Not this time of year. But as long as there's wind, it's bearable." He pointed down the lacy-edged coast, where a series of the long shallow-water docks picketed the shoreline and masts bobbed in the rising wind. "That's my place there, by the green hull."

"Wow, very nice boat. Even from here, I can tell it's classy."

"Great lines. Formosa 40. Thirty years old, real teak. Hey, another Taiwan connection."

"Must be nice being a boat person around here. Looks like there's quite a community."

"Ah, yes, we're quite the yachtie set. Pilots of the Caribbean."

As he spoke a sharp blast of wind blew the skirts of their umbrella up and strained its pole against the table with a loud creak. He quickly grabbed the pole until the gust passed. "Unusual getting wind this strong on the leeward side, instead of windward. Makes you question your whole vocabulary. Lot of these southerlies this year, maybe why the beaches are eroding. Oceanography's not really my specialty."

"I thought you didn't have a specialty."

"Not any more. I've been getting interested in why the beaches are getting eaten away, though. As one will when one has an expensive house on a beach. It might actually be water level rising. Global warming, perhaps? I lay the blame squarely on Al Gore."

"Inconvenient, if true."

Another gust made the umbrella dance again, rattling in its hole in the tabletop. Waiters were hurriedly collapsing umbrellas at other tables. The black model's wide straw hat blew off and landed in one of the pools. She paid absolutely no attention.

MeiMei watched the wind toying heavy-handedly with all the white canvas and gauze, cocked her ear to the oddly nautical sounds it was whacking out of the woodwork. "The spars creaking and canvas flapping, it's like being on a windjammer or something."

"Any stronger and it'll be like riding a helicopter."

"I like it. Next gust, grab the pole and we'll get the Mary Poppins tour of paradise."

"Or more prosaically, we can move out of the wind. Have you eaten? Tried Cuban food?"

"They have Cuban food here?"

"They certainly don't have any in Cuba. What are the three biggest successes of the Cuban Revolution?" He stood, making a motion to the bartender that produced a nod, but no check.

"There must be some," May mused as she grabbed her purse and sunglasses.

"Medicine, sports, and literacy." He held her chair for her to rise, something that rarely happens in these egalitarian days. "What are the three biggest failures of the Cuban Revolution?"

"Aside from the obvious?"

"Breakfast, lunch, and dinner." He made a courtly gesture, escorting her towards the cabstand at the street. "But Cuban cuisine thrives in exile."

A STAND UP KIND OF GUY

"**A** lot of people said a black man could get elected President of the United States when pigs fly," the President of the United States said into a sleek, matte metal hand-held microphone. He waited for the reaction to die down and deadpanned, "And check it out. I'm in office less than a hundred days and booyah, swine flew."

"Already heard that one," Weistler said around a mouthful of beer nuts.

"Don't cry to me," Monsoon grumbled. "I heard it all, while he was perpetrating it.'

"You know, once you get past the shock of the President doing a talk show," Weistler mused, "It starts to get kind of same, same. You stop rating him against Clinton or Jefferson or whatever and start comparing him to Letterman or Conan or Leno."

"Oh, I didn't tell him that about a thousand times," Monsoon roared, his florid chops shaking in justifiable anger. "Barry, you're just going to cheapen your coin, I'm telling him. And we're going to need it if you want a sequel to your act in four years. But does he listen to me? Does he listen to fucking anybody?"

On the screen above the dim twilight of the bar where watching the "POTUS Show" had become a weekly ritual for the two flacksters, Obama continued his opening monologue. "Naturally I'm not going to negotiate with terrorists." He paused and looked around as if counting the house. "I'm an attorney. I represent them and bill them by the hour."

Weistler almost spit up some of his Wild Turkey over that and turned to Monsoon, who held up a stifling hand and pointed to the screen.

"Just ask Bill Ayers He thinks I'm the bomb."

Weistler's laughter turned into an incredulous stare. "Holy shit! I figured you were just being your usual grouch about this show, but that's totally nuts."

"So glad you're finally wising up to what I've been trying to tell you. How much political capital is going down the drain here?"

Weistler regarded the screen, where Obama was mugging it up with his music director, Stevie Wonder, and pondered. "Well, I haven't paid much attention to that end of things, you know. But maybe the Chief has something. You notice none of the other talk shows have been sounding him lately. Starts looking like knocking the competition. So he kind of bought off any nasty cracks from Letterman, et. al."

"Until A-Rod knocks up his daughter."

"And there's something in being a household word. How'd you like to run a campaign for Leno?"

Monsoon's habitual scowl softened as he thought that one over. His full lips even flirted with a little smile at his inner picture of coaching Leno into the presidency. Then he grunted, back to reality. "Make it Chuck Norris and we'll talk."

"How about Will Smith and a draft choice to be named later?" Weistler shot back. But vooja de, he'd spoken too soon.

"I'm denying rumors that Will Smith has signed on to play me in a biopic," Obama off-handed into the mike, then straight-faced the expectant pause. "Hey, if Bobby Darin got one..."

There was a smatter of applause and Weistler gestured at the screen. "That wasn't even funny."

"Wait for it," Monsoon groaned. "It gets unfunnier."

"Oliver Stone did his little 'I'm more subtle than Michael Moore' number on Nixon and Bush. Apparently you have to be a Republican or get shot by half the population of the country."

Monsoon snorted in disgust. "Go ahead, toss more crap on Camelot, Buckwheat."

"Nothing on Jimmy Carter. Even with all the drama of the rabbit attack. And how about Bill? He deserves a film about his presidency. I mean other than the ones on Triple X Pay For View."

"I'd pay," Weistler chuckled.

"If they got somebody less skanky than Monica, maybe. But check this out."

"People have already compared my presidency to Bill's. I don't see any similarity between him and me." Again he strung out the wait to perfection, "I never even wanted to be Black."

He waited out the applause and laugher, then winked. "If you saw any of that bioporn, maybe you can see why Bill does."

Weistler laughed out loud. "Hey, now that's entertainment."

"Do I look entertained?"

On screen, Obama continued, "Myself, I spent my life working to not be Black. Not as hard as Michael Jackson, maybe..."

Weistler rolled his eyes and spun his stool to face Monsoon instead of the screen. "Speaking of white boys who can't keep it in their own pants, how's Hardley's kid working out down in Cancun?"

"Not hearing much from our beamish boy," Monsoon groused. "But I gotta admit, he's got fuck-all to go on so far. He's gumshoeing the A.O. but until she uses those cards it's mostly a waiting game."

"My guess is, they cancelled them about five minutes after I quit and came over here to the Good Guys."

"And we're still thrilled to have you, Jerry. But getting back to Townsend's adventures in Mexico, I don't think it's much of a problem if it's a long-term thing. He's not costing us anything, there are those who might feel better with him far, far away, and anything he comes up with will be gravy. It's a small percentage shot, but we've got to play those like we mean them. And since we're lucky enough to be working for the most powerful entity in the world, we can afford it."

"You think he got anything he could use from his old man?"

"Does anybody? I mean, not body count or whatever, but a straight answer? He was never a team player. The kid seems a little closer to what we need."

"Well, if he can get next to her and turn something out, we win. But..."

"Hey, get a load of this," Monsoon cut in. He waved his rocky scotch at the TV screen in mock horror.

"...everywhere I go," Obama was saying in a close up from the show's desk. He held up a Blackberry PDA by his face as he spoke. "They'll have to tear it from my cold, dead hands, is what I'm saying. But for anybody who isn't a security risk, it's the way things are done. It takes another Black Barry to know one."

"Jesus, he's doing spots?" Weistler burst out so loud the bartender actually paid attention to them for a minute before turning back to staring down the pettish waitress' décolletage. "That's... Is that legal?"

"Don't play naïve with me, of all people. Prexies solicit funds for speeches all the time..."

"But prime time? A straight out ad buy? This isn't like Bob pitching Dickhardia after he lost, this is... shit it's like saying the President of the United States can be bought up on the spot market."

"Been there, done that. So have you."

"Not this naked. This is..."

Joe Biden's face, created by nature as the perfect second banana, replaced his boss on the screen, holding a white version of the product beside his beaming grin. "Hey, I got one, too."

Obama was back on camera. "Yep, Joe's holding the "Whiteberry" model. It's just like mine but much smaller and instead of the internet it connects to the Old Boy network, holds just five minutes of mp3 muzak that repeats over and over, and comes complete with virtual shredder and gold-filled parachute."

Weistler turned slowly back to Monsoon, highly sobered. "Next time you talk to young Townsend, tell him to price apartments in Mexico for us."

ONE IF BY LAND, TWO IF BY SEA

*F*or some reason, people don't think of Isla Mujeres or Cozumel as "Caribbean Islands", maybe because they're in Mexico. So what is that water around them, French Onion Soup? Of course nobody thinks of Cuba as a "Caribbean Island", either. Much less Haiti.

Seagull: *The Blasé Sojourner*

Okay, so now Aphra had made Doctor Mayflower... Well, "made" in the "target acquired" sense, not in the "had one's wicked way with" way. Which was looking like an appealing way, no two ways: in the flesh, Ms. MeiMei was truly a beauty. Serene, refined kind of look. Slender and in good working condition, from the look of things. Delicate features and bruiseable lips. Cupcake tits with prominent nips. Got that Kuan Yin thing going. Goddess of mercy, mercy, mercy. Aphra getting a bit of a yen, her own self. Getting sideways, so to speak. Whole new slant on things.

Trouble being, other parties are showing signs of acquisitiveness towards her target. Namely this kind of doughy-looking little cat with prescription Ray-Bans. Trying to look like a chopper pilot instead of Asiatic software nerd or some such. Maybe not so much Asian, kind of semi-Hispanic. Oh, what else...a Flip. Plain brown Manila wrapper. Looks more like an Econ prof than a busboy or horn player, though. And sure as hell talks like one, more hand movement than an Italian, you can almost see him pointing to the board with a piece of chalk every other word. Bottom line: not much of a threat to acquiring the target, in whichever sense of the term.

Whoops, spoke too soon: he's squiring her out of the Zama, where the cutesy white muslin drapes have started billowing and snapping like the New Age Armada caught in a typhoon. Time for tried and true tradecraft: follow that car.

Definitely not a Mexican ambiance, MeiMei thought as O.B. Tuan led her to the promised Cuban cuisine at El Veradero. Much more Caribbean in feel. Like some tidewater shanty in Jamaica. Or, of course, Cuba. They walked past rusting wrecks of dinosaur-looking trucks that would have been at home in a Mad Max sequel, Tuan explaining that they were Cuban Army surplus.

"Hard to believe there's anything surplus in Cuba."

"Well these people are definitely surplus Cubans. And don't let you forget it."

She liked Veradero from the moment she walked over the rickety gangplank to get to the airy shack resting on pilings in the greenish lagoon water. The fuzzy *palapa* roof, the big plastic net floats and boat bumpers draped around the railings, the corroded bronze portholes and bell, the eaves festooned with frayed old rope of every size, material and condition. The chubby black owner nodding to them absently as if it would be the same to her if they ordered food or jumped over the rail.

Their table was half inside a horseshoe-shaped structure that had obviously been the pilothouse from some nautical failure or another. The stilthouse shack was hemmed in on the land side by the debris and detritus usual to maintenance of fishing fleets and repair of vessels. And the lagoon side was a jumble of moored boats ranging from one-motor pangas laden with coolers and nets and lobster traps to billfishermen with high spotting towers to big floating pleasure pits sleek as Ferraris and ponderous as corporate architecture.

Once orders were placed for mojitos, seabass in key lime juice, fried bananas and something called *moros y cristianos* (which turned out to be black beans and white rice, not a rematch of the Crusades) MeiMei led Tuan into a discussion of island residents and visitors. She'd already spotted where she would eventually lead him, and he was willing to follow. "It's the Last Caribbean Island," he told her. "Still fairly affordable and no image baggage. Becoming quite the place to have a home or moor your power cruiser out of Galveston or Lauderdale."

"Well it's a perfect sheltered lagoon."

"Exactly. I haul my own boat in here if anything big blows through. It's kind of like Key West, one of those spots where everybody competes for some sort of obscure status based on how long they've been coming here. Back before they paved the streets. Before the ferry service went in. Before all that upheaval back in the Pre-Cambrian."

"So is it The Caribe, or the Mayan Riviera? Seem like two exclusive concepts."

"The 'Riviera' won hands-down. A Riviera close to home where things aren't all nailed down yet. And not just the land, you know. Lots of film people lately, buying up expensive places or building monstrosities. Mostly just providing somebody we can look down on from below."

"You've got to be talking about the people who own these yachts."

"I'm actually a bit of mole in that set. Not the big power squadron types with onboard swimming pools and bowling alleys, but I can hobnob with them at the tournaments. Boats are as great an equalizer as the six-gun ever was."

"But, you're a sailor. No stinkpots for you." She recalled that term from the crowd at Leschi and Shilshole when she was dating a Boeing designer otherwise normal, but addicted to Duck Boat racing in a hand-laid Dutch double-ender.

"Exactly. I wouldn't trade my 'Boolean' for any of these sea-going condos."

And there was her opening. She pointed south, at a fenced swaging yard obviously capable of overhauling some pretty major yachts. And the mini-liner moored across the channel from it. "You mean you don't secretly crave a helicopter onboard? Be nice for making ice cube runs to shore."

Tuan rolled his eyes. "That sort of extravagance was put on earth to help the rest of us feel self-righteous and modest by comparison."

"Who owns it, the Sultan of Brunei? Donald Trump? Airwatch Traffic?"

"*Chilango* plutocrat... possibly narcocrat... named Ronchel. Not a local. Not even part-time local. Just put in for refitting. Everybody jabbered about it for a week but now we snub it."

Ronchel. That was the guy. She stared at the yacht: the Nahual, registered out of Mexico City. An area renown for its seaports. "So if it's refitting, why is across the channel from the yard? Must make it tough on the workers."

"He's been moving it every day, two pangas snubbing it over and back. Snubbing that boat is a cottage industry around here. They've got heavy security on it but seem to feel safer over there."

"Probably pirates with treasure chests and ill-gotten swag below decks." She looked at the huge blue hull again and said, "But any rival pirates worth their grog could just sneak up on the other side."

"Not likely," Tuan said, mashing his sautéed bananas into the heavy cream that MeiMei had avoided. "You're not seeing an island with trees on it over there. It's mangrove; a seething pile of woody spaghetti. You can't walk through it, nothing underfoot if you try to cut a path. It's about as impassable as any veggie patch on earth. Teeming with wildlife, of course. It's illegal to clear-cut it now. Probably why there's no condos on that side."

"Well, I guess all they have to worry about is submarines and SCUBA divers."

"Well subs and SEALS worry us all. But I'd be more on the lookout for ninjas."

"Hard to tell them apart. Don't they both wear those sinister black hoods?"

Aphra smiled at that. She had moseyed out onto the deck, shared some non-verbal sistah-hood with the proprietor and now nursed a Cuba Libre at a table within earshot, but out of view because of the wheelhouse. Thinking, You can't tell us sinister black hoods by looking at them, Chinadoll. I got the feeling the girl is steering the Flip towards something here. Well, I got a front row seat. To hear Dr. May push it a hair too far and get bit right on her curvaceous ass, as it turned out.

Staring at Ronchel's boat, where she was becoming certain her jade slab was sequestered, she was thinking out loud. "But some sort of skin diver could get over there, come up from the land side where they're not watching..."

Aphra heard the Flip geek's fork ring on the plate as he dropped it and stood. And heard him say, "I was just thinking I could hang on your every word, but you made a liar out of me. I definitely didn't want to hear that."

He came out from behind the wheelhouse under a head of steam. Over his shoulder he said, really pissy, actually, "Or any more of it."

"What???" The chink chick sounded genuinely surprised at his sudden change in tack. He turned and answered, handing Aphra a big piece of her ongoing puzzle vis-à-vis Missy May.

"You've heard about his collection, I gather. And that he keeps the cream of it on board. And come chat me up, beautiful young woman claiming to be a noted archeologist..."

"I don't know about 'noted', but I am who I say I am." She fumbled for her wallet, held up her license.

"Okay, so you're a Mayan freak and know he's got some unique artifacts. Not a state secret, exactly. And can't stand them being in private hands."

"Heritage belongs to the people." She'd been stung by the accusation, flustered because it was true, but was starting to get pissed about his attitude.

"Very good, Indiana. And he's not people? His guests aren't? The people's servants tend to lock things like that up in special collections, don't they? Where the only people who can examine them are, oh, you know, noted archaeologists."

"Look, that's..."

"So you hook me into helping you case the scene. There's other meanings of 'accessory" than cute purses, sweetie. I'm a foreigner in Mexico. Basically I don't have any legal rights." He stalked off, tossing a big bill at the waitress, but turned. "Something you might keep in mind yourself."

Aphra was thinking over the implications of all this development, getting down for her move, when she heard MeiMei speak softly to herself. "Damn. I gotta take some courses in not driving men off like an African bush-beater. Maybe there's some sort of degeeking chamber I can rent."

Got my own views on beating African bush, Aphra thought as she rose and headed around to intrude on the good doctor's table.

GETTING HER ASS IN GEAR

Xchab stared as Copper rummaged through her monster pack, agog at the tiny, lustrous, threatening clothes she was pulling out. And the velvet Royal Crown sack of exotic American cosmetics.

Winston, oscillating crossways in his hammock with head hanging over one edge, hair whisking the floor, took in his inverted view of her preparations. "Game face time? Combat-ready?"

"You got it." She whipped off her clingy sheath, and stood naked in her clunky road warrior Doc Martins. A fairly racy sight even without the fuck-me duds laying around her feet. "I need more cash than I can get spinning fire. This time of year, you know?"

Xchab, never ceasing to find new aspects of the redheaded usurper to stoke her resentment and awe, gazed wide-eyed at the tight-muscled, hourglass body. Smooth, fluid, and pale as milk from a pitcher, speckled with a firmament of strawberry polka-dots, her copper-flame patch shamelessly shaved into a snarly rooster crest.

Winston watched her pull on a hot pink G-string so minimalist as to be redundant. "Your front lawn is kinda hanging out there, Cop. Cruising BlackJack tonight?"

"Yep, my standing invitation still stands. Cross my crotch with silver and I'll tell you a fortune." She sorted through more of the gladrags, sniffing some suspiciously. "Those Plaza 21 places don't earn as much as Chilly Willy's back in the day, though."

"Nobody can climb a pole like you, Red. Especially upside-down."

"See there? We don't all look alike when you stand us on our heads."

"Now don't start up with that redhead racism, now."

She dropped onto a stool, the thong barely covered by a sequined black cheerleader-style mini-skirt, and fussed around with some breakaway tops. She chose a red one with glittery gold piping that would reveal the bottom halves of her cantaloupe-half breasts with the slightest shrug. Then unlaced her clunky Docs and kicked them off. Nabbing Xchab's all-condemning eye, she tossed the boots to her. "I think they're about your size. Find out."

The complex image conflicts that had been slapping her silly since Copper's arrival imploded under the seductive beckoning of the ugly footgear. Glancing at Winston, who was staring at the peak of the roof with stoned detachment, and Copper, who was leaning over the multi-purpose hand mirror painting herself with slut colors, she caressed the boots, smelled the blend of leather, sweat and rancid drugs, then pulled them on. They fit! That single fact was like a flare of new awareness painting the inside of her head. These ultradig shoes fit her rough *indita* feet! As though made for them! She laced them up, each movement freighted with mythology of cool. She eyed the others furtively before shyly standing up.

She felt taller, wirier, more towering and together. She took a step, marveling at the way the weight didn't drag down her stride, but seemed to power it into a more assertive, possessive kind of movement. Suddenly, bidden by an impulse she didn't see coming, much less understand, she jumped as high as she could, her hair flying up to brush the roof fronds. She bent her knees as she fell back to the deck of the island, then slammed them straight, maximizing her impact. Immediately she felt the lash of embarrassment, quickly looking for reproach from the two Americans.

Copper glanced at the source of the slam-bang and smiled. Turning to catch Winston's eye she said, "RomperStomper Room."

Winston nodded sagely, "The boots are made for stalkin'."

"And that's what they're gonna do." Copper stood up and walked towards Xchab, her barefoot height about the same as the Mayan girl's Doc-augmented stature. For the first time, she didn't shrink from the redhead's presence, just stood eyeing her balefully, unconsciously tapping a black, steel-capped toe.

"Now try this on for size." She held out a slinky black knit sheath that Xchab first saw as a child's dress, then realized in shock that she was being told to wear the thing. She did her first real comparison of the two female bodies in the room: she was shorter than the gringa bitch, but her build was stronger and more solid than Copper's whippy frame. Her breasts were perkier and plusher. And, unlike

Ms. Redpubes, she had an ass on her. But that little thing?

"One size fits all, kiddo," Copper said, handing her the tube. She sniffed it before realizing how hick it looked to do so: the sleazy, clingy fabric smelled of musk, sex and illicitness. And, for some reason, money.

As she vacillated, Copper rolled her eyes upwards and made "come on, have it off" gestures with both hands. Xchab might resent her, but she sure as hell hadn't the gumption to tell her no. Fixed in the redhead's basilisk stare, she pulled her loose Walmart shift off over her head and stood naked in the big boots. Copper sized her up, nodding in what might have been approval. "Not bad," she mused. "Not too shabby at all."

"Hands, off, ya damned rustler," Winston growled ferociously from his swinging dangle. "She's just a kid."

"That why you're jumping her, old-timer?"

He laughed and motioned at the black dress. "Hate to spoil the Puss In Boots shot, darling', but slip in on."

With no idea what either of them was yammering about, she wriggled into the black tube. Copper gave her a hand as she squirmed, Winston growling, "Okay, no grabass, hear? Two hand touch above the waist."

Copper laughed and gave a light slap on the ass that slid smoothly off one very tight, very nicely molded buttock. Xchab started and shied, but Copper grabbed the hem of the sheath and tugged it down, then back and forth a little to settle everything in.

Before Xchab could even check herself out, Copper took her by the shoulders and spun her to face Winston. "Roll over, ya old goat. This deserves your upright attention."

He rolled over in the hammock, lifting his head to take in the sight of his little sidewalk aborigine girl converted into a dark-skinned, tough-assed pillar of tight black gloss. From behind her, Copper reached around and adjusted the top hem downward, grabbed her dangling hands and moved them into fists akimbo at the waist, bumped her knee into a slight flex.

Winston applauded like a seal, whistling. "Incredible. You've totally ruined her. Where are the Matrix glasses?"

The center of approval and friendly hilarity for once in her life, Xchab mashed her gears trying to wear it all. She was not used to the feeling that she looked good. She was unused to the whole feel of the jump-up boots and insinuating grasp of lycra, of attention of this kind from another woman. She looked down, craning to see as much as she could of herself. She hooked her thumbs into the top hem and tugged it up a little. Immediately Copper smoothed it back down, to reveal the faintest meniscus of her coffee-colored aureoles.

"Winston!" Copper snapped, "Can you heave your old buns out of bed and be useful? True male role of serving feminine beauty and power?"

Chuckling, he crawled off the hammock and wandered out into the darkness. Xchab, alone with Copper for the first time, not to mention this whole First Time avalanche that was flushing her mind, stiffened. But he was back carrying an aluminum window he'd scored and never figured out how to use on a open-air proposition like the island. He draped a dark brown sarong behind it and set it on the rickety table, carefully leaning it against a bamboo roof support. Copper slid a crate of dishes forward to block the lantern light off the glass and pulled the future-shocked Xchab into a full, if somewhat dim, view of her possible new self.

She stared, transfixed. Some smoke and mirror trick made that chick look like her! She explored her appearance with a mixture of shock, horror, and a racing, visceral thrill. She put her hands on her hips and leaned forward, from off the pedestal of the clunky boots, and growled like a jaguar at the slick, sheeny, with-it slut in the looking glass. Copper cracked up. "By Jove, I think she's got it."

But there was the hair, Xchab realized after some contemplation of her image. It was still long, black, coarse, *indita* hair. She reached up and grabbed it, bunching it behind her head so she could only see a tight cap around her head. Copper gently pulled her hand away. "Don't even think about it, girlfriend. You've got killer hair. Just needs a harder core attitude."

If the dress and boots had remodeled Xchab's self-image, what she saw in the glass after Copper's do-over stripped her threads, popped her gaskets, and blew her doors. Fast and deft, Copper had gathered most of her bible black cascade behind her into a single braid as thick as her wrist, but bound with a chrome watchband a foot from the bottom to create a wide fox tail capable of dangerous swishing and brush-offs. But it was the middle two inches on top that held her attention: gelled into punkrocker rigidity, but not the usual vertical crest. Instead, it swept back in a ridge like a cock's comb, separating into porcupine spikes towards the rear as it gradually descended to meet the braid. The obsidian fin of a sea-creature, the cruel wing of a rapine bird, the mane of some equine alien. As she stared at the foreign creature that had emerged from the shell of her old tribal self, Copper shook up a can of spray paint and quickly frosted the needle-sharp tips of her crest with bright gold.

"Gonna knock those dudes at BlackJack on their butts," Copper told her, critically surveying the results of her trashy makeover.

So another terrifying/tantalizing jolt rocketed through Xchab's shell-shocked psyche. She knew what BlackJack was, had worked the lines outside with her bangles and beads until the unwanted male attention had driven her into retreat. It was a place where nasty, illegally-immigrated Brazilian and Columbian whores danced naked on men's laps and faces. It suddenly dawned on her that Copper wasn't dressing up for fun, but profit. And was dragging her into it like the sex recruiters the old biddies in the village had always warned her and her sisters about.

She backed away, shaking her head and almost stumbling in the unaccustomed Docs. But Winston was smiling and waving her out the door while Copper showed that not-to-be-denied look. Besides, she was wearing her clothes. Apprehensive and not facing the reaffirmation of the glass, she retreated into her sullen Indian shell and gave a blank half-nod. Copper took it as given, pulling a loose beach shirt over her strip whore getup and heading for the door.

"You kids have a good time and play nice, now," Winston murmured from back in his hammock and marijuana stupor.

Suddenly Copper stopped and turned to rummage through her pile of semi-clothes again. She came up holding something that looked like a chrome egg necklace and tossed it to Xchab. Who saw it was a garment for Chaac's sake; stiff, reflective silver fabric fashioned into a form-defining lid for the female genitalia, complete with a little pre-molded cleft, and connected to a forked loop of woven black cord slim as pencil lead.

"Slip into that, sportster. And we're on our way."

Xchab stared at her like a cow again, drawing an exasperated scowl and "get on with it" gesture. She steadied herself against a pillar while slipping the straps over the big boots and tugging the sub-G-string on. Actually there was something erotic in the way it rolled up her thighs.

"Nice girls don't let their pussies hang out for all to see," Copper chirped as Xchab made the final, uncomfortable adjustments of the shiny new hair up her ass. "Certainly not for free."

COSMICOMICS

Stepping from the blaze of tropical sun into the dark, tawny interior of Ganzo's *palapa* had damped her vision, so it shocked her to suddenly feel his hands plunge in under her damp hair and around her neck. But she reacted without hesitation. Her looks and gold hair might as well have been a target painted on her ass since she got out of grade school and she had learned to cope with it.

She jerked her head back and brought her fists up to strike just below the vault of his rib cage, driving both of them backwards a half step. She stepped on the edge of the door blanket and stomped down on it with her other foot, tearing it loose and letting the damp, avid light flood the shack.

He blinked once, but hadn't moved, or apparently felt, her double punch. His face showed no expression at all. His hands were still extended out in front of him, but now she saw that they were connected by a leather strand. From which dangled a white carving. He brought his hands to his own throat, modeling the necklace, then extended it towards her again, nodding gently as if teaching a baby. Now she felt rotten.

She stepped inside and looked into his open, guileless face. What had she been thinking? This guy couldn't hurt a fly if it was mugging him. And if he wanted a piece of her, he'd had opportunity, to say the least. She reached out to touch the bruise on his left side. "I'm sorry, amigo. You just startled me, is all."

But she got the feeling he'd barely felt the punch. This was one solid dude. He nodded again. No harm done. Hey, here's a necklace.

She took the dangling charm in her hand and examined it. "Whoa! This is beautiful."

It was a round piece of coral the size of a quarter, flat on one side and gracefully domed on the other. A baby coral, she thought. Only got this big before something broke it off the rocks and washed it in. The domed side was sanded smooth and bore a very subtle low-relief carving of a mermaid riding on the back of a dolphin. She was stunned by the workmanship, moved by his giving it to her. Ganzo thrust out his hands again and she didn't resist, let him hang it around her neck and clasp the ingenious shell catch in the down of her nape.

She looked down at it, then hit him with the thousand watt California billboard smile, flashing her perfect white teeth and daybreak blue eyes. She leaned for a soft kiss on his cheek and patted his pecs like you'd pet a friendly Rottweiler. He smelled like saltwrack and coconut. "Thank you. It's wonderful. You made it, right?"

She'd seen his "workbench", two fruit crates supporting a sea-smoothed chunk of plywood littered with coral, shell, rusting files, broken knives and naked hacksaw blades. But with the sudden infusion of light she could see his inventory hanging in the rustly fronds of his walls. Dozens of similar wonders hanging there, the sea treasure of a loving craftsman and gifted beachcomber. She moved over to touch them, turn them to the light.

The soft inner chaff of baroque coral chunks had been routed out to leave burnished, creamy webwork; finger-thick slabs of conch had been laboriously graven into sharks and mermaids and Mayan godheads with a faint gold backlight from the translucent shell; coconut shell disks were mounted with sea turtles and angelfish and modest nudes scraped out of scraps of bone or marlin vertebrae; hollow monkeyheart pod pendants concealed keys or wave-sculptured green glass and even a tiny pendant watch. She was hanging with an artist, that much was obvious. She turned to him, eyes shining. This was just so bitchin'.

He pointed to a set of shelves; curved, weathered planks from Cuban boats foundered on the reef resting on battered, pre-used cinder blocks. They'd just been areas of dark brown shadow in the umber *palapa* light before, but now she saw the cream of Ganzo's Olde Curiosity Shoppe.

It was a museum of seldom-seen, eye-grabbing jetsam. The bleached clavicle of an adult sea turtle, a hollow segment of the branch of tree coral, tubular sponges like panpipes made of froth, cadmium yellow razor clams still joined and filtering the tawny light down on stingray spines and triggerfish spikes and barracuda teeth, crazy twisted worm tubes colored like caramel, cowries and trochas flanking delicate conch shells of all colors, a finned trolling weight cast of lead and now encrusted with tiny bonsai trees of red coral, purplish fans spangled with miniature snails like Christmas trees. a gold-hued conch almost two feet long with the tip of the spiral sawed off. When she looked at the conch and laid it back down in a constellation of periwinkles and barracuda jaws, Ganzo lifted it to his lips and blew it like a trumpet.

The deep, vibratory sound of the conch call got to her. She felt the hair on her neck ripple a little, a slight tightening of the skin on her upper arms. It was a deeply elemental sound, not mournful so much as solemn, contemplative. It droned on like a Tibetan temple horn, as she stared. The notes were still dying out when she noticed the four big white coral blocks.

There was something about them, the way they sat on display in a little niche formed by the upright prow of a broken dingy, caught the light in obliques that seemed to raise their convolutions as if embossed. They just seemed to have something to say. She approached them as if tugged along by some invisible, somewhat pushy, usher. As the conch note shivered somberly off to silence, she reached out to touch them.

She held the coral—a slab of white calcium as thick as a brick, wide as a lunchroom tray, slightly tapered to a mild keystone—like she'd hold an infant, staring at it. It was trying to tell her something, had some secret or clue. She felt like prodding around it to find the secret drawer.

Ganzo came up beside her and she turned to him with the intimacy and respect she'd learned in the last five minutes. "How did you make these?" So softly she could barely get it out.

He shook his head. "I didn't do, I found. Big storm."

She traced the contours of the design on the coral, the twisting web of solid stone she now saw as a design. "What are they?"

He moved over and straddled a plastic milk crate padded with slubby jerga cloth. Picking up a labyrinthine piece of coral, he used a sixteen penny nail to point out the flaky star inside the tube of hard material, the delicate web of crumbly calcium that had been the polyp's fragile furniture inside its sturdy marble walls. She winced as he ground the nail into it, crunching away at the interior structure. In less than a minute he had reamed out the soft stuff, leaving a tube that ran all the way through the piece. He inserted a soft pencil wrapped in emery cloth and polished the inside to the same dull gloss as his necklaces. Suddenly she saw coral as stack of tenements, the rooms littered with flimsy trash that could be cleaned out to create a gallery of ocean sheen. And no longer as complex rocks, but as collections of baroque tubes.

He held the piece up in front of her, watching her face until she nodded. Then he took the big chunk of coral that she was still cradling and set it on the plywood and traced his finger along the raised pattern of white stone. She nodded again and he grabbed a blue school notebook from the table, whipped the sandpaper off the pencil and sketched with a sure, fine hand that once again shocked her with his hidden depths.

He held up the design and she studied it. Something familiar about it, but... Hell, her own face was familiar, "but..."

He rummaged around in his "shelves", mostly gallon plastic paint buckets stacked in rows at the wall end of his "bench", and drew out a battered metal ashtray. Cheap market souvenir for gringos, the squatting guy with his laden tumpline, surrounded by glyphs. The Mayan calendar, as seen all over the tacky little stalls off main streets in tourist dives like Playa Carmen and Isla and Tulum.

He dumped out a handful of brass findings and pointed to one of the glyphs, then back to his sketch. And it all fell in. She felt her breath catch in wild surmise. He said "Akbal," then pointed to the sketch and repeated, "Akbal."

"Oh, holy, shit," she muttered. "That's just impossible."

He nodded gravely and patted the coral affectionately. "*Coralcatura.*"

She looked at him, stunned and confused.

He reached to the "shelves" again, pulled out a musty old "Condorito" comic book, and pointed at the peppy little cartoon condor on the cover, flipped the pages. He said, "*Caricaturas.*" Then pointed to the white chunks and again said, "*Coralcaturas.*"

STRIP THE LIGHT FANTASTIC

If the idea of visiting a strip club chilled Xchab, the reality treated her to hot blasts of sheer panic. It was bad enough out on the sidewalk. Not the teeming crowd of testosterone mainliners she'd seen in high season, but even in summer there were enough bargain-hunting gringo men, narco downliners, and enough of the usual Machus Mexicanii to qualify as a crowd, milling around outside the rope trying to spring for or weasel out of the cover charge. And it turned out that a striking redhead wearing practically nothing and a Mayanita *cum* punker in slitherene and lethal cockatoo crest were crowdpleasers. The same mob that had ignored Xchab in her tribal drag now brayed their interest. With a certain degree of detail and body language. She had stepped off the bus with a degree of assurance and matched Copper's leggy strides with her own imitation of forward press femgression, but once dangled in front of the slavering maw of mankind, she balked and quivered.

Copper shot her a sidewise glance. Should have expected this. She was surprised her faithful Indian sidekick didn't drop into a submissive squat. And if she did, it was a good thing she'd made her put on the RoboUndies. The Stagedoor Juanitos interpreted the falter as a wound, calling for culling. But Copper dealt with that briskly enough. The first guy that stepped up, coming on with "Hey, *guapa*, why don't we...?" found her right in his face, wafting him a complex perfume of faux-expensive musk and curdling erotica. "You're on. Let's see the four hundred bucks."

The comment almost sent Xchab into mental arrest, but then she marveled as the fratpack parted in front of them. No child of Israel had been more amazed at the parting of the sea, nor walked through the gap with greater trepidation.

Inside of BlackJack was worse. Instead of a looming mob, it now started to look more like an organized sport where the rules all favored the team in trousers. Shirts vs skins. Xchab stared, apalled beyond words, at her first inside shot of Sodom By The Sea. The music hit her like a swollen black fist. The big trashcan thwallop of last-quarter grudgefucking, the nasty nature of the sneered lyrics obvious even to somebody who didn't speak English or rapjive. She felt it on every inch of her skin, deep in her tripes. It made her ill. Made her want to kick things.

She registered the entire, uncensored antics of men for the first time. She'd seen the eyes on the beach, the leers. And of course had put up with Winston. But here for the first time she saw what her aunts had told her all along, Brutes yowling for their meat, shoving each other aside to rub their hands on girls' privates. Holding up money, then exchanging it for crude degradation and twisted pleasure. A temple of release where cats toyed with mice and ripped the veils from their intentions. They stared at Xchab, even though she was clothed, more or less. She quailed from their eyes, unable to sort out admiration from rapaciousness, longing from lust.

Copper was yelling at her, finally grabbed her bare shoulder and shook her out of her paralysis. Numbly, she followed her twitching butt through a labyrinth of tight-packed tables, lightly packed with men. Tables on which nude girls did a stylized prance. This was what Mexicans call "teibol", she realized. Whoring from middle distance. She revised that definition when one girl jumped on a man's shoulders, calves kicking the beat on his back, hands twisting in his hair, naked crotch grinding into his face. Copper had to come back, grab her and tow her away, she locked up so bad behind that little performance. And it was going on all around her.

Copper sat them both down at a table far from the main stage, where two blondes simulated lesbian bliss, and close to the service bar at the rear. She gestured to summon a stocky waiter with a scar on his jaw and a white shirt that glowed like blue dashboard lights in the club's stutter of blacklight and discoduck strobes. He hugged Copper with obvious affection and respect and they chatted in friendly yells. Then she introduced Xchab. Who had been noticing and trying to sort out the looks she was getting from the men, but saw nothing but professional courtesy in this Manuel. Who shook hands, leaned over for the perfunctory Mexican kiss at the cheek, and went to get drinks.

Copper was speaking very loudly in her ear, "Stay at this table. The ladies' room is right there behind you. Don't accept a drink from anybody except Manuel. If a man sits down here while I'm gone, tell him he has to pay a hundred pesos each song to sit with you. And buy you some twenty dollar fake Johnny Walker. Anybody lays a hand on you, call Manuel and he'll come cripple the fucker."

Then she was gone, plunging Xchab into fullbore anxiety. But Manuel materialized beside her, handing her a Margarita. She took it with a tellingly grateful lunge. He smiled at her; a dark, dangerous face above the ghostly glow of his shirt, and waved a hand around the place. She followed his gesture: it was all Bosch to her. He leaned down by her ear, chuckling, and said, *"Bienvenida a BlackJack, 'mana. Provecho."*

Startled, she realized that he was Mayan, too.

She sipped her tequila slush and turned her attention to the girls, how they dealt with it: some bold, some reticent, all trading the ogling and pawing for American dollars. *Pura carne.* Then Copper came on and showed her something very different.

The redhead didn't mince or prance like another plate of libido chow, she roamed in like a jungle cat working up an appetite. She moved as if performing sports, an ancient dare from long-forbidden folklore. She swarmed up a polished brass pole: perching like a bird, soaring like a hunting shark, skinning around like a Chinese acrobat.

She leapt to the edge of the stage, daring and rebuking the men. She stomped on their groping hands and they threw money at her disdainful backside. She leaned down to rub bald heads, slap insolent faces. She grabbed a guy's glasses and flaunted them on various parts of her anatomy, creating caricatures of the very dumb-lust they trumpeted. She jumped from the stage to a tabletop, kicked out at the howling faces, leapt from the circle of grasping hands. She dived under a long table of conventioneers, her progress underneath it traced by men jumping back out of their chairs, laughing.

Then she popped up for a lope along the table and a long, leggy leap back to the stage. And the lights went out, sluicing Xchab with another wash of fear. But then two red eyes glared out of the darkness.

And started to move. It was the same electron dance Xchab had seen before, but now the tiny lights spun in close, their glows revealing portions of a ruddy nude anatomy. Finally the little lights—which she knew Copper had named Deimos and Phobos and referred to as her "new secret weapon"—swung around behind her and out of sight, then up between her legs from behind. She trapped them between her thighs, became an undulating patch of lurid red hairs before the little eyes winked out. The lights came up to a thunderous, stamping applause, but the stage was empty except for a busboy gathering up big drifts of tossed bills and stuffing them into a plastic bag.

Xchab felt a hand on her shoulder and leaped up in alarm, but it was just Copper, laughing at her.

The last three hours had been pretty weird, even given the location and circumstances. Perhaps the most disturbing aspect was that Xchab, barely-reconstructed teen-aged junglebunny, had gotten used to BlackJack. She wasn't seized up by ongoing atrocities on stage, tabletop and thightop any more, could actually hear Copper without straining or flinching beneath the hit parade of anti-personnel music.

Her tour guide to gringo sex hell now arranged a big sheaf of bills the busboy brought her, fanned them in Xchab's face; a welcome cool breeze with hints of sweat and illicit substances. When Manuel came by with another round she peeled off a third of the stack and handed it to him. Then gave him an American five and pantomimed him having a drink. Xchab had seen enough by then to realize that Copper was bringing in four or five times what the other girls attracted. And that it made her popular with the whole house.

And what she was saying was mostly about picking up tips from the other girls. How they did it, what worked and what didn't. Watch the Brazilians, she emphasized. They're Black as Cubans and know how to shake a booty from birth. The toughest thing about stripping isn't the eyeballs out front, it's stepping out of a G-string in high heels.

But after two more dances, with the same rain of currency, and a few more drinks, she leaned shoulder to shoulder with the younger girl and said, "Look, it's a play, okay? I see myself as an artiste, really. More than that: fire is like my religion. This is just a gig, a *gancho*, you understand?"

She took another swallow of some gold foreign whiskey and turned to talk right into the kid's face. "Thing is, it's a slippery slope."

She studied Xchab's blank look. Had to keep remembering Spanish was the girl's second language. "You understand me? A nasty business. You get around it too much, get sucked in, they start owning you. I don't have much morality... I do whatever I need to, fuck the rules. But here's Copper's Law: Whatever you're doing— dancing, stripping, marrying, peddling your goodies on the street— the big thing is that nobody owns you."

So there it was. Xchab stiffened up and blurted out, "I'm not going to dance in front of people naked."

Copper laughed and patted her forearm. "Some punker you are."

That gave her pause. Copper watched her chewing on it. Not the sharpest knife in the drawer, this kid. But there was something about her, something sort of draped around her like an invisible veil or *rebozo* that Copper responded to instinctively. Probably part of her veneration of *Santa Muerte*[28] and *La Anima Perdida*[29]. This girl's soul would have to find a map in order to even quality for being lost.

Finally Xchab spoke up, almost inaudibly under the pud-thud of the soundtrack. "Then why did you bring me to this place?"

Copper leaned closer and slipped her arm around the girl's shoulders, under the heavy rope of braided hair. Her lips just inches from her ear, she said, "I'll tell you why, honey. You live in an unstable world. There might come a day when you need some money and this is actually about the cleanest way a girl with no education and nice tits can make this much in a night. Keep it in mind. You've got the stuff. To say the least. Couple of years, you'll be legal and still tight."

There was a longish pause while she let Xchab process the whole thing, arm still around her bare shoulders, lips still at her ear. Then she said, "Here's three main lessons, Chiquita.

One, learn things that bring money. What pays, pays off.

Two, don't be ashamed of your body or being a woman. We rock.

Three, don't let them be in charge. Don't give to them, take from them."

Her lips touched the brown shell of Xchab's ear and laid down the softest, gentlest of kisses. With just the tiniest thrust of pink tongue into dark recesses.

Then she took another drink and said, "But if you happen to feel like getting up there to dance, just say the word and I'll make you a star. Maybe even a comet."

HELPING HAND

MeiMei's ruminations on her knack for blowing off men just when they were getting interesting—and useful—were interrupted by the appearance of a tall, athletic Black woman, decked out in tropical whites whose simplicity only advertised their expense. Recognizable at once as the languid lounger from Zama. She blinked into the blaze of reflected sunlight, then gaped as Aphra said, "My guess? He was too small to keep, anyway."

She swiveled elegantly and unbidden into the chair Tuan had just flounced out of and inclined her head to the chubby mama in charge. Who'd been glaring at MeiMei for whatever sins caused her to drive off a good customer, but immediately brought another wine cooler over to Aphra. Sister Power, all that.

Which was the card Aphra laid on MeiMei Chiang. "Listen, girlfriend, I heard that guy's tantrum, and his bit about skin. Skin tone caste system crap. Tell me this..." She laid her long, strong arm on the table, shining ebony against the white table top. "Where do I fit in?"

She was putting on just a slight gloss of southern girl accent that she'd found to be effective and disarming. Her mother had praised the full-on pickaninny dialect she called "Tom Tom Club", but Aphra really never got the handshake right for Steppin it.

MeiMei said nothing, just goggled at the sudden invasion of this electric model who looked like a dropout from Aphrodite and moved like a hunting cat. It was obviously her day for eclectic chat-ups.

"So we establish, I'm thinking," Aphra went on, "That ain't neither of us exactly leisure class tourists. And that you got something on your mind, don't got nothin to do with suntans or dating pools."

MeiMei smiled. If nothing else, this should be entertaining. "Just a working girl, here," she said. "And it's not working out."

"Kind of work you do? Offhand, I'd rule out the hospitality trades."

"Apparently. I'm an archaeologist, actually. And I can't seem to find the Meso-American paleontology hangout around here."

"No way! You out there finding lost arks and temples like Indiana Jones? Ah... you're here for that Mayan stuff, huh? Chichen Itza and shit. Sacrificed virgin skeletons."

"Mayanology's my specialty, but I'm more theoretical. I can barely remember the last time I got chased through a tomb by mummies."

"Well, I bought 'Mummies For Dummies", but I couldn't get into it." Aphra snapped her fingers and dug into the cloche purse that clung to her flanks. "But see what I picked up in town just today. Genuine Mayan stuff, probably made by coolie slaves in Szechuan."

MeiMei looked at the silver ashtray with bright enamel design. Homage to the ancients, she thought. Grind out your fake Cuban cigar on the face of the Gods. "Actually, that's the Aztec calendar[22]" she said. "Taken from the Sun Stone in Mexico city. The Mayan depiction you generally see is a guy squatting with a tumpline on his forehead, surrounded by twenty glyphs. We call them 'day signs'."

"Oh, and they just all the rage, these days. But you see this thing, keep hearing about all this Mayan Calendar, Mayan astrology, Mayan Prophesy stuff."

"I know, believe me. That's sort of my specialty-specialty. And the fad nonsense around it is getting pretty ripe."

"Damn, this morning I buy a calendar, ain't even got a naked man on it, today I'm talking to an expert. So, what's the skinny, honey? We talking about the end of the world? Or just same shit, different millennium?"

"It's a pop myth. A buzz like the 3K thing."

"No. Scuse me, cause you're the expert here, but I don't think it's the same thing. That 20K bizness was all inside computers, right? All those geniuses didn't know they'd need three numbers in fifty years. But it ain't really the End Of The World, what I'm saying."

"Actually, they just ran out stone during their production runs."

Aphra didn't get stopped short in conversations very often, but MeiMei was an adept of the inscrutable Asiatic straight face so the Black woman just stared at her a moment. Then got the slim, Kuan Yin smile.

"Here's the deal. You've got your main calendar, called the Tzolkin[23], twenty day glyphs by thirteen symbols called "tones". Making 260 permutations, unique 'dates' that establish a sort of holy 'year'. Nobody used that calendar in their daily lives, you understand, and there wasn't one hanging on a wall anywhere. All theoretical, only of interest to priests."

"Sounds healthier than priests being mostly interested in little boys' backsides."

"You get a lot of hubbub just over that. People with their little 'Mayan Hieroglyphic' necklaces for their birthdates. The human genome has 260 cell families, so it's mystical..."

"Shit, I've seen a whole book of stuff that the number 42 is all about." Aphra winning hearts and minds.

"Exactly. Anyway, much later when they had enough history around to need longer time lines, they developed another concept called the "long year". So you've got three numbers interacting—they generally show them like cogs on gearwheels—and it produces this

BakTun period of about five thousand years."

"You giving me the two dollar dummies tour here, huh?"

"Calendar 101. If you want more detail I can give you links to my monographs and recommend some books."

"Oh, Lord, no." Aphra fanned her glistening ruby nails defensively. "Way too much info. But that five thousand year thing's coming up pretty soon, right? Two thousand twelve?"

"Coming soon to a theater near you."

"Then we getting these tidal waves and comet hits and ninja attacks and what not, right?"

"Worse, a wave of blonde actresses with issues."

"Damn! Now that's a right dire scenario. But seriously, since I got an expert here, what's up with all that? What's your prophesy, your prediction?"

MeiMei smiled and started to wisecrack, but stopped. She looked at the calendar ashtray, then at the sleek hull of the Nahual. And said, "Believe it or not, there might be a clue to all that. And that's what I'm here looking for."

There was nothing in the taut black planes of Aphra's face to reveal the hot pulse of exultation that shot through her. This was her drug of preference, the sight of the fox tail on the moors. She leaned forward and said, "So you down here hunting up the playbook for the end of the world? Look, you need any help? I always wanted to be, like, Assistant Laura Croft."

ENNUI ON $360 A DAY

*T*he *overwhelming impression you get from Cancun's hotel zone is that everything permanent was constructed by Mayan Martians from Las Vegas. The nightlife strip is a little different, though. It's essentially an MTV pachinko machine bouncing springbreak assholes around until they fall out the bottom.*
Seagull: *The Blasé Sojourner*

Townsend's problem was being on the ground, but without anything to go on. Aphra Alisander had flown into CUN and that was all that he or anybody running him knew about it. Until she was somehow spotted or used one of her compromised credit cards. Which so far she hadn't done. So he was trying to dig her up through a combination of solid detective work and just hoping to blunder into her or some rumor of her having passed through. He was diligent in his search, even though it was a long shot that got longer the more he persisted. He might look like a blond beach jock, but he was a seriously workaholic young man. Who combed the pleasure zones of a city built to be very little else, surrounded by an invisible cloud of his own peculiar discontent. A lack of happiness that would get absolutely no sympathy from any man alive.

He'd paid a courtesy/fishing call on a low-grade local asset, a reporter named Ondera who covered politics for a tabloid rag. Ondera had sniffed around the whole concept of regional impact on the gringo elections, meticulously dissected it for any possible profit opportunities, and given a mental shrug. He just couldn't see any feasible way the Yucatan would matter to anybody else, anywhere.

He considered the possibility of making something up (he'd read Carre's "Tailor of Panama" four times since being recruited as a tag-end Agency stringer) but was dissuaded by his awareness that his ability to concoct stories was limited—witness the fact he was working for a scandal-and-tits rag like "QueQui" that made "National Inquirer" look like "The Watchtower". And something about Townsend. It wasn't like the movies, he'd long since figured out. It isn't the big, bulgy macho guys you have to watch out for. It's clean-cut, meticulous, polite robots like Townsend Hardley who disappear your ass for you.

So he worked at ingratiating himself. Towns was the first actual contact he'd had with any *Norte* operative since he was recruited ten years ago by a shaggy little spook who looked like Steve Buscemi playing a surfbum laid out on a rock in the sun for a few years. He dragged the young agent around Cancun's stunning collection of bars, strip clubs and practically nekkid beaches, margarita and *cervesas* flowing like wine. It was doubly gratifying that the young *gabacho* picked up almost every check. Meanwhile plastering the kid with information and tips, most of it totally worthless. Townsend had learned early that intelligence is like that: a flood of mindless data where a few worthwhile plums dissembled like white raisins in stale coffeecake.

One tidbit that stuck with him was Ondera's dissertation on Mexican political news. "I know, I know. You're from *gringolandia*; you think getting to the bottom of things is just a matter of throwing money and time at a question. It's different here."

It looked fairly different to Townsend as he spoke: they were sitting in lounge chairs with two young *mulatas* gyrating on their laps while his attention strayed to a pale redhead on the main stage, dancing nude and feral in a blaze of spinning fireballs. "In Mexico, there is no bottom," Ondera continued. "Seriously, it's like quicksand or some hole to China. You think you find out the explanation, but it's just another layer on the onion. And there's always another layer inside that one. *Periodistas* here just settle for the story that works."

"I don't know about journalism," Townsend replied, leaning over for his beer and getting a puffy black aureole rubbed in his eye. "But I'm beginning to think that's the way it works with spycraft."

And if Mexican politics was obscure, dire and berserk, Ondera was pleased to inform him, it was apple pan dowdy compared to the governmental structures in nearby countries he could mention. Such as Belize, Guatemala, Cuba, half the Caribbean and all of Central America. Which made an uncomfortable fit with Townsend's emerging awareness that flying into Cancun didn't necessarily mean that Mexico was the ultimate destination. There was only one major jetport in the entire region that included Belize and a hell of a lot of Guatemala. For that matter, if you wanted to go from Washington to Cuba, the only really logical route would be to fly to Cancun, then transfer to a flight to Havana. So he could end up trying to trace a sexy black woman in a country internationally famous for them, and where he would be singularly unwelcome. His dad would have said, "Major bummer."

The entire transportation thing was a nightmare, for openers. As soon as he'd mentioned checking car rentals, helipads, limos, bus lines, and such, Ondera had laughed his somewhat drunken butt off.

"Cancun," he hooted, "Is really nothing but transportation. A computer in the federal tourism office figured out this was the place, so they built a resort, then started building ways to get to it. Then the syndicates started nailing down the ways of getting around from hotels to bars to brothels to tourist traps. There might be more taxis in Cancun than in New York. Think about this thing, Town: a city of three quarters of a million residents—not counting over three million *turistas* every year—that didn't even exist thirty years ago. Where would you find anything like that in the world?"

"Bahrain? Dubai?"

"Oh, right, it's all about Arabs now. Nobody cares about us *frijoleros* anymore. You aren't even fucking with Castro these days. But listen, every *centavo* that comes into this town—falls into the Hummer dealers, the Donzi dealers, the Ferrari dealers—gets brought here by a tourist from somewhere else. Millions of people bringing billions of pesos...and none of them come here with a car."

That bit of information did what the sheer boredom of the task hadn't been able to do to Townsend's husky work ethic. He gave up canvassing transport and ditched the shoe leather approach altogether. In fact, he ditched shoes altogether. Opted to spend his time strolling the shreds that remained of Cancun's famous powdery "air-conditioned" beaches, poking around at random in the gush of sunstroked humanity laid to waste thereupon. Until he had more to go on, this was as legitimate a place to search as any other, he realized, and fell into a rather solemn and joyless beachbum life: drifting along the miles of hotel frontage, mingling with groups of funlovers, checking out the bikini corps at poolside, stopping by dozens of bars to cool off and ingest fluids.

And he actually spotted a few black women, even a couple that might have fit the bill. But not for long. He pored over the broiling, coconut-scented bodies and kept moving.

And at night he made the rounds of a staggering number of absolutely absurd clubs, disdaining the hypertrophied stroboscopic honk of the tourism mill while quietly quartering rooms where legions of exhilarated, shitfaced hedonists boogied around like corn in a popper.

The problem with Townsend—who was about as fit, handsome, and sexually desirable specimen of human male as the planet produces without ironically making them queer—was that he just wasn't that committed to the mindless philandering that flirted shamelessly with him or just stalked over to peep some cleavage and slip him a room number. He tended to feel his father's legendary womanizing as a sort of hereditary flaw, which somewhat spoiled him for the banquet of female pulchritude continually laid at his feet.

He suffered numbly from a condition that has been virtually eliminated in the American male, at least to hear the popular media tell it: a hunger for "something more meaningful". And like most pilgrims searching for meaning, he had no idea what it consists of. Up to his ears in sex, he would have liked to feel love—never suspecting that he was too tightened up to experience normal emotions. He wanted something special, something that grabbed his breath, heartbeat and balls at the same time and wrung them every which way but loose. He sought The One.

Worse yet, his bar was set pretty high. He wanted a woman he could talk to about what was really going on his head. Which meant classified material as well as secrets of being that very few people experience or understand. Somebody as stealthy and lethal and over-engineered as himself. He dreamed of a beautiful female spy who would be the only one with whom he could truly be himself. He hadn't yet realized that the only person he'd ever seen or heard of who fit the bill was Aphra Alisander.

SKELETON CREW

The darkness was full of skeletons.
Not a novelty.

Well, these were a little different from most of the skulls and bones clanking around in Winston's bummer dreams. Whole different attitude.

As he crept forward through the darkness, white grins popped out on either side, soared around overhead. Not your Day of the Dead types, not grisly Lost Temple stuff, either. More like Cemetery Spring Break. These skeletons frolicked, essentially. They paddled kayaks, balanced on surfboards far over his head, sat three deep on motorcycles, zoomed on jet skis, waved beers and margarita glasses. They wore tourist trap sombreros and NBA jerseys. They waved at him, made out with each other,

This had felt like a prophetic dream from the start, but he was beginning to have his doubts as he wafted along through the cavorting dead. He shouldered past a bunch of skeletal mariachis with old silver horns and entered another chamber, this one better lighted and painted with murals of Mexican revolutions and colonial life. Overhead was a balloon with two dead in the gondola, dressed like Villa and Zapata. Winston mentally shrugged and ghosted on, smoothly dollying in on dreamwheels.

He passed a table set with fruit and bottles, two handsome skeleton couples dressed to the nines for luxury dining. A skeleton parrot sat on the shoulder of the woman with the silvery gown. Then he saw the other table, over in the corner, and knew this particular dream was about to cut to the chase.

Four skeletons sat at this table. Two were dressed in the satire finery of fatcats in murals by Rivera and Orozco, a big-boned male in funeral suit sat across from them beside a set of gleaming white bones clothed in an embroidered peasant huipíl. A shower of gold fell from the darkness above, flitting around before coalescing into a golden, translucent skull floating above the table and regarding him with eyes like holes punched in Hell's back furnace. Winston, no stranger to the appearance of deities (benign, malign or design) in his visions and occasionally real life, was wiped out. He felt like falling to his knees in front of this pulsing, luminous creature whose eyes spoke of vision permanently focused past infinity.

In a thunderous echo owing much to The Great Oz, the skull spoke to him thus: "Are you trippin', fool?"

"Who, me?" Winston said out of reflex. "No way. I wish."

The skull's glow throbbed like wind-stoked embers. "That's what you think."

"Actually, I think I'm dreaming."

"Dream on, turkey." The skull thundered. "Tomorrow night I'll be right at this table. Be there or beware."

The terrible glow faded, and the skull diminished without relinquishing eye contact. It was almost invisible when it suddenly popped back to full resolution and fireflush pulsation. "Oh, yeah. Bring shrooms."

Winston had learned that the last thing Xchab wanted to hear, while playing house with him and waiting for a whiter knight to sweep her onto a more reliable charger, was replays of his dreams and drugged visions. But this one required some information to understand and he had also learned that the best bet in such cases was to blurt them out to anybody who'll listen. Some mousy secretary trapped on a diner stool or sodden wino slumped on the bus might just barf up the missing key required to point one in the proper direction. And bingo. He'd barely gotten into the first leg of the cavern of skeletons when she fixed him with one of her stonecarved Mayan expressions and said, in a bored tone, "Sounds like Pericos." The old fart thinks he knows all this stuff about the Yucatan, but has no clue where people party.

Not that she'd ever partied there, personally, but she'd gotten a wistful nose to the window, coveting all the toys and doggies and lollipops, on her grim treks to sell woven bracelets and shell jewelry to the choked flow of First World twerps beer-bonging their way through the feeding frenzy of Cancun's hospitality ghetto. Holding up her chintzy goods and suffering tourists to snap shots of her Mayan get-up while she soaked up the vista of all the moneyed, sophisticated, superficial glitz she coveted. Until the wait staff headed her off and hustled her back to the Yaxchitlan sidewalk.

But now it looked as though Winston, of all people, was actually going to take her there. Walk in and get a table, find out what these people eat and drink. She looked as stony as ever cruising across Palapas Park, but inside her a thwarted soul beat its untried wings.

Winston was blasted, of course, which might have explained a few things. He'd been glad Copper had declined to come along, muttering woodenly under the grip of Ketamine. They'd left her floating in an innertube, her bare bottom bulging down into the water: what she called "trolling for barracuda." Her addiction to that rather nasty and consciousness-lowering drug was a mystery that Winston found by turns annoying and tragic. He didn't like being around people who were "KO'ed": they were like amplifiers on stand-by mode, meat puppets who'd swallowed their own strings.

He, on the other hand, was toasted on some very fine Affy weed he'd scored at the hostel and augmented with just a pinch of mushroom dust, so he wouldn't have minded a third party checkoff on what he was seeing.

He'd noticed it as soon as they came into the park, little kids with ice-cream cones staring at his loose hempen duds and weedeater hairdo, adolescent hand drummers calling out to Xchab over their beats but getting her usual basalt head snub job. There seemed to be a lot of bees around Xchab. Luminous golden bees. They followed her at first, stringing out in swelling squadrons. But by the time they left the park for the alley over to Yaxchitlan the swarm was all around her, shifting their pattern to create a scintillating veil around her dark, ordered features and short body. They towered over her head, milling and buzzing in a high register that almost reminded him of tin whistles. Too bad he hadn't brought his flute. The glow from the bees lit their way through the alley.

He made one attempt to discuss this phenomenon with the girl, but she'd made it curtly clear that she didn't want to hear any of his crazy shit at the moment. She was already up ahead, luxuriating in the interior of Pericos.

Winston strode into Pericos like he owned the franchise, imperiously waving off the waiters proffering menus and the worried looks that appeared when *jipis* and *inditas* showed up amidst the carriage trade. He'd walked into too many pitiless courtrooms, forbidding boudoirs, raucous cellblocks, hellish Angel showdowns, and stonecold busts while partially decapitated by substances of unknown origin, trajectory or allegiance to quail at whatever dicey deal was going down in Chez Skeleton.

Because the dead were indeed at hand, floating around high up under the peaked *palapa* roof: real life skeletons. Up there on real motorcycles and jetskis and outriggers and crap. Far more troubling than anything in a dream, actually. Winston generally considered reality to be too weird for him: a crutch for those who couldn't handle dope.

On the other hand, it was drug of choice for Xchab. She was getting hot over the whole proximity of wealth and leisure and the ability to deploy them. She leered artlessly at the displays of money, but her rookie stun quotient was out of synch with what the people themselves rated: she might read a Rolex or Prada gown as just a timepiece or black dress, while waxing ecstatic over a ripped Metallica shirt appliquéd in gilt or some switchblade cell phone or cunningly curved cheap sunglasses. The point being: this was The Stuff. And these were The Ones Who Be Havin' Stuff. And above all knew how to get it, what to do with it, and how to evaluate and unleash it. She trailed Winston, stumbly and agog, her eyes and ears drinking the place in.

As soon as they entered, Xchab's bee escort buzzed past her, eagerly leading the way. He followed the glow of the yellow bee road into the back room. Where he immediately saw the tables he'd dreamt, except that only the first one was really skeletons. Back in the corner sat four real people, more or less, and the bees were all around them like a seething gold lantern.

He was sauntering up to a table he read as freighted with enough greed and potential violence to make many a person's "too high for this shit" lists, but wasn't fazed. Well, he was impressed by the way the bees all coalesced around a small leather backpack sitting on the table, close to the big guy in the linen *guayabera*. In Cuba a *guayabera* might mean one thing, but in this part of Mexico Winston tended to read them as, "there's a gun under these starched shirttails".

Xchab was staring at the two assholes in Melrose chic, magpie eye for the glister of expense. Winston was more interested in the guy with the pack. Muscle, but not a musclehead. Unlike, oh, say the per-diem ex-cop bodyguard sitting behind the pose monsters. And also flanking the pack, sensuous in white peasant drag, was one extremely hot *gabacha*. Hmmmmmm. Smelled like money and nogoodnikism to Winston's veteran nose. Just like back in the day.

HEADHUNTER

The spectrum of Cuevones who pass their time here is a measure of the uniqueness of Isla Mujeres as a place to live, vacation, or lam out. One day might bring Slovenian artists, Minnesota tourist families, old salts crazed by sailing over from Cuba in a hurricane, Japanese businessmen, Italian models, French guitarists, fugitives from injustice, misguided writers, or local bricklayers who just want a buzz. A guy who lives in Alaska, works in Antarctica and lives for cribbage. A Burmese couple just checking the maps. A chistoso who plays piano—reggae on the beach, chamber music for a dinner club, then hard rock at night. A Scotch dynamiter who prods everyone into dangerous diving. Ski racer, turned fashion model, turned DJ, turned CPA touring Latino graveyards. Danish writer fresh out of a concentration camp. Pervo beach photog. Cute martial artist from Uruguay. Insane Israelis. Grouchy Gringos. Then there's you.

Seagull: *The Blasé Sojourner.*

Curtsy had to martial up a major gut check before marching into Café Cueva. Damned if she'd go around wearing the Shame Merit

Badge for the duration. Of course it was Del who made the first allusion. And somehow that softened the whole thing up, put her back in charge. Must be that world-famous cockney charm.

She got the owl eye from behind the counter heaped with fresh baked goods and shell jewelry. And all the dripping insinuation he could put into, "Helloooooooooo."

"Heard you got the tin tack." He continued as he reached for her personalized mug on the rack. With, of course, the Groucho-bouncing eyebrows.

She grabbed the counter copy of "Mexican Slang 101" and leafed through it with knitted brow. "Why doesn't this thing have any of that stupid London gutter slang?"

"The sack, as you yanks would have it." Del drawled back. "Dropped like a sack of shite, is the implication."

"Yeah that was pretty much the subtext."

"And we heard why, as well." By now the leer was a pronounced as any Japanese demon's, almost covering over the redeeming twinkle behind it.

Monica turned from the espresso machine and socked her hubby on the shoulder. "Shut up, Del," she explained. She looked Curtsy towards a seat by the bookshelves and came over with the mug of steaming Americano. And, uncharacteristically, slid into the opposite chair.

"Del's hardly Mr. Discreet Empathy," she said softly. "But for guys around here, he's probably in the top point five percent. And all of them know."

Curtsy nodded glumly and sipped her coffee. With a faint taste of the *almendrado* tequila Monica knew she liked.

"Frankly," the dean of Isla's baristas went on, "I think they over-reacted. But my point's this. You know Del and I both like you, but you should consider relocating. Any guy you talk to from now, you can assume he's some rough beast cruising your reputation. You're in for a load of chaff."

Curtsy nodded. This whole thing was making her feel better and worse at the same time. Pretty much the story of her whole career on Isla. "I don't know where I'd go from here. I'm just about broke and Dolphin Dis was my life dream."

"That's rough, honey. But you're never going to get another job in the dive business on this coast."

Monica stole a look around, Del all wrapped up in serving/ogling a tall black beauty who'd come in for some complicated frappuccino variation. She leaned close and went way sotto voce, far from her usual style. "So, listen... How was it?"

"Just like with men," Curtsy said quickly. Then gave it a beat and said, "Except they're clean and you don't have to listen to them talk bullshit."

Monica giggled and started to rise, but the black customer had come over to their table, looming over them like the figurehead of the Narcissus. Saying, "You pretty sure of yourself, there?"

Curtsy and Monica, unsure who was being addressed, gave her nonverbal "Huhs?", so she hooked her exquisite espadrille—from some duty-free in the Outre Mer—under a chair rung, hauled it up and slid down into it like the fall of tropic night. And said, "No diving jobs around here, she was saying."

Curtsy wasn't in the mood to care who this Beyonce-looking broad was, just shrugged and said, "I'm sure she's right."

"Now don't be so sure of that," Aphra said, pursing hibiscus lips to waft breath across the surface of her coffee confection. "See that cute little Chinagirl over by the door?"

And sure enough, just inside the door on one of the metal chairs, was a really nice-looking Chinese woman. Del should be more frisky than normal tonight, Monica was thinking, after getting a load of these two. Curtsy just nodded to Aphra, afraid to hope.

"Well she... and I, you understand... are equal opportunity employers."

Curtsy stared at her a moment, then glanced at Monica, who was beaming. And suddenly the bombproof California girl was back, laughing out of blue skies and slapping Monica a resonant high five.

"We need a diver for a short-term venture. Pays good though. And we're just loads of fun."

Del, who'd been following it from behind the counter put in, "Oy go down a bit me ownself. Right conditions and what."

"Well, they did say short-term," Monica said, standing and giving Curty's should a friendly squeeze.

Aphra, sizing up the blonde diver at close range, also felt a strong patting impulse. But all things in their own time, as the Good Ol' Book puts it. She motioned and MeiMei Chiang got up and headed over with her cup of Earl Grey.

"That'd be the good Doctor Chiang, there," Aphra nodding her head towards the Mayanologist with whom she and her awesome powers of credit were now partners in a fairly nefarious scheme for the ultimate Benefit Of All Concerned. "I'll let her tell the tale."

"I'm Curtsy. Which apparently everybody on the island is way too aware of these days."

MeiMei nodded and sat in the chair Monica had vacated. "And I'm MeiMei. This is Aphra. But before we get into it, I'm supposed to tell you that Puch Pop misses you and sends his wishes."

Curtsy stared at her.

"And from what I saw, I'd say you should take it to heart."

TELEMPATHY

Nobody at the table seemed very happy, but that was often the peculiar case in resort fun spots. No joy on the faces of Fric and Frac over there, two metrosexual urbanoids who thought dressing down meant wearing Hawaiian shirts under their unstructured cotton Miami Vice blazers. Certainly none on the stolid countenance of the beefy, amoral cop type on their side of the table with "*Federales*" scrawled on him as vividly as "crooked bodyguard". Across the table, the slim, lovely brunette seemed to be visiting a personal tragedy. And the beefcake beside her, who should have been exhilarated to have a woman like that leaning against him and touching his arm, was nothing but a brochure on operational readiness.

And at his elbow, the small leather backpack swarming with a golden sheen of bees. Winston let the waiter glance askance as he plowed towards the table with Xchab in his wake, her fazer set on Maximal Gawk. His thoughts on the nature of the gathering at the bee-anointed table were confirmed as he drew close enough to hear:

"Look, you told me you'd go as high as quarter mil," the big muscley guy was saying. "And here it sits for two hundred grand. Just what are you sniveling about?"

"Nothing, nothing..." This from the sleeked-back weasel who looked like sniveling was probably his main function in life. "I just figured a guy like you would be resourceful enough..."

"Resourceful? You sent me out on a snipe hunt for some magic crystal skull, no idea where it was but fairy tales and Hollywood scuttlebutt. And there you sit with a nice glass of Argentine Chablis and I'm laying the thing right on your table. How much more resource you want?"

Winston had been waiting to see if the other semi-suit sounded as gay and supercilious as he looked and was rewarded beyond his expectations. "Liiiiisten, Butchy. The world lives on negotiation and wiggleroom."

"Glad you're aware of that." The big guy looking for a waiter, scribbling on his hand to signal for the check. "I've already had more attractive offers."

That lit up the two straights just the way Winston, who'd renegotiated many a stinky deal in his time, expected it would. Boiling down to the most useless question, but always the one they bleated out first: Offers from whom?

The honeypie in the *tipica* outfit broke off their sputtering with a soft comment, "I think he's talking about me. Please pay no attention."

"I dunno," Winston stuck in from his peripheral hover around the table. "As offers go, you're damned attractive."

They all turned to look at this new voice in the jam-up; gnarly old Mr. Natural with a cute little Indian trick who squirmed under their stares.

"And just who," lisped Frac, the gayer one, "Might you people be?"

"Well, I might be the Ghost of Christmas Pretend to Come," Winston answered solemnly, "But what it is, he called me so I came."

The producer turned on Bannock with a gaze a little too watery to be the Eye of Flame he hoped for. "You *called* somebody to meet us here?"

"No." Bannock rolled his eyes. "Duh. I've never seen this codger before."

"Not him," Winston said, getting the same dismissive quality without having to do an eyeroll. "Him."

He pointed at the backpack.

That pronouncement nailed Loris' attention right to the wall. Xchab stared at Winston, ready to hike up her skirt and sprint for the kitchen door.

"What? Who?" So Fric, the nominally straight dork, wasn't any sharper than the gay one. "Who called you?"

Winston just stared at the backpack for so long that everybody started fidgeting, Xchab edged towards thataway, and the straighter jerk nodded significantly to the bodyguard, who folded his napkin slowly as Bannock came on full alert. Then he said, "oXo."

Leaving Loris intrigued, Bannock flabbergasted, and the straight arrows aghast. "What the fuck is going on here, Bannock?" they bleated in unison.

"What's going on is this." Bannock crunched out the tone he hoped would carry complete finality. He wasn't above just grabbing the money and dealing with the ramifications (as previously demonstrated) but would rather not. "You sent me to get something. I got it. You owe me money. I have no idea who this ghost of George Carlin is but after a few days around that skull I'm prepared to believe about anything. Maybe oXo got a cell phone and hailed the freak so he could score. Nothing to do with our deal, so don't try to use it as an excuse to welsh."

"Know what I'm wondering?" Winston said mildly.

"What you were just talking about?" Frac minced out cattily.

"Nope. What the hell I'm doing here. Is this some sort of reality show?"

"I doubt you've showed anywhere near reality since Altamont, Mister Natch."

"So everybody's wondering the same thing," Loris put in. "Do you have any hunches?"

"I saw him in a dream. Big gold, glowing skull hovering right over this very table. He told me to come see him. Bring shrooms."

Everybody goggled a bit except Loris, who purred, "And did you?"

"Wouldn't you?" Winston shrugged. "A summons like that?"

"Won't you sit down?" Loris pushed out a vacant chair and caught the waiter's eye. "You and your friend?"

"For Christ's sake, Bannock," Fric remonstrated. "Did I miss a sign out front: Welcome Rainbow People Conventioneers?"

But by then it was pretty obvious to everybody, even their own sneering bodyguard, that it was time to cut the crap. Talk turned once again to money as the waiter laid glasses of sangria and bowls of chips and guacamole in front of the newcomers. Xchab was on the edge of her chair, inhaling the sound, look and smell of money, power, and self-satisfaction.

Winston leaned towards Loris, who met him halfway. "Excuse me, but do you happen to see anything kind of, you know... hovering... around my faithful Indian companion? Like, buzzing her, maybe?"

Loris took a measured look at Xchab, not breaking it when the girl turned to spot her gaze and twitched away like a mouse caught in the pantry. Finally she told him, "Nothing but the clouded aura of a seeker in turmoil. Why do you ask?"

Winston's turn to stare. He cruised her shamelessly, then smiled and patted her arm. "Ah. I believe we might be family."

But it was time for the backpack to be proffered within reach (straps tight in Bannock's husky grip) and the stereotype briefcase nudged forward to be inspected. Loris watched Xchab as Bannock satisfied himself that the stacks of green bills were for real: the girl irradiated by the sight of the money. *Garcón*, a glass of water and defibrillator for the *muchacha*, please. She willed a quick mental message to the Indian girl: greed is self-defeating, honey. Sit in your own skin.

But when she saw these two L.A. jackals peering into the pack, gloating over their possession of one of the world's four coveted authentic crystal skulls, she also strained to will a missive to Bannock, wishing she could speak into his head like oXo could: Remember the pistol trick, big boy? Walk out with the money and The Love?

Then caught herself. Possessiveness, grasping, force: the primordial roots of our self-immolation. Take your own advice, woman: tread the path, trust the path, be the path. She breathed deeply, in a healing cadence.

She had wondered how strongly she would feel the impulse to walk out behind the yoyos, stalking oXo. And heard his voice in her head. Not saying goodbye, but bidding her look to her left. Where Bannock sat, motionless as he watched the Californians and their goon walk out. Life's a trade-off, she thought.

Aware of her look, he turned and murmured. "I'm really sorry. But a deal's a deal."

"Life is a circle," she whispered to his ear. "I love it that you knew what I was feeling. And cared."

She heard a sigh behind her and turned to see Xchab seething with an almost religious avidity for the briefcase and Winston meeting her look with a sad kindliness. "The wheel turns," he said.

She gave him a wan smile and he reached to her ear, did a magic flourish and zippity-zap, held a mushroom between his fingers. "Think we oughta eat these babies and go for a swim?"

Bannock glanced at the darkness outside the cunning colonial windows and asked, "Swim? Where?"

"Punta Nizuc."

Rang a bell. Oh, wait. "Isn't that where Club Med is?"

Winston beamed. "Can you stand it?"

NARROWING GYRE

Just because Yaxche floated adrift in the ebbing surf of time didn't mean that all moments were equal. For one thing, her consciousness was definitely attracted and bound to the Yucatan, and seemed mostly to involve the experiences of young women. Like a person awakening in a dark space, she could sense greater dimensions around her, but didn't feel any urge to explore the darkness in search of walls and limits. It wasn't that she couldn't exist in earlier time, or in the old age of the lives she browsed through as idly as a jellyfish pulsing along on the tide; it was that her attention was elsewhere. Or elsewhen.

One limit that she was well aware of was the end of time itself. She knew where it was and what was happening there, but felt no attraction to the final taper, no impulse to savor the ultimatum.

There were even certain ephemeral moments that drew in her attention the way a lantern draws a moth across wide, dark fields: little nexi of consciousness that held her gaze and riveted her perception even amid the raucous sweep of jungly centuries.

One moment she constantly returned to (as if she ever really left) was simple, even humble, but evidently exercised some powerful esthetic for her. Bringing much of her attention to a hover just above a mosquito coil burning on a battered wooden table, it filled her "eyes"; she couldn't look away as the glowing end of the black spiral moved steadily inward, a ruddy ember circling patiently inward, consuming its fuel in a measured march towards the center.

There was something about the hot red point eating its way along its pre-destined helix, turning the toxic incense into smoke and dropping a fine line of ash on the table below it, forming an after-image, a chalk shadow commemorating its cyclical passage to the center, where it would expire from lack of fuel and further destination.

Why that particular burning coil held her gaze, rather than the thousands of them all over the peninsula, had a lot to do with one of the few males that focused and enabled her attention: Puch Pop. She was growing very fond of Puch, as anybody would understand if they shared her timeless point of view.

One thing to admire: he used his real Mayan name. Unlike his brother, Juanito, who relished his Spanish name and would just as soon forget that he had an Indian name at all—like so many Mayans with a shot at assimilation. Not that much of a shot in Mexico, where the world *indio* is a racial slur meaning "stupid" and "inferior" and where the spectrum of skin color blended up from dark to white by the blur of *mestizaje* amounted to a de facto caste system. But not all *indios* lived like ghosts in the jungle or wore *huipiles* to work cleaning hotel rooms or labored as construction *peones* for minimum wage. And the ones who didn't were called by Jorge or Maria, not Itzel or Kisin or Yum.

Even the once-great Mayan surnames were disappearing, thrust away into dark attics, buried under tiers of stone. Cham, Pook, Chal, Itza, Mams, Miss, Ek, Pop: these had been great names, royal names. Many were the names of glyphs carved into stone steles and calendars and temple walls. Now they were an embarrassment to those who tried to morph into a new mutt tribe of Gomez and Martinez and Sanchez. Or translated Ek into Estrella and moved on into bureaus or auto ownership. Was the next step moving to Florida and glossing Estrella into Star? Was that how stars were born?

And it got weirder than that. The Pop kids (the boys anyway) had gone to school at upper-middle class *liceos* and *colegios*: the result of parental scrimping and part-time jobs in Cancun, a tradition among Mexicans who pay for private rather than government medical care if they can possibly afford it, and sacrifice to give their kids a shot at being citizens of a real world rather than the illiterate *burros* the public school system coughs up. And where they ran into monied white kids who thought it was a hoot to troop off to the Mayan settlements along the strand north of town, slumming and eating *salbutes* and *panuches* they found tastier and more risqué than the normal fair in town. The more money and social pretense, the more likely for the offspring to be lolling under a *palapa* munching green tamales and tasty *kash* or *poc chuc* at "Maya-mi Beach", the Harlem of their class.

Juanito would go along, unaware of, or perhaps nervous about, the irony of it, but Puch had only gone once. He'd ordered a beer from the Mayan girl, in her own language, and fallen into a short conversation with her about what school these people went to. He turned back to his friends and caught their stares. His race was not a secret, written all over his wide face and stocky build. But he had pulled it out and brandished it. They reacted as if Twenties socialites in emeralds and pearls might have if one of their party at the Cotton Club had suddenly wiped off his grease paint to reveal himself as a Negro. It was at that point when he ended his social contacts with his schoolmates with the sole exception of faking their butts off on the soccer field.

There had been another episode he remembered and shelved next to the day he stopped "passing", also sitting next to a pretty school girl—who wasn't exactly blonde, but definitely not an *indita*—and ordering beer. Their middle-aged busboy's heavy nose, squat hunched shoulders and blocky legs announced him as almost grotesquely Mayan. He came to their table looking down at an order pad and when he turned his eyes up to them expectantly, they were a deep, shocking violet. The girl showed nothing, but grabbed Puch's thigh under the table and squeezed it in delight. Communicating a little delight to him, as well. When the lavender-eyed *mozo* left she turned to him shaking with laughter. "Did you see that? Oh my god, *que bárbaro!*"

Her friend, lighter-skinned with aspirations to being a preppy *fresa* twit and in total disapproval of her *amiga* running around with bush trash like Puch, snickered knowingly. "He saved up every *centavo* from his tips, then blew them on those contacts. Pitiful."

"But why?" Puch's date asked, genuinely bewildered. She didn't look at Puch though. Neither one of them did. The last thing they wanted was any insight into the "Mayan-don't-wanna-be" syndrome. "Who's he trying to kid?"

"Probably himself. Or just doesn't get it."

"Or maybe he knows what the deal is," Puch said as he stood up, laid a hundred peso bill on the table, and picked up his book bag. "And just likes looking that way."

It was the last time he dated a Mexican girl. He'd couldn't articulate why, but he'd had it with the race-conscious *Mexicanas* and didn't find the uneducated Mayan girls all that interesting. Fortunately, Cancun was a magnet for foreigners and he lived in a tourist attraction.

When Yaxche's viewpoint widened up and away from the eternal smoking spiral of the mosquito coil to include Puch's hundred pesos on the table beside it, she saw the incident as though through a gold filter, the soft light of gas flame lanterns in the little *"Mayami Bich"* taco bar that did business without electrical or water hookups. It was one of many moments in the Pop boy's life that she particularly cherished. Floating loose and rudderless in the whorling eddies of time, Yaxche had come to see him always in a sort of golden light, the ecstatic coloration of what he would eventually realize he had become. And her overly-distributed consciousness would pulse with ineffable love for the stout, handsome kid. If you were looking for a savior of your race, you couldn't do much better than Puch Pop.

DEEDS OF DOODS

Copper drifted deep into the night, bouyed by a much-patched innertube printed with faded images of Xcaret. Her red mane trailed from under her red baseball cap into the soft-lapping water of the lagoon, her naked ass drooped into the cool water, a length of hanky ski rope moored her to Winston's floating island, about as attached as she ever got to anything.

Her mind was addled beyond cognition, a situation of her own doing. Addle-pated was her vacation from the tyranny of detail, the persecutions of memory. When the past ate at her emotions and the future loomed ominous and arbitrary, there was just nothing she'd found like the eternal present of Ketamine. A little present to herself.

She'd just taken another massive hoover of the white flake she'd cooked out of the liquid she'd bought from the veterinary in Cancun where she was an old, if not exactly cherished, customer. She'd promised herself she wouldn't do it all up this time because she needed the money if she was going to get to Boston and twirl her flames in that Aerosmith comeback video. She'd turned cat softener into a cottage industry in her past sweeps from Mexico to The Excited States, as she called it. Hitting critter pharmacies where she knew they would sell her the stuff by the liter and not ask any recriminating—or incriminating—questions. Then chaperoning it on a flight to the Big Scrapple, an innocent clear fluid in a water bottle carefully resealed with a soldering iron. Tougher since 9/11, true, but she could still inject it into Kahlua bottles in her checked luggage. For the same old markup of several thousand percent. Precise numbers weren't her forté at the moment, riding a rubberduck bob in the perpetual "Vitamin K" nulltone and watching the moon stutter along like a film at the quirky half speed of K's noted freezeframe presentation.

She felt at home on Winston's floating folly, as good a metaphor for her itinerate life as anything. She felt swaddled and inviolable in the warm tropic night. No need for clothes here, for technology and gimmicks, for anything other than tepid water and holy fire in the damp black air. She leaned her head back until her ears were underwater, sang a few bars of her favorite healing song, "She's got all that I need, pharmacy keys..." The water closed in on her hidden membranes, softening them and massaging them with a dull roar that grew more and more insistent, a throbbing tremor that contained within it a high-pitched, bitchy whine.

Chimi, *nee* Agosto Cesar Ronchel, leaned forward over the grips of his JetSki to point in irritation, "¡Por alla, pendejo! Right over there by those mangroves." Chango was a dumfuk, all right, couldn't even see in broad moonlight.

Chango (known to his rich, dickhead parents as Aquiles Dominquero or even "Quichi") squinted into the darkness, revving his Kawasaki JS750 compulsively. He wasn't really into scoping things out, by nature. More of an action toy. He didn't see any floating island and had serious doubts there was such a thing. Wouldn't an island just sink? He gave up and plaintively whined, "Why don't we just go over there, then? Have a good look?"

Chimi, by far the most intelligent of The Lords of Xibalba, always stressed the need for reconnaissance and prior plotting, but thinking things out wasn't exactly the long suit of his band of monied, hedonistic scions. And the growling chorus around him made it clear they were all into immediate gratification. He shrugged. "Time to run that *pinche* hippie out of our ocean, *chavos*. And teach that redhead twat why to respect what a man has hanging."

A group howl answered his address to the troops, followed by the deep thunder of Corcho's glasspacked Yamaha Superjet, then the ear-splitting screams of tweaked motors driving after-market impeller pumps to blast the gang across the lagoon, a dozen white roostertails of spumed water flickering in the moonlight as the pack loped greedily towards Winston's hand-crafted homeland.

It was occurring to Copper, in that syrupy fuzzbrain Special K way, that things were getting rather loud. And the water was being uncharacteristically rambunctious around her. And that therefore, she should take a look, or (ha, ha) think about these things. In some way, in other words, react. No hurry, was her feeling. And yet...

The boisterous action of the water increased dramatically. The main drama being that it tossed her little plastic donut violently into the air. The tube flipped, flashing her soggy bare buttocks to the moon, and as her head came briefly out of the water before crashing back in again, her ears were boxed by a cacophony of demonic shrieking in a piped-up, two-cycle mode that hammered at her so hard even the K couldn't modulate it.

In fact, as she broke surface, grasping frantically for her non-approved flotation device, the Ketamine got mean on her, all pretense at psychic shelter vanishing in her frantic perception of what was causing the hellish choir of internal combustion overload. With her eyes exactly at sea level and her monkey-prune fingers clinging to the slippery surface of the tube, she was buffeted and buggered by the jet banshees, horrified to see dark shapes darting in from the night like an avenging posse of killer whales on crack.

She was very fortunate they didn't see her in the water; which she figured out much later. But her thoughts were hardly happy as she watched the Lords of Xibalba reduce Winston's floating idyll to ruin.

The Lords were frustrated that there was nobody in residence at the moment. They had verified this by the simple, if uncouth, stratagem of leaping their craft out of the water, skidding them across the deck and painstakingly created "garden", and barging through the house itself to plunge back into the water amid a chorus of catcalls and showers of flindered belongings and building material. A couple of entrance/exit wounds of that nature and it was pretty obvious nobody was around to enjoy the spectacle. Pissed off that the hippy and uppity *peliroja* weren't available to accept complaints, the Lords redoubled the deployment of their considerable talents for vandalism.

The demolition of Winston's Isle became a competition in excessive reductionism. Lords circled the island, skipping sideways in tight turns that generated wakes to provide liftoff for their comrades to get a little sky. JetSkis soared up off these wavelets then pounded down onto the funky, flimsy beauty of Winston's sovereign nation of homegrown, smashing anything that presented beneath their plunging hulls.

Corcho rocked forward as he spun around his prow, the aft jet blasting the shattered remnants like a firehose. Chimi took three tries before he managed to leave the water sideways, cutting a broadside swath of wreckage through the rapidly disintegrating superstructure. Chango got the highest jump of the night by caroming of the slanted front end of Ojo's Yamaha, actually topping the entire *palapa* roof, then falling through it like a cartoon anvil. The yahoos snatched up flotsam from the water, flaunting pieces of furniture and female garments, as they circled like amphetamine sharks, munching big bites out of the hated *hipilandia*.

Bobbing in their wakes, her head now tucked protectively inside the innertube, Copper watched the elimination of her haven in queasy spasms of terror. The K puppeted the waterbikes into jittering, frenetic motion freighted with limbic evil. She shuddered at the piston-powered hiphop and manic warwhoops of what she was perceiving as a troop of flying android monkeys, perhaps with a touch of armored pterodactyl. She would get around to lamenting the damage later, her present was now overdosing on a screaming, smoking, wrenching clamor of terminal velocity and ill-will. Somewhere deep inside her absent mind there was a whispered hope that sooner or later the Ketamine would wear off and the monsters would morph back to something normal. Hanging naked in the water, trembling with fear and revulsion, her heels moved unconsciously, driven by a memory from her disturbed childhood: click those red shoes together and get the hell back to Kansas.

FLIP SIDE

Ever since he shown her the *coralcaturas* she'd been obsessed with them. He'd come home and find her poring over them, stroking their surfaces, rotating the big coral chunks in different angles of light to study the shape of the symbols on their faces. No stranger than any other gringa behavior, maybe. Ganzo was no authority on how women acted around the house.

He paused inside the door of his rooftop hovel, watching her work on a pencil sketch of one of the coral heads, bending over his crude table in cheap panties and cutdown t-shirt, nibbling her lush lip in concentration. He stood with a stringer of fresh-speared fish dangling from his hand, trapped into immobility by the sight of her.

She finished her drawing and studied it, scowling prettily in dissatisfaction. Then became aware of his presence in the room and turned to smile at him. He smiled back and showed her the fish. She applauded silently and rubbed her bare tummy.

But when he laid the fish by the gas stove and came over to see her sketch, she turned a troubled face up to him. "I just feel like they mean something. Trying to say something, you know?"

Ganzo nodded solemnly and touched her sketch with one finger. "It mean something. This is, *Zotz*."

Her eyes widened and she stared at her sketch with new eyes. "Oh, right. It's a word. Wow! So what does it mean?"

"It means, *Zotz*."

"No wonder you call them cartoons. What does it mean in English, cutie?"

"It's... like mice, you know."

"No, I don't know."

"But they fly. Not birds. Little black wings made with leather."

"You mean bats?"

"That. Like Bacardi bottle."

"So the corals are talking shit about bats?"

He shrugged and sat down on a hardwood stump, watching her with his still gaze.

"But look at this." She turned the coral over to show him the bottom, but got no reaction so she grabbed another drawing and held it up beside it. "Look, this thing is six inches thick... it broke off right, like in a storm? But see, it's this different symbol."

Ganzo continued his serene gaze, patiently awaiting something he could comprehend.

"So the corals are like, writing these little words, and changing over time. How can that possibly be?"

"I don't know." He paused, not really giving her the impression of thinking, but some sort of search going on. "I don't understand how possibly is. If is, is possible, no?"

"No shit, big guy." He looked like a sea God, but wasn't exactly a rocket scientist. Or even a Little Leaguer, really. "But see... it's like I've seen this thing before. Like I can remember..."

"You remember something?" That seemed to make some changes in his super-calm face.

"Yeah, well, almost. I just know I've seen this before."

"Do you remember your name?"

"Baby steps, fellah," she sighed. "Baby steps. Maybe I'm better off without a name. Living like this it doesn't matter much."

"No. Because if you don't have a name, they give you one."

"That's how you got Ganzo, right?"

He nodded, everything self-evident, and she frowned. "Maybe I should just make one up?"

"Why?"

She stared at him for a long moment, causing zero discomfort to his stolid pose. "Tell me something, Ganzo," she said softly, "Why do you haul these things up here to your shack?"

"They catch me."

She waited, but nothing further came, so she made little "get with it" motions with her hands and he cranked back up. "I see many things, but then I see one thing that says take this home. It catches me, I can't leave it."

"Like me?"

"Yes."

"So I caught your eye?"

"Yes. Here you are."

She could have kicked herself when she heard her coy tone, but had already said it, "Do you think I'm attractive?"

Something almost approaching surprise showed on his impassive face. "¿*Como no*? I think you are most beautiful thing I ever saw."

"But you don't think you have to do anything about that?"

"I do. I look at you. What else to do with something beautiful? Look, feel good. Look more."

Curtsy actually felt a little dizzy for a heartbeat, there. She shook her head at him, smiling. "You're a very sweet heart, Ganzo. It's really nice."

Up to a point, she thought.

CLUB MEDS

Loris had already slipped out of her *huipíl* and waded waist deep in the warm tropic waters just inside Point Nizuc. She stood topless, lapped by gentle dark waves, arms raised as if to embrace the gibbous moon.

Winston still had on his droopy hemp pants, standing knee-deep in the water carefully counting out a handful of mushrooms. Xchab eyed him with guarded disgust. Old hippy getting set to bend his brains again. He'd be naked in a hour if her experience proved true; humming his Hindu chants or barking like a dog.

Bannock had kicked off his shoes and rolled up his Dockers, wading tentatively in the shallows while keeping an eye towards the hotels and Club Med buildings.

Xchab winced as Winston gulped down a big pinch of the dread *hongos*, then stared as Loris turned from her moonitation and approached him like a marble goddess emerging from the sea. She had been respectful of Loris from first sight: unable to pigeon her into any imaginable hole, wiped out by her beauty and whiteness and grave bearing. And now she was browsing the fungi, holding one up to examine by moonlight. The big *matón* who was obviously her boyfriend came up to watch as Winston wolfed down another dried cap.

"So what's the dose on these little beauties?" Loris asked.

"Well, based on your estimated body weight, obvious attitude, and extraneous pulchritude," Winston offered in judicious tones, "I think three or four should do you wrong."

He hunched a shoulder at Bannock and added, "Toughie, here, about the same."

"Okay, can I get eight, then? Wait, make it twelve."

"Whoa, you're a trouper after my own riddled heart."

"There are still three of us unserved, if you recall."

Winston shot a highly un-inclusive look at Xchab, who was hanging way outside the companionable circle the others had fallen into around the handful of shrooms. Then shrugged and handed Loris a dozen of the shriveled little pixie caps and gobbled down the remaining ones. He waded out deeper, staring into the shifting moondepths for minnows.

Loris turned to Bannock, cupping the sacraments between her breasts. She quietly took in his reluctance and smiled.

"You know, the first time I ate these things I was a completely different person." She stared past him, into some temporal inner distance. "They squared me away, put my life into a different order."

"I thought that was oXo's job." He spoke lightly, but was actually very interested in her past. A first for him. He wanted all of it, everything about her.

"Simplest answer; they worked hand in hand."

"So how long ago was this different person?" How much past baggage could she have at her age, anyway?

"Not as long as you'd think. I was a cheerleader, how do you like that?"

"I can see you cheering people up. Kind of unexpected, though."

"Not really. I was definitely attractive. I was also a neurotic, grasping, manipulative, shallow little rotten twat. All social, just what looks best and how can you get it. Messed up."

"Kind of typical, though."

"Worse than par, I'd say. I was a very messed-up kid. I was heading for suicide or one of the installment plan suicides lots of my friends had already signed on for."

"But you dropped acid and traded your pom-poms for tom-toms?"

"It was a process. But I'd have to say that drugs saved my life."

"Try not to give any speeches at PTA rallies, okay?"

Her only answer was holding out cupped hands full of *p. cubensis*.

"So your opinion as a professional healer/weirdo is that I should eat this disgusting crap?"

"Absolutely. Cross my heart."

"Okay, but I gotta tell you..."

She leaned in quickly, stopping him with a quick brush of her lips. "No you don't."

Bannock bowed his head to sniff the fungus in her hands. They had a little smell, but faint amid her vanilla soap, faint musk, and clean, silvery personal scent. He carefully picked out half the shrooms, then paused.

"Should I chew them up?"

"Not recommended. They taste nasty. Just get them down the hatch quick as you can."

He popped them in his mouth, bent to scoop up a handful of the lukewarm Caribe water, and lapped it like a dog to chase them home. "Well. That's that. Do I get my money back if I end up drooling in a loonybin somewhere?"

She stepped close to him and cupped his cheek with her free hand. She stared into his eyes from six inches away, luminous under the moon. "We're going to be just fine."

And he believed her. Maybe that was what it really was about her all along: he believed her.

Loris turned and approached Xchab, who was on the point of turning tail, but stuck around out of personal awe for the white girl. She dressed like a queen on the *tele* shows, took charge, didn't defer in the least to Bannock—who Xchab had immediately seen as a macho, dangerous guy—and in fact had obviously talked him into eating the mushrooms. And, don't forget, hadn't batted an eye when all those thousands of dollars crossed the table back in Pericos.

But above all, she'd been nice to her. Had noticed her, for one thing. Invited her to the table and treated her well. There was something about her that just told you she was on the right side. And now she walked up to Xchab with cupped hands full of fungus, held them out as if it was already agreed.

The Mayan girl glanced at the men, who were watching her with a careful neutrality, just wanting to see what she'd do. She wondered, herself. Then she looked back at Loris, pale breasts luminous under the moonglow, her face ancient and innocent, and couldn't look away.

"I've never thought of it as a trip," Loris said. "Always as coming home. And I'm all I've got to come home to."

Xchab stepped forward, as though putting her foot over a cliff. She held out her hands, cupped as if to receive water, and Loris poured the remaining shrooms into her grasp. Without breaking her gaze into Loris' big eyes, she swallowed them. They tasted totally revolting, like dirt and chicken droppings, but she was a jungle girl and had consumed weirder eats out in the village. She gave a deep, all-over shiver like a big dog coming out of water.

The big guy said, "So now what?"

Loris spoke and Xchab knew it was profoundly true. "Now," she said, "Is just a matter of time."

DIVERS ED.

Aphra was getting more concerned every second that Curtsy didn't swim back out of the cave. Her concerns had been a little different earlier, watching her tuck and drive down from the surface into the dark underwater cavity with lazy kicks, her buttocks bunching powerfully under the red, "Baywatch" bikini. How long has this been going on, she'd wondered. Babes underwater with tits all floaty and zero-grav, scissoring legs right at you like that? Damn!

But that had to have been over five minutes ago. She'd been extremely impressed by the blonde's condition and diving skills on the way out to the reef—she and MeiMei cheating by hauling themselves along the Avalon marker rope, Curtsy sculling along on the bottom peering at weird skindiver shit down in the silt. But this was beyond "experienced"; this was edging into "humanly impossible" and getting out there toward, "the dum ho just drowned herself".

She floated facedown, fixed with growing anxiety on the suddenly evil-looking overhang of the cave, crusted with strange growths and probably jagged teeth. MeiMei was really freaking out, taking big breaths and diving down, like she could do anything out here, and her as newbie at this shit as Aphra. Now WTF?

She was dithering between taking one desperation dive to the bottom, less than twenty feet, after all, and seeing if she could spot that damn ditz, or just writing off the money and heading back to the corral, when she heard a piercing whistle. Her head popped out of the water and she stared across the ten yards of shallow water over the top of the reef and saw Curtsy standing knee-deep, laughing her ass off. Crazy bitch.

She caught MeiMei when she breached, gasping after another of her useless and increasingly frantic attempts to see back into the cave. Pointed out the Golden Girl, posing like a Sports Illustrated cover against the infinite blue plate of Caribbean under scudding heaps of cumulous. "Must have been a back door," she said, testily.

MeiMei started to yell something about scaring the crap out of them, but realized that had been the idea. "Very cute. How do we get over there?"

"Hyperventilate for a minute," Curtsy told her, seriously. "Then drive straight down and power into the tunnel. Turn belly up. If you lose a fin or get in trouble, just crawl out along the roof of the tunnel. I'll watch for you from this end."

"Yeah, right," Aphra sneered. "That why you brought us out here, play hidey-seeky?"

"Move to your right about six yards," Curtsy told them. "See how the reef is skinnier there? Wait until a wave comes, give you a little more depth, then zip across real quick."

She watched as her pupils followed her instructions with only a few false starts and a scrape or two, then rounded them up on the other side and tipped her mask back to give them her full gaze. "I brought you out here to see how you do," she said. "See if you can handle being in the water. How you act if something goes wrong."

"So did we pass, Teach?" Aphra was over it, but stuck with her pissed-off diction.

"Not bad. Nobody panicked, nobody ran for home, nobody started yelling." She turned to MeiMei. "I appreciate your concern. You were going to try to come after me, weren't you? Bad idea, good attitude."

"Got any more caves you want to lose us in?" Aphra asked, looking around.

"Caves and tunnels and arches, oh my!" Curtsy burst out, her eyes shining. "It's what makes this place so special. The whole Yucatan is just a flat plate of limestone eaten full of holes like Swiss cheese. On land they call them *cenotes*, underwater, they're my personal playground."

"That just sounds so dangerous," MeiMei said, staring at the curl of waves out to the lighthouse, a power cruiser spanking around the point. "What if you get stuck or run out of air?"

"The technical term for that," Curtsy lectured learnedly, "Is 'crab chow'. Kind of like, what happens if you run out of handhold when you're mountain climbing. And you can't do underwater spelunking with SCUBA tanks."

Aphra nodded at that. She'd wanted to spring for tanks, feeling it would be safer and more professional than just swimming to the yacht with snorkles. But this little exercise Curtsy had termed a "test dive" had convinced her freedive was the way to go. No bulky gear, no tell-tale bubbles, no wetsuits covering up the goodies of her companions out here on this invisible meniscus between aquamarine water and deep-dish blue sky. "So." she said. "What next, Houdinita?"

"We could go out to the lighthouse if you want. It's really fun sitting out there, up in the air like that. But mostly let's screw around in here. We can go outside..." she waved at the inlets between the string of low flat rocks, waves rushing though them and occasionally breaking over the rocks, scattering gulls and pelicans. "But we aren't planning on going anywhere with wave motion, so let's mess around in here for awhile, get used to diving, learn some signals."

"Signals?" Aphra stuck in. "We aren't going to be down in the Titanic or nothing. We can just stick our heads up and talk, right?"

"Yeah," Curtsy said brusquely. "If we want people to hear us."

Aphra nodded again. She was suddenly aware that she resented not being the stealth expert. She was on Curtsy's turf and aware that the girl could lose her or even kill her out here with no trouble whatsoever. She was in the hands of a blond, for crisakes.

But she liked what she was seeing. Curtsy leading, MeiMei—in pretty decent shape herself for an egghead type—because she needed to find and ID what they were looking for, and Aphra because she was bankrolling and anyway had a long-standing prejudice towards being on the scene when the shit goes down.

And if you wanted a practice field or dive dojo or whatever, this place was perfect. She could see now that the reef with the tunnel was paralleled by the other reef, which stuck out of the water a foot or so, leaving a nice sheltered pool in between the two. To the south the strange triangle of the Avalon Reef Hotel poked up like an abandoned Lego project, to the north was a necklace of rock wreathed with a tossing lace of wave, back behind them was an immense stretch of sand-bottomed shallows.

Curtsy was no drillmistress. She led them around showing them sights. Sting rays flying along the bottom like slo-mo birds, darting clouds of Blue Tangs, a big Parrotfish grinning like his dentures hurt. starfish, fan corals. But Aphra noticed each time they examined some cool little fish or cavern or shell they were getting smoother at going down, coming up without noise as she taught them how to displace the water in their snorkles before tipping them up to sip air, learning to be aware of each other's positions and understand the others' signals and gestures. They were starting to move together, like a herd of some kind as they learned their environment. Hmmph, she thought, School of Fish, is what we got here.

Curtsy pulled them up in the lee of the largest islet, MeiMei jabbering in wonder at the fish and various specimens she was seeing. "Is the reef always this close to the island?" she asked.

"Isla *is* a reef, Doc," the blonde laughed. "A limestone reef. Where it's dry they put up houses; where it's wet the coral build on it."

Aphra was more into business than science. "You think we've got it together enough for the caper?"

"I think so. For beginners, you guys are doing fine. And everybody's in shape. Should be a piece of cake now that we're starting to move like a unit. Just remember: it's two little raids we're doing here. Yours and mine."

Aphra nodded and started to speak when they heard another shrill whistle, this one brassy and cop-like. Startled, the girls and looked towards shore, where a bulky guy in the red and white livery of the Avalon security squad was blowing a whistle and angrily motioning at them to go back into the roped-off area. All three laughed in unison.

"Not many rules in open ocean," Curtsy giggled.

"And enforcement's a bitch," Aphra added.

MeiMei chuckled. "Know what we should do?"

Moving almost as if choreographed, the three spun around, lay prone in the water, hauled down their bikini bottoms, and paddled hard to hoist their gleaming butts above water, shooting the security guy a triple-barreled, tri-tone, multi-racial moon.

They turned and lay back, finning slowly to see the guard's reaction. He stood for a minute, scowling, then laughed and started to applaud. They waved and Curtsy did a sort of water curtsy, then started back towards towels and shooters at Na Balam, laughing like schoolgirls.

"No, honey," Aphra said between chuckle spasms. "*Now* we're moving like a unit."

THE COME-DOWN

You have to fly into Cancun in the daytime to even get a clue. Miles out you look down into open ocean and it looks like desert. You're seeing the bottom because you can't see the water. That's your first clue.
Seagull: *The Blasé Sojourner*

It had come on pretty smoothly, considering half of the trippers were virgins. Xchab had fretted nervously, pacing and twitching and popping her eyes in totally non-noble-redperson tension. Loris had tried to soothe the girl, but realized she was skittish and suspicious, so she just gave her some space and concentrated on her own little pre-flight mantras and mudras.

She'd smiled watching Bannock adjusting, peering around at first; trying to analyze and guard. But after one of her prolonged dips—lowering backwards and sinking into the silky, accepting water, emerging and whipcracking her hair—she saw him staring at the pellets of water flying off her like a crown of pearls, ashimmer in the lights of the hotel zone. She waved to him and he waved back, then fell into the whole fingertip thing, wiping and weaving in the air. She giggled and kicked a spray of jeweled water at him.

Winston, of course, came on like a true slut, psychodillies as mother's milk to him. He did a boneless dance in the shallows, flapping his floppy shirt to internal music. She gave another glance at Xchab, paralyzed on the sand, and figured it was time to shed a little light. She waded in, approaching the Mayan girl slowly. She got no response, seeing eyes focused inwards and dead-centered. She stood in front of the girl motionless, beaming herself into her. Xchab blinked once, in slow motion, then met her eyes directly and without evasion for the first time. She sensed something powerful in the dark gaze, but also undirected, drifting in currents that emitted no light. She reached to her own waist and undid her soaked panties, then stepped out of them and whirled them around her head. Drops of moon-hue spun out into the darkness around them. Xchab stared at her, then tipped her head to watch the outward spiral of light drops into the night.

The girl reached out now, laid her hand tentatively on Loris' cheek as if checking to see if she was really there. Her hand trailed down the pale skin, slid off the pale breast, hung heavily at her side. Loris tossed her wet panties onto the sand and made a simple gesture.

Immediately Xchab shed her own clothes, which blew whatever was left of Winston's mind. Xchab had emphatically not been the type for public nudity. He stopped his ghost dance and stared at the two naked women standing face to face, the short one so dark and solid, the tall one so white and slim. Whoa!

Bannock stared at the pair, also. He exulted in the sight, wiped out by the beauty of both of them. But without a touch of lust, a lack he was somewhat aware of. Sublime shapes under the cresting moon. Then Loris turned and walked back into the sea. Once waist-deep, she dived, the flash of her half-moons a wonder under the lunar lighting. When she breached again, she waved to Xchab, laughing. Xchab stared then did the last thing either Bannock or Winston expected. She broke into a laugh and charged into the water, kicking up a fountain of spray until she, also, took a dive.

She came up and paddled towards Loris like a puppy, chortling in childish glee. Loris splashed water in her face, initiating a spate of horseplay that the men watched, struck dumb and motionless. Until Loris glanced at them, standing ankle deep in their street clothes, and snickered. "Wotta couple of wussies."

Winston glanced at the big guy and said, "Are we going to take that?"

"Hell no, podnuh." And Bannock was pulling off his attire and sailing it back onto the beach.

"Who's the rotten egg?" Loris taunted while Xchab cackled and tossed Mayan catcalls at them.

The two men thundered into the water like Percherons, belly-flopping noisily into the wet warmth, then swam at the howling girls with windmilling crawl strokes that filled the air with a filigree of moonwater. They slithered through the pale light like otters, basking and bellowing in the electric night over the reef.

The sky was lightening, the turquoise tint seeping into the water, and Bannock was spending more and more time underwater, watching the quicksilver underside of the surface, snatching at fish, sliding around Loris' legs like an eel. He pushed off the bottom and came into the air like a killer whale, a big male upsurge into a sky going pink but still full of stars. He stood near Loris and tossed big double handfuls of water into the sky, watching the seductive play of color in the droplets, striving to build his own rainbow. "So this is where stars come from," he murmured.

Then he turned to her, and was washed over by raw feeling. The beauty of her, rising from the water like an alabaster statue. The wonder of her, every line and movement a hint of the strong, smooth stream he'd plunged into in her depths. Then he saw that the water on her cheeks wasn't seawater, but tears, and was beside her in a minute, waiting for her words.

"We're making a big mistake," she whispered, and Bannock felt the big red balloon inside him go slack.

"I don't think so," he told her, trying to catch her eye and not succeeding. "I feel better about us all the time."

That brought her around, sweeping him with a sorrowful gaze he saw as somehow Italian. "So do I. And when I'm, you know... like this... and feel that way, I take it pretty seriously."

Winston had been floating with eyes dilated upwards and all the drive and animation of a barnacled log, Xchab also back-floating with her head to his, her lush hair pulsing around him like seaweed. He suddenly tipped his head up, the girl's hair spilling over his brow like the world's worst comb-over. "Seriously?" he piped. "Are you serious? Don't take anything seriously. Or it will take you right back."

He flopped back into sensory deprivation and Loris stepped to Bannock and laid her hands on his pectorals, her head on his chest near his heart. "I'm talking about oXo," she said forlornly. "Those guys are assholes. They're imprisoning him to exploit him."

Bannock placed his palms just where her hips curved out from her waist and spoke into the top of her head. "Did you have a vision of him chained in a dungeon begging you to come rescue him and bring some crack?"

"I just know, okay? We have to get him back."

He took a long pause, feeling her skin, the warmth of her against the hair of his chest, watching the fingers of day creep up the eastern sky over Isla Mujeres. "I don't know what the hell's wrong with me anymore, but I guess that's a good enough reason for me, too."

Winston bobbed up, eyeing them like a graying sea otter. "Good enough for me, too. Whatever you're talking about."

Bannock ignored the old hippie, who receded once again into the sea. "If it wasn't for you and ol' oXo I wouldn't have been caught dead eating this crazy shit. But now I can't believe I would have turned it down, ever. It changed me too, somehow. I feel like a different person. Does that wear off?"

She smiled softly into his wet chest thatch and said, "Not if you work at it."

"So I'm a different person now? Would you say?"

"If you say so. And not just you, either."

Bannock turned where she was looking and saw Xchab slowly rise, the water slicking down off her cinnamon body as if off sheet metal. As she came up out of the water her hair slid off Winston's head, like a stop-action of aging. She stood facing the dawn and reached out towards the faintest aura of sun, doing something ritualistic with her fingers. She turned to them and Bannock saw what Loris meant: the girl's face was cast into a firmer mold, hard as igneous rock, ductile as sand. She was a solemn priestess, eyeing them for worthiness. And spoke: "This is the place where the sun is born."

She reached down and gently lifted Winston's head, Loris noting a more tender attitude towards the geezer. He stood and looked around at them, then at the shivering new sun. And Xchab spoke again. "The place and the time."

Xchab's hand had come to rest on the green fender of the taxi as they got in, tracing the last three letters of the words "EcoCab". Winston chuckled and leaned over to tell Loris, "Cab is her surname. And the Mayan word for 'bee', wouldn't you know?"

The ride from Punta Nizuc to the other end of the lagoon had been almost entirely silent. The driver didn't know what to make of the odd quartet, and anyway their clothes were soaked and sogging up his cool Pumas seatcovers. The foursome, wrapped in the soft, brown ego-restructure of a waning good trip, had little to say, but found it very comfortable to relax in one another's company without babbling.

They got out at the gravel lot by the bridge, huddled together in the post-dawn while Bannock handed the cabbie a too-big bill and got no change. But as soon as they turned to head down the path hacked years ago through the mangroves they saw Copper slumped under the stunted trees like a sack of old clothes.

Winston moved to her, shocked at seeing her in such an abject, beaten posture: unthinkable for the ebullient, defiant redhead. Bannock was looking around for threat as he followed Winston towards Copper, Loris moving in with a calm certainty. Just as Winston reached her, she tilted her head back, her eyes puffed and tearful. "It's gone!" she sobbed. "They killed it!"

Winston looked where she was pointing and saw only a slick of oily rubbish and chopped vegetation where his home had once floated.

AFTER MATH

Winston couldn't believe Ms. Ruff, Tuff, and Hard To Snuff was in tears over mere material possessions. And not even hers. Touching, though. He'd known Copper a long time and knew there was a fuzzy heart inside the steel-belted leather shell, but it didn't get out much. Much less so since the advent of Dr. K.

They'd found a little stuff floating around. Including a pair of fire chains in her shredded backpack. Bannock found a dive mask, and improvised a strap from his shoestrings to dive for more stuff, but just got coated with gunk. And Copper's mood wasn't improving.

Winston tossed her a baggie with the absolute last of his stash of weed. "At least you got your dancing rig, Coppertop. Now you have nothing to lose but your chains." And at least all that fucking ketamine is gone.

"But how about your stuff?"

"Since when do I have anything worth a shit? You know me: if I need something, I either jack it or make it out of debris."

Loris stroked Bannock's back as he fussed around trying to improve the seal on his jury-rigged mask, but was keeping an eye on Xchab, who was doing a pretty good imitation of a Mayan stele, staring expressionless at the space that had been her only home since the hovel of her childhood. "How about the kid, there?"

Winston shrugged, "She barely owns any clothes."

Copper turned to her, snapping out of her funk. "Win likes to keep 'em bare-assed and pregnant."

The old hippie reacted in cartoon alarm, crossing himself. "Bite your tongue, bitch."

Bannock stood up, tossed the mask out into the debris-smeared lagoon, and turned back to them in a sort of military movement that got all their attention. "Look," he said off-handedly. "We've been up all night. We're wet and hungry. It's Plan B time."

Copper cut her eyes at him, lips pursed. "If you've got a plan that has a meal, bed, and shower in it, lay it on me."

"Was your visa destroyed, too?"

Copper frowned at the descent to the kind of bureaucratic reality she generally ignored. "And my passport. Chopped into fishy litter."

"Good thing I've still got mine," he said with an off-kilter grin that Loris really liked. Then he pulled out and flashed a gold-colored VISA card, which Copper really liked.

"But weren't you telling me how a deal's a deal?" Loris spoke in a schoolmarm voice, but he could see the fun in her eyes.

She had a point, though. Bannock, a little abashed, said, "Yeah, yeah. Look, I was just thinking that over in the shower."

The piping hot showers with lovely Talavera tile and mounds of fluffy towels. Which had put everybody in much better spirits than they'd experienced sitting in littoral muck eyeing the shambles of an owner-built, sovereign lifestyle.

They'd all gobbled mounds of room service hamburgers and beer, Bannock having convinced the concierge at the Gran Caribe that being allowed to entertain his friends in his room would play better with the clientele than having them troop into the doggedly upscale dining room or Riviera-style poolside café. Now the party lay about digesting their meal and possible futures. Xchab's eyes kept flitting around this room crammed with more luxury than she could have previously imagined: cataloging with equal ecstasy the full-wall high-rise-glassed view of a world as much wider than hers as the gleaming Caribbean outsized the crystal pool below, the leather lounges, the microwave and blender in the kitchenette, the absurd paintings of hip Eurotrash lounging under palms. Winston bemoaned the loss of his stash, but was otherwise typically curious as to what came next. Copper, her usual rambunctiousness mellowed by fatigue and the aftermath of shock, lay with her hair dangling off a sofa arm, tapping a foot to the piped-in Cuban jazz. Bannock and Loris leaned slightly towards each other at the clever pull-out table in authentic blond Ikea.

"So why would I honor a deal with these two Hollyweird dipshits, but not Blaster? Well, I was working for them, for one thing."

"And they're so much more honorable and squared-away than he was."

"Yeah right. No, the only difference between their brand of scuzz and his, they have money."

He looked at her for comment, but her face was as still as an underground pond.

"So is that what I'm on here?" he asked her quietly. "Ethics measures up to money?

"Bannock," Loris asked in a reasoning tone, "May I ask? Do you think about things like that very much?"

"Nope. And you can see why. It's pretty much an acquired taste."

"I told you psilocybin would be good for you."

He leaned over to cup her head in his hands, brush his lips on her cheek and murmur, "And it told me you'd be good for me.

Copper glanced up, smirking, "Hey you guys, get a room."

Bannock gave her a look. "Excuse me, but we *have* a room. There might be a place on the roof for hippies to hang their hammocks. Why not go see?"

Copper glared at him but Winston laughed and she joined him. Bannock leaned back and stretched to reach the cordless house phone on the counter. Waited, then spoke into it.

"Hey, I've got three friends here that need a room for tonight. Can you just put that on my card? Great, thanks. They'll come down and pick up the key. Oh, yeah, that's better. 516? They'll meet him there."

He slipped the phone into the pocket of his logo-monogrammed robe and said, "Let's get together for a late breakfast tomorrow. About ten? Figure out where everybody's Plan B's are falling by then."

Copper and Winston looked at each other and figured out Bannock had just bought some privacy in a really gracious way. They got up and headed for the door, giving him soul shakes and peace signs as he waved off their thanks, "Get a good night's sleep," he called out as they moved into the hall. "Exploit the facilities."

As the door closed he turned to Loris. "They'll probably get buzzed and spend the whole time joyriding elevators."

"I think the Mayan girl could spend three days just ogling the gift shop." She stood up and walked to the bedroom door, trailing her fingers along the view-under-glass as he watched her fondly.

"That's the way of you crooks, I understand," she said over her shoulder. "Rip off some poor slob, then throw it around like a sailor on leave until it's gone and you have an excuse to pull some more crimes. That the deal?"

"I was thinking we could really use a Hummer." She didn't react, so he went on, feeling his way through unfamiliar thoughts. "Seriously ... I can't explain it exactly, but I just sort of felt like we're into something together here. Do you get that? Know what I'm talking about?"

"Oh, I certainly do."

"It's like since that swim and getting the fungus among us there's some sort of.... What? Is there a word for it? We're a karass or grok or Temple of Shroom or something?"

"Nothing that fancy. We're brothers and sisters. We always have been, but when you get around cubensis you become aware of it."

"So is that where we're at here? You and me? Brother, sister?"

"Don't you feel it?"

Bannock came out of his chair slowly, moving towards her. "What I feel like, Sis, is a little incest."

Loris smiled, her robe slipping down off her shoulders, "Brother can you spare me some time?"

SCATTERED SHOWERS

Nobody had voiced any objections to Aphra relocating her little "strike force" to a cabana at the Maria Del Mar, especially since she seemed to be picking up the tab.

Curtsy was thoroughly sick of the treatment she was getting

from guys around the little cubbyhole in Colonia Electricista where she'd stashed her few possessions. MeiMei had been content at the Rocateliz, a nice place right downtown where she could indulge her most secret vice—smoking fine cigars—but didn't need being close to the search anymore and was delighted to be a couple of barefoot steps off Playa Norte. And of course Aphra was elated to have two such delectable pieces of tail there in her own henhouse.

Nevertheless, MeiMei had felt she should say something about the Black girl's generosity. Aphra waved it off. "Kidding, right? I'm one multiple-well-divorced little black widow and money's not a problem at all. And when else would I get a chance to jump something like this off? Being Indiana Jones meets Cleopatra Jones in a string bikini?"

So it was just a girlfriend party there by the beach and pool as they planned to take down Ronchel's yacht.

Thing was, though, Aphra's deep pockets had some trick stitches. She'd been cruising on cash, and her stash of travelers' checks from Gnarls Barkley of London was slimming down. Should have been no hassle, what with toting one of the most powerful credit cards in existence but she'd gotten that FYI from DC that certain hyper-hymie weasel jumped ship to the Dark Side. How often to you see a "NYJew" poster boy working for a black boss, anyway? Upsets the whole natural order of things. Course here she is, running a blonde and a chink, so what the hell?

Point is, Weistler's defection meant everybody involved was potentially compromised. And left her without any sure feel for the downside of anybody being able to triangulate on her, but her instinct had always been; In case of doubt, blackbag it. And she had a sneaking suspicion that as soon as she swiped that card it'd ring a bell for the Committee To Re-Elect, or worse—open an info-share window to the whole damn gummint and she just could end up standing there with her undies around her ankles and a virtual crosshair drawing a bead on her bush. Bottom line, she was watching expenditures, but couldn't pass up on having the previously mentioned pale tail under her immediate premises.

Not paying off as yet, but she had her hopes. Sitting there in Corona commercial lounge chairs staring off into tones of blue water—Aphra particularly enjoying the sight of Curtsy doing her workout topless in waist-deep water—while chatting up the good Doctor Chiang.

Who was coming on with her usual line of Lecture 101. "Actually, there were previous 'ends of the world'. Collapses. We talk about the 'Mayan Apocalypse'..."

"That Mel Gibson movie? Apocalypso or something?"

"More or less. And yes, having the Spanish show up and conquer them, burn all their books, didn't do much to help promote their culture, but actually there were collapses even before that."

"Build up these big temples, then everything just fall to shit and wander back off into the jungle, right? Just like in Africa. What was with that?"

"Probably ecological, most think. They pushed their population up past what they could feed."

"Well good thing we got smart and don't do that shit now, huh?"

"Oh, right. But there's another thing. They went pyramid crazy. Started pouring all their energy into building huge tombs and stele for their rulers. There are Mayans to this day, living out in the rain forest, who sneak into old ruins to burn incense in front of stone carvings on the wall that represent nothing more than dead kings. Not even rumored to be Gods. And they don't know the difference. The whole sacrifice cult got crazy, sucked off all the labor and resources."

"Maybe why they ran out of food?"

"There you are. A major reason, according to a branch of the whole theory."

"Uh, oh, hang on, I'm getting something here. I hope you ain't gonna tell me these apocollapses happened on these like, calendar-end dates. Don't be scaring me now."

"That's harder to figure."

"But you might be able to? "

"That jade codex might be able to explain a lot of that. It seems like properties of one time cycle tend to generalize to others. Trouble is, I'm not all that confident about getting away with this Charlie's Angels bit on Ronchel's yacht."

"What I hear around the Outta Town Hotties network, that boat's far from airtight. One thing, the owner's this world class horndog."

"Oh goody, so I could just show up on the gangplank in a teddy and he could Shanghai me aboard and rape me. Sounds like a plan."

"Just leave all that to Auntie Aphra. You got the target knowledge, Blondie there got the dive skills. What I'm bringing to the table is what you might call tactics."

MeiMei glanced sideways at Aphra, lounging next to naked under a light coat of oil and a wide-brimmed straw planters hat, and suddenly self-proclaimed as a tactician. She was starting to realize that she might have already seen some of those tactics at work, and that this Aphra might be somewhat deeper water than she'd previously assumed. No big...whatever it might take to score that plaque.

She listened as Aphra laid out her plan for the raid with a precision and vocabulary that seemed to veer back and forth from military to criminal. It sounded fine. Actually, it sounded kind of like the drone of the waves on the sand and the wind in the palms: the sun was not so much baking her as pressing her flat, oppressing movement and thought. A process aided by a series of what the grinning Mexican waiter in luau shirt called Coco Locos as he brought them over to their low-slung canvas chairs that seemed to sling lower with each sip of rum, vodka and coconut milk from the coconut shell cups. She didn't need to know all this commando stuff, did she? She was content to leave herself in Aphra's hands.

Which was also Aphra's personal plan for contentment, as it turned out. MeiMei was a trifle unsteady as they trailed soft white sand back into the cabana, not all that accustomed to sneakup drinking in the afternoon. Fortunately Aphra leant a helping hand, which seemed to be her main MO. And smooth enough about it that MeiMei didn't really realize just how in hand she was until she stood nude under soothing warm water in the big pink shower stall, with Aphra scrubbing away her sweat with a sudsy loofah. MeiMei actually knew that the word "loofah" meant "ribbed squash" in Mandarin, but was slow to notice that the squashing wasn't going on anywhere near her ribs. And was feeling way too good. Her eyes whipped open and served her the sight of Aphra's gorgeous, savage and totally avaricious face as she applied that helping hand where she figured it would help her the most.

MeiMei reacted instantly, with burned-in reflex, unleashing a sequence of three kata that blocked the urgent, pleasuring hands and slapped Aphra's bountiful black ass up against the pink, shell-motif tile. Aphra looked startled, then flashed a feral grin. They stood there with warm water pouring over their bodies, slicking them up, a pretty ravishing shot, all told.

"I appreciate your help on this project," MeiMei said evenly, "But I'm not really into that." Not into much lately, she was thinking. Are you really going to get all picky over feeling this good with somebody that's pretty great to look at?

Yep, she decided, I am.

Aphra generally saw domination as the route to any given solution, aided by slickery as needed. She'd spent the money, would like to have a little dirt on the Doc for later. The martial moves had been a surprise but, hey, you get that with your Asian types. And push come to shove... She reached out deliberately and cupped one of the smaller girl's luscious breasts.

MeiMei was shaking her head. "Sorry. Not going to happen."

The alcohol had been working on Aphra, too, and what she'd copped of the Chinadoll so far had gotten her damned hot. So she not only failed to relinquish the disputed breast, but moved to pincer the nipple.

A foot slammed into the side of her jaw. Damn. She could taste a trickle of blood. Which just got her that much hotter, but she didn't see much she could do about it. "Whoa, nice job, there. I'd love to see that again in slow motion."

"Then touch me again."

Aphra laughed, holding up her hands in an "Uncle" gesture.

"I couldn't stand it, anyway. Me and you fighting naked for free when there's a million guys out there would pay big bucks to watch it?"

MeiMei didn't speak, just watched her through eyes that were quickly clearing of the CocoLoco mist.

"I gotta say, hon. I'm no stranger to The Arts my own self. I was pretty bad right off the streets, before I even started workin' my mojo in the dojo. But I get a distinct feeling you're not to be fucked with."

"Exactly my point."

"Damn shame, cutie. You coulda been a contender."

Aphra steamed out of the shower boiling in frustration and superheated yen. She stood in the front room of the suite, shaking off water like a retriever. And looked up to see Curtsy in the bedroom, staring at her while frozen in the process of peeling off her bikini bottom. She turned on her heel and stalked into the room twitching a virtual panther tail.

"You could pick up a few extra bucks here, girlfriend."

Curtsy was caught off balance by that, and not just because she was standing on one foot with the other snagged in her suit bottom. "More diving?"

"In a manner of speaking." Wonder does NAUI have a badge for Muff Diver?

"Well, then." Curtsy wasn't sure how to take this whole thing, but was okay with finding out. "Lay it on me."

"Pretty much the idea."

Curtsy wrinkled her brow, glowing with the day's dose of sunshine. What was going on here? "Why don't you just tell me?"

"Two hundred cash, right now."

"For?"

"Taking a shower." Aphra gave it a beat and bit of pelvic thrust. "With me."

Curtsy took in the whole thing, the sleek black body and no-shit pose. And hesitated a little. "I can't guarantee you," she said.

"Guarantee what?"

"That I won't end up kicking your butt."

"I can live with that," Aphra told her as she wheeled and headed back to the bath.

In the shower, a lovely tropical sort of space with a wide window showing tops of palm trees, Curtsy didn't know quite what to expect. She just sort of stood there, naked under the equally naked eye of Aphra, leaning in the corner checking her out. She fiddled with the taps, grabbed the shampoo, blurted, "Okay, so how do we do this?"

Aphra reached for the shampoo and washrag on the shelf and said, "Very, very thoroughly."

LA ISLA BONITA

"Now this is America," Copper breathed rapturously. "What you truly miss when you're expatting."

Winston checked her out, slathering butter and strawberry jam on a thick slice of real (not Bimbo) bread. "Even more than having workable mail, telephones, and legal system?"

"Like I need any of those," Copper tossed back. She was mopping up some over-easy eggs with a chunk of actual non-chorizo sausage, one of those lean, effortlessly wiry women who wolf down caloric goodies unscathed and drive normal women homicidal. "You want the American Dream, it's right here: the Denny's Grand Slam Breakfast."

"Well, the local version, anyway." Loris hadn't been out of the States long enough to long for yolk-soaked pancakes and non-crumbly toast and first world pig products, so she tucked away some chilaquiles between sips of iced tea.

"That tea," Copper went on. "Made by seeping leaves in water. Not dumping some space station microdust in water. The coffee, actually steeped, not '*NoEsCafé*'. What I'm talking about. A civilization has to freakin' deliver to get taken seriously."

Xchab was less sold. She'd have gotten *molletes* and chiles, but was determined to explore gringo folkways and was therefore trying to wrap toast around eggs, sausage and refried beans as if it were a tortilla. Weird stuff, but damned good. And being here at this beachfront restaurant where couples in expensive clothes sat next to barely-clad sunlovers built like porn actors, where everything was sparkling clean and the food forthcoming forever, where stiff-uniformed waitresses came across formal with "*Usted*" but slipped her some Mayan advice under their breath.

Bannock had eaten lightly, buttered *bolillos* from the basket and a steady stream of coffee from the stylish chrome carafes. He leaned back, chewing on some train of thought or another. Loris was waiting him out.

He rolled his cup around on the saucer, then blurted. "Okay. I can trace oXo down. We'll go back up to L.A. and I'll get all over it. An agent sent me to those clowns and I can..."

"Not necessary." Loris blotted her lips and smiled at him. "Sweet and committed, but not really necessary."

Now Bannock waited her out. She reached into her Oaxaca engulf-all bag, pulled out a lurid slick brochure and handed it to him. The other three heads at the table followed it, wondering if crystal skulls had started slipping flyers under windshield wipers.

"The Mayan Riviera Underground Film Festival?" He glanced at her, then around the table. "Is this some kind of a joke?"

"Probably. Are Cannes and Sundance not jokes at a higher level of energy?"

"Beats me, but I bet you're onto something there."

She leaned over and pointed. "Look who's scheduled for the Saturday panel."

"Seminar," Bannock mumbled. "Holy crap, that little dork really is a producer."

"And we can even get to see one of his films."

"Can't wait. Looks like The Loveboat meets Freddy Krueger does Girls Gone Wild in Cancun."

"I'd pay to see it," Copper chirped, skillfully nabbing Winston's last slice of toast. "I was there two years ago. Wall to wall phonies and wannabes throwing money and pussy around. I made out like a bandito."

"I'm looking at this thing and have absolutely no idea what the hell it's all about. How big is Playa Carmen, anyway?"

"It's a tourist trap full of Italian sharpies, American dullies, and gringo-wranglers from Mexico City," Winston pronounced, surreptitiously sniping a roll when Xchab wasn't looking.

"They get money from the state and national tourism boards to do stuff like that," Copper told him. "Get their films laid off that way, too. Cheap local crews, kickbacks and downlines and shit."

Bannock gave her a long look that she slid off of by signaling for more coffee. He stared at the brochure, working a toothpick around the corner of his mouth. Then he said, "I think I get it."

"They want to move up the ladder from grinding out this crap," Loris nodded.

"And think they can do it with the right director."

"I hate to say it, but that's not a bad idea." Winston shrugged when they both glared at him. "If that sucker could direct me a dream, he could sure as hell put together a kickass blockbuster."

"But it just won't work with their Melrose ambitions," Loris said, and Winston nodded agreement as he chewed. "But even at a little festival like that one, there'll be deals to cut, bigshots to impress. So they'll definitely bring oXo."

Bannock let that sink in for a moment. "I see one problem."

"I'm so glad to hear that," Loris beamed. "Because I was seeing about a dozen."

Bannock tapped the brochure with a thick finger. "It's a couple of weeks off."

152

"True. They probably flew back to Burbank in the meantime."

"Or this joker and his buttboy could be buried up to their necks in aromatic spirulina in some health stalag," Copper put in. She turned to Loris, "The Riviera here has gotta be the highest concentration of spas and Zen centers and health hedonists in the world."

"Really?" More than casual interest from Loris, all right. "Maybe I could do some massages somewhere."

Bannock turned to stare. "You do massages? Like professionally?"

"My main trade, actually. Did you think I was just a dope dealer's social secretary?"

"Cool. Can I get an appointment?"

"Great." Copper rolled her eyes, her instinctive hostility to Bannock waning, but still worth a goad or two. "Massagist meets misogynist."

Bannock ignored her, as he'd been doing. "So we lay up somewhere then get down there in advance and scope it out, get his room number. Be sitting there when he walks in with the skull."

"If he has it with him," Winston cautioned.

"If not, we persuade him to take us to it."

Copper, after scouring the last food off her plate, and anybody else's she could reach, announced, "Well, I know where I'm going, while you guys pull your extortion caper. Place I can live cheap, hang with good people and decent musicians, and there's enough summer tourists to dance up a few bucks.

"Sounds like a plan," Loris said. "Is this a real place?"

"More or less. Isla." She pointed out over the turquoise water, still and sleek in the summer morning. "You can even see it from here."

Everybody turned to take in the low ridge of land floating on the turquoise horizon. Winston said, "Well, you know I'm an island kind of guy."

"Let's try not to get this one torn down around us." She turned to Bannock and he saw the aggressive snark fall off her. Just the redhead next door, smiling a little ruefully. "Hey, look, Bannock, man... I really appreciate you springing for the room and meals and all. That was nice and you're a solid guy, especially with me giving you a hard time."

"Not a problem, Red. Maybe we can see you fire dance sometime."

Copper reached under the table, unconsciously patting the little day pack that held her kevlar-wrapped fire chains. The fact that the chains—and even the little bottle with the last of her Coleman white gasoline—were her only possessions to survive the wreckage of Winstonia was a powerful spiritual statement to her. And only the latest of many.

"So what's the chances of us bumming a few bucks to catch the ferry over, get bunks in Poc Na for a few nights until I can dance up some cash? Like a hundred bucks, maybe?"

"We can do that. But tell me a little more about this Isla place."

"Oh, it's the max. You know those Corona commercials? Couple in hammocks under palm trees on a beach, chuck their cell phone in the ocean? They shot those on Isla Mujeres."

Bannock turned to Loris. "I don't know about you, sunshine, but I've always dreamed of living in a beer commercial."

Copper quickly told Loris, "And there are plenty of spas there, too. Massage pavilions on the beaches. Look, whatever you guys do, you're this close to Isla, you should get to know the place. It's really, really special."

"How about this?" Bannock said, eyeing the tropical isle floating between sky and sea. "We all go over there. You guys get situated, pick up a few bucks, figure out your next move." He turned to Loris. "We'll play tourist for awhile, then head down to Playa Carmen to scout the festival, look up Mr. Crystal."

Loris looked at him with a cryptic smile.

"Hey, I was angling for the money before I met you. What do you think I had planned? Sitting on a beach for a long time, surrounded by fun people and beautiful women. So it's not like it's a stretch."

"Best thing is, hotels are cheaper there, "Copper said. "The Villa Ki'in, a cabana for like eight people costs less than your room here did. And their pool is amazing."

Nobody bit, so she had to finish it herself. "They call it the Caribbean Sea."

RAIDERS OF THE LOST CHANCE

"Well they sure don't look harmless to me," MeiMei said. "Those underslung jaws are bad enough, but their eyes have that attitude like, you know... Just start something, bitch."

Aphra wasn't that crazy about the big school of barracuda either. In fact, she wasn't nuts about snorkeling in dark shallows at night with the only light some sort of gizmodo halogen thing Curtsy had brought but didn't ever seem to want to turn on. But she let Ms. China Syndrome do the whining.

Curtsy wouldn't have turned the light on at all if she'd known it would show a big bank of silvery killers hovering around them like a sardine can full of primordial hard-eye. But she steadied MeiMei up with a chuckle. "You know how many people have ever been killed by barracuda around here? Zero. You know how many barracuda I saw roasting on a beach bonfire last month? Thirty. So who's the dangerous ones here?"

She'd gotten her bearings straight and figured her team of Gnarly's Angels was about as comfortable with dark water as they were going to get. She splashed the surface and when they looked at her, she pointed the direction.

Aphra did one more nervous adjustment of her mask, muttering, "I don't see why we gotta swim around our elbows to get to that asshole. Plenty of docks over there by Rolandis."

"You didn't want anybody to see us going in," Curtsy told her curtly.

"Or more important, coming out," MeiMei threw in. She was aware that the plan had been built around Aphra's tactics, so the Black girl was probably just doing a little mood-lightening. What worried her was coming back to the cul de sac where they'd left their rented, street-legal golf cart. The heavy current in through Sac Bajo had made getting to the mouth of Macax Lagoon almost a waterslide, but coming back they'd be tired, possibly in a hurry, and fighting that surge. But she had faith in Curtsy. Their "test dive" had impressed her with her underwater abilities—about what you'd expect of a woman enamored of dolphins. She had figured that impressing them had been part of the reason for the maiden run. So now she blindly followed the blonde into black water between even blacker shorelines.

The thing that really creeped her out was having things brush her legs. Weeds, plastic bags, seagrunge, flesh-stripping monster tentacles: hard to tell until it was too late. It was getting easier to see as they moved down the lagoon; streetlights, waterfront bars and restaurants, work lights in the marinas, various glow from boats. She'd been nervous in the dark, but the gradually lightening of their little swim reminded her that the main thing was not to have anybody see them. That's why she and Curtsy rubbed that black gunk all over themselves. Curtsy had said that wetsuits would just be too hot in the summer backwaters and had turned down Aphra's offer to help her smear the blackface all over her bod.

She didn't have much kit on her: a workmanlike chisel-tipped, serrated diving knife sheathed on one leg and a black fanny pack full of tools she assumed came in handy for unauthorized entry. Aphra had a knife that looked less like a tool and more like a prosecution exhibit in a serial murder trial. And a watertight packet of electronic doodads strapped around her waist. Curtsy seemed mostly clothed in ropes, various rigs to get them up the daunting sides of the yacht. Last resort stuff, Aphra had said: there would probably be lines or an anchor chain or some sort of fantail ladder. But, as she'd pointed out, "Best you be prepared."

And when Curtsy had said she must have been a girl scout, Aphra had given her a private grin and said, "Actually, I still kinda am."

So they were ready. And moving past El Varadero. MeiMei stuck close to the mangroves across the channel, even though that increased her contact with "things". She could see the fat Black woman carrying two buckets of beer to a couple of guys so authentically salty and seafaring you just knew the closest they ever came to boat ownership was sloshing a schooner of draft. The soft, golden glow of the restaurant and rollick of Cuban *son* and mambo made her wish she could just ditch this whole craziness, swim over there and get some shrimp and beer, maybe run into that Tuan guy again.

Then it hit her that passing Varadero meant they were almost to the swaging yard. She looked ahead, shaking her mask clear to look for the Nahual. There was a dark hulk in front of her, listing into the water. She remembered the half-sunken ferry she'd seen. She started to move between it and the shore, but the tight gap gave her pause. A lair of vicious Things if she ever saw one. She moved around the foundered boat, trying to stay low in the water with only the tip of her snorkle exposed to harsh lights from the repair yard. She trailed her gloved hand along the wrecked hull to keep oriented, rubber-ribbed fingertips sliding along rough, slimy timbers without giving her any splinters or queasies. She felt a change in the curvature and realized she had reached the taper of the stern. She swam a little faster but couldn't resist poking her head up for a look.

And bumped right into Aphra's hard ass.

She and Curtsy were vertical in the black water, finning slowly while staring at the empty place where the Nahual should have lain. MeiMei jerked her head to the left, checking the boatyard. No gigantic mega-yacht there: she would have noticed it right away.

The Nahual had left the building.

Aphra turned to them, calm in the face of a total fuck-up. "Slight change of plans, kids," she said. "Follow me."

"*Cariño*, if you trying to 'pass', you need to look around, some better kind of make-up," the Varadero owner told Curtsy, laughing her bulbous butt off as she trundled off to fetch a bucket of Superiors.

Oddly, they hadn't drawn that much attention climbing up on the deck; three hot, dripping women in swimsuits and facemasks, two smeared with back goop, all three lashed up with commando gear. The Varadero probably gets all kinds, MeiMei was thinking.

She'd been shocked when Aphra headed towards the lights of the restaurant, swimming fast across the channel where there might be boats coming through even this late. But when they'd all three reached the dock, she'd explained. "Nothing to hide at this point, fellahs. No crime, no foul. And I'm pissed off and need a beer."

Sounded reasonable, so here they were sitting around a table under clusters of fishnet and starfish and faded *Revolución* posters like the Back Up Singers From The Black Lagoon, tinking beer bottles together and chugging thirstily.

Nobody seemed to feel like talking about it until halfway through their second Superior apiece, when MeiMei figured it was time to mention deep topics like, Now What? and was about to pose that very question when she was startled by the raucous voice of the owner.

"¡*Hola*! Where your little Chinee ass been, anyway?"

She jerked around, Excuse me? on her lips, but saw it wasn't a Chinese being addressed at all. Close enough, though. "O.B." Tuan DeTomaso stood by the cash register with a friendly smile for the owner, but an evaluating gaze for MeiMei Chiang. He took in the girlz's dress code, the ropes and riggings, the burglary tools on the table where MeiMei had dumped them while ransacking the fanny pack for her little waterproof necklace of mad money. The look he gave her was knowing and somehow sad.

Then he stepped out on the deck to glance at where the Nahual was conspicuously absent, looked back at her, and cracked up.

CLOSE... BUT

Seagull, though as about as establishment-unaware as they come, still found his art, such as it was, driven by economic realities. One of which was that songs mocking out tourists are not favored in places that pay one to sing. So he rather relished serving up his latest opus for the select.

They come to the Island in the winter time
Drink tequila on the beach with salt and lime
They swing in their hammocks and laugh 'cause they know
Everybody back home is covered with snow.

    They're only here for six months or so
    While the weather back home is twenty below
    They're out in the sun with a smile every day
    They're the snowbirds down from the US of A.

They put on a sweater at the first sign of fall
And give their travel agent a telephone call
They wait 'til December, see what Santa Claus brings
Then they pack up their bags, and they spread out their wings.

    They're only here for six months or so
    Until the hurricanes are starting to blow
    They're out in the sun with a smile every day
    They're the snowbirds down from Ontario way.

There's Canadian sunsets and Indian summer
But Northern winters can be quite a bummer
They wait until the Superbowl and Grey Cup are lost
Then they head for the airport, whatever it costs.

They're only here for six months or so
While Old Man Winter puts on his show
They're out in the sun with a smile every day
They're the snowbirds down from New York and LA.

They wear oil and bikinis, every woman and man
So they can fly back up north with their Yuca-Tan
It's tropical heaven they all can time share
And nicer than freezing their butts off up there.

They're only here for six months or so
When hell freezes over they're ready to go
They're out in the sun with a smile every day
They're the snowbirds down out of Canada, eh?

It went over better in summer, when there were fewer gringo snowbirds in the Café Cueva, though you never knew how the sunburned, silvertipped resident set might take it, either. But the place was pretty full for low season, and incredibly hottie-loaded. That one table over by the bookcase was one hundred percent over-the-moontang and he'd add on a few points every time the big black chick made a move. Not that he'd kick little Miss Saigon out of bed, either. Hell, he wouldn't even toss Curtsy back to the dolphins. Amazing bunch and he was playing to their table, hard.

But not to ignore those new faces on the sofas around the coffee table in the back corner, by any means. A slender drink of water slipping around in a cotton shift that made it pretty clear it was just there like the veil on a sculpture: temporary shroud for some amazing shape. Sitting right by the cutest Mayan chick he'd seen yet. I'd buy a bracelet with my name on it from her for a dollar, Seagull thought as he strummed an instrumental break. Even sing one just for her, like "You're sixteen, you're beautiful and you're Mayan,"

And a familiar face amongst them. Not to mention familiar tight tits, tough ass and red head. The fire-dancer he'd almost hooked up with in Uxmal two years go, but she was traveling with that sexy lezzy with the rattletop djembe. Damn! Maybe I should set my axe on fire and play with my teeth.

Copper was unaware she was being scanned by a potential musical collaborator, traveling agent, and bed-partner: she was just relaxing in the mellow, sweet, innocent Isla vibe. She'd always doted on the Island: the perfect combination of her kind of laid-back and unspoiled, but with a decent number of gringo dinks with enough money to make spinning her fireballs an exercise in profit, not just exercise.

Beyond that, she had a certain affinity for a place where she had her own church right on the main square. Well, not really her church, though to hear some people tell it...

The combination of her name and hair color brought a spark of recognition everywhere in the area, but nowhere more than on Isla, where the main church on the plaza principál is dedicated not to the Lady of Guadalupe like everywhere else in Mexico, but to the Virgin de la Caridad de Cobre. Unusual in Mexico, where you gradually find out that it's barely even a Catholic country at all, in the normal sense, but manifestly a goddess cult in which Christ is revered mostly because he's the favorite son of the original Latin Lupe Lu. But the Charity of Copper virgin cuts her action on Isla, where Lupe's church is much smaller and located out in a colonia. Well, okay, located on a clifftop with Caribbean view, but prestige-wise, Copper Charity is the go-to deity on Isla and Copper got a kick out of it.

A deeper kick, that still hadn't completely settled in the lamina of her subcon, was that in Cuba, where the Virgin originally hailed from the town of Cobre, she carried a second ID, a persona she found fascinating. To a practitioner of *Santeria*—the Latin Caribe's answer to voodoo—many Saints are merely hosts for powerful id gods, AfroCarib spirits that ride people like horses but reside inside Catholic canoneers like parasite eggs injected into host grubs. The Virgin might have her sparkling white chapel and muted bells in the main square, but over the flickering lanterns and fresh-spilt blood of sacrifice she was the Goddess Oshun, and far, far from a blushing virgin bride.

Xchab had absolutely no idea what sort of place her bizarro new companions had dragged her to this time. It was obviously a gringo/Euro kind of place but showed none of the flash she associated with that in Cancun. In fact, it was downright shabby: old sofas, used books piled all over one wall, rough floors, burlap ceilings, counters and shelves made of what looked like driftwood or at least heavily distressed lumber. They didn't even make your coffee for you! They brought these little glass cups of grounds in hot water and you had to push the plunger down to pour the coffee out. And how about the entertainer? He looked like a clown with his big puffball of sandy hair and his tramp clothes and taped-together glasses. And his guitar looked like it was not only used, but abused and grafittied by some crew of miniature gangbangers. And if he wasn't a clown, just a singer, then his act really, truly sucked.

Loris was totally happy, not that she was a hard person for happiness to get in touch with. She was running with maybe the best man she'd ever met, was on the trail of oXo, and absolutely loved Isla Mujeres. Their cabana at the Villa Ki'in was like a dream to her; funky living room with posters of Kahlo and Zapata opening out on a patio with cane loungers that gave onto a powdery beach sloping down to a little lagoon of calm water flushed by waves breaking over a reef. The water was clear as the air, and shallow enough that she could wade over to the reef and peek down at tiny wrasse darting in Technicolor. She'd lazed on the beach all afternoon with few words spoken, just drinking in the sun and Bannock's presence. Just watching Copper and Winston frolic in the water while Xchab strode solemnly around at waist depth, her long man's shirt floating around her as she peered into the crystal water like a stalking heron. Just resting a hand on his hairy arm and feeling him relaxing, too. And, okay, yeah, downing a few Coronas.

And chilling in this charming little café with the cool Brit couple and the knucklehead slacker singer and the Yucatan coffee and rich brownies and the feel of a sort of hideout from reality, some forgotten niche in development where you could be unwary and human. The people who came in for coffee seemed to share that feel: uncoiled, yet aware, happy to be here. The other table there, those three model-looking girls—Black, Asian, and blonde—look at them. Just young, beautiful and not a care in the world.

MS. THE BOAT

The table talk among the three hotties without worldly cares was starting to run out of room. Aphra was getting a little testy, having exposed herself by swiping her credit card—yet ending up without a boat to show for it. And this on a tiny, tacky little rock with more boats than tortillas. Understandable, she assumed, out here in the middle of the damned ocean. But if there were all these boats, and this such an underprivileged country—half of 'em slipping into the States to be gardeners and shit—why didn't they want to rent her one? And she said as much: "What the hell's wrong with these losers? I'm paying triple-list and nobody taking it?"

"They'll rent you a boat." Even the perky Curtsy was dispirited. "Just not without a crew. Makes sense, you gotta admit. The boat is their whole gig, their livelihood."

Most un-lively 'hood I ever checked out, Aphra thought, but said only. "I gotta agree. If we couldn't cut a deal with that Tony cat, we're probably stuck."

"Wasn't he a little sweetheart, though?" MeiMei had been the last to give up on Captain Tony. And he'd be a great guy to blitz around the ocean with. Aphra was right: it wouldn't do to have anybody witnessing this little tea party. But Tony had really caught her eye. "I just wanted to scratch him behind the ears and pet his tummy."

"Honest, open, charming," Curtsy nodded. "A real cutie pie."

"How do people like that survive?" Aphra tossed in. "Perfect height, though. His mouth would hit me right around the nipples."

One of Aphra's two drawbacks as a spy was her innate, undisguisable flamboyance. Deep black six-footers with her look and athleticism don't do surreptitious. She'd compensated of course. Sometimes the best disguise is prancing around in the spotlight. But meanwhile she was striking out while playing her strongest card: the crypto-Fed MasterOfTheUniverseCard. "It ain't like money's the problem," she fumed. "That card is Beyond the Valley Of Gold And Platinum. It's, like titanium, baby. Strutonium. Kryptonite Kard. I offered to post the price of a new boat as deposit for shizzle sake."

Curtsy just shrugged. The black rug-muncher had been ballistic after SeaHawk Divers, a great bunch of guys she'd chosen as the most professional dive outfitters on Isla, had charged back her three thousand dollar rent when they found out she didn't want any pilot on board. She'd talked her into keeping the tanks and camera and other gear, though.

The digital camera in its waterproof housing was an interesting addition to the pile of gear the *triciclo* had trundled over to the Maria del Mar—especially since it wasn't normally rented out and Aphra had paid a stiff bonus to get it. Curtsy had inspected it and nodded, MeiMei wondered out loud why it would be necessary. "This thing you hunting up," Aphra had responded, "It's not like you want it for itself, am I right? It's like the information on it."

MeiMei frowned. "Well, it should be returned to the..."

"Yeah, but that maybe ain't gonna happen," Aphra broke in. "Maybe it's in some sort of Tom Cruise-proof case but you can get a shot of the hieroglyphics or whatever?"

MeiMei paused but had to agree. "Yes. Push comes to shove, I want to see those glyphs."

You and me both, sweet thing, had been Aphra's main thought. "So if it start getting shovey out there, the one thing we're hanging onto is that camera, right?"

So they had their tanks and gear, they had their camera, they had— by some mysterious means—a Blackberry with an app that updated the longitude and latitude of the yacht. What they conspicuously didn't have was a boat.

"Well, there's always the *sindicato*," Curtsy said, as much to raise her own mood as to mollify Aphra. "We'll talk to them tomorrow and if they don't spring for it, we'll figure out something else. Hotwire a ferry or something."

Honey, anybody could hotwire a fairy, it'd be you, Aphra mused. But said, "Dealing with the Syndicate. Just like back home."

"*Sindicatos* are unions," Curtsy explained. "This is actually a collective. Fishing and seafood co-operative."

"What do they call it again?" MeiMei asked.

"Social Justice."

Aphra hooted. "Well, I wish 'em luck on that."

"Man, talk about your vulgar boatmen," MeiMei bitched bitterly. She almost didn't want to finish her shrimp cocktail after finding out what a bunch of greedy, grasping, sexist dickheads the collective guys turned out to be. Almost. She glared out from under the restaurant canopy at the aqua stretch of bay between the co-op dock and Cancun and munched another shrimp, but under protest.

"Glaring contrast to Cap Tony, all right." Aphra muttered darkly. "Evil power politics badges just hanging off them and can't wait to get some sweet innocents like us out on the water and bait our chum for us. Gotta figure anybody paints 'Social Justice' on their wall is about a week away from getting measured for brown shirts and jackboots."

"So what now?" Curtsy asked plaintively. She could see this miracle gig going up in smoke over one small detail. Okay, a major detail. Not fair, dammit. She waved off the leering waiter and stared south along the palm-lined stretch of waterfront, trying to coax a plan out of a brain that had never been good at coming up with Plan A's, much less more advanced letters. "I'm stoked for this play. And don't forget my recip."

"Tit for tat, Blondie." Aphra said in a way that made it unnecessary to add the, "So to speak" part.

Curtsy glared back and MeiMei quickly broke in to track things away from discord. "What would you call that architecture?" She pointed at the inverted triangle shapes of the new headquarters of the Fifth District of the *Armada Mexicana*. "I can't decide if it's inverted early Miami Cokelord or something by Marvin the Martian."

Curtsy glanced across at the weird upside-down buildings and said, "One of the cabbies told me it's called 'Militarized Mayan'. Sounds about right."

"*Militarized* Mayan?" Aphra exclaimed. "Shit, that's all we need, militarize the damned Mayans. Most people say they out to win your hearts and minds, they more interested in your mind. These cats tear your hearts out and eat 'em or something."

"That's not actually..." MeiMei's lecture ground to a halt as Aphra leaned forward over the table, getting both their attentions, then arched an expensive fingernail towards the other dock.

"Correct me if I'm wrong now, girlfriends. But am I not sitting here looking at a big crowd of boats? Big, fast-looking suckers with two or three motors apiece?"

And sure enough. Several dozen big, lean bluewater speedboats: NorthSeas, Bayliners, Maxums, Invaders. All mounted with double and triple doses of Evinrude 200's and Johnson 115's. Right under their noses the whole time they'd been sipping bottles of Sol, noshing on seafood and trying to deal with the *sindicato*.

"Oh, yeah," Curtsy said defensively. "But they aren't rentals. They're like seized."

"You mean confiscated?" Aphra was all focus now, talking in clipped tones nothing like her affected ghetto locution. "Grabbed 'em for running drugs? Wait, running drugs *into* Mexico?"

Curtsy laughed and shook her gold hair, throbbing the hearts of three lurking waiters. "Funnier than that. They smuggle illegals in from Cuba. Bring 'em to Isla, dress 'em up like tourists and send them to the mainland on excursion boats."

"Okay, now I know you're jiving. Smuggling wetbacks into Mexico?"

"Wetbacks?" MeiMei chuckled. "Why, that's... racist."

"Sis, I'm too racially-abled not to." Aphra scanned the fleet of locked-down aquatic hotrods again, pondering. "So, who's in charge of them? The DEA or the Mexican Migra or something?"

Curtsy gestured at the Military Martian headquarters and guarded dock. "The Navy, I guess."

Aphra leaned back and tipped her Aviators back down over her eyes. "Sailors, huh?"

Petty Officer Teofilo Agradez—or rather *Segundo Maestre* Teofilo Agradez—couldn't believe his eyes. After midnight on a Tuesday, boring *pinche* watch, standing there in spiffy whites when nobody would come by and see him, stainless steel Colt .45 automatic holstered like somebody might trespass on this dippy dock... and out of nowhere comes this *bombazo* in a skintight red sheath, wearing sunglasses at night and swinging her *trasero* like she meant business. She had to be a *Cubana*. Not just because she was black: get a load of the ass and attitude on her. And the look she was slapping across his kisser; like, Go to hell, stud. Not to mention, Come and get it.

So his interests swung in areas different from security as he stepped over to accost her at the gate to the dock.

Where she lowered the moviestar shades, gave him the scorching eye, and said, "Hey, there, sailor."

BADGER GAME

*H*ow many times to I have to tell you dweebs not to use your *plastic in Mexico? Why would you want to put a couple of fifty cent tacos on your MasturCard, anyway? Even if they didn't run it back in the kitchen and swipe it on four different machines? Use your ATM card to get pesos. You get the best rate and don't have to keep doing math for every purchase. Don't give credit where debit is due.*

Seagull: *The Blasé Sojourner*

Townsend woke and had the cell phone in hand before the subtle alarm tone could even wake up the Wisconsin cheerleader sprawled bare and prone beside him in the ransacked bed. He always woke up all at once like that.

It was just Weistler. Town's attention sideslipped a little, to the plump, sculpted, muscled, lightly peach-downed ass at hand. Damn fine, he was thinking. Varsity tested. Luscious.

He felt an odd upwelling of affection for this nameless girl while he listened to the Weasler buck and wing through his usual opening jive. He was way too jaded to be heavily moved by sex and/or love anymore. But something about the sheer perkiness of those slumbering buttocks invoked a sweetness in him. She was just walking around in front of it, unconsciously strolling and jumping and mosh-dancing through life without even getting to enjoy the view of something really, truly beautiful. He felt a moment of fondness not just for her, but all the sun-lushed flesh about to wake up and spread itself on the beach, all the fetching bounciness of the All-American booty. He made a note to give it a nice kiss before slipping out. Then Weistler got down to business and his interest drifted.

"Apparently a diving shop," Weistler was droning on. "Runback turns up scuba gear, 'fill', whatever that is…"

Probably filling the tanks with air, you dip, Townsend thought, even as he sat up and sorted out his clothes. Hers tossed around like hurricane droppings, his neatly draped on a chair. Pistol and phone neatly tucked under the mattress without her being the wiser.

"And get this," Weistler continued as if imparting the infotel of all time, "Translates to 'hire boat with hands', but got charged back."

"Sounds like I better get in motion, pronto," Townsend said and he pulled on his shorts one-handed and slipped into his nice new leather huaraches that were much less comfortable than they looked. "She might be heading out to sea."

"Or, apparently, not," Weistler corrected him. "But what's important is where the dive shop is, right?"

"If it's not in Mexico we wasted a lot of taxpayer money."

"No worries. Isla Mujeres."

"That's a day excursion from here," Townsend knew that from all the beachboys pimping the excursion, but didn't know exactly which way the trips went. "Must be really close."

"Good thinking, Golden Boy," the weasel sneered. "You can probably see it from your balcony if you get the pussy off your face."

"I'm there." Townsend was heading for the door, pulling his shirt over his other arm. "Text me the address and phone."

"Now why didn't I think of that?" Weistler hung up.

Town hit the bathroom on the way out, ran his fingers through his hair and checked to see if the gun under his shirt was noticeable. He turned to go, but spotted a carmine lipstick laying on the washstand. He picked it up and scrawled on the mirror, then headed for wherever the hell Isla Mujeres was.

When Jodi Trent—sweetheart of Fond du Lac and delight of the Badger backfield that had gone a sorry 5-6 last season but scored a solid 100% with the ebullient Jodi—bumbled into the restroom still very bleary regarding the previous night, she found the mirror decorated in what she first thought was some sort of "RedRum" threat, but blinked it off to read: "Absolutely Grade-A ass. U.S. Government inspected."

She didn't really have a very clear recall of Townsend until two hours later, not to mention two beers, three glasses of orange juice, and a handful of vitamins and iron, but when she did, she gave a golden Midwest smile. She didn't get swept away by studly guys much lately, but the memory of her mysterious disappearing lover gave her a minute of sunny affection before she headed back into the surf and sun.

DRUMMING UP BUSINESS

The Hidalgo stretch used to be good for buskers, but now it's a victim of its own excess. You've got your fake Mayans in blackface and peacock feathers blowing conch shells, your fake Peruvians with bells and whistles and "¿Que pasa, Condorito?", your phony mariachis doing "Tears In Heaven" on trumpet and violin... it ain't over 'til the fat man with the guitarrón sings. If you're not wearing a costume or setting fires, nobody even notices you.
Seagull: *The Blasé Sojourner*

Seagull rattled his battered blue enamel "*ranchito*" cup like a crapshooter and spun his tips out on the counter of the takeout pizza joint next door. Hmm, not too shabby for summer. Whoa, that USD bill from the Beyonce babe in the straw hat was actually a fiver! Hot damn! He could have afforded a nice *barbacoa* sandwich at the Cueva. But he pocketed the bill and counted out enough for a slice of pizza. He slapped the coins down on the counter and said, "There it is, hotstuff, change you can believe in."

The beautiful Weejun (with the unfortunately big Weejun SCUBA boyfriend) who handled the counter at Aqui Estoy! scooped it up, gave him a heartstopping smile from the midnight sun, and before popping his pepperoni and chorizo slice into the oven for a quick remelt said, "Be the change you want to sponge in the world,".

That was it right there. If he wanted a change of gears, he was going to have to do it. Every stick has to shift for itself in this brut-assed world.

He was alone on stage for his second set, Congón having presumably split to Poc Na with that sanpaku Argentine hippy chick. Always hostel-friendly, our Congón. Leaving him with only what rhythm he could beat with his feet. And the crowd, if that's what you want to call three tables, had that "heard it before, twice" look about them. The Grace Jones negress had split (and thanks for your support) but the other table of hotties was still there to be schemed on. Especially the redhead. He had some ideas in that direction. Meanwhile, when your feet are in the stirrups and your ass is on the ground, best bet for a crowdpleaser is to sing about drugs...

Well I have run a few guns across somebody's enemy lines
I've flown in a few tons of sinsemilla in a B-29
I've done Swiss-made watches and leather *huaraches*
Sometimes I've even moved a little Coke..... a Cola
I'm just supply demand without the duty or the excise man.

Not bad, hit em with a hooky chorus and it's chicken in the pot.

I'll be makin' a break from takin' over contraband
I might trade you this hash for some cash and a Volkswagen van
I'll be heading for the border with my papers in order
Taking my departure south of Puerto Vallarta
Gonna get myself nice down in Smugglers' paradise.

And now the bridge to Tipville.

There are rusty old freighters sitting down at the dock
Full of Panama red, full of Peruvian rock
Seaplanes loaded with their quota of imported booze
There are shadowy bars with flamenco guitars
Señoritas with their eyes like stars...
I just think I could use some kind of tropical kind of a cruise.

It's just the right site for living high while you're lying low
If you're feeling flush or had a brush with the Border Patrol
So mellow out on that beach and reach for that Mescalito
Drink something cold and wet and watch the sun set
On Smugglers Cove.

Just gimme one more shot of that Jose Cuervo
And I'll be headin' on down, to the boundry of Mexico
One more bottle of Tequila to go
I'll find the salt and the lemon and the women
Down in Smugglers Cove

He hit the retirees up front first, and glommed a couple of bucks out of sheer confusion. The Aerofloters chipped in a few kopeks or buttniks or whatever the change house wouldn't accept, then he was moving on the Babetable. The big guy with the DeNiro head and Hulk Hogan frame wasn't around, which emboldened Seagull considerably. That guy looked like he could strike highway flares on the tip of his dick and crunch your ass up like a stale dinner mint.

But present company seemed nice enough. The Andie McDowell-looking brunette gave him a five and TKO smile, the *indita* stared but didn't take his scalp or anything, and the redhead—what the hell was her name? Cooper? Coop? Something like that—dropped him a few pesos and that *simpatico* look you get from other people who work for gratuitous gratuities. So he laid it on her. "I remember you."

She fluffed her pile of coppery coils, pushed her chest forward almost imperceptibly and drawled, "Most people do."

"Great fire dancer. You were working the tourbus crowds at the ruins with a guy playing a samba rig."

"He was hot, too. Shame he was a total asshole."

"Who's drumming you now?"

Another lingering look. Looking mostly down. "I don't really take applications. As such."

"Look I can do the beat. I'm not in the league with Congón there, but not many are. And I'm only a partial asshole. Forty percent, tops."

The brunette chuckled at that, a soft song like a creek turning pebbles. Copper—that was it! Copper!—gave a half smile and said, "Gonna beat on your box?"

"I drum, too, you know. I've got a dumbek and I'm not afraid to use it."

He could see the blowoff coming, so he blurted out. "Look, I know where we can make some good money before high season. I'm starving here and I'm guessing you're not doing much better. There's gonna be a film festival down in Playa..."

"So I hear."

"Couple of weeks off. Meanwhile, we could work sunset at the beach, do a wedding or two I know about, after hours at the CasaBlanca. Make some coin, shake down the act, go down and wow the mini-moguls."

Copper gave him a long evaluation this time. He stood still for it. You work with somebody like this, truck the road together, it's not like a blind date or something. He saw a slight softening in her face, a semblance of a yawn.

The brunette saw it, too, said, "Would you like some coffee or something?"

Then he felt the bruiser behind him, a sort of dark heaviness he associated with a rough hand on his shoulder and footwear up his butt. But Copper looked past him and smiled at the guy. Said, "Hey Bannock, this is Seagull. We're going to be working together."

Hey, she remembered him, too!

WHO LET THE DOLPHS OUT?

"Is there some sort of name for this crap?" Curtsy asked with a trace of disgust. She'd smeared the black paste (the composition of which Aphra hadn't shared with them) on all her exposed skin, but didn't much like putting it on her face. For one thing, it smelled like an evil science lab.

"Blackface makeup," MeiMei said offhandedly as she put finishing touches around her diving mask. "Put on your Al Jolson game face."

"Pigment envy," was Aphra's reply.

MeiMei smiled, but was getting a whole different slant on Aphra. Hard person to pin down, she was thinking. First she's the aloof model, then the wealthy patron, then wants to get into your panties, now she looks very much at ease getting ready to go commit a commando felony in Mexico. On the other hand, since this was just a prelim to her own felony theft caper, she couldn't really object.

And she was really glad they had the boat. The big, insanely fast, criminally modified Cigarette-style ocean racer that rumbled powerfully under her bare feet like a tiger purring before a pounce. This was one piece of engineering with "getaway" and "eat my wake" writ large in every detail of its design and execution. And had scared the crap out of her when she'd taken its wheel for about thirty seconds during their test run around Sac Bajo. Fortunately Curtsy had a relaxed, natural calm about rocketing across the slight chop, running without lights at speeds ranging up towards "bat out of hell".

And you know, there was a little extra frisson in knowing they were bombing around in a hinky-snagged aquatic hotrod with a criminal record before they even got around to perpetrating anything illegal themselves.

"I was a water skier," the insouciant Curtsy had explained. "Pretty competitive in high school. Drove a few half-fast boats."

Aphra had said, "Know what, Gidget? You got one great ass and tits that don't stop, but I do believe you're crazy."

A thought that MeiMei echoed now, rocking in the dark, menacing boat, staring at the lights of Dolphin Discovery. But, she reflected, is this crazier than what I want to do?

They all had their fins on by then, Curtsy with the nylon bag slung over her shoulder. There wasn't anything else to fool around with, no more excuse not to jump it off.

Aphra had the same thought. She had been watching the horizon for anything backlit against the distant lights of the Cancun hotels, but now sat beside Curtsy on the gunwales and motioned MeiMei to join them. "Let's get this done before the moon comes up, shall we ladies?"

She put her hand over her mask like Curtsy had taught them, then toppled over backwards into the dark sea. MeiMei heard the second splash as Curtsy keeled over, then rolled back into the water herself. She touched muck: the boat was anchored in about four feet of water with a grassy bottom. She stood on the tips of her fins and eyed Discovery in the distance.

"Got a bit of security, I see," Aphra said as she moved her snorkle slightly forward.

"Guess that's my fault," Curtsy said. "They didn't used to have watchmen outside like that."

Aphra turned and you didn't have to see inside the black mask to know she was rolling her eyes upward. "You take lead," she said, and again MeiMei got the impression it wasn't the first "job" this woman had been on. Curtsy adjusted the gym bag over her shoulder and moved smoothly and silently towards the pier, barely a shadow in the night sea.

MeiMei hung on the chainlink, breathing through her snorkle with only half of her mask above water. She was finning lightly to maintain her position, but a harder kick would alert the girls just below her feet that there was something to be aware of on the surface. The "watchmen" seemed to be mostly watching their cellphones. Thank Christ for texting, MeiMei thought. She could hear each little snick as Curtsy squeezed the bolt cutters on the fence links below, but knew that was just because her ears were under water. Aphra rose to breathe, then went back down. Curtsy didn't seem to need air. She must be spending five minutes underwater with each descent.

She could feel a slight vibration in the fence with every snip, but there was no change in its general rigidity. She heard a sharp snort and almost levitated right out of the water. She calmed when she saw the sleek surge in the water inside the inner fence. Of course. The dolphins had been aware of them since they showed up and were in there checking them out.

Probably some alpha males up close here, vigilant. The rest back in the center of the pool. Two more slick backs moved in the water like waves, then there was an entire head above water, staring at her with eyes she had to admit looked intelligent. And kind of sexy. She got a glimmer of where Curtsy was coming from. These things were super-touchable and definitely should be set free.

Then Curtsy was beside her, her head right behind her ear. "That's Bongo," she said. "My favorite. Take a slow, deep breath and come on down here, we're going through."

MeiMei took a few breaths of increasing volume, then bent at the waist and stroked down with her arms. She grabbed the fence like Curtsy had told her and tugged her way down into darkness. She felt a hand on her shoulders, nudging her forward and to the right. Where there was no longer any fence. She didn't know that Aphra had wired the cut fence back, leaving a triangular opening like parted curtains, but she knew she could move through... and then get back up to the world and score some air.

She remembered to tip her head back and exhale as she rose, then tip forward to bring the purged snorkle out of the water without having to blow it out. She sipped in air, then took deeper draughts as she breast-stroked under the catwalk to the inner fence. Where she could just reach out and touch the four dolphins that waited on the other side of it. Wow!

She stroked Bongo's head, marveling at the smoothness. Like a wet watermelon, she decided. She saw the sharp little teeth, as if he was smiling at her. This was worth the whole caper, right here, she thought.

This time MeiMei felt the fence give as Curtsy cut it. And realized that Aphra was bundling the sides away, binding them in position with the baling wire from the gym bag. She felt the fence shudder as the first dolphin nudged through it and slid along her calf as it emerged. They were out here! Right around her! She could hear and feel more movement as the herd, or whatever they call them, moved out through the gap in the fence, exploring this new breach in their captivity. She shook all over in a visceral spasm to realize she was surrounded by them. Then she heard footsteps on the catwalk above.

She froze, wiped out by adrenal rush of panic mixing with whatever endorphin spasm the dolphins had triggered in her. Caught! Shit!

She looked up as three smooth heads broke the water to stare upwards with her. Curtsy hit the surface holding some sort of abs workout device, all metal tubes and surgical rubber. Which seemed so surrealistic that she looked closer even as her throat pinched with fear.

Not helped when she realized that it was really a stubby spear gun in Curtsy's hands, pointing up at the measured footfalls on the planks above their heads. Tracing those steps with a black shaft that ended in a sharp device that had "alien ninja death dart" stamped all over it. She gave up on processing information, just lay in the water shivering while the feet passed overhead, then moved on.

At some point she felt Aphra's hand on her gooseflesh shoulder. "It's okay now, sugar. Alls we gotta do is go out the other fence and swim off."

She looked at Curtsy again, still pointing the speargun with a grim sniper look and pose. Which relaxed as she turned back to the other two, grinning. "Pablo. Still texting that Canadian chick, I'll bet."

She saw MeiMei staring at the speargun, smiled and moved the spearpoint closer to her. "Tranquilizer head. Put a man to sleep even faster than a dolphin. My own professional equipment."

"Well, don't forget we gotta get the gun back to SeaHawk," Aphra muttered. "Now can we, oh, I don't know... get our butts out of here? Less you want to fuck your buddies goodbye?"

Curtsy's head disappeared then re-appeared outside the fence in a remarkably quick time. MeiMei stared as the water around the blonde churned with fins and whorls, the big mammals frolicking around her. MeiMei repeated her dive under the outer fence and came to the surface sliding through glossy bodies. She surfaced a few feet from Curtsy, who had pushed her mask up on her head and was joyously slithering around the escapees. Watched as she grabbed the side fins of a big male and pushed her lips to his glistening back.

As the others watched, she surged off into the night, lying on the beast's back with the side of her face pressed right behind his dorsal fin.

"Getting a tow job," Aphra said from behind her. "And people be callin' *me* queer."

MeiMei watched as the dolphin pulled Curtsy south towards the boat. "She's so happy. She's really, like, in love with them, isn't she?"

"Looks that way. They say once you go sushi, you never go back," Aphra said as she nudged her into motion. "Now all we gotta do is go get what makes you happy, Chinatown."

ROOD DOOD

Chango rocked his scorpion-tattooed wrist, dialing off and on the "R's" that impelled his Kawasaki JS750 watercraft in sharklike lunges, emphasizing the jagged white teeth newly painted on the prow and cowl. Rich, bored, and stupid, the punky scions of the Domingero clan were secular saints to Cancun's hop shops, aftermarket purveyors, and thieves. The custom pitched Solas Dynafly impeller—his latest and most noticeably effective modification—growled savagely as it punched out a firehose column of water, jamming him in toward the beach.

But let's not forget the Blowsion mat kit with side lifters, Rule 500GPH bilge kit, R&D billet angled spacers for the V-Force Delta 2 Carbon reeds. the blast fine-tuned Wamiltons scupper and pump mods, Jetworks mixture screws, 6° ignition advance kit, pro-tuned Factory Wet Pipe—all screaming psychotically from the gleaming throne of a magnafluxed Girtled head kit, electronically torque-balanced to the overbored case. And all of it protected from the bumps and grinds of its owner's crazed desire to break the world down to size by ODI filters, ride plates and intake grates.

With only the assistance of two dozen technicians he had single-handedly tripled the cost of a massively overpriced personal watercraft. And what had it bought him? Less than *nada*, as a matter of fact. He had lost the race to the point and back—his fellow Lords of Xibalba being just as spoiled and feckless, and also better jockeys—so he had to run to land for more Tequila and key limes. Smarting under the humiliation and jeers of his so-called *compass*, he tore to the sand like a buzzbomb, threading between terrified swimmers and hysterical children before driving his hull up onto the wet sand.

He paid no attention to the shrieks and insults of the people he had come within millimeters of impelling into fish chow, and even less to the police officer in snappy pith helmet and dorky white shorts who was approaching him as he sauntered towards the *palapa* bar for provisions. He was a gold-filled "*Junior*", his parents were bulletproof and omnipresent. He and his class paid no tickets, obeyed no signals or sirens, copped no shit. He was shocked when the cop grabbed his shoulder and spun him around, giving him major stinkeye from under that raked white brim and leather strap.

Of course, he not only wasn't up in Mexico City, frolicking with impunity among his fellow *Juniors*, he wasn't even in Cancun, which his caste saw as a sort of beach extension of the Capital. But he assumed that even hick Cozumel cops could read status and unimpeachability off his light skin, frosted hair, and smug attitude. He waited until the cop wound down his rant about aquatic safety, smirked, and turned back to the counter, pointing to the top shelf Tequilas and holding up five fingers.

Imagine—if not delight in—his amazement when the cop jerked him around again and sunk a hard, fast-moving fist into his gym-sculpted abs, right on the button known to anatomists as the solar plexus. The amazement was a brief flash, followed by gasping pain, fear, and rage.

When he could breathe again he raised a flushed face to the cop, who waited serenely flanked by a big crowd of pissed-off almost-victims of his approach to land. He hated the creaky, babyish voice with which he attempted to intimidate, "Do you have any idea who my father is?"

"Nope," the cop laughed. "Does your mother?"

The crowd ate that one up, as they did the encore: he grabbed Chango by his collarbones and jerked him to his feet, then held his throat in one hand as he slapped and backhanded his face to punctuate his concept that he wouldn't tolerate any such driving around the swimming areas and if he ever laid eyes on Chango again, it might be the last time anybody had the dubious privilege. He then dragged the boy to his jet ski, hurried the awkward launching of it with kicks and cuffs, and tossed the kid on it. But held him for a parting moment, rough hand deep in the spiky hair. While he whipped out a radio and gave a quick description of the miscreant and his hyper-priced toy. The kid was going to drive very slowly out to that huge, ugly yacht, the cop told the listeners, and was not going to leave it again unless he was swimming. Otherwise he was hoping the listener could sweep in and arrest him, if not just run him down. He released Chango to a ragged, heartfelt cheer from the mob of beach-goers and *chilango*-haters and stood waving as the little delinquent crept back out to the Nahual in something so far beyond humiliation that he would have needed intravenous self-esteem to get suicidal.

Chimi would be the worst, playing host/God on his old man's yacht while Ronchel *pere* was conferring and hobnobbing ashore with bigwigs who had flown thousands of miles to meet him and wouldn't even get to see the already famous yacht. It had seemed like fun, the Lords hoisting their wetbikes aboard and setting out in ridiculous luxury to ply the waters and women of Cozumel, but it had turned into a pain in the tush and he couldn't wait to get the hell back to Cancun. And was suddenly wondering just how that was going to happen, anyway.

He looked up and there was fucking Chimi, standing on the helipad laughing his candy ass off. And the other guys drifting out of the aft bar to whoop it up over him creeping back in like an old lady. He was so pissed off. He wanted to have that cop killed, wanted to pound on his "*amigos*" with a piece of pipe, wanted to fuck somebody to death.

SHOUT OUTS

Curtsy was in a bit of a state by the time they reached the long dock at Casa O's, swinging between a wild elation at having free-ranged "her" dolphins, sadness at knowing she'd never see them again, and dread that the ocean might not be totally hospitable for newbies like the Discovery Gang. She was biting her lip and frowning by the time she nudged the rumbling Narcruiser up to the dock. MeiMei suffered from no such equivocation: she was scared stiff they'd get nabbed for the dolphinbreak and already piling up dire outcomes from chasing after the Nahual.

Aphra scanned the dark restaurant and sniffed the air for unexpected perils, then hopped out onto the dock. Her second drawback as a spy was a steep susceptibility to seasickness. She'd been a little queasy shooting around the relatively open water off Sac Bajo, and had no doubts how she'd feel a half hour into blasting off for points south. She was screamingly apprehensive about letting the Chink and the Twink set off without benefit of chaperone, but there was no way for it and she just had to put a game face on it. "Got your communicator handy, there, Ensign?"

Curtsy held up the clear, watertight Pelican case that protected the unbranded, highly modified satellite phone Aphra had given her (along with instructions she made sure were also heard, and therefore comprehended, by MeiMei). "Aye, aye, Uhuru."

Another thing right there, letting a piece of gear like that out of her hands. A big bleeding trail right back to her and full of incriminating shit right up to its touchscreen crammed with quasi-pirate apps. Oh, well.

"Have a fun trip, kids," she called down from the dock. "See you in a couple days." Hope to hell.

MeiMei tried to take an edge off her jitters (or just delay setting out). "That Marine acted like he expected a few privileges coming when we bring the boat back."

"I'll straighten him out on that when the time come."

MeiMei had laughed, "Brash, baby. What street were you working up stateside?"

"Easy street, bee yatch."

Curtsy, figuring that was about as sentimental a goodbye as they

178

were going to get from Ms. Lez Be Friends, nudged the throttle forward. The big launch slid ahead smoothly, then put on a little thrum as she aimed it at South Point and dialed on a few more RPM's.

Aphra stood watching, shaking her dandelion-coiffed head as the Maxum moved off into the darkness, grumbling with the urge to flex its over-tuned muscle. She heard the pitch change at the point, Curtsy putting the throttle in the kitchen and bringing the little thunderboat up on a spanking skim across the higher waves out of Isla's lee. She caught a fleeting glimpse of it just as it passed the point, a streak silhouetted by the glow trail of the rising moon. She stood for a minute, staring, then muttered, "Just bring it back to mama."

She didn't yet know, as she walked the planks back to Casa O's, that her golf cart had been sabotaged by local taxistas as an expression of their deeply-held belief that tourists should go to downisland restaurants in public transportation, not rented flivvers. When she did find out, she didn't even go particularly ballistic, just took it as an omen.

Oddly, the pounding sprint across open water had a soothing effect on MeiMei's nerves. She even stood up, taking the wind in her face like Curtsy. Which, she quickly realized, was also better on her kidneys and other assorted innards, which had been getting butt-kicked by the bucket seat every half-second. The walloping became a soundtrack at that point, a drummed mantra that calmed her as she stared into the silvery trail the rising moon was drawing across the black Caribbean as if for their particular benefit. She looked at Curtsy, smiling into the blast of warm, wet air as her moongold mane whipped behind her. She pulled off her black watchcap and shook out her own hair, joining the rhythmic scalp massage to the bucketing beat of the hull, and found herself smiling as well. Where did Aphra get a black watch cap in Mexico?

For that matter—she snagged the sealed cell phone and gave it a closer look—where did anybody get stuff like this? She was pretty sure you couldn't get satellite positioning of individual private vessels from the iPhone app store.

"What the hell is this thing?" she yelled at Curtsy.

The blonde girl turned and shrugged, probably her response to a lot of questions, was MeiMei's guess. Then she proved her wrong by yelling back, "I think she's some sort of spy."

MeiMei must have showed her astonishment because she yelled

again, "Some things I saw in her room." Just never mind what she had been doing there at the time. Or not doing. Or whatever it was. Turns out chicks aren't even as interesting as men.

MeiMei digested that one for a shocked few minutes and shouted. "We didn't find her did we? She found us."

Another shrug. MeiMei opened the case and held the phone behind the little windshield to examine it. The whole GPS was just wrong, somehow. Like a military graphic on TV. Some of the search apps were also just a bit too knowing. And the rest she couldn't even figure out at all. Hmmm. She looked back at Curtsy, who nodded, then turned her face back into the slipstream.

Around three-thirty Curtsy spotted the fins.

She pointed back astern—where she'd been casting an occasional eye throughout the trip—and MeiMei stared blankly, then saw a black back cut the water, the dorsal fin knifing up and through the waxy moonsplinters in their wake. She felt a thrill she couldn't identify and smiled with pleasure. "Think it's your pals?" she bellowed at Curtsy.

Curtsy shook her head and leaned toward her. "No chance. Dolphins swim like fifteen knots, cruise at seven or eight maybe. Top speed maybe twenty."

Well that settles that question, MeiMei thought. And actually, she'd been wondering, "How fast are we going?" Fast as a motherfucker isn't really quantitative.

"Fifty, fifty-five, knots," Curtsy called, pointing to a speedometer that hovered around sixty MPH.

"Fun idea, though," MeiMei shouted. "Your buddies tagging along."

She wasn't prepared for the sad look on the blonde's normally cheerful face. "I mean, they obviously really like you. And you seem to..."

She broke off then went ahead. "I've heard a few things. You love those animals."

Curtsy turned a searching look on her, then grabbed the throttle. All three hypertrophied Evinrudes toned down a few notches and the boat settled into a powerglide. Suddenly they weren't jamming from wave to wave. They were still moving damned fast, but going up and down with the shape of the sea, not hopscotching across the peaks.

She gave MeiMei another look.

"I mean, if you don't mind my asking."

"Well, I dunno," Curtsy said guardedly, sizing her up. "Does anybody like talking about their sexual perversions?"

"I've met people that's all they want to talk about. And I mean some creepy ones."

"You consider being queer for dolphins creepy?"

"I think it's kind of cool, actually." She'd been surprised to first realize that, but there it was.

"It's got its drawbacks."

"I feel like I'm talking to a lesbian or something here, but... were you always this way? Did something happen to make you...?"

"I don't know. It's not just mammals, it's animals that move sleek in the water. Sharks and manta rays. Killer whales? Whoa! Wet panty time." She stared straight ahead, but MeiMei could sense something welling in her. She probably didn't get to talk about this much.

"I worked at SeaWorld right after high school, the one in California."

"Sounds like your dream job. Why didn't you just stay there?"

"You can't guess? Fired for illicit conduct with Shamu." She pouted a moment, upset at the sheer injustice of love that can't speak its name. "Who by the way isn't even the real Shamu. Kind of a Scamu."

"Killer whales? God, how macho can you get?"

"Big. Black. Slick. Free willies."

She drove on in silence for awhile, laid her hand on the throttle grip, then changed her mind. "I was like a little girl... maybe the first time I ever felt anything sexual... I don't know. We went to the Children's Pool in La Jolla. There were all these seals and sea lions there. Baby seals are sooooo cute, I had little mask and fins even then, when I was maybe eight. Paddling around seeing these animals flashing around me, I got all excited. You know, like flushed and my tummy flipping..."

She shot MeiMei another look and started backing out. "I don't know if you've got a morbid curiosity or just want to find out why a cute California blonde with great tits doesn't have a boyfriend."

"Maybe I'll get to that after I figure out how a cute little China doll making six figures a year doesn't have a boyfriend."

"So what are you queer for? Stone gods with curses on them?"

"Actually only goddesses get The Curse. But I don't know... I just don't meet any guys that trip my trigger. In high school I went through a phase with big football studs. I was like four foot nine, maybe ninety pounds and I dug the idea of a guy who could pick me up and toss me around. In fact, I liked the actual act of being picked up and tossed around."

Curtsy seemed to be listening, so she went on. "But I grew out of that. I just like a guy I can talk to at all levels, you know. I always wanted to meet a guy smarter than me who wasn't a founding member of geekville. I met enough academic dorks in college, but I end up comparing them to..."

"Indiana Jones?"

"Something like that, maybe. A guy who knows things, can blow my mind. But can also move, you know. Around universities, you meet some pretty cool guys, but nobody with the creative flexibility."

"*Creative* flexibility? That's your idea of where men are at?"

"What, that's kinkier than waterproof skin and breathing out the top of your head?"

"Got me there."

"Ironically, I met a guy recently who seemed to fit the bill. Had me all intrigued. Then he sort of morphed into a jerk and blew me off."

"Really? Why?"

"Well, he somehow got the idea that I was planning some sort of ninja raid to steal a relic from a rich. powerful Mexican yachtsman."

"Dudes! Where do they come up with this shit?"

LOOSE ENDS

It wasn't so much what he did as what he didn't do. Elementary tradecraft to Aphra, learnt at mother's knee. And other lowdown joints.

Now I got as much vanity as the next girl, she mused while lounging in the full exposure of the Acantilado, staring out to sea from the cliffs at South Point and wondering where her wandering chicks had blasted forth in search of treasure and intel. And with good reason. In a gold bikini fit to die in, wispy wrap, huge plastic shooting glasses that could only be called "high yaller" and this straw hat with a brim the size of a Verizon footprint. And thinking it's not out of line to expect a man to check me out a little, not give me the old furniture treatment. Now maybe if this was a Lakers Girls tryout or something, but here and now I think you gotta say I'm worth a look-over, but he don't look especially gay and is coming on with the chopped liver take. Tell you what we do about unwanted and highly suspicious lack of advances back where I come from. Sashay over there and sort things out.

Not a bad looking man. For, you know, a man. And a super-honky at that. Oh, and look, now that I'm walking right on up to him, sashay la femme, with my barely gold-covered crotch at eye level and augmented musk mist carried in on the sea wind, now he's letting on that I might just exist.

Townsend looked up at her a minute, taking it all in while she posed as motionless and out-of-place as the livid sculptures strewn down the Point, closed his copy of "Wired", and motioned to the chair beside him. As three waiters sprained themselves vying to be at hand, he said, "What took you so long?"

She laughed out loud. Gotta hand it to the boy. She made sitting down a scene to remember, waved off the waiters, and leaned forward with eyes wide and lips moist. "So what's your main MO?"

He leaned in too, holding up the "Wired". "FYI, I'm the CEO of an IT .com, trying to keep the IRS and ICC off my IPO. Name's Roger Parker. NMI."

"LOL." She waved flaming fingernails at her luscious breast and said, "And I'm Chlamydia Washingtonian-Huitlacochl. So pleased."

This time Townsend laughed all the way, something he hadn't done in awhile. "How about you call me Town?"

"And you can call me when I'm in town," she purred lasciviously. "My name's Aphra."

Thing she'd learned, if they're onto you, they already know who you are. And half the time don't care if you know who they are.

"Nice name. Fits, somehow." If he hadn't known her name he'd have snickered over that Aphra thing. Sure baby. Hyphen American, right? But hey, here they were, secret squirrels on first name basis.

"Ever hear of Aphra Behn?" She dialed off the vampy, got a little more real. "Not many have. Even though she was the first woman to ever write a novel in English. A black woman, dig that, back in seventeenth century London."

"So was it a regency romance?"

"No, it was a Tudor romance full of silk bodices and codpieces. What the hell you think it was? About being a house-nigger slave of the crown."

"Sounds like a good beach read."

"Mega-bore, actually. But that's where I got stuck with my name. One thing I figured out pretty young was I won't gonna be no slave, baby."

"I might still be working on that."

Now that earned the man a little deeper look. Here he was, golden runway god with the bod to back it up, had some wits about him, and maybe he wasn't all that fulfilled. Or not. She decided to tiptoe out on a limb.

"I took me longer to figure out that my mom and her Mickey Maoist cronies could enslave my ass just as quick as anybody else. Fact, they had the inside track."

"But you stuck with the hairdo."

Hey, it's a wig, whiteboy. But he had a point there. Was she as free from her roots as she liked to think? "Cain't do a thang with it."

"I like the look. I like everything I'm looking at, actually. Just thought I'd get that in." He motioned to the hovering waitstaff and pointed to her empty glass, creating a stampede. "It suits you. And sort of says 'retro-proud, non-iconic, activision' without coming right out with it."

"Hair is just so political, don't you think?"

"Is it still? Was there ever a lefty with a Jheri Curl?"

"Lefty? I look like some relief pitcher to you? Seriously, you think I'm a leftist you shoulda met my Mom. She was like SDS before she was a student. Five minutes after they formed the Weathermen she was like Eyewitness Weathergirl. Pointing out low repression areas and encroaching fascist fronts with a 'fro as big as the Apollo."

"Red diaper baby? It can scar worse than being Catholic."

"God yes. She wanted me to be a bomb-lobbing MaoMau like her. Thought I was a rightwing Nazi when I registered as a Democrat."

"Well, I was, too. The opposite. I don't think they have a word for being raised by actual rightwing Nazi wolves."

"Brownshirt diapers? Kultur Kinder?"

"My dad pegged me as Commie faggot for registering Republican."

"Well, now." She smiled, then looked away, sweeping the sloping spur of ground that was South Point before it plunged over the cliffs into a blue-green stretch of Caribbean kissing blue-blue horizon. "Quite a pair to meet up here at the end of the earth. Assuming we're not both full of shit."

Townsend turned to look at the ogling waiters. "I think we both already got made as full of shit just from the way we're dressed."

You don't know the half of it, peckerwood, she thought. But realized that it might be the other way around: he might be all over her ass and she didn't have a clue where he was coming from. But for now, she'd assume he was connected somehow to the Weaseler and therefore to The Chief. And was sitting up nights figuring a way to turn her over and find out what she knew and what it meant.

Given that assumption... "Look, I gotta run. But could we get together for dinner?"

"I sure hope so."

"Yeah, me, too. How about that Sunset Grill place around eight?"

TEAM TRANQUILITY

Spotting the Nahual in the Cozumel harbor had not been a problem. It dwarfed the other pleasure craft anchored in the roads, looking more in the league with the huge cruise ships than the dinky sixty and ninety-footers around it.

They'd watched the yacht most of the day with Aphra's nifty little Swarovski binoculars, taking turns getting some sleep under the shade of the NarcoCraft's skimpy bimini top. Lots of bodyguards and a clique of truly obnoxious younger guys drinking in the aft lounge and daring each other to dive off higher and higher locations. One idiot was trying to climb onto the helicopter while waving a bottle, but two big bodyguards dissuaded him and cut off his protests by heaving him over the side. Which got a lot of applause from his chums.

Ronchel hadn't showed up until late in the afternoon, up on the flying bridge with a big amber glass and a couple of bimbos. MeiMei got to watch him get a tagteam blow job, initially slumped in the pilot's chair, then rousing to stand in the King Of The World pose for his money shot. Then *he* tossed one of the girls into the sea, where she floundered around pitifully until being rescued by the entire group of slackers from the aft end. MeiMei couldn't believe she was even thinking of setting foot on that floating orgy, but that was the plan. If you wanted to call it that.

Their timing was good. They'd watched the bimbos get sent back to shore around sunset, in a launch with three bodyguards, who seemed to be jealously guarding their bodies. Shortly after that exercise, the jumping monkeys fired up the jetskis that had been bobbing around in the lee of the yacht and headed into town with the expected degree of whoop-up and Stupid Jockey Tricks on their pricey screamers.

MeiMei wanted to let things chill out aboard, but Curtsy thought it would be good go get there before the bimboguards got back, which made sense. So they hove up to the little bathing deck at the aft waterline, engines chunking and spitting due to Curtsy having stuck pins through several of the spark plug wires. And got a lot of friendly help from tough, liveried retainers as Ronchel piped them aboard practically rubbing his hands together in glee.

And if you wanted an evening glee club to drop by, it would be hard to top the duo of MeiMei and Curtsy: brushed glossy, made-up to kill, flaunting minimal bikinis and a light coat of fragrant coconut oil. About three seconds elapsed between explaining their "engine cutting out" problem to the torpedoes gawking over the aft rails and getting a warm personal invite to come on board and get sorted out. It took about ten minutes of playing Ronchel to get a personal tour. Curtsy had a sling bag aboard with her, which was immediately searched, revealing marine gear and the speargun. She was graciously told that they'd diligently watch her bag for her.

So here they were at last; holding generous drinks, batting their eyes outrageously, tolerating equally outrageous pawings of whatever spilled out of the little slut suits they wore for the occasion, and getting to oooo and aaaah Ronchel's personal collection of rare and extremely important pre-Columbian art. He was saving the other gallery—erotic sculptures ramping up from cute to sexy to totally revolting—in the adjoining cabin.

Curtsy was genuinely impressed. This stuff had to be incredibly valuable and significant. She gazed at framed sections of ancient codices on the wall, their colors kept vibrant by special filter glass that had a slight red tinge at the edge. She gawked at statuettes and pottery, all selected for beauty as well as archeological importance and sheer visual power. She stroked a jade statue of a woman giving birth to some demented little god. Holy moly, was pretty much her take; this guy is loaded and knows his shit.

MeiMei was having a hard time keeping up a front. She was recognizing piece after piece that had mysteriously dropped off the catalogues over the years. She saw two Olmec[34] sculptures that were identical to pieces she'd personally seen in the Denver collection[35] and at Dumberton Oaks[36]. She had a feeling she was looking at the real thing and the museum pieces were forgeries. This Ronchel was like a cartel boss for pilfered antiquity. She delicately touched a small jade figurine he'd handed her, making sure to make salacious contact with the little thing's huge phallus. "I just love jade," she simpered. "It's a legacy of my people, too, you know? You must have some very rare pieces."

"Everything I have or do is rare," Ronchel murmured to her. "And precious and astounding. I see you like that little Toltec guy."

"He'd make a great tattoo," MeiMei mused, studying the little pre-Colombo porn piece from various angles. "I'm thinking of getting one... well... somewhere kind of secret."

"It would have to be pretty tiny to be secret in that suit," Ronchel said suavely.

MeiMei just smiled knowingly. And, of course, maddeningly. "But what I'd really like is a skull. Do you have any, you know, ancient Aztec skulls I could look at? Maybe kind of 'tribal' ones?"

Ronchel, practically licking his lips, motioned her to a curtained oblong doorway. She let him squire her to it, hand resting possessively on the swell of her hips and tending to slide southward. She glanced back at Curtsy, who was examining some white objects in a cabinet in the far corner. "Come on Kurtz," she said, "He's got some tribal skull art in here."

Curtsy turned and headed to them, but her brow was furrowed, "I don't get it. Everything in here is so special and beautiful, but those things are just hunks of rock."

"Hunks of coral," Ronchel told her, trying to decide which of these he should take first. The blonde was the real treasure, of course, a big mouthful of gold hairs was his guess, and maybe should be saved for desert, after plundering the *chinita*. On the other hand, both at once didn't seem too far fetched. And make them do each other. Then get some of the crew in here and take videos. This was really his lucky day... stuff like this just sailing up to volunteer. "They're very special in their own way."

He tweaked back the curtain to his inner sanctum of extra special treasures and MeiMei saw it at once, front and center in the rear, surrounded by gold, onyx and more jade. There it was, just steps away. She took two steps forward. Ronchel moved up behind her and let her feel his tumescence tucked up against her flimsily-sheathed butt cheeks. "Lovely, no? Would you like to examine it more closely? That's what we should always do with lovely things: examine them in total detail."

She squirmed around to face him, keeping a smile on. Behind him Curtsy had her hand tucked into the band of her own bikini bottom and spoke in a languid, bedroom voice. "It's sure hot in here. Okay if I take my top off?"

Ronchel spun around to look at her, tits already out on display as she strode toward him. MeiMei was ready to grab his elbows, but no need. Curtsy pulled that wicked-looking Pneu-Dart tranquilizer spearhead out of her waistband in mid-stride and plunged it right into his stomach without any pause or preamble. She held it between her fingers, tumped against the heel of her hand. The blow pierced his abdominals just below the sternum, injected the entire 6cc's of sodium phenobarbital/diazepam/ketamine cocktail in the same motion.

Ronchel swung a vicious blow at her face, trying to smash his cocktail glass into her eye, but Curtsy had already danced back out of reach. He threw the glass at her, which she ducked, then looked down at the Pneu-Dart sticking out of his stomach like a banderilla out of a fighting bull. He growled and took one step towards Curtsy, murder in his eye.

MeiMei jumped up and came down on the back of his knee, kicking with all her weight to snap his kneecap down against the carpeted deck. He grabbed his knee in pain and Curtsy stepped into a powerful soccer-style kick that bloodied his nose and knocked him over sideways. He lay there without moving.

"Jesus, did you kill him?" MeiMei asked in an undertone.

"Afraid not," Curtsy snapped as Ronchel emitted a gurgle that turned into a rackety snore. "He should be out for an hour."

"Shouldn't take that long," MeiMei said quickly and turned back to the jade on the wall.

Curtsy was keeping a disdainful eye on the recumbent Ronchel but scoping the wealth festooned on the walls around her. "Hey, May, think we could get some of this gold and shit out of here? I could use the payday."

MeiMei turned as she pulled her camera out from where she'd clipped it to her brastrap, under the cascade of her thick hair, and scowled, "We're not stealing antiquities, Kurtz."

"Well, just the ones *you* want," Curtsy pouted. But the more she thought about it, she couldn't see how she'd unload a zillion year-old tomb treasure. Just land her right in prison, most likely.

MeiMei had swung the frame out from the wall on a concealed hinge. She could see alarm wires and hoped they could be dealt with, but mostly busied herself getting shots of the rear side of the plaque. It was like Puch had said, a skull with an actual cartoon balloon full of glyphs. She used the manual over-ride to get a bracket of several exposures, the lens already capped with a macro attachment to allow focus from eight inches out. She turned to Curtsy to ask what she thought about hacking the alarm... just in time to see Ronchel rise unsteadily to his feet behind her. He was holding a remote in one hand and she could hear feet pounding into the room outside the curtain. Limping slightly, dripping blood from his nose, he glared at the two intruders and rasped out, "You fucking cunts are going to die in agony for this."

MINOR DISTINCTIONS

Her given name was Delicia Martinez Pau, but nobody had called her anything but Deli since her older brother Gabo hung it on her as a baby. But it was strictly co-incidence that Lori and Polo had hired her to work the counter at the Blue Iguana, serving up bagels and sliced lox to gringos who missed delicatessen delights. So of course she was now Deli del Deli. And had an eye for gringos.

And something about that pair sitting out front on the wooden sidewalk caught that eye. Couple of fashion models, had been her first peg. Statuesque black Catwoman and hunky Mr. BlueEyes. Then she'd watched them move around a little, browsing the shelves, checking out the glass-front cooler, and she was thinking more like, athletes. He's the no-nonsense relief pitcher who can also hit for the cycle, she's a dirtywork power forward in that black woman's basketball league they have in the states. But now, watching them eat and talk, and the way they watched everything else, her big thought was: cops.

"Not bad at all," Aphra was saying, sitting out front with all the little golf carts and scooters and Euro mini-trucks passing by like they were hanging in LegoTown. "But I heard the food's really special over there in that Mango place."

"I just can't see waiting in line to get into a place that's crowded," he answered, methodically munching his turkey breast on egg bread.

Aphra would have couched it in terms more like, "lines are for chumps", but she nodded in agreement. Matter of fact, she was finding the guy extremely agreeable. And damned sexy. You know, for a man. "They said come by Monday night for Jamaica jerk barbecue."

"It's a date." He looked at her a second as he said it. Was that what it was?

"Be sure to remind me." She'd moved past any doubt this guy was after her ass, and not in the usual way. Just a feeling. It's smarter than street-smart, her Momma had told her: it's bush-smart. You work the street, it's a good thing you stay a little bushy. And her vibe was telling her that bush wasn't all this cat was after. Although, he was starting to get a little gleam in his baby blues. And she'd thought sitting around waiting for her jack-girls to show up with her intel was going to be boring.

But here was this mega-cute guy sitting there, everything he said to her making sense: not her usual experience while chatting with square white breeders. It's almost like they were in some club, waiting until it was okay to flash the secret handshake.

Meanwhile, Townsend was having similar feelings about the situation. He'd been around this woman three times and each time felt more like she was the only woman he'd ever met that he could talk to. She was a colleague, really. And damn good at the craft, apparently. The idea of having a woman he could talk to about the big features in his life and be understood, have a conversation between equals while lying in bed together, just floored him. What would that be like?

It was the first time he'd ever had any sort of attraction of the human kind for anybody he was working. Of course he was still young: his old man had apparently humped everybody he came into contact with. And that's who was kind of on his mind here: another topic that got under his skin but he couldn't talk about to anybody.

"Well, I'm doing okay in my work," he told her. Which he'd said was "Information consultant." And it was actually true, wasn't it? "But thing is, my father was kind of a legend in the same field. I get around the older guys in the company and I feel like they're talking to me as an extension of him. Like he's throwing a big shadow over everything I do."

"I know exactly what you mean." And she did, that's what was weirding both of them out. "Except it was my Momma who was the stuff of legends. And everybody around her seemed to just be waiting for me to grow up and be a pale copy of her. I might as well have been called 'Junior'."

"So how do you deal with it?"

"Got out from under, hon. Went my own way. She got nothing to do with what I'm doing now, Communications facilitator." True also, no? In the same way.

"I've considered that, but I really like what I do. It's really who I am. And all I really know."

"I hear that. And I know other stuff. But I'd be bored shitless being an exec or model or whatever. Porn star."

She was smiling when he glanced at her. "Well, I considered that, of course," he said, "But the smut leagues took me so low in the draft..."

"I had plenty of offers, believe me," she said. "Some from my Momma's friends and colleagues, too. Makes you say, Hmm. But I didn't have to change what I was doing, just took it down the street, you know? Highest bidder. Then went indie."

"That's crossed my mind." Hell, it had been burned into his mind on a couple of occasions. Double up, triple up, work for a cartel, for the Mob, for some Wall Street asshole. "But, I don't know. I guess I plan on just growing up and making a bigger name than Pops."

Hmmm. There was something to be said for that one. But you didn't really make a name in the private spy gig. "Well, at least you learn a lot when you've got 'rents' in the field, huh?"

She sure had. All sorts of useful shit around the house, Debra's main men *du jour* falling by with their guns and berets and rad-rap. Rapping at me some in between jamming Mammy. Talk about a glass ceiling, though. Stokely—who she had a brother named after, by the by—always said that a woman's position in The Movement was "prone". Not supine, you notice. Gotta have that fine ass up top.

"Yeah, there's that," Townsend acceded. Dandled on the knees of killers and cold warriors, picking up the lingo and tips as he got older. Realizing later that some of his conversations with some of his dad's butthole buddies, little fireside chats that moved from his touchdowns or freethrows last week to his future career plans, were really more like pre-job interviews.

She stood up and stretched like a panther, then looked down at him, patted her belly and smiled. "Yummy nummy in my tummy." And it hit him, an active, probing hunger for her. He'd never felt anything like that for a woman since about eighth grade. He imagined stroking that tummy, licking that navel. And what not. Whew.

He stood up, carefully dusting any crumbs off his lap. He looked at her and said, "Hey, we ought to have a drink or two, with a view of the sea. How about we go to my place at the Avalon for a while?"

She turned her head towards him, inclining it slightly forward. Looked him over good and proper. Said, "I got a better idea, White Boy. How about we go to my place, poke our toes in the sand?"

Deli watched them walk off towards the main street where the cabs passed, not quite leaning toward each other, but with a connection you could see a block away. Heading straight for bed, she thought. I'd like to see a video of that little hookup. Then she went out to pick up their plates and two really generous tips.

TEACHING TOLERANCE

When the bodyguards burst in through the curtain, suddenly overwhelming the studied "real museum" décor with a whole lot of very practical-looking guns and scowls, Ronchel grabbed a big stainless Ruger .357 from the nearest goon and stepped towards the girls, who had cowered back against the wall. He caught the slightest, quickly hidden, flicker of amusement from these professional tough guys; seeing him rendered limping and bleeding by two women. He advanced on the girls with the gun held straight out in front of him, shaking with fury. He placed the muzzle on MeiMei's lips and pushed her back until her head was against the wall. "Open up, you sneaky little gook."

MeiMei, surrounded by machine guns and ill will, saw little option. She opened her mouth wide, hoping to avoid any chipped teeth when he perpetrated the obvious violation. He slid the big, cold muzzle into her mouth, rattling it around a little until the front sight pocked against the back of her throat, triggering her gag reflex.

He spoke in a low, insinuating tone. "Now suck it."

MeiMei closed her lips around the barrel and osculated them a little, trying to breathe and swallow around the steel abrading her epiglottis. The men behind Ronchel laughed and made appreciative noises. Then he yanked the gun out, cutting her upper lip. He turned to stare at Curtsy, speaking to his men without breaking the hateful glare he was focusing on her. "Strip them both."

Probably their all-time favorite order. Although maybe they stripped women for him every weekend, who knew? Rough hands jerked the thin strips of cloth from the women, leaving red marks where the fabric dragged and broke. Ronchel continued to glare at Curtsy as his minions whooped it up, making comments on MeiMei's sparse thatch and the blond fuzz of Curtsy's pubic crest. One watchdog stepped up and rubbed his hand through the blond curlies, smirking at her as he did. Curtsy spit in his face.

He instantly backhanded her across the tits and pulled back a fist.

"No! I want to have plenty of fun with them while they're still beautiful," Ronchel barked. He reached to cup the Curtsy's nape and grip her hair, pulling her head back and tapping it against the wall. "Later you animals can do whatever you want."

He stepped back, stiffening into as much dignity as he could muster with his dick hanging out and blood smeared on his face. "Take the *güerita* to my quarters. And the Chink down to Three."

Curtsy didn't bother looking for a way out of the master stateroom, which was kind of "Hugh Hefner meets Captain Nemo in a Vegas Whorehouse". There wouldn't be a way out. And she didn't bother putting on any clothes. Instead she started ransacking the place for weapons. A live-in situation with a drug dealer during her brief post-highschool coke slut phase had hipped her to the way these things worked and she went under the pillows and king-sized memory foam mattress first, then all over the drawers on each side of the bed.

She was going through the dresser drawers, bottom to top, when the door opened and Ronchel stepped in, his face cleaned up, an Ace bandage around his knee, and flourishing his big shiny gun in one hand and his little purplish weapon in the other. He locked a deadbolt behind him and smiled at her, dangling the revolver off his finger. "See anything you want to get your hands on?"

He leaned back and thrust his pelvis out, leading off with his whole engorgement. "How about now?"

Curtsy laughed and shook her hair, which left Ronchel a little nonplussed. "Hey, I'm sorry I tranked you. okay? It was the slope's idea. She was paying me and I needed the money."

She moved closer to Ronchel, tentative little-girl steps, but otherwise a blazing gold advertisement for the female race. "Look, you seem like a pretty cool guy. And you've got a great set-up here. I'd love to hang out here with you, you know? Go places, live good. Fuck your brains out. Gimme a break, okay? We just might want the same thing."

Looking into her guileless blue eyes, Ronchel could almost buy it. Gringas were like that, was his experience. Sluts who would do anything to be around money. And she was a prize piece, no doubt about it. He'd much rather break her down on the bed there, give her a taste of what the *macho Mexicano* could do to a woman, than just rape her a few times and toss her to the hounds. He eyed her narrowly, reserving his judgment.

Curtsy moved in closer, encouraged by his silence and lack of movement. "It's more fun when I'm into it," she told him, with a look that promised untold delights. "We could really have some fun if you'll overlook my shooting you up."

194

A slight frown flitted across her face and she looked at him curiously. "Hey, what's with that, anyway? Those drugs should have put you out like a light. They would have put a bull to sleep."

Ronchel laughed. "When you have mountains of money and nasty habits you build a heavy tolerance to just about any drug you can think of."

Curtsy nodded, happy to have it all explained. "Wow! See, I could tell you were my kind of guy. I hope you keep some coke around the bedroom here. Do they call it a bedroom on a ship?"

Ronchel was already calculating the greater pleasures in having Curtsy while she was out of her mind on dope, versus whimpering in pain and not doing anything to help out. Close call. Then she stepped right up to him. He put the tip of the barrel right on her temple, raised an eyebrow at her. She giggled. She was fun, he had to admit.

She lowered to her knees, leaning in to brush him with her hair as she went down. This was a weakness of almost all Mexican guys, as she'd heard from a lot of girls. Fellatio was practically a sin for Mexican girls, sticking your business into somebody's teeth when they weren't having it was dangerous, and getting willing head was a grail quest for these assholes. She cupped his balls and examined the goods, cocking her head to one side.

I'd bite the damn thing off and let him bleed to death, she thought, but it would hardly make a meal. She said, "Looks yummy. You mind?"

Ronchel had no real objection to getting sucked off. But sticking your dick in somebody's mouth was something you didn't want to do unless you knew they were friendly. He could shoot her after she bit the tip off, of course, but that wouldn't help much. He said, "Lets go over to the bed."

She hopped up with a sunny smile and led him with a hand around his cock.

"You didn't have to mess it up like that," he said with mock admonishment.

"You think it's trashed *now*." Curtsy tittered. "Just wait."

He lay down and dragged two pillows under his head, his gun hand laying off to one side. "How about we start off between your tits?"

Everybody has lips, he was thinking, but how many have tits like this? And tits don't have teeth.

Curtsy was down with that suggestion, and knelt low over his thighs as she massaged him between her breasts, giving it enough variation to make it interesting. Let's get him groaning, was what she was thinking. Enjoying himself at full volume.

And sure enough, in less than a minute, she had him calling out audibles. Probably exaggerating a bit for the benefit of the guards outside. Then she hunched up and started working up his body, finally straddling his crotch and looming over him like a blonde goddess, working her hips back and forth to rub her gold fur over his erection without denying him a view of the color of her damp hair. He was eating it up and getting pretty vocal about it.

Curtsy raised up just slightly, teasing his lunging member with a little contact prior to entering the main event. She leaned forward, tossing her tits from one side to another, and stretched out her hands to support herself as she eased down on to him. Rested her hands on his arms, actually. While initiating the famous fate worse than death. Just imagine that he's Flipper, Kurtz, she was thinking as she started showing a some spasms of her own, rhythmically clenching his arms as he groaned and heaved.

Then she clenched down hard, holding his gun arm down, and snapped her head forward, her wide forehead smashing into his already-injured nose. He screamed, but she figured it wouldn't get much attention at that point in the proceedings.

She jumped off to his right side, keeping the gun hand pinioned to the mattress. She grabbed his package in her right hand and squeezed so hard he spasmed and squeaked and went limp. She slid her hand down to strip the Ruger out of his hand and jumped to her feet. She swung the gun against his temple with her full strength and ran to the door.

She stopped there, listening with her eyes on Ronchel, who wasn't moving. Finally she took a deep breath and silently turned the knob on the deadbolt. She opened the door slowly, not seeing anybody in the passageway. She peeked sideways and could see cowboy boots in both directions, the bodyguards standing there listening to the show. She stuck the gun against the wall at about the level of her own heart and pulled the trigger.

She was out the door, facing the other guard, before the first guy even hit the opposite wall and spattered arterial blood all over it. The other asshole was too shocked to even raise the little submachine gun dangling in his hand. Curtsy put a round right through his face, blowing the back of his head down the wall to create a delta-shaped Pollock impression. She spun back the other way, pointing the gun, but there was nobody in sight. She ran down the passageway with the gun held out in front of her, hoping the reinforcements wouldn't arrive from behind her.

She glanced at the bronze plaques on the doors as she passed, but they were all cute little names, no numbers. She was only six feet from the end of the hall when the door opened and a guy came through it at top speed, holding an UZI. She was on top of him almost simultaneous with the bullet that caught him in the sternum and blew him backward. She ran over him like a doormat. There was a shot from behind her, but she was already out the door, running aft to where the boat was tied. She heard steps and yells in the passage behind her, could see bodyguards running on the deck below. She wouldn't have had time to start the motors and cast off anyway.

A bodyguard in a white guayabera, toting an expensive Fabrique assault rife, looked up and saw her, a gorgeous blonde athlete running like a deer on the upper deck, her hair flying out behind her and firing like she meant it. He threw his gun up and blew a chunk out of the teak handrail, but doubted he'd hit her. He ran up the starboard stairs three at a time, but when he could see down the deck she wasn't there. He came all the way up and moved to port, where he heard more shooting.

He came around the corner and looked forward just in time to see the blonde vault up onto the railing and set her feet to dive far enough out to miss the lower deck. He took a bead on her, but just as she jumped he heard a pistol shot forward and she dropped the gun and spun off into the night, off-balanced and slack. Now that was a hit, he was thinking as he ran forward to look down into the dark water. He almost ran into Sr. Ronchel himself, still naked, and looking even worse than before. Not to mention totally crazed. The Boss snatched up the Ruger and leaned out over the edge looking for a shot. He was afraid his jefe might fall over and stepped up close.

Ronchel turned a twisted face to him and screamed. "Get us out of here, *idiota*."

He gaped a second and Ronchel hit him the chest with the gun. "Get under way, *hijo de puta*. Now!"

He turned and ran for the bridge, pulling his walkie-talkie out to call ahead. Gotta say, he was thinking, if I was getting that bad beat up by a piece of ass, I think I'd just let somebody else nail it for me.

ULAMA RAMA DING DONG

Paco had thought summers were brutal back in Sinaloa. Ha. It got damn hot and soppy in Mazatlán and Culiacán, but nothing like over here on the Caribe. It was like being in a hot towel all day and most of the night. Your shower, the water's lukewarm and you're sweaty before you can dry off. He was getting really, really tired of always having his balls dripping with salt itch.

But sweltering here in Quintana Roo had two big advantages. He had a job. Which was not something to be lightly sought over on the Pacífico coast. Seasonal, underpaid, silly... but it was a job and occasionally attracted a few groupies.

And he could devote himself to The Game.

It's funny but he had always thought of it as "The Game" even though everybody knew it was called *ulama*. But over here everybody just called it "the prehistoric ball game" or "the Mayan ballgame." And even funnier, he hadn't met a Mayan yet who actually played The Game. Or even knew how it was played. But that was the great part, really. In fact it was downright *chidisimo* because that meant when Xcaret—which he thought of as the Mayan-Gringo *Disneylandia*— wanted to stage games on the authentic phony ball court they built, they had to import players from Sinaloa. So here he was. Digging it.

Another funny thing, Puch knew more about the history of the game than he did, and he was a star player in the top league in Sinaloa. They'd played at the carnival in Mazatlán, the second biggest in the world, for the Governor, for the U.S. and Canadian Ambassadors. And took home beer money. Or less. Here he was making a living and scoring with chicks from like Norway and Japan and Alaska and all those places.

Puch said *ulama de cadera*, the style they played, was a direct descendant of the oldest ball game in history. How's that for *chingón*?

Centuries before anybody played baseball or *futbol* or *basquet* or, whatever, golf. And think about it, where else were they going to get a rubber ball? The only rubber in the world was here in the Yucatan. And playing The Game wasn't just something to do on Sundays, have a few beers and go humiliate those *nacos* from the Guasave team: it had been like a religion. Kings and warriors and priests. Sacrificing the losers. Or was it the winners? Anyway, it was a big deal.

And look where he was playing now. Well, during high season, anyway. A brand new court made to look like old stone, colored lights on the game, cute Mayan "cheerleaders" (actually those *porristas* were about as Mayan as he was... mostly *Capitolino* kids who wanted to get on with *foclorico* troupes up in Guadalajara or the D.F.). Stars, they were. Fireworks and big applause and flashes going off. Get nice tips for posing with people. Sometimes some really nice tips from various *gringas* and *Europeas*. And everybody here was a major stud from back in old "Chinaloa", too.

They hand-picked the best for this—after all, they paid the best. Xcaret didn't assign teams, let them clump up on their own. So it was pretty much the top players from the Coast against the cream of the hillbillies. Mani had said it, and it was true: Xcaret was the SuperBowl of *ulama*. Right here in Mayalandia, where it all started, then died out.

Puch told him that wasn't uncommon for this area. He said horses got started there, then went to Spain or somewhere and died out here. But the Spaniards brought them back. It was how things worked over here, is the way it looked. Like the *Judios* going back to Israel or something. And now it looked like Puch was building his own ballcourt.

It started out when Puch—who they knew because he led snorkle tours at Xel Ha and Xcaret and was a very solid guy, *muy gente* and *buena onda*—invited a bunch of players over to this Crocun place to eat and suck up a few sixes of Superior. Tasted like dishwater compared to Sinaloa's own Pacífico, but it was the local fave, *La Rubia de Categoria*. And they all came back. You would too, if you tasted Señora Pop's chow. ¡*Riquisimo*!

And they'd started playing down in this big pit behind the restaurant. It used to be a stone quarry, but had been scraped out and there was this pond at one end where some crocodiles and iguanas hung out, but the rest was this almost perfect box where they could run around, practice passing the ball from hip to hip, take shots at a basketball hoop Puch had mounted sideways on the wall of the quarry, instead of the traditional stone ring.

They taught Puch the game, and he wasn't bad at it, either. And he taught them a lot more. He'd been off to study at *la uni* but mostly he just ran around learning stuff about his people and his country here. And they'd all tidied up the quarry a little. Puch conned some guy with AguaCan to bring a little mini-dozer in, but they did a lot of moving rocks around, pounding the floor of the quarry flatter with big mauls. The way they'd cut the stone out, there were already tiers, and sometimes their wives and girlfriends and an occasional stray tourist chick would sit up there under this *palapa* Puch had set up, watch them play and toss them a cold *cheve* now and then.

There was something different about playing here. Not like Xcaret, which was more a spectacle than a sport, like those cape and mask bruisers in the *Lucha Libre*[30]. And different from back home, where it was this community thing. Here it was straight-out *sportiva*, man on man, teamwork against teamwork. They loved playing down here and came over every Sunday, and a lot of times during the week, maybe just to help groom the court. It was actually starting to look like the real thing. And hey, wasn't it the real thing? Weren't they indigenous Mexicans, weren't they true players?

Lately it had been more fun because a bunch of the dancers and musicians had started showing up as well. Not wearing the whole feathers and animal head drag like at Xcaret, just jeans and skirts and sometimes swimsuits. Nobody swam in the croc pond, though. Nice bunch of kids, mostly from like conservatories in Merida and Mexico, girls studying dance and playing Xcaret for the money, like us. Not a real Mayan in the crowd.

They'd been doing a little grooming of their own recently, making a sort of platform above the goal end of the ball court, trying out routines up there, dancing around a fire at night while the *musicos* jammed and we sat around and watched and clapped.

The weird thing was, you couldn't have paid him to do stonework in this heat. Be a damn *albañil* earning the *minimo*[31] for sweating like a *negro*. But they were doing it for fun. It just sort of felt like something they should do. And if they needed to get rid of a rock, there was always a place for it. And if we needed rocks, they could just pull them out of the slope of the hill. Puch sort of set aside areas to take rock and fill out of, one on each side of this outcropping above the end of the cancha and dance platform. One day Mani was standing there bumping a ball up and down off his hip pads, and pointed up the court, said, "This place is starting to look like Palenque or something."

And it did, like they were carving a Mayan site out of live rock. Paco mentioned this to Puch and he just smiled. Told him, "Stick around."

BUNG FU

MeiMei tried the door, but it was securely bolted. Locks on the outside of stateroom doors, she thought, always the hallmark of a true gentleman. She cased the whole boudoir without much hope of finding the Secret Weakness Chamber. This guy probably does this all the time. A lovely bathroom (do they call it a "head' on this class of boat?) with bidet, no less. But a notable lack of scissors or blunt weapons. The closet had nothing but some frilly nightwear and sleek lounging robes. In what looked like child's sizes. Yuck. As she examined the barred portholes, she checked to make sure the camera was still tucked up behind her neck, the little lanyard securely lashed into her thick black hair. The one thing she desperately wanted to have if she got out of this fix. Then she heard shouts and shots. Followed by a splash.

She jumped to the porthole and saw bodyguards pelting by, armed and rancorous. Oh, damn, damn, damn! She was practically jumping around with anxiety when she felt a tremor run through the yacht, then an almost subliminal sensation of movement. Another glimpse out the window confirmed that she was under way. Ronchel probably figured there might be more of us raiders. She wished. She wished, in fact, that Aphra would suddenly show up, swooping down on a parachute, blasting from the hip with twin UZI's, and kicking pervo peckers off with Seventies go-go boots.

Instead she got Ronchel. He slammed the door open, making her jump, then back away until her butt hit the bulkhead. He came into the room in an obvious fury. Along with other emotions equally obvious by a casual glance at his bulging crotch. He stared right into MeiMei's eyes, neither looking at nor speaking to the two bodyguards who flowed into the room behind him. They immediately moved towards MeiMei, who held her hands in front of her with her fingernails coiled like talons.

Ronchel laughed and raised his right hand from beside his leg, demonstrating that it clutched a huge stainless steel revolver. Which he pointed at Mei while the two thugs moved in and patted her down (pretty diligently, she thought) for nasty surprises. One of them nodded to Ronchel, who motioned them out of the room.

Quickly, MeiMei said, "You really think a big, tough guy like you needs that much gun?"

Ronchel laughed. "Need? Not at all. But it's much more fun."

As the torpedoes closed the door behind them, he moved close to MeiMei, staring with obviously growing pleasure. "Not bad, not bad," he said. "For Plan B."

"You can also choose two dishes from column A," MeiMei said, holding his gaze while standing tall with no attempt to cover herself.

"I can choose whatever I want, Chinita. And I've got all night."

MeiMei sighed and shrugged. "So why do you still have your pants on?"

"Good point." He pulled the string tie of his pants and let them fall. Had to help them get around his dick, but then they fell to the floor and he kicked them at her, standing there with rampant hard-on and brandished firearm.

"I can see right now it's true about guys with big guns trying to compensate," MeiMei sniffed.

"I think I'm big enough for chink pussy," he said stalking towards her like some sort of matador/flasher. "Are you getting a little excited?"

She raised the back of her hand to cover a yawn.

Ronchel grinned tightly and stepped close enough to extend the pistol within inches of her chest. With excruciating slowness he put the muzzle right on her nipple, her tan flesh sliding inside the gleaming barrel. She could feel the sharp edges of the rifling. She shook her head sadly. "Pitiful."

Without any expression he flipped the gun sideways, hurting her tender tissue as it raked away, then swung it back, towards the side of her head.

MeiMei made two moves at once, a high *Bang Shou* block of the gun and a plain old *Chin Tom Toy* kick to the area she was thinking of as *gao wán*, rather than "nuts", since she always switched over to Chinese when practicing the arts her father had drilled into her from the time she could walk. A move one of her boyfriends had once referred to as *"Hung Wun Low"*.

He fell to his knees making retching sounds, turned away as if trying to crawl for the door. She took cold aim and kicked him as hard as she could where his left hand was cupping his outraged basket. He screeched like a woman, threw up, and lost consciousness. MeiMei grabbed the gun and pointed it at him. She even inched the trigger back a sliver. But knew she couldn't do it.

She stepped over and stood behind his knees, knelt and positioned the big gun right on his anus. Then shoved if forward with her full strength, taking savage pleasure in the feel of the front sight tearing membrane as the seven-inch barrel plunged into his rectum. Again she felt the impulse to pull the trigger, but knew she wouldn't. She stood and dithered a moment. God knows how long he would stay unconscious: the guy was like one of those movie monsters, kept rearing back up when he was supposed to be out of the picture. Finally she grabbed the most substantial-looking of the robes from the closet and ran to the door, shrugging into the diaphanous white kiddyporn loungewear.

She had her mental fingers crossed as she tried it and gave a deep sigh when it opened. She dared a quick peek into the hall, hoping she wouldn't have to run back over there and draw a shit-smeared sixgun to deal with bodyguards. This whole bit was just not her style at all. She slipped out and ran for it.

She hit the main rear deck frantic for an escape plan. The boat had to be gone. She had unfortunately omitted helicopter lessons from her postgrad curriculum. If there were lifeboats or escape pods, they weren't in plain sight. She heard the snarl of two-stroke engines approaching and looked over the rail to see a half-dozen JetSkis coming into the wake and drawing up to the water-level stern catwalk. She realized that there had been a radio or cell phone call to notify these little dickheads that the mothership had weighed anchor.

As she watched, Corcho jockied in close, jumped his Yamaha up onto the little bathing deck and grabbed a dangling line from a davit. The other Lords were queuing up for docking procedure. All six of them would be up on her deck in minutes, and they looked like even less congenial rapists than her host had tried to be. She stared at the scene below as the Dood they called Chango eased his Kawasaki in close enough to snatch at a float-tipped mooring line Corcho had tossed astern. And heard shouts behind her, the soft putter of running deckshoes. Without giving herself time to think better of it, she jumped up on the teak rail, leaped off, and plunged from view.

The Lord known as Chango was in some ways very fortunate. Other ways, less so. After his humiliation ashore on the previous day, it's unlikely his psyche would have been able to handle awareness of what happened as he leaned over to grab the floating polypro mooring line. Namely an aerial bombardment by a bitch. MeiMei fell almost thirty feet, trailing her shiny white robe like a geisha butterfly. At about the point when she would have reached terminal velocity, her feet impacted the top of Chango's spine, the right heel striking at the point known as "the atlas". The immediate result of her landing on him, smashing his chest into the hand-rubbed finish of his garish tank and cracking his jaw against his custom "ape hanger" handlebars, was that he promptly ceased to be an impediment to her desire to leave the area. Beyond that, he ceased to be alive.

Her landing cushioned by the abolishment of Chango, MeiMei fell to her knees on his shoulders, then quickly slid down his back into the saddle. In the moment's grace bought by the sheer novelty of her arrival—naked Asian poon from the heavens being rarer than meteor showers in that area—she tugged the inert Chango around, grunting dojo monosyllables at the exertion of heaving him into the drink while his buddies watched, stunned.

Fortunately—as we've seen—operating a JetSki doesn't exactly require top-drawer intelligence, so she quickly figured out where to put her hands and what to do with them. The hopped-up response of the super-souped Kawasaki JS750 literally scared the piss out of her when she racked the throttle around. But even more so "Chimi", wastrel scion of the Ronchel lineage, whose SeaDoo RXP-Turbo was directly in front of her. The hyperactive Kwaski hunkered down and bolted almost out of the water, the hull mostly dry as it smashed into Chimi and ran right over him, converting him and his RXP into an ad hoc ramp for an awesome jump that brought cheers from nearby yachts where attention had been gathered by the gunshots. She blasted straight over Chimi, carved a turn to port that terrified her, and became the proverbial blue streak.

Stung by having frozen up, infuriated by the demolition of their two comrades by some gookporn ninja who was pretty blatantly a mere woman, the remaining Lords recovered their usual aggressive velocities and pelted behind her. She headed back down the wake, eyes peeled for Curtsy.

And caught a glimpse of her, lolling over a swell, hair a faint yellow carnation floating in her headlight, surrounded by a nimbus of blood. She saw no signs of life—quite the contrary—and quickly realized that if she stopped the only result would be both of them falling back in the hands of these assholes, and if Curtsy wasn't dead already, she would be soon enough. She blasted by her accomplice, the Kawasaki's wake rolling her over into a face-down float that spoke of finality.

Leaning low for less resistance, MeiMei felt tears being torn from her face by the force of the wind. The California girl had just been so cool, so vital, so... alive. And now? Last seen face-down in a slick of blood. Because she got sucked into this lunatic Mission Improbable scheme. She cried silently as she shifted her weight, searched out a position of low profile that didn't kick her butt as she skimmed the waves, a kind of jockey crouch.

The jounce across the open sea was once again oddly soothing. After a half-hour MeiMei had regained her usual inner calm and outer watchfulness. She had realized that she had an slim edge over her pursuers. Her craft was just a fast as theirs—in fact, it dawned on her that in a male motorhead ratpack like that you couldn't have a slower vehicle or they'd sneer and drum you out—but she was substantially lighter and offered less wind resistance. There were no tricks or techniques that would help them out in open water: this race would be to the swiftest and she had an advantage. The problem was... race to where?

And while she was browsing tropical destinations, there was also one of those niggling energy questions that pester us all these days— did she have enough gas to get wherever she dreamed up to go? She guessed she'd live or nastily die on whether the Doods had topped up their tanks on their trip to shore. And that she had the same reserves that they did. There was no way to know and her weight advantage would apply to fuel consumption as well as speed.

She didn't look back at the Doods: she instinctively saw glancing over the shoulder as bad prey behavior. Learning while fleeing. She experimented with the controls—at one point touching a button that released a blast of "La Cucaracha"—before finding the switch that cut her running lights. She understood that the Lords would have to keep theirs on so as not to lose her: another edge that wasn't much but numbered among the small advantages she held and hoped to maximize. She hung back from the handgrips with a stern grimace as she fled into the night. Run straight, dark and swift, was her mantra, her glitzy robe billowing out behind her like a superhero's cape. She worked the camera out of her hair and placed in securely in the receptacle where the mp3 deck had been before she popped it out and lobbed it over her shoulder in hopes of clobbering one or more JetSki jockeys. Then she ran out of things to do and just hung on for the duration.

HOUSE CALL

MeiMei had fortunately headed the right general direction and when she saw the glare of lights from the Cancun hotel zone she used them to guide her jouncing flight from the pursuing gang. Twenty minutes after starting to look for it, she made out the outline of Isla Mujeres and headed straight for the South Point lighthouse. She'd gained some lead on the thundering Lords, but could hear them, relentless, behind her. She headed in close to the lee shore of Isla, aiming past the dock lights at Garrafon Park, trying to run closer to land. The Lords followed, keying on stray light catching the white robe that flapped out behind her like a comet's tail.

She'd figured out the only place she really had a chance to find safety. Anywhere she tried to stop, those goons would be right on her, and there was small hope of any cops or vacationing Green Berets being around at this hour. So she nosed in close, meanwhile making what few preparations she could think of. She retrieved the camera and knotted the little lanyard around her left wrist. She used her teeth to tear a big strip of whatever Victoria's Secret Weapon material the robe was made of. She had experimented a little once she figured out the Doods couldn't catch her in a straight-out race, and learned that releasing the grips caused a deadman switch to cut power. But not when it was lashed down tight with the fuzzy, glittery hem of the robe from the Roman Polanski Collection.

Which made it easier to shrug out of the robe, which had been impossible when her velocity required her constant grip. She knotted the sleeves of the robe, looped them on her right elbow, and nudged in closer to shore. Which was scaring the hell out of her because at the speeds she was going there would be no chance to avoid any sort of obstacle. Hope nobody's out skinny-dipping tonight, she thought as she rocketed along the coastline, threading under the series of long, high docks that extended out over the silty shallows along the sheltered side of the island. Then she was there.

She reached under her butt to tuck the robe's sleeves into the grab strap on the seat, then had only a second to set the Kawasaki on a course that would take it out away from the other piers. Then, as it passed into the shadow of one of the lower ones, she jumped off and splashed quickly to cling to one of the crusty pilings. She ducked her head under water as the four vengeful watercraft screamed through the gap under the wooden walkway, none of the Doods capable of being craven enough to run outside the piers when a mere bitch was slaloming under them. Once the Lords of Xibalba had careened past she headed madly for the shore.

As soon as the fugitive Kawasaki came out of the moonshadow of the island and broke into the relatively open water off the Turtle Farm it was obvious that it had become an unmanned projectile. The sudden deceleration of howling jetskis caused them to nose into the water, expertly flipped into little dive/turns by the various surviving Lords. Corcho, who'd trailed them because he'd been on the yacht when they took off, pulled up and summed it up. "The bitch bailed. We backtrack." All four of them revved up and whizzed back along the shore, keeping their wind-burned eyes peeled for naked castaways.

It was only thirty yards to shore, but tougher than she would have guessed. The bottom was gooey and gross, with creepy grass and God knew what else. But swimming was no picnic, either, especially in the dark beneath the pier, where odd floating Things bumped squishily against her. Finally her crawl strokes were brushing relatively clean sand on the bottom and she put a tentative foot down to stand up in waist-deep water. Only to bellyflop back as she heard the first jetski return. The Lords were moving much slower now, their tweaked two-strokes muttering as they poked along, shining headlights under docks and scanning the beaches. MeiMei crawled in further, seeking the deeper darkness where the dock met the beach. When the last of them putted off to the south, concentrating their search around Casa O, she jumped up and sprinted for the house.

Which was totally dark. Maybe nobody was home. Setting up her next exercise: how to get out of this area and back to the Maria Del Mar in the middle of the night with no money and no clothes.

She approached the small side door, not wanting to be silhouetted slinking past the big sliding glass that covered most of the front. Once there she couldn't decide how to perform the simple act of knocking on the door. She hadn't seen anything to cover up with and was too anxious to get out of sight to do a lot of searching. She located a spot under an arching bougainvillea, moved to the door to pound on it loud, long and desperate, then dashed back to the cover of the magenta bower. Where she waited shivering and exposed and generally ready to freak out. She'd done a damned good job of keeping it together, she thought. Getting caught in a crime, then being an attempted rape victim and seeing her friend shot to death, then—face it—probably killing those two water bikers, then leading a hound chase across open sea at night, most of it stark naked. So what she wanted was to achieve a spot of relative safety and security, get some damned clothes, and exercise the exquisite luxury of falling completely apart.

No such luck. The door didn't open, but three huge lights came on, the big kind they use for ballparks and prisonbreaks. One of them was directly over her head, so the bougainvillea provided no shelter at all. She grabbed one of the leafy branches, only to discover that it was covered with sneaky thorns. Then the door opened and Tuan DeTomaso stepped out, holding one hand behind his back and staring at the nude honey who had decided to call on him at four in the morning.

There was no point in being coy at that point, MeiMei decided. She stood up straight and walked over to Tuan as naturally as if she'd been wearing her jeans and lab coat. As he gaped, she said, "Help me, O.B. Tuan. You're my only hope."

Mitsy Fortnum liked lolling naked in the warm dark water. Last night it had been a real turn-on; sneaking out of their rooms in the wee hours to do a "From Here To Eternity" number in the gentle waves on the sheltered beach at Rolandi's. But that was last night, and now it seemed, well, so Last Night. Tommy was all over her, as usual, but she just didn't get that same forbidden tropical fantasy kick and was starting to fret. It was nice to go with a guy who had a Porsche and could take her places like this, but she was starting to wonder about the wisdom of a continued relationship with a guy who was basically just a dull ex-jock, when you got down to it. And was proving less and less capable of lighting her fire.

She tapped him on the shoulder as he moved over her in the warm shallows, incidentally grinding her Pilates-honed booty against some kind of unpleasant vegetation that had washed up there. That didn't work so she grabbed a handful of his hair and pulled his head back sharply to make eye contact. "Listen, Tommy," she said, but didn't get any further than that because something came whooping and screaming out of the night.

It was big and black and she caught a flash of huge white teeth in an evil, gaping grin as it thundered up on them with a deafening roar. Whatever it was just missed plastering them or gobbling them up or whatever its hell-sent mission was, but might have grazed the back of Tommy's thighs as it whined past them. He jumped to his feet in one spasm, popping out of her like a champagne cork. As she turned to see what it was—her stomach doing flipflops and triple axels—it rained all over them from this fireboat waterspout out of the sea avenger's ass end. Just before it tore up the beach like that Normandy movie, knocked a couple of tables and umbrellas from there to eternity, and smashed into the stone wall supporting the restaurant deck at what must have been close to eighty miles an hour.

Tommy was standing there staring, all those lovely muscles clenched up, shaking like a wet Spaniel. She lay gaping, her innards doing odd things, her fists and anus clenched tight as a streetfighter's fist. Then the Kawasaki burst into flame.

That brought her to her feet as well... you could see burning gasoline splattered all over the beach lounges and massage tables, and even floating on the water. Holy shit, would they get burned in the *ocean*? She stared at the flames, her mouth lolling open and her belly churning.

Tommy turned to face her, no sign of that big, proud boner now. The fire seemed be spreading and lights were coming on in the hotel. She looked down and saw a play of hot colors all over her wet, beautifully augmented torso. "Come on," he whispered urgently as he tried to pull her over to the lounger where they'd left their robes. "Let's get the hell out of here."

"Are you out of your mind?" Mitsy asked rhetorically. She turned to him and just tackled him like a blitzing linebacker, grabbing him around the knees and carrying him over backwards into the water. "This is getting me so fucking hot!"

She broke off communications at that point, taking advantage of her position to get a mouthful of action and start the process of working herself into an oblivious frenzy.

PIQUE A BOO

"Well I never mind getting my feet wet a little," Aphra said, deadpan enough that she was sure the innuendo got through.

Town had paid off the cab at the entrance to the wood bridge to the Avalon, and then kind of mosied around, leaning over the rail and staring down at the water beneath. He'd pointed out a barracuda to her, and three pearlescent cuttlefish flitting through the cone of light under the span. Then he'd looked around and said, "I kind of hate to go inside, it's so nice. And this beach is just so perfect. Am I crazy to want to kick off my sandals and take a little moonlight wade?"

So get their feet wet they did. He kicked off his sandals and sloshed along the waveless shallows. She hiked up her skirt, to the desired effect, and fell in beside him. Slogging around the shallows by Na Balam, bumming along North Beach, chatting nicely, Aphra had to wonder. Did he know he was standing right in front of her place, talking about not wanting to go over to the Avalon? Stay down here on the sand and all? Be interesting to find out if he's even registered at the Avalon. Definitely reading him as competition at that point.

And he kind of had her. Obviously she'd rather snoop out his room and he'd rather do hers. But was she going to say, No, to hell with the tropical beauty, let's go into your hotel? But sometimes it's just, See one, play one. So she hit him with the wet feet line, then sunk it with, "Know, what? We could have those drinks on my front porch. Right up there, behind the palm trees."

"You're staying here? Man, that's so cool. I booked an all-inclusive over there, but now I see this place right on the beach, nice old buildings, I wish I'd known."

Well come on over for some all-inclusive, Casper, Aphra thought. Said, "It's a great little spot. You drink rum?"

"Don't they call it grog around the Caribbean?"

"All I got is some Coke." That was a probe, of course, but not a flicker. So, "Why do they call rum and Coke a 'Cuba Libre', anyway?"

"Government secret. I think they can pull your passport just for saying it."

"Nah, the Democrats are in now. My man Obama be down there swapping spit with Fidel, sending 'em tractors and Mastercards."

He spotted a round flat rock in a foot of water, picked it up and skimmed it on the surface. Aphra admired the clean, powerful delivery, the rock skipping completely out of sight. Man didn't just look good and talk shit, he could move himself, huh? She had another of those weird moments when she looked a man over and thought; Not bad, not bad, oughta give it another shot. Whatever else he was, he was damn sure pretty.

Meanwhile, Townsend was getting almost alarmed at the way his intentions were zigzagging between taking care of business and wanting to just wrap himself around this big, smart beauty and hang on until he knew how it came out. Fortunately, the two urges coincided at the moment, and were headed in a mutually promising direction.

And it got more promising after two drinks, when she slipped inside to "visit the ladies" as she put it, and he could take a quick scan. He ran his Art of the State iPod-disguised transponder over her purse and got nothing. Maybe it was reading something out in Langley or wherever its hyper-tech innards were routing things. He turned up the field, broadened it to maximum cardiac pattern, and got a blip or two from inside the room. He quickly slipped on the stylish sunglasses the guys called "X-Ray Spex" and leaned over to peer through the window. The displays fired in his left peripheral vision, and he spotted two different hot spots: the nightstand drawer and the pocket of that robe hanging by the bathroom door. Which was opening, so he ducked out of view and pocketed the shades and bug-buster. It had been a quick glimpse of the reads, but she was using some pretty trick stuff, herself. Then she was back on the porch. Wearing the robe. So much for heading for a whiz and copping her feed. On the other hand, he was electrified by the fact that she was standing there in a bathrobe.

And even more so when she said, in a rather smoky tone, "Know what I like about this place? Makes it easy to do a little skinny-dipping at night."

He felt an unaccustomed, and not really desirable, leap in his chest at that. Damn! He was already on his feet. Totally ready to strip off and follow her delectable ass into the water. Leaving all his toys here in his clothes, and once they came back there wouldn't be much way to snatch the stuff up, would there?

Among the characteristics Town shared with his father, that proved advantageous in his line of work, was the ability to make very quick decisions to take uncalculated risks. He stood up and faced her, looked straight into her eyes, and said, "How about we save that for after?"

"After, you saying?" she put a lot of arch and English on it. "After what, may I ask?"

"After all," he said, and stepped right up to her: touching her breast with his, reaching to hold that wiry waist he could almost span with his hands, lifting his thumbs to loosen her robe's terrycloth belt. "After us."

She fixed him with a steely eye, from six maddeningly scented inches away, and said, "Will you please remove your hands from my private parts, mister?"

Well, you give it your shot, he was thinking as he let his hands fall to his side and trotted out his boyish, sorry-ma'am grin. Which she wiped off quick by shrugging the robe off her shoulders and letting it slide down her to the ground. And saying, "That's better."

He actually took a step back. Taking her all in. Jesus frickin' Christ on a crutch, was his assessment. Holy freakin' shit. She smiled and tapped her foot. "Backin' off already, white meat? I kinda thought you had more developed ideas."

She stepped up to him with her hands cupped over her smooth, shaved crotch. Then cupped on his crotch. His impression was not unlike sticking his main unit into a light socket. He went to full erect position so fast he was surprised he didn't fall over from the venous pressure drop.

She smiled appreciatively. "Now, that's the kind of idea I'm talking about. Sometimes more is just damnwell more."

AFTER YOU

"**I**'d say you're nude, screwed, and tattooed," Tuan said over this shoulder. Then turned away from his workstation, with its racks of radios, computers, and possibly mad science death nukes, to say, "Old Navy expression. Picked it up from my mom."

MeiMei, dressed in bad-fitting sweats and cupping a warm mug of chai, curled on the couch as if trying to diminish the very volume of space she took up. She felt subdued and chastened, trying to damp out the shock and terror of the night by keeping things light and flippant, and not doing all that well. "I like to see a man with a hobby," she said brightly.

"Monitoring the news is sort of hobby," he told her. "Scanning police and navy bands is sort of a crime. You sure know how to pick 'em, lady."

"Well, if you'd only warned me..."

He laughed and wagged a finger at her. "Told ya, told ya."

She gave a rueful little smile and pointed to several cellular phones on the sweeping desk that seemed to take up half of this sealed-off, dehumidified bedroom: geek heaven, piled with gear and laced with no-nonsense cables. "Maybe we could call somebody. Find out..." Uh, oh; he was already shaking his head.

"Who owns Telmex?" he asked her, as if drawing a student out using Platonic methods.

"How would I know? Oh, wait, I do know. Sort of. Carlos something, also owns all the television networks."

Carlos Slim. Richest man in the world and he's a Mexican. You have any idea how deep a level of corruption and omnipotence that speaks to?"

"And he's tapping your personal phones? That's kind of flattering."

"Ronchel probably plays golf with him. Is probably related to him, *padrinos* to each other's kids, same clubs, same corporate boards, buy up the same officials and pass them around. It's how it works."

"Oh, man. Another fine kettle of fish I've gotten me into."

"I think you should just assume from this point on that any move you make will almost certainly bring you to his attention. He's combing the coast for you."

"What, the navy and cops and everybody? But he's a criminal!"

"No, he is one of a handful of the owners of the Mexican legal system. And you, apparently, assaulted him, attempted to steal his property, and killed several of his people. I'm nervous just being in the same room with you."

"And he's turned the whole countryside out after me."

"Like I said, you can pick 'em. It gets better. One of the young guys you terminated was immediate family. You apparently ran over him with a personal watercraft. Before turning it into a bomb that assaulted Rolandi's, who'd probably be the richest and most influential people on the island if Ronchel hadn't helicoptered in to direct the manhunt for you."

"Woman hunt," she said in a small, meek voice. She looked around the room, then back at Tuan, who was sipping calmly and eyeing her with patient expectation. She kept her voice calm as she said, "What am I going to do?"

"Flee," he told her flatly. "You are certainly welcome to stay here, like, indefinitely. But my guess is there will be house-to-house searches."

"*What?*"

"They have to know you bailed off that little hummer somewhere along here. They can do anything they want. I keep trying to impress that on you. Anybody he tells to do something, they'll do it, whatever it is. Whatever."

"I'm starting to get the picture." She set the cup on a pile of papers, books and gadgets that probably had a coffee table under it somewhere and drew her knees up, hugged them. For dear life, she thought. "But you said any move I make I get screwed and tattooed. The nude part they already managed."

"I noticed that right away."

He smiled softly and it warmed her somehow, like the long shower he'd treated her to before he even asked any questions, and the long, deep sleep she'd fallen into on a soft white bed in a guest bedroom. She'd slept all day, wolfed down two plates of eggs he scrambled for her, and was starting to get past the ragged edge hammered onto her by the hours of fear, by seeing Curtsy dead, feeling that boy's neck break under her feet. She looked at him for answers. There was nobody else. "So fleeing presents some problems."

"I've been working on that," he told her in the same flat professorial voice. "And I think I have it figured out. You're going to hate it."

"It's been that kind of trip."

"To cross the great water furthers," he said, trying to look owlishly Asian.

"Been there, done that," she said.

He set down his cup, stood, dusted imaginary chalk dust off his hands. "This'll probably be worse."

MeiMei skulked in the shadow of the wide porch, staring out over the bay in her baggy black clothes and slouch hat. She'd even rubbed her face with the champagne cork Tuan had scorched. Pigment envy, she thought. She wished she could get to Aphra for help. Face it, she wished she could get to her Mommy. She pointed to the end of the dock, where the trim lines of Tuan's sloop made it look like it was dancing even under moorage. "Why can't we just sail off in the Boolean?"

Tuan was standing on a table, undoing straps that snugged some long black hull to the bottom of his second story porch . He pointed further out in the bay, where small craft zoomed about and spotlights played around somewhat larger craft. "Those aren't fishermen out there," he said. "They're coastal patrol cruisers, and it looks like they have some volunteer help. Guess who they're looking for? And guess what they'd do if somebody put out at night. Especially somebody who's Navigating While Asian?"

"Well, when you put it like that..." she said, and moved to help him lower the hull. It was long, sleek, and black, with a curved, raised skeg like a surfboard. He laid if over two tables and rolled it over. She'd expected a Nanook-style kayak with a skirted cockpit, but this had a long cockpit with two seats. He pulled two double-bladed oars out of the hull and checked them out. Pointing to the pile of waterproofed nylon sacks on one of the tables, he said, "Stow them there in the stern. Push them as far back as you can."

She grabbed a sack, which he'd apparently packed while she slept, anticipating her decision. She dumped it into the hull and started tamping it back into the tapered cavity as he did the same with the other pile of aqua-luggage. It just seemed like a lot of stuff. She said, "How long is it going to take us to get over there to the mainland, anyway? I hope you put in my flannels for shuffleboard."

He pulled his head and arm out of the forward portion of the hull and grabbed another sack of canned goods. "The mainland won't do. I told you: it's not Isla you have to escape from, it's Mexico."

"So we're going to paddle to... Where? Cuba? Key West?"

"Belize."

Oh. Well that made sense. But then what? Suddenly she realized she didn't care what then, didn't want to think about it or know about it. For the first time since childhood she just dumped the responsibility for taking care of MeiMei Chiang onto somebody else's shoulders and bought a ticket for the ride. If felt surprising good, actually.

MeiMei was getting into the rhythm, stroking in a gliding cadence with Tuan, who sat behind her in his own blackface/ninja get-up moving his paddle right behind hers in a sort of rotary water ballet as the long black hull slid across the dark water. They'd left an hour after nightfall to get some distance before moonrise, and hugged the coast all the way to the point. As she heard the thrashing, sucking sound of the currents rounding South Point, she realized that it was Land's End: they were leaving terra firma, and also any illusion of shelter or safety. Once again she was putting out to open sea with dangerous pursuers somewhere behind. This could get old, she was thinking.

No such thoughts concerning Tuan DeTomaso, however. Man, what a guy. Had anybody ever, in her life, stepped up so utterly and effortlessly? Putting his own butt on the line for her, too, she assumed, though he'd been circumspect about that part of it. It's almost like he was just waiting for her to walk into his life. Cut that out, Mei, she told herself.

"You seem really prepared for this," she said over her shoulder. "Are you some fugitive, too? Always ready to bolt off in your eskiboat?"

"Well, I do a bit of cruising and camping in it," he said, "The lucky thing was that I had any clothes to fit you."

If you want to call this fitting me, she thought. And they had the faint odor of Some Other Female.

"But actually," he went on, speaking in the same unconsciously hushed tones people use when fishing off piers at night. "I always had this dream of fleeing by night, chased by evil antagonists, in the company of a beautiful woman."

That stopped her, but she didn't want to let the thought hang there too long.

"And I finally showed up."

"Yep. So I guess you'll have to do."

She was about to make some cute response when she felt the boat rock under her, then roll sideways. Then there was a blurred moment ending up with another plunge into black water. She struggled, trapped as her own buoyancy pressed her up into the confines of the hull. Then hands grabbed her, pulled her out... and clamped tightly over her mouth.

INVERSE PROPORTIONS

MeiMei's face emerged from the water and she gulped air through her nose. Tuan's hand was still tight over her mouth. She was in a close-feeling cavity, darker than the night itself. She felt Tuan take one of her hands and guide it to a hard, rounded grip. The kayak, she realized. He flipped it over and they were underneath it, inside it.

He spoke calm and low into her ear, "Don't make any noise, okay? Hold on to that and start swimming straight ahead, pushing it."

She nodded and he released her. She put both hands on the inverted cockpit rim and started doing a frog kick, pushing the boat along ahead of her. She felt it move faster as Tuan joined his propulsion to hers. In a voice barely loud enough to be heard, she said, "So they spotted us?"

"They were about to, I'd say. They'll still see us, but I don't think they'll pay much attention."

As he spoke, she saw the dark hull around them glow slightly, the black-painted fiberglass translucent to a powerful spotlight beam. Now that was scary. She almost laughed out loud at that. You've been stripped by goons, had a gun shoved down your throat, threatened with undersized rape, chased by water-bikers... and a *light* was scary? She realized what the light was revealing to the Marines or mafia or whoever was out there: a sleek black shape with dorsal fin, moving forward at about the right speed. She wished they could dive.

"Is that why you put that fin on top?"

"On the bottom, actually. No, it's an ongoing experiment in hydrodynamics. Find the right size and shape to stabilize your course without interfering with turning. It just happened to end up looking like Flipper. Or a shark fin, I suppose. I hope not."

MeiMei wondered why that would matter, then it hit her. You're a bored sailor or cop cruising at night on a wild goose chase, holding a machine gun... and you spot a shark. What do you do?

"Well, actually," Tuan went on, sensing her tension, "Not 'just happened to'. The shapes of the natural world obey and utilize the same physical logic as the ones we engineer. Resemblances are hardly co-incidences."

But MeiMei was still a little hung up on the idea that people might still be trying to gun her down.

"Jesus, they really are looking all over for us. For me, anyway."

"Go with 'us'. If they catch you, I'm just going to become an inconvenient bystander. Disposable."

"Are you serious?"

"Are we swimming in dark seas trying to avoid capture by armed men or did I get it all wrong?"

"And they might just shoot us up anyway. Any second."

"In the midst of life..."

"This would be a pretty weird place to die."

"Most people worry more about the time factor."

"I'm site-oriented. A professional deformity."

"Well, time's all relative, anyway." And not to change the subject, Tuan thought, but let's do. "We're not in the spotlight anymore. I'm going to duck out and take a look-see. Don't wander off."

"I'll be in the forward stateroom. Please send up some tea."

"Okay, but no entertaining in your room."

Then he was gone. She could feel the sudden absence of his breath, of the air space his head had occupied. She kept stroking along. I'm the motor of a fake dolphin, she thought. You know who would love this? A quick pang of hurt and memory flashed over her. Damn! Dead in the water. Well, let's just hope he doesn't go two for two.

Then Tuan was back. entering the little space silently. "They've moved off, but are still too close for us to get righted. We'll just keep dog-paddling away for awhile. We've got all night."

She kicked along for a few minutes, leaning her head against the underside of the deck while scissoring her legs. Got all night. Great. Then what? She said, "What you said about time being relative? How can that be? I mean in real-world terms?"

Tuan chuckled, glad to see her distracted from their current perils. "You know what Einstein said about a minute on a hot stove seeming like an hour?"

"Did he mention padding underwater while waiting to get shot up?"

"Actually his example was an hour seeming like a minute while kissing a pretty girl."

She let that hang for a minute. Was she catching this guy's eye? Well, hardly the time and place for that. Relatively or not. "But how can that be? Time is... well, it's what the world is organized on."

"In archaeology textbooks, yes. All those little charts and time lines and dating and all. But not in physics texts, no."

"But..." she thought about it for a few seconds. Hmm. "But what else is the world structured on?"

"Well, you've got your matter, of course. Most people would sort of pick that as what things are built of."

"And it's relative, too, right?"

"Both factors of the speed of light. Which is also relative."

"The Mayans were obsessed with time."

"So they carved it into stone, right? Tried to nail it down and own it. Can't be done. I mean in, you know, universal terms."

"By nailing down matter."

"The human impulse. Every molecule on earth with its own deed and legal title. Monsanto has patents on biochemicals that occur naturally in the soil."

She nodded, unseen in the total darkness under the turtled hull. After a minute, Tuan heard her giggle.

"Lots of people find that Monsanto thing funny. I've thought about building a stand-up routine around it."

"No, I was just thinking. We look like a dolphin moving along here. What if some male dolphin sees us and decides to mate with us?"

Tuan laughed softly, glad to see her mood lightening. "So is getting mated by dolphins a big concern for you?" He realized instantly it had been *a faux pas.*

"Not as much as some people I know," MeiMei said glumly. "Knew, I guess."

"The Dolphin Discovery girl?"

"Yeah. Curtsy. And I guess that's how everybody will think of her. If they ever do. Perfect tombstone epitaph: 'Dolphin Discovery Girl'."

But she won't have a tombstone, will she, MeiMei thought. What was it she said, herself? "If you screw up, you're crab chow." She couldn't think of that beautiful, lively body sloshed limp across the seabed, nibbled by animals. And reduced to bone, then to calcium dust, she reflected. Pressed down by more of it, becoming part of the limestone slab of the Yucatan. Maybe that was better than being dropped down in a box.

Her silence resounded in the close dark of the inverted hull, and Tuan could guess its source. He hoped he could lift her out of that. Hell, he hoped he could keep her from getting killed in some gruesome way by the remnants of Mexico's "Perfect Dictatorship."

He counted off a hundred frog kicks before saying, "You've had a really rough time. And it's going to stay rough for awhile. We'll be able to turn upright and start paddling pretty soon. And once we make the shore, we'll blend in with the vacationers along the Kukulkan strip. The further south we get, the easier it'll be. Once we're in Belize, you'll be safe and things are really beautiful. It's going to get better. Okay?"

"Then what? Can I come back to Mexico? Ever? My work is here. How will I get out of Belize without any money or a passport?"

"I brought a lot of money. Which gets accepted as a passport if you pick your spot. Belize has airports and borders with other countries. But don't worry about that. For now just take it day by day. Hour to hour until daylight, actually."

Just take it as it comes, she thought. Paddling through paradise with this guy. Not the worst fate in the world. "Thanks, Tuan. Thanks for everything."

"I told you. You're my fantasy come true. Thank me once we get out of this pickle."

I think that can be arranged, she thought. She continued to kick steadily, each time she spread her legs wide, then thrust them back together giving her a subtle reminder that Tuan was right behind her. One kick at a time, MeiMei.

SHOP TALK

Oddly enough, Aphra was thinking, it was kind of good for me, too. Almost makes me see why so many other girls would want to screw with these penis-bearers. She rolled on her side and reached out to tousle a thick handful of curly caramel hair, smile back into the wide blue eyes that were regarding her with a flattering air of wonder. Put it this way, she thought, I just wish every time I had to get jam up and jelly tight with some breedin' fool it was as easy to put up with as this one. You put in your day's work, might as well be in attractive surroundings. And vice versa.

And work is what it was looking like. She affirmed that on her little trip to the can to slip into something more comfortable. No sooner turned on her top-of-the-line TruthSeeker than it started telling her the tale. Which was Agent Blue Eyes had been out there reading her gear like an old magazine in the dentist office. So he was a job now. Or at least she was his job, which was the same thing.

Still, though. It wasn't that creepy being in bed with this cat. He was a real hose-monster once he got loose to it, but mostly he was just so damn gorgeous. She could have done a photo album on his abs alone. His *asshole* was cute, for cryin' out loud. Like a little pink chrysanthemum. They were wasted on each other.

But the big thing was, and this was starting to really get up on its hind legs and worry her mind around: he was "in the life". On somebody's varsity somewhere, was her estimation. Possibly not unrelated to a recent hymie rat deserting the Big Ship. That was kind of exciting in itself.

She shared that with Townsend, like so many other things. She didn't have anybody to talk to either. Her sex life was as empty and transient as his was. She also longed for some vague image of sitting around talking shop to somebody as good as herself (like there was any of that around), somebody you could go nuts in bed with, then giggle about the intricacies of turning folk out and selling their ass down. She was actually pretty good at snap risk-taking, too.

"Hey, look here, honkyshines. I kind of like your act. Makes me wanna come a little clean, you know. Tell you the tale."

Townsend couldn't wait to hear this one, pushed up to lean on one elbow and give her his undivided. As she made a performance art masterpiece out of standing up, stretching and padding towards the bathroom. "Soon as I get back."

The door was still clicking shut when Townsend came up off the bed in a smooth uncoiling of long muscles. He fished his gizmojo from his pants pocket and the Men In Black spex out of his shirt in less than two seconds. And did what you do with super-expensive, over-designed dirty tricks like that: spied.

Her robe read null, but he caught the e-glow from a vase on the dresser. Lead glazed pottery: good thinking, SuperFreak. But soooooo last year. It wasn't interesting anyway, now that his proximity let him cop full disclosure. It was about the same as what he had, purely feed read. So she was already onto him. He could bug it, and maybe even so she wouldn't find it, but why bother? The big news was still over there in the bedstand drawer. He went back to the bed, watching numbers and indicators bounce around on the lenses, amber digitals superimposed over the dusky view of the room through the multi-coated dark glass.

Oh, yeah. It was reading as a GPS, but that was just a ruse his cadge-gadget was all over from go. Tracking. Very long range tracking. Augmented by satellite feed from... not a familiar registry, but it didn't matter. She was keeping tabs on somebody using a cloaked tracer he couldn't have bought with five years pay. He sweated out the 'sponder tumbling the crypt, already hearing a muted toilet flush behind him. There it was! He pushed the fake Apple selector wheel twice and glommed the target co-ordinates and register. He was back in bed, the shades and iSpy under the mattress in one catlike move, just as she came out and stood there with the light behind her. He locked his hands behind his head and laid back to stare at her with unfeigned pleasure and admiration.

When she quit posing and flicked the light off to come back to the thrashed, reeking bed, he said, "You were saying something about secrets and making a clean breast?"

"Clean breast? What you think I was in the bathroom for, honey?" She leaned over to place a thick purplish nipple in his mouth. "Taste clean from where you sitting?"

He gave it a noisy kiss and patted the bed beside him. "I'm all ears."

She crawled up the bed on all fours, swishing her tail like a panther. Sliding down beside him, she grabbed a handful of very attentive genital. "All ears? That what you calling this business here?"

"I'm still holding that thought."

"Yeah, well, see..." she paused, staring blankly at the meaty shaft in her hand. "You ever heard of Oracon?"

"Cleans clogged drains as it slays household pests?"

She shook his meat briskly enough to hurt a little, "Don't play that shit. Like I said, it's time for keepin' real."

"Yeah, I've heard of it. A think tank." He paused just long enough for her to scowl slightly, then continued. "It says here. Actually they're pretty much the blue chip outfit in industrial espionage. Spooks R us."

"No honey, case you didn't notice, spooks B me. Both kinds."

"And you decided to tell me this. Because high-grade professional snoops always have a deep-seated urge to blurt it out to whoever they're fucking."

She gave a full, titty-jiggling laugh at that. "Only when I'm in bed with a colleague," she chortled. "Who's about one second from getting kicked out of said bed."

"Okay, you made me."

"I sure did, sweetie. Got tired of waiting for you to put the make on me."

'OK, here we are. White spy and black spy, just like that cartoon. What now?"

"What *now*? We *rap*, niggah! We talk about the shit we pull. When was the last time you talked about that crap to anybody? Much less a woman?"

He'd been thinking that same thing, hadn't he? Pretty much same time he was socking it to that little cheerleader from Michigan or wherever. Hmmmm.

"Okay. You got it. You're all over it like static cling. So where do we start? How about at the beginning? I think I got some issues there."

"Issues, huh? Well, the beginning is always good. For openers, you know."

"See I got into this because my old man was into it. He was like this star. Worked like CIA, Secret Service, DEA, you name it. I didn't really think about doing anything else. Well, pro ball for awhile. Might have worked. Or might not have. I was practically recruited before I was out of high school."

"Damn, child. What's the chances? I got same kinda shit going on. Did, anyway. My mama wasn't just a 'lefty', wasn't just 'radical'. She was like a Movement unto her own self. Fuck whitey in every aperture at once, you know? So I was learning about weapons and stashing shit and funny money and trailing drops right out of the crib. I was spyin' before I was in high school. Used to pick up cops and sound them for information. Or let them make a move, then use it to twist them up. How you like these pictures of you with your hand up a thirteen year-old's skirt, Mister Pig? Wonder can they print the whole thing in the newspaper or have to crop out the good stuff?"

"So you pioneered that whole 'Bust A Diddler' TV show? Out-predatored their asses?"

"Best you know it. I did my first industrial spy-by when I was seventeen. On my own hook, too. The Mama would've hit the fan if she knew I was whoring my talents out after capital instead of some righteous bullshit." She lay back on the pillow, unconsciously mimicking his hands-behind-head posture, stared at the ceiling. "I cooked it up, walked in and sold it to some Ofay idiot wouldn't a thought of it in a million years. And even yet, only reason he hired me for it was hopin' it might snow in hell sometime and he'd get into my pants."

"Man." Townsend breathed. "Man, oh man. Know what, I'm going to hit the washroom a minute and sort this out in my head."

She watched the way he sort of uncurled out of the bed, the clench of buttocks as he moved towards the bath. "This might shock you," he said from the door. "But you're not quite like my usual date."

"Mine, neither," she said as the door closed behind him.

COASTER BREAKS

"**L**ook up, smile, and wave." Which was the opposite of what MeiMei had been doing. But she lifted her head to look at the hovering helicopter, so close its downwash was ruffling the water on the off side of Tuan's kayak. Gave them the beauty pageant smile and window-wiper wave she hadn't used since she was Miss Academic in the Miss International District contest her sophomore year. The chopper bobbed in what might have been a return salutation, and moved down the coast, perhaps seeking more smiles, waves and cleavage shots from tourists frolicking in front of the big hotels.

"When you're hiding, it seems like everybody is after you," Tuan said. "So you end up acting like somebody they're looking for."

MeiMei continued to paddle in the oddly lilting rhythm she'd picked up and honed during the hours of skimming across the dark water of the Bay. Interrupted by two repetitions of the turtle/dolphin gambit. With the coming of daylight, they'd hugged close to the hotel zone, blending in among swimmers and players with other expensive water toys. MeiMei had so far exchanged waves with three jetskiers, two paddle boats, several other kayaks, and some weird AquaTrike that looked like a lunar lander with huge fishing floats for wheels.

"You seem to have some experience in this whole fugitive thing," she said to Tuan over her shoulder. "Is there a one-armed man in your life?"

"Just one more example of generalism," he replied. "And of course I've been a fugitive from the laws of thermodynamics for years."

"On the lam from the Entropy Cops?"

"As are we all. In the end they corner you when you're too feeble or stupid or unlucky and then these withered old people—or maybe splattered stiffs—take you in hand and lead you back to homeostasis."

MeiMei laughed. It was kind of fun carrying on conversations with a man she couldn't see. With Tuan seated behind her, matching her waterbug paddle strokes like some sort of Chinese sync teamster, she didn't have to maintain eye contact, didn't have to make appropriate facial expressions, could just talk and listen to his fascinating line of gab. It's like the internet, she thought: pure expression with no meat involved.

She glanced down to see if the sun was getting to her skin yet. They hadn't exactly had time to apply emollients while fleeing the forces of justice, homeostasis and rape/murder/artifact theft. Not to worry, her arms already had some tan and she was catching some shade from the brim of the big ugly cloth hat Tuan had given her. The hat that could be twisted down into some moebius disk that sprang out into a hat because it had a wire sewed around the brim. Perfect topper for a generalist/inventor/geek. And her neck was protected by the bright yellow T-shirt stuffed under the hat, but draped around her shoulders. Covering her hair, was the main point there. At last, she had thought, I'm a sought-after blonde. Fortunately the arrangement of the T-shirt didn't show its logo, a dweeb on a beach sporting a huge bulge in his trunks, a bevy of adoring mammaries, and the legend, "Girls Love A Guy With a BIG JOHNSON". It figured to be a long day, after a long night. She was starting to get lost, she felt: her life cut down to the chase.

"Tuan, will I have a life after this insane goose-chase?" She asked over her shoulder as he did a little something with his stroke to guide them around a gleaming Donzi anchored in front of the Ritz Carlton. It had no visible passengers but was rocking in a staccato rhythm that, taking into consideration various sound effects being emitted on board, suggested that somebody was getting shtupped in the scuppers.

"Did you have one before?"

More or less, she thought. Unless you consider "life" to include a circle of friends, sex within the last year or so, romantic moments, maybe even kids and dogs and that whole bit. But hey, that's life. "Well, I had a career, anyway."

"Been there, done that. I get so much more work done since I retired. But yeah, we're going to get you out of this mess and back home."

"But I'm washed up in the country I specialized in."

"They say Cambodia is the new Mesoamerica. Archi-architecturally speaking."

"Oh, good. I'll pick up some Khmer and head right over."

"Look, you don't know how this is going to play out. That guy could get shot by a narco cartel tomorrow. Or get yacht-jacked by Somali pirates. Or he gets caught on camera and extradited to a U.S. prison for something totally unrelated. It happens."

She rather liked the pirates angle. Bet Aphra could hook that up in a jiffy. Figure out a way to get that pilfered museum off first. For about the tenth time, she felt an almost sexual yen to catalog that collection. "And aren't they overdue for another revolution or coup or something? But I guess it's one of those 'one step at a time' things."

"One stroke at a time, anyway. Exactly what I was going to suggest. The future looms less when you focus your awareness in the present. Look at this: we're paddling along in wonderful limpid water, with a great view. All those teeming idiots are paying big bucks to be here, fifty pesos an hour for kayaks. Wait until we get past the buildup, down into the biosphere reserve. It's breath-takingly beautiful."

"You're right. And thanks. Be here now, right?"

"Once you start seeing time as relative, it's a quick step over to it being illusory. Increasingly I'm starting to view the physical world in exactly the same terms I heard from this old Sufi master in Iran twenty years ago. The world is made out of attention."

"What did he mean by 'attention'?"

"Exactly what I asked him. And he said, 'Attention means attention'."

"Was he a drill sergeant? I guess that's too deep for me. Or mystic or cryptic or deficit spanned or something."

"Don't make me show you the equations."

"Any fate but that."

"This whole thing started because you wanted to find out what's beyond the end of the world, right?"

"World according to a stone calendar by a vanished civilization, anyway."

"Okay, you look around and see the world. Close your eyes and you see a lot less. Get really focused and you see more, more detail revealed as you pay closer attention. Now you go to sleep. What happened to your world?"

"It stepped out for lunch with that lonely forest tree and the refrigerator light. So this is one of those subjective/objective things?"

"That's a distinction that's been falling apart ever since Heisenberg's Uncertainty Principle."

"You sound pretty sure of that."

"Absolutely certain of Uncertainty." He smiled happily, watching her flex and reflex in front of him, her flawless cocoa skin glistening slightly from the heat of the sun. Fun companion for The Lam, he thought. And feeds me straight lines: I like that in a woman. "So what are you paying attention to while you're asleep?"

"I don't have dreams," she said. Then quickly added, "I mean, I don't remember them if I do."

"So what's the difference, then? Somebody watches a needle plotting a graph of your brain rhythms and clocks your eye movement and concludes you're in there swinging aboard a Viking ship full of clowns and naked schoolteachers, but just don't know it."

"Yeah, I guess. I have trouble with the Deepak Chapra view of physics, but I can see it about time, I guess. We kind of made time up ourselves, didn't we?"

"We didn't make up days and years, but hours and minutes are completely artificial. But I guess I'm saying something like, let's say you're drifting down into sleep. Your view of material things is fading out, sounds are dropping off into silence, your speech ability is going to nothing, maybe you're talking nonsense to yourself. Thoughts slowing and winking out. All your charts of the world are crashing down to the zero ordinate. Where's the zero point, your end of time?"

She thought about that for awhile, then stopped thinking about it. She took his advice and drank in the scenery, the pleasure of the slick knifing motion of their boat, the calming rhythm of paddling; like a physical mantra moving forward by means of the rotary swing of paddles. Her arms pulling the paddle around the air/water like a geometric cone, an hourglass of movement with its motionless center directly in front of her solar plexus. This is now, that's then, she thought.

After about ten minutes Tuan spoke again. "Once we're south of the airport we'll put into a little mangrove hole I spotted last year. Eat, get some sleep. I think we'll take the next leg of this little jaunt by night."

"Works for me," she said. "Day, night, what the hell? Merrily, merrily, merrily, life is but a dream."

Tuan tsked disapprovingly. "Just row, row, row your boat."

CATCHING HER DRIFT

She was hanging suspended. There was no time, no space, no future or past. No more pain.

Rising and falling, a face looking sightless at the stars, surrounded by a sargasso of gold hair streaked with blood. Naked, mindless, a child of the currents and swells.

Then came the nip on her ankle.

Then the slickery slide around her legs, the caressing brush by her buttocks, the playful nudges in her stomach, then her groin.

Then the big, muscular body surging up from beneath her, forcing her dangling legs apart. The tensile fin raking across her crotch.

And her eyes opened again.

Slowly, she moved her arms forward, dragging through the resistance of the water, moving like sluggish bottom creatures, all soft and slow. She felt a slight touch at her knees, then the sleek torso rubbing up her abdomen, rubbing her breasts as she moved her arms around into a barely conscious hug. A hug she held for a long moment, clamping herself to that big, streamlined body. Then she was pulled underwater, a quick shallow dive that shocked her awake, brought her to the surface coughing and sputtering. She loosened her embrace and looked at the conical head riding the surface, nudging her throat, laughing at her. "Bongo!" she yelled. "You made it!"

There was no hint of her directing anything or calling any shots. After she had greeted the whole pod one by one—the males crowding playfully in, the females reticent, but sliding by to greet her, Mayab nuzzling her head, concerned about the bullet furrow—they started moving away and she rolled prone in the dark water to attempt to move with them. She was stiff, weak, finless. Pinoccio, the big alpha, pressed up from below her, sliding under her stomach. She grabbed on, letting her hands slide back to the base of his flippers, extending her elbows until she lay on his back, head beside the dorsal fin. And he moved out in a powerful lunge, his flexing trunk moving beneath her chest. His pistoning flukes brushed her calves until she raised her legs to the surface, trailing widespread as he led the pod west.

She'd ridden Caruso and Bruto and Bongo, lying in rapture on their backs. They'd come for her! She hugged them tight to her heart as fragments of the night came back, crashing into her head unbidden. Those cocksuckers had left her for dead! And God knows what they were doing to MeiMei. She'd shot some of them. Good. They'd left her dead in the water! But her true friends, her real lovers, had come for her. She shuddered on the undulating back, salt tears streaming down into the sea. They came to rescue her!

A hour later, she was laughing into the night, howling at the moon. The instep of her left foot was pressed against Pinoccio's fin, the right foot on the throbbing back of Yaqui, standing erect with spread legs as they blasted her forward through the night like a water-skier. They'd done this dozens of times at Discovery, Curtsy's looks and figure quickly vaulting her into the showpiece slot for riding on dolphin beaks. But this new pose worked better for long hauls and the beasts were practically frisking with the fun of romping her across the water like a moonlit golden goddess.

They passed a small boat, very low in the water, and the people seemed really excited as she blew past, waving. Later she waved to a fisherman, who damned near fell out of his boat. They were close to shore then, she could feel it. When she could see the dark shadow of land, strung with human lights like a diadem of sparks, she looked for landmarks. And finally made out the park at Tulum, the unmistakable ruins. When she saw the lacy white break line at the reef she jumped off the backs of Guido and Bruto, almost pulling off a flip before hitting the water.

They were all around her at once, whistling and nudging. She laughed and stroked them all, slapping the guys on their melons or shoulders. "This has been so great, guys. I wish I could just take off with you, hang out forever. Come back when I've got my fin, okay?"

Pinoccio bumped up under urgently, but she chuckled and disengaged.

"I can't let you take me inside the reef, there, guys. There's already going to be fishing boats out and they blast around at top speed inside there. And they might even shoot you." She waggled a scolding finger, "You keep biting fish out of their nets, you're not making any friends."

Finally, she swam towards the reef, which was close to the surface at this low tide, getting nudged and bumped and felt up the whole way. Once her feet brushed the reef, she knew they wouldn't follow her any further. She could make it in from here easy. Get some clothes and food and... They Came For Her!

She paddled until she hit a gnarly coral head, found footing on it and stood up, raising her out of the water from her nipples on up. She clapped her hands and saw a dozen beaks break water, looking at her. She felt like singing them a song. She blew kisses and waved, "Good bye, dudes. And you're welcome for all the fish."

She made it about halfway to shore, tiring and in a dicey state of mind as she did her lazy crawl. So the panga was on top of her as soon as she heard it.

She reacted too slow, diving as deep as she could, but not deep enough to avoid the bottom skeg of an outboard motor hitting her head and grooving the scalp right down to the bone, like a plow. For the second time in eight hours she drifted like a corpse; tawny naked flotsam the waves hustled towards the beach south of Tulum.

HALFWAY MEASURES

It's a little pretentious, don't you think?"
"So fire the architect."

MeiMei chuckled. She kept thinking she'd run out of awe and wonder at the "Mayan Riviera" coast she was seeing from Tuan's kayak and was starting to toss out contrary remarks just to see how he'd get them back over the net. "I mean, 'Sian Ka'an Biosphere Reserve'? It's, what, a couple of acres of Mexico and they're talking about having a very special reserve on the whole biosphere?"

"I think they're hoping to get a patent on the life forms," Tuan replied. Not that it'll help them with all the pirating going on."

"PhylaPirates of the Caribbean. Johnny Depp and Michael Moore together at last."

"I've come down here just to see birds," Tuan said. "It's amazing. I've been trying to formulate a theory of latitudinal pigmentation."

"And you haven't yet? I'm astounded." She'd heard a lot of his general theories over the past days, his restless mind trying to tie everything up into larger and larger packages.

"These things take time. Those equation theories are easy. But there has to be some factor behind the fact that the closer you get to the equator the more color the biosphere flaunts. At the poles everything's in black and white: your penguins and polar bears and such."

"Orca," MeiMei added. She'd been awed by the huge fish as a girl in Seattle. Infatuated, maybe. That whole idea led her to a place it was too sad to go, though, so she chatted brightly, instead. "Formal wear. In keeping with the cooler emotional state of high latitude numbers."

"The temperate zones; a lot of brown and gray and earth colors. The slightest flash of color, like a robin's breast, and people get all excited. But down here? My God."

"I see what you mean," MeiMei said thoughtfully. "And it's everything, isn't it? The fish are Day-Glo, the birds look like a Peter Max fantasy, the flowers almost glow in the dark."

"So why? I always assume there's a reason."

"Even people," she teased. "Everybody's hunched over in Minneapolis and Seattle, with their loden green Gore-Tex parkas and black raincoats. By the time they clear the airport here they're wearing shirts and bathing suits that would blind a Hawaiian."

"It's hard to find an evolutionary advantage to going around flaunting bright colors in everybody's face. Sort of the opposite of protective coloration."

"I assume it's all about sex, somehow."

"Everything is; isn't that what they tell us?"

"Well, it's certainly a motivator." Or is it, she was thinking. She'd gotten the idea that Tuan had been at least somewhat taken by her, and she was certainly willing to move in his general direction. But so far this trip had been pretty tame in that regard. The general feel of flight from danger had faded and now it was just a routine of racking up miles, sometimes at night, sometimes by day. They had taken turns sleeping in the boat, leaning over the deck in a decidedly uncomfy posture. They had put into hidden inlets and grabbed snoozes on cusps of sand, slathered in bug spray. They had actually tented out last night: in addition to oodles of very good chow, Tuan had brought a tent and light cotton sleepsacks, it turned out. But sleeping with

Tuan around hadn't led to even an intimation of "sleeping with Tuan". White knight syndrome? Was her breath bad? Was he as gay as he looked? Stay tuned. And avoid leading comments.

"There's a devious attractor in there somewhere," he said. "And it'll turn up. Meanwhile, I just enjoy it."

"Me too. This is incredible." The Riviera to the North had been stunning in it's way, but so much of it was high rise hotels and resorts these days. Most of which they'd slipped by at night, often a half mile offshore. But this was Raw Nature On Parade. Beach backed by sheer jungle, inlets teeming with life, aflutter with birds. If nothing else, it would be a trip she'd remember vividly the rest of her life. Which she had evidently decided would continue at some point because she found herself thinking ahead at times, especially when Tuan was silent, just stroking behind her like a machine. And frankly, it was starting to look like things were going to be very different in that future that would arrive once they paddled through enough of this screaming, travel-poster beauty.

"It's not just the natural aspects, either. There are over twenty-five ruins inside the reserve, some of them fairly significant."

"I'm not too hot on ruins and antiquity lately, OB. Sorry." What it was, she got too frustrated and bummed out thinking about it. And knew that until she got her camera somewhere to see the glyphs on the jade plaque nothing she'd studied would really be all that significant to her own general theorizing. The Future was trumping The Past for the first time since undergrad.

He nodded. That was why she hadn't cared about cutting past Tulum at night, he thought. And hasn't even mentioned archaeology the whole time. It's gotten ugly for her, or she's moving past it. He took a good look at her, the slim body sun-browned to the point that she looked darker than most Mexicans, even than the Mayans. Good. He wished he could bleach her hair or something, but the hats and towels were working. He felt a strong impulse to reach out and stroke the cleft between the long muscles of her back. She was truly exquisite. But he'd decided anything like that would wait. He wasn't going to hit on her while he was still trying to keep her alive. Take her on the rebound from fear and death. He had a feeling that would keep, anyway. Just a feeling. Nothing theoretical.

He spoke in the tone she'd learned meant, Take a look at that. "See the inlet there?"

She could make out the green streak of water, a tiny gap in the trees she had learned would widen as they approached, open up to the basins of brackish water that were the font of so much of the wildlife proliferation around them. "It looks bigger than the one at Xel Ha. Maybe the biggest we've seen?"

Tuan laughed. "To say the least. It's the mouth of Ascension bay. Huge. We've actually been cruising along beside a big finger of it for miles. Right behind that peninsula."

"Is there a town?" She'd come to associate towns with hassles, with snapping back from footloose waterbug tourists to fugitives.

"On the far side. Puerto Madero. I think we'll just cut straight across."

"Good. Will the town be a problem?"

I'm trying to figure the timing to pass it at night. I can get a better handle on that once I see it across the lagoon."

"It's been a long time since we saw a boat."

"Good news, right? I have a hard time thinking they're patrolling this far south, but I sure don't want some drug patrol craft to radio in that they've spotted a couple of *Chinos* in a kayak. If it was high season we'd be seeing all sorts of tour boats, other kayaks. That's why we're running this by day. Tourist kayaks are common here. But not so much at night."

"I was thinking when that squall hit us yesterday." That had been a little scary. In fact MeiMei was well aware that if she'd been alone, without Tuan's steady hand on the steering and steady voice behind her ears, that little tantrum of wind and shoulder-high waves would have scared the crap out of her. Which could get messy in a kayak. "What if a hurricane came up?"

"Too early for that. September a long shot. October, not such a long shot. But they aren't that common even during the season."

"What would we do?"

"A really big blow? Head out to sea and balls it out like men."

She bumped her paddle against the side of the boat on her backswing, a little kayak gesture she'd picked up.

"Anything big enough to really, like, you know, kill us, and I'd haul into shore, pull the boat well into the bush, lash it down, get underneath it. Have a little hurricane party. If we were near a town, I think I'd just put in, leave the boat and catch a bus south, maybe rent

a car. They'd have a lot more on their minds than us at that point.
Cross into the free trade zone on a shopping excursion bus, pay off
some border guys to let us cross into Belize proper from there."

That was what kept her calm, she thought. He already has a plan
even for something totally unlikely. And couched in details. Details
that expand her awareness of her current situation. Good guy to
have around.

"But what I was going to say," Tuan continued his train of thought,
"Is that it means we're now halfway to the border.

MeiMei looked ahead, saw only more incredible turquoise sea,
sugar white beach, violently green vegetation. Under too-blue sky
and slowly piling thunderheads out to sea. How about that? she
thought. Halfway there.

SECRET ASIAN MAN

Denny Mercer sized up the Worthy Oriental Gentleman who'd
moved stealthily into his office. If the tattoos peeking out
at the cuffs and throat of the bespoke Nathan Road suit, the two
missing fingers, and the Dragon Lady slinking in behind him hadn't
been a clue to this being a major Triad warrior, the outline of the
oh-so-concealed hatchet under his burly arm would have been the
big tip-off. Denny looked up at him coolly, if not actually coolie, and
spoke around the crumpled unfiltered Camel, "I suppose you're the
longest dong in the Hong Kong tong?"

Narrowing his already narrow eyes, the sinister Celestial nodded
with understated menace and pushed his calling card across the desk.
Of course his real calling card would be one of the shirikin stars in the
glove leather sheath up his sleeve. Denny got ready to bust a move.

Meanwhile, in real time: Denny slouched in his chair concealing
the still-smoldering roach of the spliff he'd just obliterated, staring
through glazed pupils at the slightly-built, middle-aged Chinese
guy in work clothes and his dumpy, shuffling wife. It's not like he
really owes you any explanations, but it's a boring job and Denny is
prone towards a rich fantasy life. It's why he become a Confidential
Investigator in the first place and doing the computer skip-tracing

and photo peeps that Seattle offers to freelance snoops hadn't slaked that impulse toward the melodramatic, so he trips out a lot. Weed just aggravating the situation.

He picked up the card. Roosevelt Chiang, Landscape Consultant. He eyed Roosevelt and his wife, who immediately dropped her eyes and shrank a few inches. "Let me guess," he said slowly. "You want me to find something or somebody?"

Both nodded, Chiang keeping modest eye contact. "My daughter."

"I do that," Denny said wearily. "But I gotta tell you a few things up front."

The two Chinese stood motionless and expressionless, staring. Denny motioned towards the two rather beat-up wooden straight chairs in front of his dilapidated desk. He had shopped carefully for banged-around furniture he felt reflected a proper P.I. office. The hatrack had been the hardest to find. "Please, take a seat," he said in his professional tones. "Can I offer you coffee? Water?" Lapsong Souchon tea in a paper-thin porcelain cup, perhaps?

The couple shook heads in unison, but sat and continued to regard him blankly. Fresh off the sampan, was Denny's offhand estimation. "Number one: I can give you three addresses right now. A donut shop on Capital Hill, a coffee shop—slash crackhouse—in the U. District and this weird sort of tea and mp3/anime joint behind Uwajimaya in the I.D. You cruise those places every night for a week and I bet you spot your kid."

Not a peep or blink out of PapaSan and MamaSan.

"Two: if I take the file, first thing I'm going to do is turn you inside-out for any child abuse reports. If you see what I'm carefully not implying here. Sorry to put that out in front of your wife."

"She not speak English."

Oh, not as eloquently as you? There's a surprise. "So are you new in town?" Town, in the sense of, The Occident.

"No. Thirty one year here. Just not talk much to..."

Roundeye demons. "I understand. What I meant, though, where'd you come up with my name? It's not like I run bilingual ads in the International Observer. Turns out the characters for my name are some smutty pun."

"Oh, same almost everybody. Chinese very fun language."

A raff a minute, all light. "So, were you referred?"

"No need. I already know you great master. You smart, figure things out."

Whoa, great master. Cooooool. "Uh, sorry, but are you kidding me a little there?"

"Not joke. You same Dennis Mercer, best Guest Guesser."

That one ground Denny's wheels to a halt. Yes, he was an avid player of the Post Intelligencer's football prognostication contest. And he'd excelled, having played it every year since the Seahawks cranked up with Largent and Zorn and Smilin' Jack. He did well calling the college games, but was murder on the pros, especially AFC. In fact. betting on the NFL in the Frigate Tavern made him more money each year than his P.I. business. He'd been in the Top Five fourteen times and had won two of the grand prize trips to Superbowls, more than any other guesser in King County. Well, actually tied for first with some guy named... WHOA!

He snatched the card up and looked at again. Omigod. He regarded the inscrutable client and said, "There's an R. Chiang here in town, you know. He's the top guesser, drives me nuts."

"Not top," Chiang replied modestly, even bowing slightly. "Your humble student."

"Holy Cannoli! Amazing!" Denny slammed his chair down and ran around the desk with his hand sticking out, then changed his mind and gave the same deep bow that he'd gotten from the pair when they came in. "Man, this is great. Hey, how do you do that, anyway?"

"Game very interesting. I study."

"I hope to shout, you study. But how can you barely speak English... due respect... and manage to read the Raiders upsetting the Chargers in December?"

"Charger linebackers very low morale following arrest. Opportunity for new tight end. Need prove himself fast or back to selling cars. He play for same college as JaMarcus for two years."

"But he wasn't supposed to suit up for that game."

"He clear waiver very fast. Dolphins need salary cap. Groundskeepers at McAfee Stadium know things, tell me."

Gawd, the lawnmower spy network, no less. "But how'd you get the Giants over the Patriots? Nobody saw that coming."

"You saw coming."

"Yeah, but I... and hey, you were three points closer calling the score. Come on, how'd you do it?"

"Have black belt in Guess-Fu from Monastery in Chou Wei mountain province."

Denny rocked back, his butt hitting the desk, and stared.

Chiang gave a sliver smile and said, "Now I make joke. We from Taiwan. Fortune smile on me one day, on you some other day."

Denny laughed. "Look we should get together sometime, talk..."

"Yes, very nice, you come to my house. But my daughter. Hard to concentrate with baby girl lost."

"Well, don't you worry about that, Mr. Chiang. I'm on it like white on lice."

"Good. Tell me how much, I give check now. Fortune smiling on you now, find my girl."

"You bet. She's as good as found Mr. Chiang."

"Friends call Rosie. My wife, Emily."

"An honor to meet you both." Denny moved behind the desk and poised at his keyboard. "Your daughter's name?"

"May Flower Chiang. But everyone call her MeiMei."

Imagine that, Denny thought as he typed in the name. "Age?"

"Twenty seven."

Baby girl. Okay. "When did you last see her?"

"Three weeks she not call. She always call twice a week when she out of country."

Out of country. Aw, shit. He looked up and said, "We might have to discuss some prepayment of expenses."

Chiang nodded. "I understand. She call from Mexico. State of Quintana Roo. Place Che Tu Mal."

Wherever the hell that was. They must have planes that go there. "Why is she in Mexico?"

"She study Mayan pyramids. She expert. Doctor." His wife understood that word for sure, started nodding and beaming.

"She investigate something there," Chiang went on with continued pride. "Twenty twelve."

"Twenty twelve? Oh, wait, that B.S. Really? Do you know anything about it?"

Chiang gave a minimalist shrug. "Year of Dragon. Superbowl

Forty Six. Indianapolis."

"Indianapolis in February. Ridiculous. Anyway, let's get through the information here and I'll book a flight. Your girl is as good as found, Mr. Chiang. I guarantee it."

"Life has no guarantee. Nothing but guess. You good guesser."

"Thanks, 'sensei'. Listen, I'm sure your daughter is fine. Just having too much fun to remember her folks. Probably frolicking around the ocean right now, safe and sound."

SECOND LARGEST DRAGSTRIP

"Are we there yet?" MeiMei asked in a plaintive whine. "I have to pee."

"You should have thought of that before we left Grandmother's house," Tuan answered from behind her.

Actually the peeing issue had been a little weird at first. The solution to such bodily processes had been to get out into the water, do whatever business was at hand, then climb back in. Kind of refreshing, and saves bundles on toilet paper, MeiMei had decided, but lacks a certain decorum. Could be worse, she had thought the second day of what Tuan called their "Paddle Our Little Butts Outta Here Tour": she'd been spared dealing with even less decorous sanitation needs. Although about another week and that would be an issue as well. Meanwhile:

"You said we were half way to Belize, back by that bay. So we must be over the border by now." The next big bay had been Chetumal, no doubt about that. Which would mean they were cruising along Caye Caulker. Definitely Belizean territory.

"Well, there's an explanation for that."

She'd learned he'd make her ask what the explanation was. So she did. And he said, "I've decided it makes more sense to sell you out to the bad guys."

"Well you should have thought of that before," she said reprovingly. "I might have brought a higher price before I got all sun-gnarled and prune-fingered and fright-haired and callused."

He didn't keep running with the gag, like he usually did. He was silent awhile, and she was aware of him moving cyclically behind her.

Then he softly said, "I was thinking that it would be a shame for you to be this close to the reef cayes, in a small craft like this, and not get a chance to see them."

"But you didn't get around to mentioning the little scenic detour until I asked?" She found his reticence charming but spoke in a scolding voice.

"Well, see," he continued to be flat and sincere. "I thought you might not go for it. And I was hoping you would."

MeiMei thought about that for a hundred yards of smooth glide over the slight wind chop, then said, "And you don't want this to be over, either?"

She could hear him blow his breath out, but he answered steadily. "As far as I'm concerned, we could keep this up forever. I'm having the time of my life and enjoying the company."

So he'd made her ask about that, too, she thought. Men. She said, "I only see one immediate problem," and made him ask her about what it was.

What it was: "I actually do have to pee."

She felt the subtle deceleration of the hull as he pulled his stroke and turned his blade sideways under the water. As the boat came to a halt and nosed nicely into the three inch riffle, he extended the paddle to stabilize the boat while she carefully stood up and prepared to jump flatfooted over the gunwales. But stopped and almost lost her balance when he spoke.

"Know what bums me out?"

"God only knows. You sure seem to take disasters, risks, and small bladders in stride."

"There's no way to have a plank."

She stared at him. Was this some nautical term that didn't really mean what it did on dry land, like "head" and "galley" and "sheet"?

"So you could walk it," he explained as if it should be obvious. "I took an internship in Piratical Sciences, and it's how these things should be done."

"First get an eyepatch, then worry about the niceties," she said as she jumped daintily overboard in order to piss daintily into the ocean.

"It looks like a parking lot!" MeiMei protested. Or maybe a post-apocalypse freeway. This was the Belize Barrier Reef, second largest in the world, one of the single biggest objects on earth. And it looked like a dirty parking lot after a storm.

"Thanks for pointing that out," Tuan said from the back seat. Because now that she mentioned it, it was like a two lane strip of gray limestone across the ocean, low waves on one side, lake-smooth on the lee side where they slid along as sleek as a Teflon steam iron. "The polyps just keep building higher and higher, into the sunlight and nutrient streams. Then they hit the surface and can't go higher, so they spread laterally. And the top looks like old cement."

"And it's all littered. Where does that junk come from? Those tree trunks and stuff?"

Tuan made a tiny adjustment on his next stroke, turning the blade almost imperceptibly to glide the kayak closer to the reef. "Those 'trees' are coral, too."

"No way!" But she saw it. Like enormous stag corals. But laying around broken and battered, cluttering up the parking lot like trees after a tornado. Which, she realized, was exactly what they were. "They got broken off and tossed up here by hurricanes?"

"Exactly. Hard to imagine, isn't it? And once they're there, there's not much is going to move them off."

"God, I guess not. It's incredible though, like flying along the top of a mountain range. And knowing it was built up by googillions of little animals."

"Mountain range is a good analogy. If we were flying by the top of the Rockies or Alps we'd be seeing bare rock. There aren't many animals above the treeline and the peaks don't even have vegetation."

"Let me guess, you're a mountain climber, too?" Like half the profs in Seattle?

"I tried it. I don't have much of a head for heights. But anyway, you move down the slopes, below the treeline, and the bare rockpile starts looking like an ecosystem. It supports all those life forms, and conditions their climate. Same thing here. Start down the slopes and it's one of the richest, most beautiful bio-communities in the world."

MeiMei peered over the side into the clear water. "I wish we could. Go down the slopes, I mean. See what lives right on the reef."

She felt the kayak lose thrust, do that little nosedip she'd learned meant that Tuan had stopped paddling. She laid her paddle across the cockpit and turned to look at him. To see him pulling a mask and snorkle out from under the deck behind him. He brandished it in front of her face, grinning. "Thought you'd never ask."

"Ever thought of asking me one of these days?"

"I've been giving it a lot of thought," he said, then grabbed the gunwales and flipped the boat again, turning them both out into the warm, blue-streaked water.

MeiMei broke the surface, flipping her snorkle forward to clear it. She looked directly across at Tuan, his mask inches in front of her. "It's unbelievable!" She didn't care if she was gushing. The test dive back at Isla had been a staggering introduction to tropical underwater, but this was like some different universe. She'd been soaring over brain coral heads the size of SUV's, sponges she could almost swim into and hide, schools of fish all turned out in Tuan's not-quite-formulated "Tropical Pigmentation Protocol". She was stunned and thrilled at once, excitement shining out of her eyes.

Tuan smiled, watching her with the same sense of wonder that had been growing in him for two weeks at sea. So delicate, so beautiful. But brainy and fun. A real treasure. He moved towards her until their masks touched. MeiMei stared into his eyes from inches away, the two of them opposite ends of a tunnel of translucent silicon, divided by two panels of transparent lens. He finned lightly and reached out to rest his hands on her hips, delighting in the cool give to the flesh, the sudden stillness that took over her Moon Goddess gaze.

He said, "I've been meaning to ask you something."

She smiled and moved closer to him, hands on his shoulders and behind his neck to hold their heads together behind the double glass divider. "It's about time."

SINS OF THE FATHERS

As soon as the door closed, Aphra was in motion, rolling out over the foot of the bed like a sleek black bullwhip uncurling on the floor. She grabbed the pants she'd tossed over a chair back and snatched out what looked like a pocket electronic translator—and could actually do a decent job of turning English words to Spanish and back if anybody cared to—and punched in sequences with a blur of ruby-tipped fingers. Smiling as she read the screen, dowsed around the room.

Under his side of the bed there. He had her rumbled but good, no doubt about that. But what she wanted wasn't coming up very quick. That was some trick-ass hardware there. Oh, wait... no, what the fuck was that all about? Ah. Oh, shit. Who is this guy, CIA? NSA? What it spelled out was, "Super Fed". Well, that's live, she thought. No point messing around with the second string. She was back in the bed seconds before he opened the door, tucking her scanner under her side of the mattress and giving him a come-hither glance and centerfold spread that should be frying every receptor he had.

"So I'm still working my way up the bureaucratic ladder," Town was saying as he moved back to the bed and got in, kneeling over her for a long moment, drinking her in. He reached down and brushed his hand lightly over the narrow furze of nappy pubes she hadn't lasered, waxed and Veet'ed out of existence.

"One thing I like about fucking white boys," she said. When he raised his eyebrow she gave it a beat and said, "Pubies don't sound like Velcro."

He laughed and bellyflopped on the bed like a kid, rolled a pillow under his chin and gazed into her face. "I'm doing okay. But maybe I wish I'd thought of going wildcat myself. I don't mean to brag, but I've had stuff go through my hands that people would pay big bucks to get their hands on."

"Or make sure nobody else did, right?"

"Exactly. Deep Six stuff. The Ex-Files."

"Sometimes I get the feeling over half of industrial snooping is negative like that. Find out what they don't know. Make them think the wrong thing. Find it and bury it. Get that damn disk back. Find the negatives and destruct 'em without looking at 'em. What'll it cost to shut that bitch up?"

"I'm in it for good, though. Something about dealing with countries and global outfits and... I don't know. I just want to be the best at it there is."

"Better than your daddy, right?"

"Probably a lot of it. Yeah. Shit."

"Well, listen, hon. Sometimes I think everybody's into everything for messed-up reasons they don't even know about. Now it's me who 'doesn't want to brag'—wink, nudge—but I might be at the top of the game right now. I coulda been one of the top ten industrial analysts in the country at Oracon. And now? I don't know. I wish somebody would come along and pay me to turn them over. I think I could do it if anybody could. But I might be top gun right this minute. That's the pisser: you never find out. There's no standings or like quarterback ratings or anything."

"Top gun, private division. I can believe it."

"Division? Hey boy, I wonder a bit about that shit. Who's really the champs? What I've been seeing some of those Federal types pull off lately, I think maybe us NGO squads could win the SnooperBowl if they had one. You think the CIA's smarter than I am?"

"I kind of doubt it. Ever think of going over to the public sector? Do your duty for God, Country, and Some Asshole In The Whitehouse?"

"I oughta have a big 'A' tattooed on my tits, sugarboy. Standin' for 'A-political'. I'm only it for the green flash."

"Well, I'd make it a triple A. Alltime Awesome Ass. In years to come they might just search out the finest butts in the world and give the best one the Aphra Alisander Trophy."

"You might qualify for some sort of Heisman yourself. The High Man trophy. Hey, what's your last name, anyway? And don't give me no Double Ought boogie-woogie."

"Well, it might not be bad for that trophy. It's Hardley."

Aphra bit her laugh off halfway, her face suddenly hardening. "So wait a minute... oh, fuck, you saying... So your daddy, big time fed agent and shit, his name was Hardley, too?"

"That's how it works. For white folks, anyway." He gave it his best smile, but she wasn't buying.

"First name Davis? Well, Jefferson Davis? Jefferson Davis Hardley?"

Townsend stared at her. Was this taking another turn that he had no handle on? What...

"You asshole motherfucker!" Aphra went from supine to standing on the bed in one explosion, as though launched by hidden springs.

"You douchebag!" She screamed. "You rabbit-assed whiteboy twat!"

Townsend was also on his feet by then, standing by the bed erect (though a lot less erect than moments before) and staring at a woman who was now a nostril-flaring, eye-blazing, talon-brandishing column of gleaming black rage. He opened his mouth to reason, and realized that would be really pointless. Whatever happened, it wasn't something you could talk away.

He squatted and reached under the bed to grab his gear. Aphra took a step on the mattress and kicked him in the jaw so hard he saw white flashes, landed back against the wall. He stood, holding his electronic goodies behind him, and she leaned back to power a karate kick right at his throat. He blocked it with his free hand, but felt it. She knew what she was doing and was very fast and strong. He leaned over as though to pick up his clothes and she fired another kick at his face. He was ready for this one, grabbing her ankle and twisting it hard while pushing it up towards the ceiling. Her other foot came off the bed and she fell, trying to twist, but he controlled her with his grip on her foot. He grabbed her other ankle, jammed it with effort behind her opposite knee and bent her calf down to trap it, controlling her with one hand while he snatched up his clothes with the other. She snarled and yowled like a buggered cheetah.

He had everything in hand and was holding her without risking damage, but stood there staring at her, writhing and flexing on the bed. her ass cheeks sweating and clenching with her effort to do him harm. His erection came back just like that and he felt an extremely powerful impulse to grab her other foot and fuck her thrusting, heaving head off.

Instead he gave a sudden heave that pulled her towards him, rolling off the bed. The same movement gave him impetus towards the door. Even with his head start he beat her to the door by a very slim margin. He was outside on the sand, trying to step into his pants while holding his gadgets in the other hand, while she stood in the door shaking with hated. The sight made an impression on him he'd carry with him all his life: filling the door with sheer animus and animosity, her body perfect and lethal, her face like a jungle cat, baring sharp teeth.

People were starting to gather, lights coming on. He had his pants on and stuck his stuff in the pockets. No sandals. A shudder passed down Aphra like a ground tremor and she was suddenly icy, razor-edged calm. She stared at him in contempt and said, "Tell your asshole daddy that Debra says, Fuck yourself to death."

She slammed the door and he stood there staring for a long

moment. Then he turned to face a circle of dumbfounded faces and shrugged. "That time of the month again," he said and walked away, bummed to the max.

He was across the bridge and entering the Avalon lobby before he figured out what it had to be all about. He stopped like he'd walked into a solid left jab, turned and stared at the *palapa* on top of the Maria Del Mar. And hoped to hell he hadn't just been getting it on with his half-sister.

HAIR TO ETERNITY

"So what are your theories on The Big Bang?" MeiMei spoke softly from down in her throat. Pensive, ultra-relaxed, but still playful. She held a homemade "CocoLoco": rum from a metal flask in the seemingly endless stores in the kayak's hull, mixed with the milk in the shell of a coconut he'd found on the beach and chopped open with a machete from that same floating warehouse. She felt absolutely and stupendously great.

"I thought it was fantastic," he replied lazily, lying with his head outside the tent, staring up at more stars than anybody else would have any use for. "I think it's the most singular thing that ever happened. And I'm hoping it'll happen again soon."

"Men," MeiMei murmured in his ear. She had rolled up on one elbow to sip from the coco, but now reached across his bare torso and slid her equally bare breast along his rib cage. He bent the wrist that passed under her waist, cupping her butt in just the nicest way ever. She didn't really feel like lying here making cool repartee. She felt like jumping up and down and whooping and hollering. Had actually done quite a bit of that a few minutes before. Not to mention some tremulous shivering of timbers, clenched toes pointing at the sky, and quaking like a flushed fawn under aspens. And not to mention some various groveling and gesticulating and walloping of the kind a decent writer wouldn't think of mentioning by any means. And now that single touch of his hand on her ass had caused her to consider the possibility of another such episode in the fairly foreseeable future.

"If you'd read the brilliant monograph I co-authored with Steven Hawking, you'd know I espouse the Steady State theory."

"That's fabulous, OB. Do you or Steven want to go steady?"

"I'd go with him, if I were you. They say he's hell on wheels."

"Oh, that was tacky. Even from a hard scientist."

"Well, less so, now. Hard, that is. Still plenty tacky."

MeiMei set the coconut down and nuzzled him a little, sniffing him out. She still had a hard time believing that she was not only getting laid, but even edging over towards those Harlequin Romance sort of trappings she'd had so little time or opportunity for in her life. Smart, famous, funny... what else? Oh, yeah, rich and owns a sailboat. All that and pretty good muscle definition and a pronounced stamina. *Those pussy pirates probably killed me after all,* she thought. *And I must have been a damned good little girl.*

It hadn't exactly been sudden. To say the least. He probably could have had her however long ago it was that she knocked on his door naked. Brought her a towel in the shower, stepped in, and stepped up. She kind of doubted she'd have made much objection. Swimming along under the inverted kayak with the searchlights, motor launches, and blue beanies out there had softened her outlook, as well. She remembered thinking it had to be the sort of situation where the imperiled heroine ends up under four-poster damask with an improbable bustier and a side order of pectorals.

Then there was that moment this morning, when their masks had touched and he'd just put his hands on her. Like you'd walk in and put your gloves on the side table. Just touched her in a way that obviously had no practical intentions, but seemed so natural she'd barely registered it: just looked into his eyes behind the wet glass and knew they were almost there yet.

But for some reason, it was late afternoon when she'd known for sure that she was going to bed with him that very night. If you want to call sprawled on a beach "bed". Not, she thought as she stared up through the scented darkness into the deepening cup of stars and listened to the wind rustling the palm fronds in syncopation with the rhythm of the low windward-side surf just yards away from them, that any silk sheet Tempurpedic setup could compare to this.

They'd beached the kayak and pitched the tent, eaten a light snack of coconut slices and canned salmon, of all things, and gone for a sunset walk along the confectioners' dust beach, wading in and out of the transparent water. She'd spotted an odd stick that looked like a stringbean floating vertically in the shallows, then realized it was some sort of pod. It bobbed along in the wavelets of the lee shore, bumping its bottom end along the finely fluted sand bottom. She'd picked it up to examine, turned questioning eyes to Tuan.

"Glad you asked," he said. "Because that's a very interesting part of a pretty relevant process."

"Shocker."

"It's a mangrove seed," he proceeded serenely. "Falls into the water and goes with the flow. When it gets into shallow water, it does what you just saw. Sooner or later, with a little luck, it gets stuck, stands there in the water. And starts putting down roots."

"Ah, I get it." MeiMei just loved it, put the seed back in the water and squatted to watch it keep on bumpin'. "Then it grows up and puts out those limbs that turn into roots and roots that creep up and become trunks."

"Exactly. Even if the reef wasn't built up to the surface yet, that seed could snag in five inches of water and start growing vegetation."

"And then it would catch silt..."

"And birdshit and floating junk and whatnot. Start creating its own currents, where silt gets dropped on its lee side."

"And you've got a swamp or something out here in the middle of the ocean." She thought about it. "And it would look like land, wouldn't it? Like a little island. We saw some of those yesterday."

"And pretty soon it would be a real island, real land. Start having little beaches. Waiting for the next opportunistic traveler."

"A guy from Fodor's guide?"

Tuan led her up the beach to the edge of greenery and picked up a coconut. "Toss this on the beach," he said.

She made a show of shot-putting the coconut almost to the waterline, where it rolled to a stop.

"If you keep tossing it, it'll always end up like that," he told her. "Notice the way it's shaped, not really round, but not really conical. It's a shape that lets it roll into position automatically any time it's washed ashore."

"And once it gets settled in, your island has trees."

"Which means things stay put a lot better."

MeiMei thought of the huge stone trunks she'd seen lying on the bare reef, but could see what he meant. "It's all about design."

"That, what you just said right there, is at the heart of my whole general theoretical meandering," he said lightly, but she felt the serious import of it. "You look at coral, they're little jelly creatures the size of barley. Screening the sea for calcium to build a skeleton to protect them. But it doesn't protect them from death, and the next one that drifts along builds his little shack on their remains. And you end up with one of the largest things in the world. Then you get things just happening by on the next wave and the way they're made, the way they're shaped, ends up building land out of the sea."

"So you just take the right décor group, add water, stir and you've got a continent."

"I woke up once in grad school. Whichever grad school. Berkeley, I think. Slumped over some cubicle desk in the library stacks and there was this note written on my knee in felt tip pen. It said, 'Who designed the city of coral?' Want the punchline? I couldn't find a felt tip pen anywhere around the desk."

"Intelligible design?"

"I'm still working on that. I'm not the only physicist who realizes he's just one equation or variable away from getting into theology."

She walked down to the water and stared at the mangrove pod, still pogo-ing along. And kept staring. It was a message sans bottle, she felt. She looked up and he was looking right into her eyes. "You just get the right elements, with the pre-existing design, and set them afloat," he'd said. "Then all it takes is time."

And from that point, it had taken exactly one hour and seven minutes until she'd tossed her head back onto the sand, moaned, and felt the docking procedure complete itself.

And now here they lay. Building an island?

"Something you said yesterday," she said, speaking almost directly into his ear. "About the universe not expanding out forever, but like reaching limits and starting to contract? Is that what you mean by steady state?"

"Not exactly. And I have to admit it appeals to me in a non-scientific way at the moment. Kind of, oh, I don't know...a romantic folly of sorts."

"Is that anything like a sweet nothing?"

"Yes, but more mechanistic than rococo, like a BMW. I look at the idea of the universe inflating into Everyness, then deflating to what Nothingness would be if there were even a nothing to think nothing about and what hits me is…" He leaned forward and touched his hand to her shoulder. "That in millions of years, this net of time that is unfurling around and through us will recoil, and we will once again be here, together, right on this beach."

Mei kissed him, then said, "But in reverse motion. Shouldn't hurt the sex part any."

"But then we'd paddle away backwards, I'd end up in my living room wandering why a genius millionaire with Abs Of Semi-Steel should be sitting there alone, and you'd be dashing away into the night on a backwards SkiDoo. And we'd wander off to separate lives. Go through our childhoods, once again without appreciating them, and end up as gleams in our fathers' eyes."

"But then the yo-yo would hit bottom, wouldn't it? And start reeling the string back in."

"And here we'd be again. And not even bored with it. This moment has legs. It won't go away."

"More like it's one of those moments that keeping going away, but you know they'll come back without even calling first or warning you to get dressed."

"I'm warning you right now. Don't even think about getting dressed. I like your concept though. I'm trying to think if there could be a theorem for it. Chiang's Law of Conservation of Eroticism."

"Physics, pah. It fades in the light of antiquity. It's the Myth of Eternal Return."

"Got a ring to it. Joseph Campbell?"

She shook her head, whisking him off with her sun-damaged hair. "Eliade, Trask and Smith. Princeton Press. But the first time I heard 'eternal return' my immediate thoughts were my mother terrorizing Nordstrom's and The Bon shopping for clothes… oh my God."

"You can just call me OB. I mean you've seen me naked, and all."

"My mother! I haven't called her in three weeks! She'll be frantic. She'll call out the Marines! I have to get to a phone."

"Okay. Tomorrow we'll hit Tobacco Caye. They'll have something. Probably a soup can with a string."

"Tomorrow's great."

"Which leaves tonight. What's left of it."

"Well, speaking of Return and Steady State and Infinite Expansion..."

"Have you ever wondered what came immediately after the Big Bang?"

"Oddly, no."

He reached, then handed her their tropic isle cocktail. "The big coconut."

She pushed the drink aside and moved over on top of him. He felt her breasts flatten on his chest, her legs straddle him. She leaned her head forward and all that thick black hair fell around him, like a cloak of starless night that engulfed them both and wrapped them away from the world.

PARALLEL CURVES

The way these things go, Townsend could have shown up to catch the same ferry as Aphra. But he didn't. Maybe if he'd walked out of the Avalon Reef ten minutes sooner, or if he hadn't gone the long away around, walking North Beach in front of the Maria Del Mar with his shoes slung around his neck and his general grasp of the situation dragging ass on the bottom.

Was she his sister? Or half sister, technically? He wouldn't be surprised if he had a whole army of half-siblings out there from his father's scattergun semen distribution program back in the day. What else would have caused that sudden fury and rejection just from mention of the name?

He stopped under the palms. facing the hotel's beach portal, and felt a deep sense of loss for something he'd never really had. He didn't know just how greatly he hadn't had Aphra, of course, but even if he'd known her interest in him was pretty emphatically not sexual, he'd have missed the conversational links they'd been forming. And if he'd known just how much Aphra had dug him, even as a lesbian from birth, he could have taken some pride in it, maybe.

He stood halfway up his calves in the slow lap of the wavelets, staring without focus into the courtyard of the Maria Del Mar, then shook it off and put on his game face. Whatever else she was, she was the target and needed to be re-acquired. He walked rapidly up

Playa Norte and around the point, cut in through Sergio's to slip on his shoes and grab the return ferry ticket out of his duffel bag, then headed down the *malecón* to the dock. He didn't know that Aphra had left on the previous boat, and had no way of finding that out. He'd tagged her tracker to re-echo, but she'd apparently re-flummoxed it and he got no blip.

He figured there was no way she could have affected the pickup from the sender she was following: all he'd done was nab the codes. He was showing nothing as he looked at his "iPod" sitting on the bench in the terminal, idly glimpsing at the other docks where off-season tourists filed off windjammers and a huge, surrealistic pirate ship. It might be a sender that functioned intermittently to avoid detection, sending pulse bindles at given intervals. Might be smashed to pieces somewhere. When the Magaña boat eased up to the dock he stood up and slipped his little electro-tail in his shirt pocket. Holding his ticket ready as he moved towards the gangway, he socketed in the earbuds. Nice thing about this cryptoPod, it actually did play music. He clicked twice and stopped on "The Sky is Crying" by Stevie Ray Vaughn.

He had no way of knowing that Stevie's widow, Lenny, lived on Isla Mujeres and he and Aphra had gone right by her house on the way to The Blue Iguana. There are definite limits to Intelligence. No limits whatsoever to Coincidence.

A concept Aphra pondered heavily as she disembarked on the Cancun side at about the same moment that Town was boarding the other boat on the Isla side. What the fuck were the chances of her ever running into a son of J. Davis Hardley? Much less the chances that one of the very few men she had ever willingly screwed and hadn't much minded it, would be the self-same fortunate son?

She brooded further in the cab to downtown, where she damned well planned on renting a car. Her card was blown or it wasn't. She was totally fed up with public transportation and cheap hotels. Was there some subliminal signal between her and White Bread, one of those things you pick up on without knowing why, like the cute little trick down at the Baskin Robbins that time, with about twenty hotshot boyfriends coming by in their muscle cars but was actually so bi-curious it was about to ooze out her ears?

Or was it worse than that? They knew and had sicced him on her because of that? There must be records of the whole shitaree. If not on paper or hard drive, at least in the elephant memories of old spooks and *agents provocateurs* still around D.C. And he'd end up screwing her just like his old man had screwed her mama, then busted her.

No way I'm telling Ma about this. No way. She'd snatch out that old sawed-off Weatherby double-barrel she always claimed Eldridge gave her to hold for him and never came back for. Lots of her men never came back for it. Saturday night special, that's my mama. Surprised she only got knocked up twice. Then it finally hit her. Oh shit!

She started doing some really quick math, straining to remember exact dates. Let's see, the Feds took Mammy dearest in right after the bombing. August of '75, wasn't it? So that's more than nine months prior to '77, so I guess I didn't commit incest. Okay, half-incest. Unless he was nailing Moms during her stretch in Danbury. Which didn't seem likely. So she was off the hook on that one. Still...

She got out of the cab in front of Sanborns by the big bus station. Car rental right next door, but she needed to have some coffee and mull things over. Half way through her second refill she realized that she wouldn't have been so pissed off if she hadn't been liking the guy. How messed-up is that? She could have spent a week hanging out with him and swapping licks about parents and cloak/dagger shit. Screw it. Think about something a little less kinky than getting hung up on a straight man whose daddy fucked over my mama and is spying on my still-skintight ass at this very moment.

One refill later and she felt a slight vibration in the pocket of the red capris she'd shimmied into that morning and pulled out her crystal ball. Mirror, mirror, she thought as she flicked the reflective screen to display mode, where are my wandering girls today?

And at that exact moment, while she frowned at the co-ords she was reading, trying to make sense of them, Townsend was rounding the traffic circle in a newly-rented Jetta, only a hundred yards from where she sat. He'd caught the same pulse and was working it out. Both arrived at the same conclusion at the same instant: moving south along the coast... but very, very slowly.

HIGHS IN THE MID-FORTIES

He paused on the last metal step, cold gray eyes quartering the misty runway from under his snapbrim. He stepped down, turning up the collar of his trenchcoat against the wind that rippled the oil-slicked rainwater on the tarmac. Behind him the engines of the big Trimotor kept turning, staying warmed-up for the jump into the altitudes of oblivion. Was she going to show? Or would he climb back up those steps and disappear into the dark, dank blankness that should have been their future? Denny Mercer looked around, took a last pull on a rumpled Lucky Strike and tossed it into an oily puddle. One thing you could count on about dames: you can't count on one thing about dames. No, wait, that must be her now. And, whattaya know, mighty easy on the eyes. Heading right over towards him with a great big smile. Looks like trouble. The usual kind. Female.

Lluvia had no trouble spotting Mr. Mercer in the Chetumal bus station. He was the only gringo climbing down out of the bus from Cancun. But he didn't seem to see her. Looked a little dazed, in fact. She walked up to him and said, "Mister Mercer?"

Denny did his usual slip-shift out of his fantasizing (aided this time by a joint shared in the washroom of the ADO bus with two shaggy kids fresh out of the Israeli Army and cruising Mexico for thrills). He'd spoken to Lluvia once, calling the museum from the CUN airport to give her an arrival time.

The museum staff had arranged for an English-speaking secretary to pick him up and assist him in his inquiries into the Dr. Chiang situation, which they clearly saw as potentially embarrassing. And who else but Lluvia, who'd been very concerned about Doctora Chiang and uneasy over the way she just vanished three weeks ago.

She stood looking at Denny, waiting for his response, while he looked her over. Both liked what they were looking at, but neither thought of it that way. Some guy passing through on business, some skirt who'd be there when he strode off into the sunset. He said, "A guy on the bus told me Lluvia means 'rain'."

Not the sort of opener she was used to, but then she wasn't used to seeing men walk around in the tropical summer wearing belted raincoats and felt fedoras, either. Maybe reporters from the United States always dressed like that. "Yes," she said, flustered that there seemed little to add. "Do you have luggage?"

Denny hefted the pre-war leather satchel he'd carried on. "This is it. I'm a man who travels light."

She nodded, then for lack of any further conversational ideas, pointed to the wide from portal. "I have my auto out front."

Denny headed for the door beside her, swinging his bag. "Nice of you to come pick me up. I guess it beats sitting around the office, huh?"

"I voluntaried to come," she told him. "I liked Dra. Chiang. And yes, to getting out from the office."

"So you're going to help me out? Translate for me?"

"Yes, it's my assignment this week. Help you of investigate."

"Sounds good. Can we go where she was last seen?"

"I booked a room for you in the Ucum hotel. It is cheap and near Museum. If you don't like it, I can..."

"Great, great. Thanks a lot. But..."

She wasn't there. He looked back and she was unlocking a jaunty little red Tsuru. He came back and got in, immediately breaking a sweat all over. He took off his fedora and wiped his brow as she backed out and headed out of the parking lot. It looked like quite a ways into town. Kind of weird for a bus station. He said, "I was thinking I'd go straight to the museum, maybe get some leads. Where she was last seen, that stuff. Detective kind of stuff, you understand."

She cut her eyes at him. "You're not a reporter?"

Oops. He'd forgotten about that. Either the heat or the strangeness of Mexico or this cute interpreter was taking the edge off his usually razor-stropped brain. He looked at her and lowered his voice so nobody else in the car could hear. "I'm an investigator," he told her. "Helping people who are concerned about Ms. Chiang. I have my suspicions, you see what I mean? It's what I do."

It actually impressed her. She was a fairly simple girl, all told, and an addict of American films. Had seen "Casablanca" seven times; not that easy in Mexico. She paused, then plunged. "I have also my suspicious. Please can we go somewhere first, talk? I want you to know the Museum... situation... before you go there."

"Sounds good to me. I can see you're going to be a big help."

"I know a really nice coffee place."

"Perfect. I'll knock off for a cuppa java any place on earth."

Lluvia giggled. "But this place is not on earth."

MEANS OF PRODUCTION

OXo was on a pedestal. Literally. And not the first time in his experience, either. In fact, this hand-carved hardwood planter holder from India, supporting him on a brass disk held by the trunks of rampant elephants, was fairly cheesy compared to various niches and alcoves from which his blank quartz eyes had stared. But it was a nice gesture. For a tract house in Van Nuys. Which might have summed up Kenny and Gareth's whole film career: decent props from Pier One housed in an off-the-rack structure built right on a fault line.

Kenny was currently meeting the leveled gaze of those transparent eyeballs without seeing much except the color of the wall behind them. ("Melba Toast", a rather insipid shade of beige.) "I just don't get it. This thing is supposed to be such a great communicator."

"No, that was Reagan. And you actually produced that spot for his campaign, for the fat lot of good it did you."

"But he's our director!" Kenny was edging over into what Gareth thought of as his "turbo-whine", the way a airliner engine can suddenly jump up from mere noise to something truly deleterious. "How's he going to direct if he can't talk to us?"

"Well you have to admit that a director who doesn't shoot off his mouth is refreshing."

Kenny smoldered awhile longer, staring into the twin crystal balls and trying to make his own eyes go out of focus, like when you try to see the design hidden in those tacky posters. "I try making my mind blank..."

"Not exactly a stretch."

"Bitch. How do you find his wave length?"

"You mean, What's his frequency, Kenneth?" Gareth chuckled like a jealous deb. "No messages from the ether? He wants points on the back end? He wants you to meet this girl?"

"Are you doing any better, SuperHag? I'm more receptive than you are and you know it."

"Yeah, receptive at both ends."

"Two apertures, no waiting. But, you know..."

"If I knew, would I be asking *you*, for the luvva gawd?"

"Well there is one thing I've noticed... I don't know... Probably nothing."

"What?" Gareth glanced around in a frenzy. Maybe a crowbar? "What?"

"I just keep thinking about this place, sort of seeing this... you know, place. I think I might have dreamed about it last week."

"Glad you came forward with that bit of data. So, what kind of place? A leather bar?"

"Oh, please. No, it's like it's in the jungle. But there's this building."

"A pyramid? Some kind of ruins?"

"Oh, nothing like that. It's beautiful. Like... Robinson Crusoe. Or Rivendell. Or you know that plantation Clark Gable had in 'Naked Jungle'?"

"No. Because Gable wasn't in 'Naked Jungle'. That was Charlton Heston. You're thinking of "Mogambo"."

"Oh, riiiiight. Ava Gardner. But I think I mean Heston's place."

"Good, so we can rule out the House of The Seven Gable. Can you tune it in a little more? Any details?"

"Like the date on the cornerstone? What can I tell you?"

"Nothing, apparently."

"It's like a daydream, stupid. A vision. Not big on production values or rolling credits." Kenny stood up and flounced off. Or as much as one can "flounce" wearing a 1890's bathing costume with wifebeater straps at top and mini-shorts at the bottom. Canary yellow with baby blue accents. "I was just trying to help. I'm going to go tinkle."

"Try it standing up. It's very butch."

"Oh, sure, and make a big splash. Which guess who's the only one who'd clean it up?"

Gareth stared at oXo some more, fuming. Not getting even a jungle daydream or Kung Fu flashback. Then Kenny was back.

"I just can't get that place off my mind. Like some stupid song you just can't... oh, snap!"

"Do tell."

"Well, this might not be..."

"TRY ME!"

"There was this sort of theme song. Well not song, really. I just remember this little background vocal thing, maybe like you used to hear these harmony chicks doing stings for radio stations? Like, 'The highly successful sound of Radio Loooooooondon'. Or 'Rollin' with the rockin'est...'"

"Would you spill it!"

"If you'll quit shouting, maybe. It was like 'Something, something bids you go... to Falcon Oh...'"

"Is that like the letter 'o' or a zero or what?"

"How could I tell, you simp? I just heard it. And what does it matter?"

"Because," Gareth snapped, heading for the Mac terminal, "I have to type it in to Google."

"Oooo, good idea. Look in 'Images'. I don't suppose Google has "Visions".

"Not according to Bill Gates, they don't." Gareth was madly typing, zipping through pages of images. "Was it 'Falconhurst'?"

"Of course not. I'd have recognized that one. It was on a river, by the way."

"No help."

"Oh, and you know..."

Gareth looked up at him as if ready to throw his smart terminal at his stupid partner.

"It might be more of a 'b' word. Like 'balconies' or something."

Gareth moaned and typed more. Then stopped with his fingers poised, staring at the screen. "Kenny, come here,"

"Oh, yes, master. The way you're acting I'm better off over here talking to this piece of rock."

"Get your well-reamed butt over here, goddamit. Look at this thing."

He spun the monitor sideways as Kenny dawdled sulkily across the worn shag carpet and was rewarded by a piercing shriek: "That's it! That's It! Oh my God!"

"Blancaneaux Lodge, apparently."

"So it's real? Where is it?" Kenny was practically jumping up and down.

"Give me a minute. Oh, Christ! Guess who it belongs to?"

"If I could guess would I be pleading with you to tell me?"

"Whoa! This is pretty spooky."

"Oh, you noticed that. My fantasies are on the internet. I wonder if some of the sexier ones made it. Google..."

"It belongs to a film producer."

"Oooo, that is spooky. Does it say who?"

"No it just says, 'Belongs to a famous director, seen one, you've seen 'em all'. What do you think?"

"So tell me you... felchmonster!"

"See how it feels?"

"One phone call. That's what it would take to have you killed."

"Did that Brando thing awhile back."

"Oh, that's really... Wait, you mean Coppola?"

"You got it."

"Wow, that is spooky.

"Reading on down it gets even spookier."

"He didn't die, did he? The third one after..."

"No, listen. He has seminars at the lodge. Bigshot writers and producers, like a dude ranch for film wannabes."

"You mean like people pay to go?"

"Duh... would you pay to go hang out with Coppola and, hmmm, lemme see, Buck Henry?"

"Buck fucking Henry? Jesus, how much?"

"Or lessee, Shane Black, Michael Klawitter."

"Who's Michael Klawitter?"

"Producer for just about every Pacino film except the Godfather ones."

"Holy shit, Pacino? Would we get to meet Coppola? Where is this place?"

"That's what I meant about it getting spookier. Belize."

"Belize, Belize... Africa, right? By the Ivory Coast?"

"You bet, Miss South Carolina. It's like a hundred miles from a little place in Mexico you might have heard of."

"Acapulco? Cancun?"

"Close. Playa del Carmen."

"Oh, God that is spooky! When is it?"

"That's the spookiest part yet."

"Oh, Lord, don't tell me."

"Okay."

"Fuck you, Suzy! It's during the festival, right?"

"Nope, three days later."

"Well, we just have to be there, is all. How much?"

"Seminar plus a week room and board, $3,275 per each."

"Ouch. But it's doable, right?"

There was a pause while Gareth squinted at the monitor and fidgeted his fingers across the keys.

"Excuse me, I said, That's doable. RIGHT?"

"Well, look, we've been socking those credit cards pretty hard..."

"Cards? What happened to... call me old fashioned but... cash flow?"

"Good question, now that you bring it up instead of running into the night at the mention of paying those two..."

"Okay, okay. Don't bring that up and snivel about it another three months. Basically, we gotta go and that's that."

'So that card we got from PayPal should be good for the sixty-five hundred. And how much to get there?'

'That's the point, idiot. We'll already be there. We'll grab a bus down from the Playa for like twenty pesos and a tortilla with a picture of the virgin on it."

"And take oXo. Absolutely. Bring him into the circle of stardom."

Hmmmph." Kenny turned to regard oXo, luminous with faint afternoon light. "I think he's already there, don't you? And did you ever get the idea that maybe he is bringing us in?"

"Sorry, I just used up my spooky quota for the whole week."

CHERCHEZ LA BLONDE

People who didn't know Ganzo might have thought of him as a good foil for the cute blonde he'd been showing up with in the bars, beach cafés, and restaurants along the glorified highway strip that Tulum thought of as the town of Tulum. Striking, if decidedly odd, couple. The vacant young artisan and his rivet-hot jewelry model.

Those who knew Ganzo didn't know quite what to make of it. The first time the question came up in the bar at the Paraiso one wag said, "He probably found her washed up on a beach," and got a mild round of laughter out of it.

The blonde was kind of drifty too, in her own way. Don't try getting her life story, that's for sure. Even the total sharks around the cabanas had quit hitting on her. She was like a million dollar house that hadn't had the electricity connected yet.

Women found her congenial, though, and Ganzo charming enough in a closed-circuit sort of way. She was in Paraiso talking to this American girl with glasses and frizz, a studious geek type. looked like Velma from Scooby Doo. The blonde animated and perky as usual, like a high school cheerleader who spaced out graduation. Saying, "Hey, it wasn't just like *I* couldn't believe it: those mariachi guys about fell out of their sombreros when you started jamming with them like that."

"I don't think those guys even read music, frankly. They just learned the parts for each song: no clue about improvisation. Trumpets are pretty simple when you're used to tooting tubas and sousaphones."

"That is just so cool, Celia. I never even knew any of those girls who played in the band."

Because you were out there shaking your pom-poms and booty and nailing all the cool guys while we band geeks got the chess club dorks, Celia was thinking. But this dumb blonde didn't really seem like that. Nice, not a "Heather" or anything. "Those guys were here again, earlier. But they didn't let me play with them again. Too bad, I had this sort of Souza meets Gershwin riff that would have fit right in on top of that Cielito Lindo number."

"I wish I could do something like that. You've really got it going on."

Celia was floored. Here was Scarlett Johanson's stunt double calling *her* cool? Whoa! And now she's pulling out that gym bag, probably got more of that darling jewelry her Rain Man boyfriend made. But wait, what the hell is that?

"I almost forgot. I brought this for you."

"What is it? Oh wow, it's a seashell on steroids!"

She laughed and brandished the big conch, eighteen inches long even with an inch of the tip sawn off and polished smooth by Ganzo. "Yep. It's a *caracol*. Ganzo did the hole in the end there."

Celia moved the conch around in her hands, but when she pointed the cut-off end at her mouth, it fell into place. She could hold it up with one hand and blow into it. "Unbelievable! He reamed out the embouchure there and polished it."

"Yeah, you know. You put your lips on it."

Which is what Celia did. The big shell was light and resonant, with an open chop and exponential expansion like a flugelhorn. She did a few exploratory notes, ran some quick riffs. The conch had a unique, mellow sound and was hilariously easy to play. She did a line of Brahms, a quick hook from Herb Alpert. Everybody in the place was looking at her. She stood up and nodded, headed into a luminous, soulful take on Night In Tunisia. Curtsy stared at her with her mouth half-open and eyes shining: Ganzo watched with what might have been a smile. She did American Patrol, a sort of medley from The Music Man, and nobody seemed tired of it so she started screwing around.

The conch was a natural for muted, post-bop cool so she went into a sort of Virtual Miles thing, then started stutter effects and tonguing. She put her hand into the huge, flaring bell of the horn and moved it around, experimenting. Pulled her clenched fingers in and out, messing with bent notes and falling tones. Did a wah-wah riff with her hand moving in and out at an increasing frequency.

The blonde was delighted, clapping her hands and laughing. Get a kick out of fisting, do you, Goldilocks? But Celia felt bad at the thought: this girl was a true fan, open and alive and buying every bit of it. She blew out her cheeks like Gillespie, went way blue.

Aphra had been solidly pissed off for over a week. She'd figured out that her bug was giving such intermittent pulses because it was moving so slowly it had lapsed into a totally lackadaisical refresh rate. So yeah, she was pissed. She just couldn't figure out why those bitches were cruising so slow. Or where or why. She'd come to the conclusion that the boat was adrift. No power, maybe nobody really at the wheel. But who the fuck knew?

So she'd been moving down the coast in a truly stupid little rental

Volkswagen called a Bora. More like Bor*ing*. Like it mattered when she couldn't go anywhere. Get a reading, head down the weird multi-lane highway south of Cancun, drive off on some wretched little road to the ocean and look out there and see nothing. And nobody else had seen anything, either. She knew better than to be asking about any blondies or chinkies, but had managed to figure out nobody she was looking for had been through. Once, just south of Puerto Morelos—odd little spot with an English bookstore and great Chinese restaurant, of all things—she'd gotten a possible scan about a hundred yards out, middle of the fucking night. Maybe saw some sort of boat out there, just at the edge of the beam from this bizarro lighthouse, tilted over like the Leaning Tower of Pizza. Since then, *nada*.

She'd been around Playa Carmen and that whole tourist trap, Riviera-wannabe scene for almost three days. They were out there, but she couldn't close. It was driving her out of her ever lovin' skull.

And now Tulum. What a pit. All about Mayan ruins. Near as she could tell the new stuff they'd slapped up along the highway was just ruins that hadn't gotten around to being totally ruined yet. On the road to ruins, so to speak.

And of course, a washed-out two-laner full of potholes and speedbumps in the middle of nowhere going down to the beach. Which didn't seem to have any big powerboats sitting there with her little runaways waving welcome to her. Mostly had all these shacks full of European hippies running around naked and stoned to their eyeballs. Some of it not bad stuff, come to that. She saw two sets of tits there that looked pretty toothsome and she got the feeling that if they didn't swing her way yet, they might be susceptible to the right swing vote.

Which would have been just copasetic if she hadn't been too pissed off to get into it. It had been an hour since she caught a squeal on her little ElectroFink gadget and it sure as shit looked like those 'ho's were right here, right now. But here she was, stalking down a damn beach in the damn dark, in her bare damn feet, is what she was doing. Fuck it.

She'd decided she could use a drink or three, maybe see what kind of chickadees were in these little cabana bars along here, when she heard this just other-world music. Coming out of little bunker over there with the cute candles in paper bags out front. Some unreal riffs, she was picking up. What was that axe, anyway?

And what's the beat, there? Tropical bebop? Trop-bop? One minute sound like some Tibetan temple thing, next minute it's like Freddy Hubbard trying to do Delta. She turned and walked up the beach to the Paraiso.

Huh, what it was, was some white chick with nerd glasses playing a conch shell. Figure that out. Nice, though. Defly diff. Crowd of euro-wonks getting into it, nerd girl doing a sort of reggae/calypso thing now. She shills seashells from the Seychelles.

Then she stops and takes a big corny bow and there's some nice applause, Aphra putting her hands together, too. Gotta hand it to Four Eyes. And this blonde groupie up front just jumping out of her well-shaped hide over it all, nice looking stuff. Wish she'd turn around.

Which she did. Holy fuckin' shit on a stick!

Aphra practically ran across the room and faced the smiling blonde. Who looked at her without a flicker of recognition. What kind of wack game is this? She leaned into her, scowled, "Hey homey, don't you know me?"

Evidently not.

The blond was looking at her like some oblivious livestock of the cud-chewing food group. Slight smile, looking expectant. Aphra was about ready to slap this bitch, snap her out of it, call her play. Instead she slumped slightly, met the big blue eyes at their own level. Said, really loud, "Yo, Curtsy! You in there girl?"

Evidently not.

Fuck.

On an impulse, Aphra reached out and cupped one of those nice firm titties under the loose T-shirt, then stepped close and reached down to clench a tight buttock, long fingernail just barely like brushing the Promised Land, there. Aphra's patented Full Nelson Mandala hold. Pushed her lips up to hers and started going all tonguey. There was a shocked hush in the room, then she got a bigger applause than the conch girl did.

She broke it off and rared back, looked into Curtsy's face. "Bring anything back, girlfriend?"

"No, well, wait a minute..."

Aphra snorted through her flared nostrils. "Now I been called a lot of things, especially afterwards. But never forgettable. Meanwhile I coulda just sworn you and the little chinkette headed out of Isla on a boat I paid for and never saw again. Ring any bells? Wanna cut the shinola and play nice?"

She saw something pass inside the baby blues, a sort of flutter that got her thinking that whatever this was, it might not be an act. "Hey girl," she said in a friendlier tone, "Give it up."

She watched as Curtsy's expression seemed to crumple, then fall away like loose stucco. Her eyes widened, then moistened, her lips started trembling. Suddenly she dashed herself into Aphra's arms, shaking violently. She threw her arms around her neck and clung for dear life.

"What up, baby?" Aphra asked her softly, patting her shoulders in a sisterly way. Looking over the heaving shoulders she could see this decently cute Mayan guy staring at her. In a kind of impersonal way.

A quick spasm shot through Curtsy and she pushed away from Aphra and faced her, definitely all there and aware. And not one little bit happy about it. Her eyes filled and spilled and she started sobbing. "I killed those guys, Aphra! I shot 'em and they're dead."

Aphra reached out for a soothing stroke on her upper arm. "It's okay, honey. I'm sure they had it coming." Whoever "they" were.

Curtsy's sobs slowed down and lessened in volume. She held Aphra's gaze, looking like a miserable little girl who totally knows her whole life is just ruined for the moment. Then it was like the sun coming up behind the sky blue of her irises. Aphra had always noted (and coveted) the girl's innocence and girlish enthusiasm, but at that moment she saw it go off the charts. It was Christmas and Birthday and First Prom in there. Curtsy beamed, wiping tears and laughing.

"But they came for me," she almost yelled. "I knew they would."

She grabbed Aphra's upper arms in her powerful grip, practically jumping up and down. "They came, Aphra! They came and saved me."

DOUBLE OVER TIME

They didn't get that early a start. Because what with one thing after another, they hadn't gotten a whole lot of sleep. Around five in the morning, under a setting cusp of moon, MeiMei had lain with an ear to Tuan's chest, trying to modulate the throb of his heart with the soft beat of the waves. And it came from her mouth unbidden, "Our whole time together has just been sort of a big honeymoon, hasn't it?"

And immediately cringed. First night with a guy and you're saying "M-word" type words? Why don't you just tell a guy you're planning a felony caper the first time you meet him? Oh, wait, did that one, too.

But Tuan immediately stroked his hand up into her hair and drew her forehead up for a kiss. "It feels that way, doesn't it? We should package this experience, offer it with all those 'Wedding In Paradise' hucksters on Isla. We could hire some vicious pirates and patrol boats for the thrills, give them sunburn with UV wands and little packets of sand to sprinkle into their cracks."

She felt her laughter moving her breasts around on his ribs. "Would it be too trite to say I'd like to just stop the clock right here and now?"

"What? You're Chinese and your mother doesn't have any grandchildren yet and you're talking about arresting time on circumstantial evidence?"

Whoa. Now he was talking kids. Grandkids even. For two people who just spent a couple of weeks sleeping together in cramped quarters and peeing in each other's presence, but didn't hook up until a few hours ago, they were sure shifting up to cruising speed in a hurry. She looked at his silhouette in the fading moonlight and thought, hold that "Whoa", though.

"If you stop the clock, everything just freezes, right?" Tuan was softly stroking her flank, but was obviously focused elsewhere for the moment. "Just stay in the moment, don't change. Of course we can probably move around, right? Walk, eat. Various motion-driven activities. But time will cease to be a factor?"

"Kind of a snooze button for aging and nagging reality."

"Well what would happen if you stopped the calendar?"

What that line stopped was her whole train of thought. She'd never really entertained the concept of an actual end of history. Real and, well, literally carved in stone. "Well," she said after a few minutes of mental sifting and composing, "I guess if it froze up on only one day, you'd want it to be a good one."

"Good point," Tuan said thoughtfully. "Nobody wants to stop the clock during a root canal operation. You'd definitely want a Kodak moment at the tip of your time pyramid."

"Time pyramid? Is that a real concept or one of your home-made bombs? I guess I tend to think of Mayan time concepts as circular. Wheels within wheels and all that."

"And where you find those stone calendars, how far do you ever have to look to see a pyramid?"

"The end of your nose, more or less."

"Have you actually counted the steps of the Pyramid of the Sun? Are there really 365?"

"At Chichen? Sure. There are 365 going up and 3000 coming back down, is the joke."

"Ah, narrow little steps? Strait is the gait. There are students of the Gizeh pyramids, like Thompson, et. al. who say the design there is essentially a squaring of the circle. Pi meets phi. And that they are calendars."

"I'm more partial to the Invaders' Landing Pad theory, myself."

"Well, the thing is... can you stand another big egotistical general theory lecture?"

"Only if I thought it was leading somewhere carnal and libidinous."

"One step at a time, my dear. That's what this little jot of verbal jazz is all about."

He shifted his weight slightly and made sure she was comfortable. Then looked up into the starfield and said, "Squaring the circle has always intrigued the great minds. Over the years one form keeps suggesting itself to solve the various mathematical, engineering and mystical problems involved: the pyramid. Pyramids, wherever and whenever, tend to be seen not only as landmarks, but as calendars: anchors and signposts in time and space, breaking infinite sky into numbered days. Carving our steps into numbered stones."

MeiMei, having learned she could toss solos into his jam without disturbing the flow, said, "And nobody measured and numbered and named the moments of the heavens as precisely or as obsessively or as impressively as the Maya."

"Possibly," Tuan returned, "Mayans are the 'New Egyptians', in pop culture, aren't they? But we get so fascinated with the Mayan Calendar and all its interlocking wheels, intricate design, and exotic symbology, we often forget that we have our own ways to enshrine time: equally complex wheels carving not the time of the heavens, but the cycles we invented ourselves."

He raised his arm to press a wrist to MeiMei's ear and she heard the almost inaudible ticking inside the plain steel case she had noticed the first day she met him was a Rolex Mariner.

"Our years stack up, one on the other," he said, "Like squared-off steps. While Mayan years revolve like seasons. We set hours and minutes and seconds in endless circles around our square grids of days and years, often unaware of the tiny cogs that mesh beneath the machined surface of our lives. These mechanisms of our own minds replace the sweep of worlds through the skies above us, names of Gods get lost in the tyrannous proliferation of mere numerals."

He stopped and MeiMei nuzzled him a little, said, "Not a bad monologue, but I think it needs some more laughs. And sex."

As it happened, Tuan agreed with that critique and bent to the task. But paused to say, "You know, we all tend to see time as being like a chunk a day, and they just sort of pile up into this infinitely rising tower. Each newly-minted block of time kind of pushing the old ones back. But there's another way of looking at it that I rather prefer."

"This better be leading somewhere hot, moist, and nasty, amigo."

"Bear with me four point five seconds."

"I'm bare and as with you as it gets. What's on your mind?"

"The idea is, time is actually pulled forward by the future. The time dimension doesn't really come with a little 'This way up" arrow. It's possible that it tends towards a singularity that has already happened, or is always happening and waiting for us to catch up to it. The way a dream happens instantaneously and the whole plot and pageant of it is just dragged along over how long it takes for your consciousness to make the transition."

"Yipes. You silver-tongued devil."

"Well, what I'm trying to say is, you have an idea that a single moment can turn everything that led up to it into a curtain rising, all past just prelude for the major, singular event."

He moved over her, burrowing between her waiting legs, cupping his hands around her head and looking directly into her. "The moment we first touched. Like this. It turned everything leading up to it into a honeymoon."

MeiMei didn't say a word, just crushed her mouth to his and used her hands, feet and everything she could muster to draw him as deep inside her as she could and hold him there.

WIDE TRACKING

Townsend couldn't help smirking each time he ComSatted the read out of Aphra's transponder. And got back analytics and vectors from Langley or Eustis or Cheyenne Mountain or wherever the hell they bounced the stuff around. Yes, he was thinking, the often-vilified public sector still has a few tricks up its sleeve, bitch. He was getting better dope off her bug than she was, unless he missed his guess, and a better idea of where it was.

One thing he knew, after computing the various aspects of the bounce, the velocity and positioning *vis a vis* currents and depth charts, and whatever else they threw into the algorithms, the "career", as they put it, of the device was consistent with human powered small craft. In other words, he mused, they've got a rowboat or a canoe or something out there and have been paddling for almost four hundred miles. Averaging about 4 miles an hour during times actually in motion, consistent with a fairly long, efficient craft of some kind. Stopping sometimes by day, sometimes by night. Sometimes waiting for a few hours, then sprinting by built-up areas by night. Pattern pretty clear to him. On the lam. Running and not wanting to be seen. Either that or a tourist with really peculiar tastes in when and where to picnic.

Another thing he knew that she probably didn't was that whoever or whatever she'd tagged had just crossed a line. Specifically, into Belize waters. Bummer for him because the DEA, and in fact the U.S. in general, had a lot less clout down there than in Mexico—where he could practically order dinner and some Mexican cop or Marine would bring it and not ask for a tip.

But the thing she knew and he didn't was gnawing on his butt. Namely, who the hell had that tracker and what the hell it all meant. Without which nothing made much sense and he was at a loss. Extremely frustrating.

For a guy most people would see as having everything anybody could want, and having done a bang-up job of accomplishing everything he'd ever undertaken in life, Townsend Hardley led a life heavily beset by frustration.

Like right now, for instance. The guy was about to show up any minute who could put him right on top of the thing, but not knowing what was going on, he didn't know how he could use it.

Show up here at the oddest, possibly coolest café he'd ever seen. In Chetumal, Quintana Roo, Mexico, of all places. The guy had said he couldn't miss it, and there was no doubt of that. "La Flota" reminded him of the long, slim houseboats he'd seen moored on the rivers in Amsterdam and Paris. But was moored alongside a municipal pier near the fishing fleet and some grey hulls with big white numbers that had "interdict" apparent in every detail. Below in the skinny hull, the galley was hip-wide and six yards long with two cramped tables. And four more... not really tables, more like counters... in the open air on the upper deck. Giving views of the jade green lagoon, the tangled mangroves to the east, and the wide sweep of Chetumal's park-like malecón. Townsend lounged, the only customer at four in the afternoon, and looked around sipping some really good coffee alleged to be from Yucatan. And wished the guy who'd said he'd meet him there would hurry up and meet him there.

At about the same time, just one time zone to the east, the Far Right Honorable Elijah Jacob Weatherwax was pitching a fit.

"Who else is onto this thing?" he bellowed at quivering underlings who tried unsuccessfully to slouch down below the line of sight over his precariously cluttered desk. He brandished a wad of graph paper with lines plotted in three different colors, shaking it at them while his jowls rolled around like varicosed pit bulls. "You can see it here, right here, shit, all over the place here...it's getting pinged and it's squealing on us like a stuck shoat. And not to anybody we know and admire. Probably reading it contemporary, like the frigging scores crawling across the screen under Mushburger and Madden's faces. Jesus!"

"The tech morlocks down there told me her transmitter isn't linear-secure. Whatever that means."

"It means they're all over her ass like her little sister's pantyhose, that's what it means. It also means something like, you know, we just might be cornholed and hornswaggled here. End up running round hiding our faces and crotches, trying to find some deniability to scootch down behind. Or just end up sucking hind titty on whatever she's down there trying to root out."

He took another look at the plotter paper and threw it at them. "Did you just pull that stuff out of NSA stock and give it to her?"

"No, she uses her own hardware. Software, too, I guess."

"Great. Just so all-fired great I could dance a Sunday jig. We're down there with a bluelight special from Spies R Us and she's getting her crack sniffed by... well, golly guys, I wonder who it might be? The Creep, maybe?"

"I don't think they call it that anymore, Senator. Just The Committee."

"I was referring to a defector from our bosom, now employed by that self-same committee, with an end to getting another four years for President Osama-bama and pissing in our pockets as we all go down."

"Could be," Hutchins said. He'd about had it with this cornpone ass-chewing. This guy couldn't really fire him. "Or maybe the Cuba Cigar Cartels. Or the Kremlin/Vatican hookup, or that Al K. Eeda guy. Or the Elders of Zion..."

"Oh, very humorous, sonny. They are onto her is what I'm saying. Because you let her go down there with a slingshot."

"Senator," Collinsworth said, drawing courage from Hutchin's sarcasm, "I don't see how you can blame us for this. Even if we'd given her the best stuff we could get, she'd still be in the field with available technology. And she'd still be up against..."

"The Committee, yeah, yeah."

"I was going to say up against the United States Government."

"Well, sheeeit," the Right Honorable said, deflating into his chair. "Ain't we all, these days?"

271

THE MEDIUM IS THE MASSAGE

"So was it worth it?" Kenny bleated. "Was it worth the money, the trouble, the flesh-pressing with these slimy, delusional third world... glamballers, the humiliation? Walking around a week with our ball sacks dripping sweat and fungus?"

"I thought you were getting your nads de-sweated by that child who thinks he's a cameraman... and that you're a director." Gareth looked around to see if there was a sufficient audience of young and bi-curious noshing the dinner buffet around the pool at El Faro to bring out the full flower of Kenny's pissiness. Saw nothing but tepid, wind-down conversation at the pool bar, micro-mini-mogulettes and mogulitos slacking off after ninety-six hours of everybody pretending to be at some branch eye of the Glamorwood tornado.

"He's twenty, very talented—if raw—and if I'm not a real director of our real film, then what aren't you?" Kenny somehow managed to give the impression of stamping his feet even though sitting down. Actually so slumped in a lounge chair that he could barely glare over the tabletop into Gareth's tired and bloodshot eyes.

Gareth sighed. "We got that award."

"Ooooo, we got an award. A Plexiglas trophy made out of melted-down six-pack thongs for our excellence in cultural portrayal of jailbait poontang wearing nothing but rectal floss and gallons of ersatz blood! They love me, they really love me. I think I spotted one of the busboys who didn't get an award."

"Well, I can see somebody got up on the wrong side of the bidet this morning." No point in trying to talk to the little cumbucket when he was like this. "Tell me when you can do enough of an impression of a sentient being to discuss how we're going to handle meeting Francis Ford Fucking Coppola and trying to get him in on our film."

Kenny started to say something twatty, but stopped. He seemed to sort of shake himself off, a Springer Spaniel quiver that shed a rain of petty fuckwittedness all around him and left him reasonably in the clear. He looked at Gareth grimly and said, "We've got to grab their attention up there. All of them, not just Mr. Godfather. We have to come on, you know."

"I know, I know. I just don't know how, know how. All I have to do is impress a bunch of world-class impresarios."

"Well think about it. I'm hatching an idea myself."

"You're going to think and scheme all evening?"

Kenny stood up and squinted towards their cabana. "I am going to take a nice little nap. What do you think?"

He grabbed his linen "man purse" and turned to mince off, then turned for a smile he thought was naughty, but actually came off as sort of desperate/degenerate and said, "And star in a little film production of my own."

"Kenny," Gareth said, and something naked and plaintive in his voice cutting through his partner's usual camp-out. "Can we get the hell out of this tourist trap piece of shit?"

Kenny started to say something flip, but Gareth slowly stood up and approached him, shaking his head slowly. "You're right. The award was a sick joke. This whole fiasco was a waste of time, money... air. We've got two days until we have to be up at that lodge. Let's go somewhere quiet and simple and regroup."

"But Jorge..." Kenny started to say, then stopped and gave Gareth a rare genuine smile and foppishly punched his shoulder. "You're right, he's not near as talented as all that. Nor as hung as I'd like, either."

"Look, how about Tulum?"

"Perfect. Let's just pack up and check out, right now. And maybe that way we can also lose..."

"Fat chance," Gareth said in a hollow tone, gesturing towards the deep shadows under the *palapa* by the steps to the beach. Where a pair of long, lovely legs led up to a white swimsuit filled out by a classy brunette. Beside which sat a hulking figure looking right at them with a relaxed vigilance.

Kenny stiffened, and his whole poise fell apart again on the spot. He lunged over towards Bannock and Loris practically howling. "Bannock, we told you. That first night."

That first horrible night, Gareth thought, as he followed Kenny over to the man who had dogged their steps for four days. Check into our room and here's the Angel of Contusions sitting there like he owned the place. Which I suppose he did. Unless anybody wanted to contest the title.

He was past being afraid of Bannock, or even angry. He walked over and pulled up a chair, plopped down two feet in front of him as

Kenny stood there quaking and making little gibbon faces. He started to speak, but Loris rolled over, graced him with a beautiful smile and passed him a cold beer from the bucket on the table. He took it and nodded to her, genuinely grateful. Something in the gesture redefined the conversation before it even started.

"Look, Bannock," he said wearily, "What I told you is true. We don't have it... him. We shipped our gear on ahead so it could clear Belize customs. Oxo's already in Belize. Safe and sound. There's nothing you can beat out of us and no point in following us, really."

Bannock nodded amiably. He was in no hurry. He was like the Mounties or something. Always got his skull.

Kenny finally subsided, sanking into a lounger muttering to himself. Loris offered him a beer, too, but he just shook his head and kept on shaking it for awhile.

It was Loris who finally spoke. "Gareth, why don't you just invite us to come with you?" she said.

Gareth and Kenny stared at her, dumbfounded. Why not just invite us into your bank so we don't have to fret with all those pesky details like breaking in? Gareth could only think of saying, "It's by invitation only. Francis' invitation."

"But you need an entourage," Loris told him, and he realized they'd heard what they'd been saying. He opened his mouth, but didn't get very far.

Loris swiveled gracefully, stood, and walked over to Kenny. "Sweetheart," she said, "You're a bundle of nerves. Lie down." Kenny obeyed, numbly. "No, on your tummy."

Kenny obeyed silently and humbly, as if he was in the habit of taking orders without thinking about them. Loris moved to his head, knelt, and reached out her hands to cup the back of his skull. The other men watched without speaking or moving: she seemed to broadcast a wave of silence around her, calm spreading out from her like ripples on a pond. As if independent creatures, her hands began to move.

Kenny lay on his back, eyes closed, smiling slightly and radiating a deep, organic peace. Gareth stared at him: the man seemed taller, more substantial, the lines of his face altered by the lack of ego-grubbing and drama. He looked at Loris, sitting beside Bannock on the other lounger. She said, "I've been around film people before. You're a nervous lot. This guy used to take me to parties with him, once to this retreat up in Santa Barbara. I gave massages to whoever wanted them. He said it made them easier to do business with. I thought it made everything more sane and human, is all."

Gareth stared at her with wonder and even a trace of trepidation. Not only had she heard his prayer, but yea, she had answered.

Loris stood smoothly and motioned him to his feet. "Let me show you something, she said. "This great little club off Fifth."

Bannock stood up as well, darkening the glow of pool lights and luau lamps, from Gareth's point of view. He gestured at the raptured Kenny. "Think the hotel will lend us a stretcher?"

FLOATING WORLD

"You see?" Lluvia asked proudly. She swept her hand around, offering the view from the upper deck of La Flota. "It's not on earth, it's on sea."

"*Sí, sí,*" Denny said, looking up the malecón at the State government buildings and the accoutrements in the park. "When you're right, you're right."

A slight breeze off the lagoon alleviated the heat that he experienced so intensely because of his moronic insistence on keeping the trenchcoat on. This was his first foreign assignment and he meant to look the part. Besides, Seattleites feel naked without their raincoats.

She sat, poured Lala half and half into her Americano (chosen instead of her usual sweet cappuccinos and lattes as a tribute to her companion) and motioned him to take the other chair. She handed him the cream and sipped from the cup, almost sighing with pleasure. This was how it should be, she was thinking. In a nice place like this, with a nice-looking, interesting man who treated her like something other than furniture or a potential love doll. Having foreign coffee drinks. She felt sophisticated, not a common feeling for her.

There was only one other person on the deck, another gringo. Long odds on that. A handsome blonde who looked like a movie star. In The Picture, was the way she felt. She didn't realize it yet, but she had at that point totally and permanently lost interest in Luis.

At the offshore end of the deck, Townsend had given them a cursory scan when they came up the ladder. Pretty girl, looks nice and fun. Guy an obvious dumbass from the sticks. I mean, a trench coat? In Mexico? He turned his attention back to the boats at the Co-op dock and wishing that turkey Montez would hurry up and show. He was already fifteen minutes late.

At the shore end, Denny was basking in the interest and general approval rating of Lluvia: the only place he generally ran into pretty women hanging on his words was in his nouveau-rich fantasy life. Continuing to speak fluent Chandler/Gumshoese, he grilled the dame over the lowdown on this Luis mug. "So he takes her to this Cobá thing and she never comes back. Nobody had any questions about that?"

"Yes. Well, only I. And he never answered. I was very preoccupied about her and nobody would say anything. I called the office at Cobá and they wouldn't say me one word. Even the Director called them and they are saying nothing. Something is going here. Not right."

"Well getting to the bottom of not right stuff is what I do for a living, sweetheart. Has anything, anything at all, come up about Dr. Chiang since she left with him?"

"*Bueno*.... Ah, there was a woman who came to look for her. I talked about that and she said she was going to Cobá to look at Dra. Chiang, but she never arrived there. I thought that was a strange thing."

"A Mexican woman?"

"*Uy, al contrario*. Sorry, I mean to say, no. In no case was she Mexican. An American, I think. But she had a strange accents. She was very *negra*, a black American woman."

"Really. Did she look like police? Scientist? Reporter?"

"She looked like a cinema star. Like Iman or Beyonce or Shakira or some person of that form. Beautiful, but I don't know.... Dangerous, like a big cat in the *circo*."

Badda bing! A chair scraped at the other of the deck and the men's wear model sitting there got up and came back towards them, threading along the narrow space between the chairs on the starboard side and the handrail to port. He smiled and nodded. "Hi, I'm Town Hardley. You're American, right? May I join you?"

Lluvia blinked, trying to take him all in. Thinking of Brad Pitt, Keifer Southerland, Gael Garcia. Denny paused. He was starting to get really fond of having Lluvia's undivided attention and, like most males, had the sneaking feeling that if Townsend was around female attention would be hard to come by.

But Town gave them the hometown ballplayer grin and said, "Hope you don't mind. I just heard somebody speaking English for a change and she mentioned Beyonce and well, I'm a fan, so I thought I'd come over and say hi."

Within five minutes of joining them at the table Town was enjoying a half-hearted rapport with Denny and a warm display from Lluvia. And had the conversation firmly routed back to the black woman and the good Dr. Chiang's mysterious non-whereabouts.

"Why would this doctor go to Cobá in the first place?"

"I don't know. But it was something about an artifact there. Maybe something from our collection, but before I came to the work here. I'm from Merida and they sent me here directly from the *Autonimo*."

"She didn't say anything about it?"

"I heard Luis say he would show her the *placa*. That could mean a plaque or badge. But on the phone to Cobá I heard him call it a *calavera*. That means, you know a *cranio*."

"Skull," Town offered.

"That. A skull. I think they don't want him to see it, but he got authorization from Mexico and took her there by any ways."

"Quite a mystery," Townsend offered.

"There is no doubt. A disappearing woman, a skull, a guilty bureaucrat. I would buy the ticket and the popcorns, definitively."

"Everything's a mystery, kid," Denny said out of the corner of his mouth. "Until it's marked solved."

Townsend nodded appreciatively at that bit of hard-boiled wisdom, thinking, Christ did this guy fall off the turnip truck last night, or this morning? Wonder if he's "packing" a "roscoe"? He said, "So you're trying to find her? An investigator?"

"I'm just interested in the Doc. She's a noted authority, you know." Which Denny knew because Lluvia had told him on the way over. He saw her glance at him, catching the discrepancy from what he had told her. She seemed to take it as part of the mystique.

"Well, I'm kind of interesting in finding somebody, too."

"And we know who, don't we?" Denny was not always as stupid as he seemed and had tumbled to the sheer lack of idle co-incidence. "You're looking for her, too, aren't you? Tracing her."

"What? Tracing who?" No way, Townsend was thinking in full alarm mode. No way!

"MeiMei Chiang. We're colleagues, aren't we? Same line of grift. More like competitors at the moment. You've been playing us pretty cute, but you slipped up."

"Oh, really?" Townsend said. Rhyming it with "chilly". Can you believe this dickhead?

"Yep." He turned to Lluvia who was practically gaping, trying to follow the plot without a scorecard. "Hey, doll, does this guy look like a Beyonce fan to you?"

She studied Town seriously. *Chiin, que gringo bonito.* Then said, "I think all men would be fans of Beyonce."

"Well, then, *amigo.* Can you tell me this?" Denny paused while Townsend smoldered. "Name me the title of a single Beyonce song?"

That pissed Townsend off more than anything he'd run into in years. More like, ratcheted up his frustration. Without visibly gritting his teeth, he said, "Okay, you got me, Señor Intercontinental Op. The black bitch pulled a one-nighter on me, then ripped me off for some important stuff and took off. I've got to get it back. So I'm after her ass."

Lluvia nodded to herself. Yes, this looks like the kind of man who would go to the bed of a woman like that. She'd buy the popcorns to watch that, too. In a heartbeat.

"Okay, look. Don't ask me how I know this, okay?" Denny gave an overacted, "just between us pros" take that Town felt like slapping off his face. "But I think she found Dr. Chiang and is trying to rip her off, too. This thing is big. Like treasure, okay? Maybe. But I can't say anything more than that. But if you help me out here a little..."

Denny was so practiced and fluent at producing fantasies for his own amusement that lying to others was a sort of performance art for him. He wasn't as good at it as he thought, but lies work best when people are really motivated to believe them.

"So here's my proposition. "We team up, pool what we've got, go find these broads, turn 'em up and sort 'em out."

Oh yeah, I'm going to pool info and work with this clown. "You sure turned me over there, pal. You're some sort of pro, huh?"

Denny pulled out a wallet and produced a rather fancy laminated document with gold seal and goony picture, making sure Lluvia saw it. Townsend took it, but butterfingered. "Whoops, sorry."

He ducked his head under the table, hand coming out of his pocket with what he thought of as his "Phaser" to scan the license as he emerged from under the narrow table. Handed the card back to Denny saying, "Wow, Washington."

"Washington State," Denny corrected.

As Denny chattered toughly about the "case", Townsend flitted his fingers across the keys of his reader, looking at everything they had on this yo-yo Which wasn't much, but certainly established just who exactly was the chump here. Wrong Washington, asshole, Townsend thought. On the other hand, he did seem to have some big chunks of this. And wasn't about to just give them up.

"So where do you think Dr. Chiang is?" Denny asked. Neutral, baseline question, like that course he took in San Francisco had trained him.

Townsend paused, apparently deep in thought, actually scanning data on Mercer. And coming to a conclusion. Namely, What the hell? He just couldn't come up with a reason why this guy would pose any threat or problem. So he smiled and said, "Okay, let's share. She might be heading down the Cayes in a rowboat."

A bit of a leap, but whatever or whoever was at the other end of that electronic connection was of extreme interest to Aphra Alisander. Unless she'd dumped the bug on some old salt trying to row a dingy to Brazil or something.

"Belize?" Denny wasn't the worst-informed American alive: he knew where it was and what it was. Another country, for one thing. He just didn't know jack about it other than that. He looked at Lluvia. "If I go to Belize can you come along? Keep helping and translating?"

Something he caught in her expression gave him pause. "Wait, how many people in Belize speak English?"

She wasn't sure if he was serious or playing some gringo game that was over her head. She said, "They all do."

"It's the official language," Townsend said, his heavily neutral tone a rebuke in itself.

"Oh. Well, great. How do we get there?"

"The bus runs south from the same station you arrived," Lluvia told him.

"But probably doesn't run out the reef?" Townsend looked at her a second and gave it a shot. "Is there any sort of town out on the Cayes?"

"Well, Cayo Tobacco has some hotels, maybe a bar. Docks."

Ah. He'd seen some docks on the satellite shots from GoogleEarth, but had figured they were all just places fishermen tied up because he'd seen no buildings. He now figured there were thatched-roof shacks in under the palms, a good assumption. They almost had to be heading there. They couldn't have three weeks of supplies in whatever they were rowing and definitely hadn't hit any towns on the way. He looked at Lluvia again, not an unpleasant place to look.

"How could I get there?"

Dangerous Den Mercer, fedora crammed back on his head and machete clenched in his pearly whites, jumped off the wing float of the long-snouted Grumman Widgeon into waist deep water. Kicking aside a crocodile, and holding the pesky Artifact over his head, he waded up the beach towards an adoring Chinese beauty tied to a palm tree by four unsavory pirates bent on plundering her. They glared at Denny truculently and went for their side arms. Denny...

"Seaplanes aren't legal there."

He was wrenched from his vision by Lluvia's comment. Damn, no seaplanes?

"Why not?"

"I think they outlawed them because *narcos* were using them so much. You understand, trafficants of drugs."

"Shut down flight on the whole coast so U.S. junkies can pay more for their dope," Denny scoffed, further pissing off Townsend, who'd been with the DEA for a year and was probably going back on detached liaison with them after this fiasco got closed out.

Lluvia turned to look at the rows of boats moored south of the municipal dock and waved her hand. "It's illegal to go over in boats, too. But the fishermen do it all the time."

Townsend looked at his watch. "I'd been hoping for something a little more efficient," he said, then looked up as a shifting of the hull and footfalls on the ladder signaled that Montez had arrived at last. "And hey, this must be the guy now."

ENTOURAGE

*T*he *club I play in Playa is called Posada Xi Ka'an. Don't worry about the weird name. In the Yucatan a name like Xi Ka-an (from the Mayan: "Place of the Site of the Location of the Spot") is no big deal. They have places around here named Oxkutscab and Tixcogob, man. Dzilbalchan, Dzinup, Xclakal, Xul-Ha, Hochob, Holbox, Xkaladzonof, X-Masil, Chikinzlofla. There's even an Xpo, but it ain't pronounced like they do in Montreal. So do what everybody else does, fake it. The Mayas themselves can't pronounce these things. I mean, come on...Xclaf? They just put the names on the map to confuse invading armies. It didn't work. But it sure freaked out my spell checker. Check the website, hztlp://www. Xzkcl.ctlom.*
Seagull: *The Blasé Sojourner*

Seagull could cover a mind-numbing number of songs, and had written a few of his own, but he was at his best—and remember, it's all relative—when jamming his own lyrics on existing tunes. Such as Jimmy Buffet's "Margaritaville", of which he had done dozens of vamps, including the one he was singing at the moment...

I spoke with the waiter, he said, "Be by later"
I've been here an hour with two lousy brews
They say "*ahorita*" or "*un momentita*"
And leave you alone with the "*mañana*" blues.

I'm wastin' time again in Ahorita-ville
Waitin' for my damn dinner and drinks
The waitresses say they'll be back sometime today
But you know, that's not what I think.

They said they'd bring it in a Mexican minute
But two happy hours have already passed
I ate all the corn chips, the salsa and bean dip
And nibbled the salt off the rim of my glass.

    I'm wasting away to bones in Ahorita-ville
    Waiting for my waiter to come through the door
    Some people say he just snuck by with a tray
    But I think he don't work here no more.

I called for the cuenta, they said, "*un momenta*"
If they're back in an hour it'll be strange
I paid a few pesos for my *chile con queso*
And everyone's vanished to go hunt for change.

    I'm wastin' half my life in Ahorita-ville
    Waiting for this damn dinner to end
    Some people say it's just the Mexico way
    But by now, I'm all hungry again.

A crowd-pleaser, especially among "sophisticates" like this film festival scuzz, who congratulated themselves for knowing what the Spanish lyrics meant—unaware that everybody else in the world did, too, even the Mexicans. But the waiters just hated it.

As soon as the meager applause died out, he ditched his multi-forgeried guitar and grabbed his dumbek, tossing the strap around his neck so it could hang right in front of his crotch. He pounded a quick, bright staccato on the rim, then moved to the slap and went into his watered-down, generic, but energetic Afro beat. And Copper was suddenly just standing there. Staring at the crowd with her arms hanging at her side, trailing chains. Slowly she lifted her arms and held them over her head, the Lost Soul dangling her chains like a broken puppet's string. Then suddenly, somehow, they ignited and she stood between two crackling balls of fire. She paused a beat, then swung the fireballs around her, the excess white gas blasting parallel tongues of fire onto the floor like hot rails to hell. As always, she danced a trance inside the sphere of holy flame.

At the front table, where you could actually feel a little heat from the blazing poi, Loris turned to Gareth and said, "Think about it, you show up with some music and entertainment, and hint that it's what your film's about. Hand drums and fire-spinning: hot totems for today's youth."

Gareth leaned back and scanned her. "What makes you think that's what it's about?"

Loris smiled. "What do you think?"

Gareth, mindful of her close rapport with the rock head he expected to direct his film, nodded sagely. But please, show up and try to impress Coppola and Shane Black with a hippy fire dancer? How about a mime, just to round it all out? Maybe an organ grinder? Kenny might like that angle.

The gas was just about exhausted in the tight-wound Kevlar balls at the end of Copper's scything chains. And suddenly they flew off her hands. The crowd gasped as the chains flew across the floor and out the open door to the deck, pinwheeling alongside each other as their fires guttered out.

And between the flying sparks, Xchab walked into the club not looking at anybody, just doing a very Indian-like shuffle-dance to the beat of Seagull's drum. She held her arms out from her shoulders, swept slightly back like a jet's wings. She moved slowly into the room, shuffling and stamping, her taut young body weaving dreamily.

There were twenty parrots in the entryway to the Xi Ka'an, their wings clipped, their scintillating, psychedelic feather moirés somewhat dulled by captivity in huge wrought-iron cages. And suddenly, for no reason, the birds were out of their cages. And flying on chopped-down wings. Xchab danced into the center of the floor, her arms rising and falling as she bobbed, her hands making circles in the air. A squadron of brilliant birds hovered behind her arms, forming big, flat, iridescent wings that moved and wavered and pulsed behind her as she danced without knowing her arms had become the leading edges for a flying wedge of determined, silent birds. Or that a huge blue papagayo with gold chest and white circles around its red eyes, was hovering unerringly over her head, fluttering back and forth as she nodded her erect head and shook her gleaming jet mane.

Winston entered the room unseen as people froze with cigars halfway to their lips and icecubes lying in their mouths, gawking at the Mayan girl dancing as the focal point of a wing of flaring feathers.

He put a six-hole cane whistle to his lips and started piping. It was a shrill but soothing sound, a highly Indian tattoo of chrome notes as clear as icepicks, broken up by a slightly breathy counterpoint. Music from the Chiapas highlands, a splashing Lacandon rain over the tight metallic beat of the dumbek. Copper shook a bundle of goat hooves, producing a dry tambourine-like sound that reeked of stone temples and yellow eyes in the jungle.

Suddenly Seagull rattled off a sharp burst of rimshots, Winston reached into the highest register for a sustained scream from his whistle and Xchab threw her arms over her head to bring her hands together. The birds flew up, spiraling into the high rafters of the club. Then the lights went out.

Copper was working the tables with professional cool, her tin can wrapped in woven ribbons, clanking and whispering as it filled with loot, Kenny was staring like a man envisioning tongues of fire, Gareth slowly turned his face to Loris, eyes wide and mouth sagging open.

She chuckled and touched his forearm on the table. "They'll just love us," she said.

SINS OF THE MOTHER

So they decamped a bit late and languid, paddling along just inside the reef, passing strings of islets like an emerald necklace strewn along the spine of the sea. Talking the multi-level language of new lovers, saying some pretty silly stuff for noted scientists. But in the mid-afternoon, Tuan pointed at a somewhat larger clump of greenery far ahead and said, "There should be a phone there."

"Oh, yeah, the phone." MeiMei felt one more stab of guilt at having neglected to call her parents. Then had the sudden thought, "How about you, OB? Isn't your Mom worried sick by now and just waiting to make you guilty about it?"

She was unprepared for the bitter grunt from behind her. And the harsh way he said, "She's dead."

She stopped paddling and looked over her shoulder at Tuan, who continued to steadily paddlewheel the kayak forward. She thrust her paddle out so his would strike it, and held it there until he stopped moving and stared at her. She said, "You're generally pretty good at talking. Tell me about it."

He drew a deep breath and looked past her to the horizon. "My father was as All-American as they come. He was in the Navy. Retired now. He's probably responsible for my noted 'generalism'."

"A sailor," she said, just marking time while he got to it.

"An officer on a nuclear submarine. Most people don't realize it, but submariners are the most educated military personnel in the world. Every man on a U.S. submarine is cross-trained to every other job on the sub. In a disaster, people get killed or sections flooded, so any man on board has to able to step in and do the job of any other crew member. No other branch of the service can make that claim."

Intrigued with the size of that despite herself, MeiMei said, "Wow. So the cook knows how to run a nuclear reactor?"

"Exactly. Dad was a navigation officer going in, but after a couple of years on the Ashville and New Orleans he was also a mechanic, cook, gunner, nuke physicist... during the Carter admin he wanted to be physicist and peanut farmer. And he just kept on learning. He's in school now... I think he wants to cross-train with everybody on the planet."

Let's get back on the hot topic, MeiMei thought. "So he met your mother in the Philippines."

"Yep," his voice had taken on some animation, but slammed flat again. "Subic Bay. Ever heard of it?"

"Don't think so. A navy base?"

"A huge navy base. 'Pubic Bay', the swabbies called it before Aquino kicked us out. And with good reason."

He stopped for a minute and MeiMei waited him out. Then he shrugged, still without looking at her, and said, "San Diego has such a big Filipino population because a couple of generations of sailors married prostitutes and brought them home, then they dragged their families over."

"Come on, Tuan." She didn't care if it was an exaggeration or not, she could see the hurt starting to ooze out of it.

"My mom, the war bride. And she didn't change her ways much after she hit the States, apparently. Very common, you get these Flip fleet widow places, ex-Luzon whores hanging out looking for kicks and tricks. And Mom was the queen of the pack."

"Oh, Tuan. That's really a..."

"...shame? I felt that way at the time. Got me in fights. Might have driven me to the books. Definitely drove me to martial arts."

"Any in particular?"

"Aikido, mostly. I always thought the best offense was a good defense."

"That's a good one all right."

"You too?"

"Yeah, my dad was a devotee, used to teach me. Sent me to Roger Chun's dojo—the most brutal sensei in Seattle. Then he developed other martial interests."

"Such as?"

"NFL football."

"Ah, the Way of the Empty Helmet."

"Tuan..."

"Ah yes, our backstory continues. Dad divorced Mom and kicked her out when I was in third grade. He told me she was dead."

"Harsh. But maybe easier on you."

"Possibly. I saw her a couple of times later and know what? He was right."

MeiMei palmed the paddle to brace her hands on the gunwales and carefully turned around to face him. He stuck a blade into the water for more stability as she pulled off the tricky maneuver and ended up on her knees, facing him. She slid her hands along the hull until her face was a foot from his. She hadn't had any idea of what to say, but as she faced him it bubbled up out of her.

"Give me time, Tuan. I'll make it up to you."

He let out something that could have been a cry of joy or a sob of pain or anything in between and reached to embrace her.

So they tipped right over into the sea.

Bobbing in the water, both of them laughed uproariously. He grabbed the turtled boat with one hand and pulled her close with the other.

"I've got all the time in the world," he said. "And it's all yours."

Three hours later they were sitting in a bar on Tobacco Caye, laughing about the sign in fluent Belize Creole, "Ef you doan got 18 yeahs, you caan drink likah heah."

And listening to the short, shiny-black barmaid tell them that nowhere in the tumble of little shacks and stilt buildings that comprised Tobacco Caye was there a telephone except some ship-to-shore rigs. They were on their second bottles of yeasty Belikan beer when they heard it coming.

Unmistakably some sort of aircraft. Tuan saw the Belizean girl's face furrow in concern. Not seen as a good thing. He stepped over to the wall of the bar, the top half of which swung up on a hinge to provide major ventilation and shade out in front. It came in low and fast, stopped on a dime beside the long, rickety dock, and settled down on pontoons. A large, military grade chopper, was his impression. All white and painted with obscure arms inside the logo "Armada de Mexico". Almost certainly not a favorable indication.

He looked at MeiMei, who stared at the helicopter nudging up to the dock. Where their kayak was tied, bobbing in the propwash. Calmly he said, "I'd say we're going to end up talking to them."

MeiMei nodded, her face drawn tight. She stood up, visibly squared her shoulders, and walked over to take his hand. Together they walked out of the bar and down the dock towards the patrol helicopter.

Two men hopped to the deck and nothing about them made Tuan feel any better. Except that they were obviously not Mexican Marines. One looked like the guy with the Ferrari on the old "Miami Vice" program, the other was wearing a trench coat and a very hard look.

In a low voice to MeiMei he said, "These guys look like the law. That might actually be a good thing."

Yeah, right, MeiMei was thinking. She hadn't cowered in terror under an inverted hull in the night hiding from gypsy ninjas. They'd been cops, too. In Mexican military craft. She gripped Tuan's hand harder as the two walked towards them.

As they came up, the one with the forties' hat stared at MeiMei and slid his hand inside the breast of his trenchcoat. Tuan gathered himself for a doubtless futile leap and felt MeiMei doing the same.

Then they were right on top of them and the trenchcoat said, "Are you Doctor Mayflower Chiang?"

Mayflower? Tuan thought, as MeiMei gave a guarded nod.

Denny Mercer pulled a cell phone out of his coat, handed it to her, and said, "Mind giving your mother a ring?"

CULT FOLLOWING

It wasn't easy sorting it out, and Aphra was about to give up, when one of those thunderbolts of luck hit. Most people in espionage had an almost superstitious belief that all success came from hard work, training and, well... superior intelligence. But she'd always seen a heavy streak of crap-shoot in it all and felt like you won if you were ready to go with the roll. Which was good, because she was getting absolutely nowhere trying to get into the blonde's scrambled head.

"So you saw the jade thing?"

"Yeah, yeah. And all these heads and gold and *coralcaturas*..."

And off she went, babbling to her beach hunk about coral. Aphra shook her head and knocked back some more brandy. She looked around the Paraiso and scowled. It was going to be a long night, and it looked like it would be right here in this beachbum dive. Where the seashell-wailing chick had split and now their idea of fun was some wispy hippy playing drums and this retro-hip/goth/vamp redhead spinning fireballs around. In a place with a thatch roof, no less. Fairly fistable redhead, though.

She tried once again to corral Curtsy's exploded attention. "So the jade thing was a skull?"

"Yeah. Kind of talking, you know, like cartoon balloons? MeiMei took pictures..." Then she plummeted off the re-recognition buzz into another weeping fit. "MeiMei. They... those fuckers! They..."

"When did you last see MeiMei?" Two steps forward, one step back.

"They stripped us, then they dragged her off. The guy, the yacht guy... Oh, man, is he ever a total piece of shit. He was going to rape us!" She touched her head and went ballistic over another memory fragment. "He shot me! He must have thrown me in the water. Those *assholes*!"

She was practically screaming at that point, and her boyfriend didn't try to calm her down, just watched her like she was a circus act. Aphra tried to think of how to play her, then she veered off again, California smile breaking out through the tears. "But they came for me! They saved my life. It was so beautiful."

"Not the same 'they' as the assholes who shot you?"

"Of course not!" The very idea was offensive. She smiled and simpered like a middle-schooler in love. "The guys. My guys came and got me and brought me home. Oh, wait, I fucked that up, though."

"Your guys?" Aphra didn't mind admitting to being totally lost at this point and was starting to wonder if the head injuries Curtsy had apparently been piling up over the past week had done permanent damage. Hard to tell, though. How do blonde brain cells die? Alone.

"Yeah. Bongo and Bruto and Pinoccio and Caruso and Mayab. Well, Mayab isn't a 'guy', really, but she's cool and..."

God only knew what that rant was all about. What she had to show for this whole fuckup was that MeiMei had seen this jade skull, had gotten pictures, last seen in captivity by some guys who didn't mind raping and shooting girls who took pictures of their skull collection. And she just couldn't think of any further ways to pursue questioning without the blonde's wackness getting contagious. She took another sip of brandy and went rigid when there was one of those sudden lulls in bar chatter and she heard somebody at the table behind her say something that snagged her attention like a number ten triple-snelled fishhook.

Kenny had done nothing but bitch ever since they came in the place—*quelle surprise*—and was starting to get on everybody's nerves. "This hovel is deader than those ruins," he whined loudly. "I thought you said the beach scene here was, you know, active."

"Meaning, of course, cruisey," Gareth replied. "Look it's a cheap place to kill two days until the workshop starts. And there are some lovely women here, get a load of the table behind me."

Kenny's petulant gaze skittered past the knockout ebony/ivory pair and lit on Ganzo. "Not bad, I guess," he pouted. "But he's just..."

Loris, who'd been watching Copper spin fire with interest, turned to him and said, "We're here, Kenny. Who could be more interesting than that?"

Kenny, confused, stopped to sort it out, and shot yet another covetous glance at Bannock, who had tuned him out. Xchab couldn't even understand English and she was ready to slap him silly if he didn't shut up.

"Okay, let's talk about this trip to Jungleville," he whined at Gareth. "What are we really going to accomplish?"

"Maybe get greenlighted for a real feature, not another one of these dorkploitation reels."

"But how? That's all I'm asking." His voice raised as the real source of his recent vapors came to the surface. "What? We waltz in there with a stone skull and tell him it can talk to us? If it would really talk instead of all this stone innuendo, we could at least figure out where the bottom line is. Get a picture of the ending. Get a budget. Take out insurance."

Which affected Aphra in the manner already mentioned. She turned slowly as if scoping out the scene and took a look. Two flitty-looking chipmunks in resort wear, very tasty-looking white girl in a white linen shift, DeNiro-looking cat coulda been the collection department for a loan shark, possibly yummy lil Injun gal, and a sixties burnout. Quite the crew, all right. And she remembered now that they'd come in with the little drummer boy and his *tres* lappable redhead flamethrower.

She excused herself, walked past the washrooms that she wouldn't have set foot in on a bet, and eased out to the crushed shell lot where she'd parked. Didn't take a rocket surgeon to spot the white passenger van with rental plates so she sashayed over, slipping one of the new tracers out of her purse. One-day Fed-Ex to Cancun, cost somebody bucks, delayed her a day to pick them up, but she didn't see any way Hardley or the White House could have tumbled to them. She squatted quickly to click the sender under the fender of the van. As she walked back into the Paraiso, she did a quick check on her receiver. It lit up, tossed blips and digits around its touch screen, and basically told her, "Follow that car." Don't mean shit getting a wild break unless you've got it together to follow your shots.

Curtsy stood in the dark parking area fidgeting and chewing a fingernail. First they follow a yacht, now Aphra wants to follow a van. She'd been seeing Ganzo as provider and protector ever since she could remember. But now she could remember a whole lot more, and he suddenly seemed inadequate to the task. Aphra could swing about anything like magic. On the other hand, her last trick had played out totally ugly.

Finally Aphra leaned over. pushed the door open and patted the seat. "Come on, girlfriend. Where else you got to go?"

Curtsy dithered a few seconds more then jerked the back door open, prodded Ganzo into the tiny back seat, and slid in after him. She looked at Aphra in the rearview mirror and said, "Okay, what the hell? Get us out of here."

Aphra bobbed her head as she turned the ignition. "Oh, yowsuh. Right enuff, Miss Daisy."

CHOPPER MAMA

MeiMei estimated she'd have about thirty seconds to talk to her father before the line was overwhelmed, so she blurted out an apology and incredibly lame alibi. She heard herself say, "I didn't want you to worry," and caught Tuan's headshake and half-smile. What's to worry about having your youngest daughter chased on the high seas by murdering booty bandits, harried by gunboats and having unprotected sex with a strange man?

She turned to Denny and said, "My father says thank you. He knew your guesses would be correct." She frowned slightly and covered the phone with her hand to say, "Is that something about that football pool craziness?"

Denny placed his palms together under his chin and bowed from the waist. "Tell him it was the least I could do in service of a true master."

MeiMei started to say something about that silliness but her head jerked as she heard the upstairs phone—the ivory-yellowed Princess sitting amidst the dark, carved/lacquered dynasty pit of her parent's bedroom—pick up. She braced herself for the gusher of shrill Mandarin endearments and scoldings that blasted into her ear. She loudly blurted out, "Duì bù qi, MuMu," and leaned back to ride it out. She was sorry she couldn't meet her father's eyes and do the long-suffering eyeball roll they'd been working on since she could talk, but she knew he was seeing her do it.

At last she tried another old ploy, pitching her voice below the slipstream of her mother's ejaculations and speaking quickly in English. "I'm fine, Daddy. I'll call every day until Mom settles down. Oh, I met a great guy. I hope you can meet him."

"I will guess," the co-champion Guest Guesser of Washington State said over the tenuous connection of electron-bouncing satellites. "Narcotics king? Pirate of Mediterranean? Ancient stone warrior?"

"Very funny, Dad. He's a doctor of..."

The tirade of relief/blame came to a halt so suddenly she thought the line had gone dead. Then her mother purred, "He doctor?"

Among the pantheon of attributes of the Chinese race, few rank higher than Increased Offspring and Filial Obedience.

MeiMei clicked the phone shut and handed it back to Denny with a grateful smile. Behind him and the Sonny Crockett stand-in she saw a pretty girl who a guy in Mexican Marine fatigues and flight jacket stenciled "Montez" was trying to chat up and getting conspicuously nowhere. She turned back to Denny and said, "Say, think my friend and I could hitch a ride back to Kansas?"

Denny looked around: the Gilligan shacks on the Caye, the clear water of the lagoon lapping the piles of the swaying dock, the screaming green of Tobacco, the lines of tiny isles running out in both directions to create a false horizon between the profound blue of the Caribbean and the unfounded blue of the sky. He looked back at her and said, "You sure?"

MeiMei was having a hard time concentrating, rather than staring out the windows as the helicopter wafted along the reef. Leaning slightly to starboard to give a better view.

Denny hadn't paid enough attention, on the flight out, to Lluvia's thrilled reaction to her first flight. He'd been more interesting in jabbering at Townsend, asking questions the spy found inane and sharing nuggets of detecting experience whose wisdom had reduced Town to a hair away from throwing him out into the sea. But on the trip back, he leaned forward, tapped Montez and asked if he could fly lower and slower so Lluvia could enjoy the scenery. She had rewarded him with a melting smile and the flyboy had enthusiastically welcomed her into the front seat to better enjoy the incredible view of the water and stunning proximity of one damned cool pilot.

But there were questions to be answered and MeiMei wasn't dissuaded by her difficulty in getting anywhere with her interrogation. Denny had no idea how she'd been located and didn't want anybody to know that; Townsend was professionally reluctant to reveal his methods and gizmos. And didn't want to tip his hand by being extremely inquisitive as to what had made this pretty, slight, seemingly innocuous Asian woman important to Aphra Alisander and therefore the GOP. That would wait until they landed. At which point he'd have her detained for questioning if he had to. He'd had it right up to his dreamy blue eyeballs with not knowing what he was involved in.

Tuan had been uncharacteristically silent, just holding MeiMei's hand as she drilled queries at the two snoops and got nothing out of it but frustration. He'd given up on figuring it out, other than the obvious role of surveillance devices and a pretty good idea where they were concealed, and his usual curiosity was bubbling up in the thrumming frame of the copter. He leaned up to ask the pilot, "Why doesn't this thing have tail rotors?"

Montez, striking out bigtime with Lluvia, was proud to spiel his machine. "Not required. Channels draft to side thrusters. I direct it here." He touched a bluntly military joystick. "This is a beautiful ship, MacDonald Douglas 902 Explorer. We have six of them, patrol for *narcos*.

Well, more for illegal immigrants from Cuba lately, but that wasn't very glamorous and he didn't like the smug looks and snickers when he told Americans the Mexican armed forces were patrolling to keep out wetbacks from poorer countries.

"Do the thrusters create any ground effect when close to objects?" Tuan asked. "If you are heeled over on landing, for instance?"

Montez was delighted to discover he had a passenger who actually knew something about aerodynamics and would sit still for him rattling on about it. Tuan listened, nodding and absorbing while MeiMei fretted at her inability to get straight responses on how these two jocks had turned her up. She wouldn't have been all that shocked to learn they were delivering her to Ronchel's yacht's helipad, but had made her peace with that risk.

Townsend meditated on how he could turn his possession of the hotly-sought Dr. Chiang into something he could take home wagging his tail and Denny kept his eyes fixed on Lluvia's face as she drank in the beauty and exciting swoop of the littoral terrain below. She gawked out the window like a child and at times would turn to him and point something out below, her eyes shining. Denny had decided that whatever this McChopper had cost, it was well worth it to keep that light lit.

THE URGE TO CONVERGE

One's moving away from you on a road that only leads one place, the other one you've been chasing for weeks is coming toward you. Which signal do you follow?

No decision at all, Aphra decided. She'd felt the insistent shimmy of her tracker and pulled it out for a look. Ought to keep the thing tucked in my thong, she thought, let that vibration do some good. She read the little touchscreen, frowning, then broke into a shit-scoffing grin. Her little sender was heading straight towards her, and at a really good rate of speed, sending steadily now, not the little dribbles it had doled out to her for day after hair-tearing day.

Almost as frustrating as trying to vet that ditzoid Curtsy on what happened to her raid. Lil Barbie in the back seat now, you could almost smell her brain cells burning while she tried to put her shit back together. Or as together as she ever had it. And her pet MayaBoy just sitting there, staring out the window like he'd never been in a car before. She almost thought of Ganzo's take on travel as "like a little boy", but not quite: there was that solemn gravity about him. But pretty well just along for the ride.

All she really had was that the boat was long gone, there were pictures of the jade skull but God knew where they were, and that MeiMei was last seen being dragged off naked by some goons. Well, that little Chinadoll could damnwell take care of herself.

And since the sender in the camera seemed to be coming out of the cold, she evidentially had. Unless somebody else had it now. In which case they would need to be spoken to. The slim Detonix .380 she'd brought incountry inside a lead-lined clock/radio had been under her seat all the way and she was almost wishing there would be somebody to shoot up. She was fed up with this whole gig. She took one more look at the screen, the green dot coming right toward the Chetumal lagoon, and grinned again. "Yeah, baby. Come on in to Mama."

The Navy chopper zoomed in low over the lagoon and hovered over the military pier for two minutes before skipping sideways to set down beside the municipal dock, where several fishermen gave it dirty looks and unappreciative hand gestures. Aphra stood at the edge of the dock, looking for all the world like a tourist, one hand in her stylish Biaggio purse—handy to the grip of the pistol and a few other devices she lumped into the "rotten surprises" category—the other holding up a little digital camera, taking pictures of the nifty little helicopter sitting on pontoons in the middle of a self-created storm like a tempest in a washing machine. She moved the camera away from her eye to admire her shot, thus scanning the read-out identifying its position in the Mexican armed forces and Jane's abstracts... and a taint of DEA. Hmmph, she sniffed as she resumed "shooting" to conceal her face behind the camera, honkies in the woodpile.

The slick white MacDoug popped back up and skittered sideways to land on the city pier. She saw why it had hit the water first: the big, finned, black pod she'd seen between the floats was now revealed as a kayak, bobbing in the water with a guy paddling it in towards the boarding float. His face was hidden by a big hat, but he looked Mexican. And she got a piece of the picture, right there. Her nifty little transponder had been *paddling* south for three weeks! She just hated these third world scenes.

But wait, who's crawling out of the helicopter now? Well, on the side toward her, a clown in a trench coat. Seriously, a trenchcoat in the tropics. And a Bogart hat to top off. Now handing out a cute little *señorita*... whoa, there! What was her name? Yullia or something. Worked in the damn museum. Aphra was getting that feeling.

Looking under the aircraft, she could see a man's legs on the other side, then a pair of female calves. Something familiar about them, too. Getting a feeling...

The aircraft just hopped straight up in the air, but leaned towards her a little. She saw the pilot giving her the eye, and a thumbs-up of approval. So glad I pass your checklist, sucker. Then she looked down at the passengers and couldn't decide whether to do some sitcom double-take or whip out the pistol. MeiMei fucking Chiang and Townsend fucking Hardley, standing there staring at her!

She pointed the camera and took advantage of the fact that it could actually take a picture when it wanted to. This was a keeper moment, for absolutely sure. She wanted to hold a cool pose until her quarry and nemesis walked up to her, but she heard the door of the Bora fly open like there'd been a bomb inside and the pitter-patter of feet sprinting up behind her. No need to make the obvious guess: Ms. Mayflower also started running toward her, and now both her crack commando teammates were yelling and squealing like sorority girls at homecoming.

But she was paying attention only to Townsend Hardley, stalking up the pier towards her like a gunslinger coming after the blackhat and by no means amused. She had her gun and whatnot, but Christ only knew what he was packing. Probably some button he could push and she'd get taken out by a hotty-seeking missile fired from an NSA death star. She stood and waited for him, while Lluvia and Denny's eyes were ponging back and forth from the laughing/crying/hugging girls to the classic showdown poses of their mysterious coffeehouse chum and the Grace Jones lookalike over there. Who also drew the incurious gaze of Ganzo, sliding out of the car and taking it all in.

Not to mention Tuan, who had tied up the kayak and come up the ladder to see the two spies stop and eye each other with a palpable truculence. What went through his head was; Draw, varmit. He saw a simmer that was quite likely to get ugly and realized who Aphra must be. He looked at MeiMei, jerked his head toward the embattled Negress, and got a confirmatory nod. Combined with a touch of trepidation. He knew she had the camera, snapped into one of his waterproof gadget boxes, in the little kangaroo pouch around her waist. And that she'd been pretty clear about not surrendering it to anybody at all. He walked over to the two snoops and tipped his floppy sunhat.

"Hi. I'm Tuan, but call me OB. Hope everything's okay here?"

Town ignored him, but Aphra pulled her dagger-stare away and actually smiled at him. "Oh, yeah, the Flipster. I think I got it now. She made it back to you, you grabbed your canoe there and headed south. I'm not as clear on how you hitched a ride here, but we got time, right? Glad to see the Doc's OK, by the way. We were worried about her."

Tuan nodded empathetically and she could read his unspoken attitude even through the semi-Asian inscrutability. Along the lines of: Yeah, sure, you lying niggah ho who obviously had a bug on her all this time and is just interested in getting your hands on the jade. It was nice to be understood sometimes.

Meanwhile, the lying, etc. had been doing some fast thinking. Along the lines of, Gonna be a bitch getting into Belize with Curtsy not having identification and Ganzo, near as I can tell, not even having an identity. But here's my main man with a chauffeured government helicopter. She looked back at Townsend, who was obviously pissed, hostile, and—whether he knew it or not—hurt. Kind of touching, actually. Despite all the weirdness, and him being on the wrong side of the sexual fence, she had a hard time not feeling a certain fondness for the guy. She looked him right in the eye, spread her hands in a disarming/apologetic way, and said, "Look, we should get along."

He stared at her, apparently entertaining mixed emotions, and she motioned for him to walk beside her as she strolled towards the far side of the pier. He fought it out, then followed her. Whatever the hell else she was, she was still The Key.

She stopped at the edge of the dock, peered down into the murky water. "Hear me out, okay? I know where it is. The skull."

She looked up at Town and saw that his neutral expression wasn't just a studied mask: he really didn't know, did he? He had MeiMei, but didn't know what it was all about. "What you're after, right? What we're both playing for."

"If you say so."

She smirked knowingly. "Fine, play it that way. But you got any questions, ask the good "Doctora" there, would she like to hook back up with a talking skull."

Townsend turned on his heel, went and did just that. When he came back to Aphra he had to turn twice to motion MeiMei to wait where she was and not run after him.

"Okay. You know where it is."

"That's right. I got a trace on it." She pulled out her receiver and held it up. "My 'HomingBoy' here's all over it. And you didn't get to sneak in and diddle this one."

"Didn't have to. I tumbled the one you're holding. All cc direct to me."

"Nice try, whiteboy. We all nice and virgin on this end, dig? So you wanna play? Or you want me to go cop the real goodies on my own?"

Townsend seemed to have frozen up, running the parameters and trying to rule out his own feelings. She stepped closer to him, gave him a little of the eyes. "Listen here. She trusts me. Well, more than she trusts you, anyway. Maybe we can both get what the fuck we're after and look good, huh? Or maybe one of us can get well and leave the other one SOL. All's fair, and all that shamizzle. But why can't we be buddies?"

She looked up at him, a portrait of inner conflict and incredulity. She laughed and tapped his upper arm with her open palm. "Look, I figured out you didn't know about my mama and your daddy. So that's all cool. Sorry to kick you out of bed. Oh, and I did the math."

She left it hanging, but could see he knew what she meant.

"There's almost no chance we're related."

"Great," he finally said. "Peachy keen. I feel better already."

"But look ahere. Maybe whoever put you on this knew about our folks? Didn't happen to mention it to you?"

Townsend glared at her some more, then looked away down the lagoon. He seemed to suddenly unclench, looked back at her and said, "Oh, it's even more humiliating than that. My old man says they probably picked me for my looks and my way with women."

She stared at him and broke into a big, wide laugh. "Way with *women*? So much for their grade of intelligence. And you think that's humiliating? Listen, I got looks and have my way with women. And the last thing I feel about it is humiliated."

"Well, good for you."

Aphra waved it off, smiling at him earnestly. "I just think we could be friends. Who knows what sides we'll be on for the next gig? Meanwhile, I got off on talking with you. We should do lunch."

"You mean we can still be friends?"

"Oh, no." She got it then, and almost felt like patting his cheek, giving him a hug. "I get it. Well, that's extremely flattering. But it wouldn't work out. We have some pretty big differences. I mean, you're Baptist and I'm Rastafarian."

She saw a trace of smile and stepped closer to him. "Let me tell you something else, sugar. I like you. And I liked you even when you were dicking me. Not a common occurrence. So maybe you can take a little ego from the fact that a stone cold dyke finds you attractive."

"Whoopee. Can you send me a letter for my commendation file?" He stopped and looked down, kicked a scuzzy lead weight into the water. "But yeah. Buddies. Let's do lunch. I'll buy."

She beamed at him, and meant it. "We'll dutch it. I don't have many men friends." Don't have many friends, period, come to that. "But first let's scamper up there to the Godfather's and see can we get to the bottom of this shit."

He thought it over, then nodded. He stuck out his hand for a truce shake, but when she reached for it, he jerked his hand up and smoothed his hair.

She laughed and moved past him, towards the helicopter. "Too little, too late, homeboy. That copticopter got your hair so blown out, you might need to borrow my pick."

Montez had wound down the big Pratt Whitney turboshaft and stood beside the cockpit door, staring blissfully at this little gathering of international pulchritude. When Town asked him about heading for inland Belize he grinned and said, "Totally illegal and a violation of international law and airspace sovereignty. When do you want to leave?"

"As soon as I can herd all these cats. Mind lifting us all?"

"Of course not, I can't stand being in small spaces packed full of beautiful women." He seemed reluctant to add, "But we won't all fit. I'd suggest leaving all the men here."

"Don't count me," Denny said. "I got paid as soon as Ms. Chiang made that phone call."

He moved off towards the land end of the dock, where a fairly large crowd had gathered; fishermen scowling, joggers ogling, and tourists snapping pictures. Aphra had noted the way Lluvia had brightened when he said he wasn't leaving (and that he was getting paid) and the way she held his elbow as they said adios and walked away. When the Mexican girl passed her she winked broadly and said, "Did I say you could do better than that Luis fool?"

She slinked up to the helicopter, whose rotors were starting a slow, lazy rotation, and nodded at Tuan when he offered her a hand into the cabin. He'd heard most of Curtsy's blurted and fragmentary version and smiled as he handed her up over the pontoons to the deck. "Why are you the only one of these Angels that doesn't show up naked?"

"Oh, she does naked when it suits her," Townsend griped from inside. "She's just not as upfront about it."

Montez turned in his pilot's seat to look over his shoulder and get a better load of Aphra. "Does she want to sit up front?" he asked innocently. "Much better view."

LODGE BROTHERS

Francis Ford Coppola was the last one to walk out on the balcony of his Edenic retreat and gawk at the sleek white helicopter that was carefully working its way up the narrow valley, slipping in under the rain forest canopy to approach the lawn in front of the main lodge. He sized up the sexy frame of the 902, a man not without professional experience of military helicopters. Characteristically, he didn't view the noisy intrusion of the chopper as some fresh hell barging into his lovingly created paradise, but as just one more invitation to view something weird with wonder.

The rest of the invitees to his film conference had different takes on it, though. The muffled chop of the rotor had busted up the afternoon seminar on independent script development, the conferees stumbling out into the blaze of mid-afternoon sun to squint at this rather flamboyant intruder.

Most of the paid attendees huddled together on the porch, or leaned over the lashed cane railing for a better view into the tinted windows. Nicholas Cage and Marty Bregman were joking about the chopper, John Milius calling out over the rising roar, "Hey, Francis, what is this? Apocalypto Now?"

Shane Black rejoined, "If they start shooting, better look around for Andy Garcia."

Bannock motioned for Loris to go around the corner of the house—which she ignored—and moved towards a stone stele that might offer a little cover if things got as messed-up as they often do when Marine helicopters show up without tickets.

Kenny and Gareth stood somewhat apart from the rest, a condition they had experienced—and despaired of—from the first. The collection of filmdom's heavy hitters at the lodge had been more bemused than impressed by the entourage that Black had termed the "Jerque du Freak". Bregman had been taken by Copper's flame art, Cage had snuck off for a splif or two with Winston, and Coppola himself had expressed admiration for Xchab's sheer Mayan-ness, but mostly they were seen as a road company publicity stunt. Loris was winning hearts, minds and musculature with her massage, but nobody was taking the Burbank Bros. seriously and flaunting oXo did little to improve their shot at support. Kenny had been increasingly frantic as the first day of conference moved along; the helicopter was about to push him over the edge into babbling paranoia.

Winston turned his back to the propwash and lit a doobie.

The ship set down on the main lawn, bouncing on its pontoons. A uniformed pilot opened his window and waved.

Silenced and nonplussed, the guests and speakers (and gypsy camp followers) watched Townsend jump out and look around, every bit the central casting action hero. He reached up to help a Diana Ross type out of the front door while a beautiful, bouncy blonde swarmed out the other side followed by a hunky Mayan kid. Then an Asian beauty, handed down from the cabin by her vaguely Asian retainer.

None of this did anything to unstun the watchers on the porch.

Gareth was first to speak, slapping Kenny on the arm and chiding, "I told you we should have brought a cameraman."

Kenny returned a limpish slap and said, "And I told you we don't have the money. FYI, it's the blonde and Noble Savage from that dump in Tulum."

"Oh, right, and the black babe. Christ, how'd I forget her?"

Coppola heard them from the deck above and leaned down, "You know these people?"

Gareth took a deep inner breath, shook 'em and rolled 'em. "The film I was trying to tell you about? That's the cast."

Kenny nearly fainted from the sheer audacity, but recovered quickly enough to add, "The rest of the cast. It's multi-racial, multi-cultural, multi-sexual. It's... you know... The Yucatan Lives."

Coppola looked back at the new arrivals. "Interesting."

All right, Kenny thought. He thinks it's interesting.

Oh shit, Gareth thought, anything but the dreaded "interesting".

The copter lifted off again, Montez doing a fancy backflip and blitzing away much faster now that he knew the route. Townsend studied the group on the porch. Curtsy and MeiMei gave shy waves and smiles, Aphra cocked a hip.

Tuan recognized Coppola at once and tipped his sun hat in tribute. MeiMei took in Copper and Xchab and Loris, all looking pretty cinematic, and the Burbank Boyz, who looked genetically Hollywood. "What are they doing?" she asked Tuan, "Making a film here and now?"

Tuan looked around, said, "Do you see a camera?"

"No," she replied quickly. "And nobody gets to see mine."

"I gathered that. Well, shall we go mingle?"

"You bet your booty we mingle. I can't believe I have a chance to meet the man who wrote 'The Conversation'."

Tuan gave her an amused sidelong look. "But what he really wants is to direct. It's always weird seeing people like this in real life. He looks so…"

"So patriarchal?"

"So real."

She turned and put on a supercilious expression. "Where have you been? Sorealism is like totally dead."

DREAM ON

Loris rose from the green water, sliding upward naked and glistening like the storied blade. It was not so much dark around her as a crowding, clamoring green. There was a dim glow in the water below her and she knew she needed to return to that light. In fact, the thought made her feel soft and dizzy with anticipation. She continued to rise out of the dark water, hovering upward, water falling from her pointed toes now, radiating ripples the gold color of the light on the dark pool beneath her. She floated sedately upward through shades and tints of green.

Through vegetation: broad leaves and clambering vines of primordial jungle that broke the daylight into shifting camouflage shades of yellow and green, like layered veils over the water below. The tangle fell past her eyes as she rose, an avalanche of seeking greenery trailing tendrils into the water at the bottom of the big natural well.

She rose past more veils: green scrub, red-green streaked leaves of trees. She lifted slowly past the canopy, seeing only miles of more treetops in a circle around her, a horizon of jungle striving upward.

That sphere fell away as she continued her ascent, revealing the sea in the distance. Not that far, she thought. Not so far at all. She rose further, could make out the emerald necklace of cayes along the reef.

Then she was high enough to see the outer slopes of the reef, falling away like foothills under the clear water. She was miles high by then, passing white wisps of cloud, brushing through one wispy cool wipe as she rose higher.

She could see the sweep of Caribbean coastline then, unmistakably. The inland cayes to the north, Guatemala's coves to the south. She knew exactly where she was. She raised her hands above her head like a ballerina, linked her fingers together like a little girl at prayer.

Then she fell.

Loris slid smoothly into consciousness as usual, white wisps on blue sifting before her eyes, then dissolving to a view of Bannock, lying on his back with his right arm stretched out as if reaching for her. She lay watching him, storing the dream away and scanning it in the light of her waking life, as she always did.

She'd been big on dreams since childhood, had made a cult of it for a while, and was still a believer in their power and message. What she'd never believed in much Men—and with plenty of reasons. Now she regarded the man who was currently sharing her dreams.

 Not much to look at, but that didn't mean much to her. A legitimate tough guy and she didn't yet know if that was better or worse than the guys who pretended to be tough. But there was this: he had brought her here, where her dreams had beckoned her. He had brought oXo thousands of miles, perhaps to where he belonged. He seemed to respect and like oXo and didn't seem to mind being a vehicle for the wayward skull, rather than trying to use its powers for his own gain. Well, other than the two hundred thousand. It would bear some thinking about.

She had the strong impression that Bannock was alone in the world, but that he wouldn't mind changing that. She knew what that was like. He seemed like a very odd choice for the first man she could trust and believe in, but he might do.

She rolled softly onto his outstretched arm and without waking he curled it, drawing her to him. She moved her leg over his and lay listening to his breath and breathing his scent. She wondered what he was dreaming.

LES FOLIES BLANCANEAUX

Gareth's voice was almost inaudible as Loris' fingers smoothed their way outward from his vertebrae. He was floating, but Kenny insisted on talking, so he talked. "It's like a family reunion," he said. "Look who's around: Nicholas Cage, John Milius"

"I'm just glad Talia Shire isn't here," Kenny said with an overacted shudder. "She gave me the creeps in the Godfather series."

"The scary one is little Sofia. Won an Oscar for a goofball script and she isn't even a stripper."

"This is just a dude ranch for the starfucked," Kenny pronounced darkly. "Put in a million quarters and get a ride on Nic Cage or Buck Henry or whoever. Take pictures home."

Loris paused from tenderizing Gareth's shoulders and looked at him reproachfully. "Why would you be so negative towards a business that pays your rent, Kenny?" He tried to avoid her, but she caught his eye. "It's a beautiful artform when you see it from out here. It adds fun and wonder to our lives, so of course people are going to want a little piece of it for their mantelpiece, keep little autographs that connect them to the magic."

Kenny stared at her. He couldn't remember the last time he'd heard anybody defend Hollywood. How gauche could you get?

Loris turned her attention back to Gareth's knotted trapezius but added, "Don't be so hard on yourself. You'll get inside some day."

Kenny stood up with effete dignity and stalked out of the gazebo where she'd set up her massage temple. But he did a drama queen turn and pointed dramatically to the dock on the creek. "Just don't go fishing with anybody named Fredo."

Winston sat on the rail of a rustic Meiji Meets Tarzan bridge, sharing a bowl with Nic Cage. "Here's what I don't understand," he said after a soulful exhale. "Guy like you; quirky, funny, offbeat. Moonstruck, Raising Arizona: just these unique, righteous films.

Then they make you into an action hero with butch guns and blowing shit up."

"It's part of the process," Cage shrugged, carefully blowing ash out of the bowl and lighting it again. "Career trajectory. Plus I get to buff up and impress chicks."

Winston laughed and took back the stone Indian pipe for more inhalation therapy. "So if they have to make humorous heartthrobs like you and Banderas and Willis into Rambo clones, why do they take the genetic muscle guys like Arnie and Diesel and Ice Cube and turn them into wimps getting their asses kicked by kindergarden brats?"

"Career trajectory cut both ways, Grasshopper. If I do one more role with no shirt and killing a million guys I have to do one where I'm a pregnant househusband. The cinema gods have a harsh karma of their own."

Winston nodded sagely, tamped the ash out into his hand and rubbed it onto the leg of his shorts. "Tell me this, then. Godfather III. You're Sofia's cousin in real life, right? And family of, like, half the rest of the cast. So why'd they get Garcia to play the nephew instead of you?"

"Well, Andy had the choice of working with a Who's Who of industry greats and playing opposite Sofi, or making something where he'd wear a headband and two hundred pounds of firearms." Cage stood up and stretched, drinking in the pristine valley below the bridge. "So we flipped and I won."

Gareth's daily sessions with oXo continued to frustrate him. He knelt on a cushion in a draped pavilion under a sunburst of bougainvillea and stared through those glassy pupils and saw facets of nothingness. He turned to Copper and Curtsy, who were watching him curiously, in hopes of something dramatic in the way of kosmic trooth transmission, and snorted in exasperation.

"I'm just not used to talking to crystal heads."

"I sure am," Copper said from her hammock. "You should have tried communicating with this boyfriend I had in Bakersfield. My TweakGeek from hell."

Gareth broke his gaze into the echoing profundities of oXo and looked at her. "Crystal? Oh, you mean, speed? A meth head? Why would you hang around somebody like that?"

Look who's talking, Copper thought. You live and work with the pissiest little queer in captivity. She said, "How much do you really know about tweak? Effect on human beings?

"Uh, not much I guess. Kenny did it a few times when he couldn't score coke. Ended up crawling around with his nose in the carpet."

"Know how long an eightball lasts when you shoot it up? Like all day and half the night. Did you know it'll keep your dick hard that whole time? And that it makes women horny, pliable and crazed? Not to mention multi-mega-orgasmic?"

"Okay, I didn't know that."

"So now you do. What was your question again?"

Curtsy stared at her, eyes wide. "Yikes, girl."

Gareth suppressed a shudder and dropped a piece of embroidered Guatemalan cloth over oXo's stare. "There," he said, "You *can* hide your Mayan eyes."

Whatever qualities had made Xchab apprehensive about Copper (her looks, her insinuating confidence, her foreign—even exotic— appearance, her talents, her attitude, her unabashed fuckability) were far surpassed by her take on Aphra. Here those qualities were amped up to a feral, carnivorous, gleaming sensuality that led the Mayan girl to regard her much as a rabbit would view a neighboring jaguar. Her skin alone... In Mexico, where fair skin is ascendant over dusky in a de-facto racial caste system—thus dumping Xchab at almost the untouchable level—Copper's milky complexion topped her burnt umber like an ace played over a deuce. But Aphra being even darker didn't drop her into the cellar: it elevated her to a status she'd never seen before. Uncharted, alien, a black hole through the Newtonian physics of Xchab's dermal universe. And here she was, looming a head taller, wet-shining naked, standing a half meter away. And smiling with sharp, white teeth.

Xchab was trapped in the bathroom of the still-somewhat-under- construction family units that Coppola himself had shown the girls to and bid them welcome. A hospitality that might have had something to do with Bannock proffering some sort of payment, or perhaps the earnest conversation he'd had with Town Hardley, but was probably just a measure of the man's apparent generosity and boyish invitation to all things novel and beautiful.

None of which was at issue as she stood with her bare brown butt against the warm, wet amber tile and tried not to gawk at Aphra from carmine-tipped toes to exploded dandelion hair. Much less the thrusting breasts, musky groin, and enveloping arms.

There had been no conversation at all. She shut off the water, turned for the towel, and was startled by Aphra standing there naked, fixing her with that hungry, commanding stare. When she stepped back against the wall, the *negrona* had followed her, turned the warm water back on, and started soaping up a washrag while ogling her carnivorously.

Highly unaware of complications and roads less traveled in the sexual wilds, Xchab still had a very nervous feeling that something was happening that she would either not like one little bit or worse, might like a lot. She had to do or say something but couldn't think of much to do against this anthracite amazon. So she said, "Please. I am already clean."

Aphra gave a wolf grin and said, "And no sooner you do, it's time to start getting all dirty again."

She extended the sudsy washcloth to Xchab's shoulders and did a surprisingly gentle mopping motion, watching the soapy water run down the smaller girl's breast and drip from her nipple. Xchab opened her mouth to protest but just couldn't think of what to say. The washcloth ran down the side of her left breast, across her tummy with a little digital dipsy-doo at her navel and ended up in a soft, but pressing, swipe across her almost hairless crotch.

"Yo, dark meat. Put down the candy and move away from the child."

Xchab glanced past Aphra's shoulder and was humiliated to see Copper lounging in the doorway, still wearing the bikini bottom she'd been swimming in with Black and Milius and a couple of the paid conferees. Aphra squeezed the cloth out on her other shoulder and watched the milky water again trickled town to its nipple cascade. Then turned to Copper and said, "The more the merrier, red meat."

Copper laughed and shook her head, "Nope, redheads are the Other White Meat. But look, why don't you pick on somebody your own disposition? And weight class? And orientation?"

"Well, you put it like that..." Aphra turned to face her, spreading her legs, putting her fists on her hips, and squaring her shoulders back to hammock up the mass of fine titty. The effect was spoiled as Xchab bolted past her, almost knocking her off balance, threw a look of total confusion at Copper, and dashed past her out the door. Aphra called out, "Bye, ya, Maya. Looks like I gotta buy ya to try ya."

Copper turned back, hooked her thumbs in the bikini bottom and said, "I think I was saying I'm kind of bi-curious."

"Curiosity, huh?" Aphra snorted. "That what killed the pussy."

"Yeah," Copper continued. "I'm always curious why so many men hit on me and so few women. Don't you like redheads?"

"Redheads?" Aphra guffawed. "Shit. You claimin' colors here?"

"What, want me to flash my bush so you know I'm not cheating?"

Aphra waggled a noncommittal hand. "I could live with that."

"Fair's fair. I just wanted to see yours first, make sure you weren't 'passing' on me."

Aphra smiled and raised a single red-taloned finger to beckon her in under the water. "Careful," she said. "Don't want to get those pants wet."

"Too late," Copper said, sliding the bottoms off and back-kicking them against the wall. She nodded at the bar of lime soap on the rack and said, "Who gets to do the honors?"

"You offer your honor, I honor your offer," Aphra said, reaching for the soap. "And all night long I be on her and off her."

"Now that's a script I can work with."

Aphra spread her hands wide and curled her lip in a defiant snarl. "Come and get me, Copper."

LES FOLIES — DEUX

John Milius sat up, beaming mindlessly. Loris knelt in front of him, smiling. "I'm a writer," he said, "I should be able to think of something to say other than 'Oh, wow'."

"That's what I said when I found out you wrote 'Apocalypse Now' and 'Dirty Harry'

Milius grinned as he slowly stood up. "Let me ask you," he said, still beaming. "Do you only massage people with superb physiques like mine?"

She laughed. "Tall, short, skinny, fat, broken. Each one its own universe."

"Well, screenplays are the same way. Each one is totally different. But when I sit down and crack my fingers, they're all made out of the same stuff."

He turned and walked to the door, feeling two inches taller and floating an inch off the floor. He opened the door and turned to say thanks and good-bye, but was immediately nailed by Kenny and Gareth, who must have been lying in ambush for a half-hour.

"I think you've seen we can bring a show," Kenny gushed. "And these girls and talent here are in the film. Are the film, really."

Milius hid his wince at having his serenity crash down to Biz with these two yapping yorkies, maintaining his manner. "Does that Mayan girl even speak English?"

"Xchab? No way. She's authentic all the way. Tribal. Magically realistic."

"She'll play the Mayan princess," Gareth yammered. "Speaking Mayan, English subtitles."

"Except in, you know, foreign distribution," Kenny tacked on, nodding.

"Didn't Mel Gibson already do that?"

Gareth shook his head forcefully. "No way. He was just spouting a bunch of drunken bullshit and they subtitled him with a booking number."

He rounded the corner to where the main deck gave views of the gardens and down the tiers of enchantment to the river below. And saw their host standing at the banister, intent on the lawn below. He moved closer to speak, hoping it would scrape the Valley Boyz off his shoes since they were desperate to importune Coppola, but too intimidated to even cross his shadow. He saw the hand held up in warning and stepped quietly to the rail where only he could hear the soft, "Have you seen this, John?"

He looked where Coppola was pointing at Copper, practicing her firespin with two tennis balls on her chains, each trailing three feet of bright ribbon. The chains spun a web around her, the ribbons defining a twisting sphere of influence as though trying to weave themselves into a solid ball of color.

And three paces behind her, Xchab continued her apprenticeship, moved with the flame dancer step for step, her arms echoing each movement.

And each of her moves was traced by a hovering cloud of hummingbirds.

A brilliant buzz in the green-tinted sunlight, the flock meshed and morphed behind her, tendrils of vivid, blurred wings outlining every motion of her hands, a mantle of iridescent feathers spreading and whirling behind her like a cape.

"That's the really amazing thing up here," he said quietly to the writer. "Things happen in real life that would be preposterous to try to bring to the screen."

Gareth cleared his throat and stepped forward, holding up a timorous finger. "Excuse me, Mr. Coppola, but we actually have some ideas on that..."

Aphra figured she could get in, grab the goodies and be back at the well-provisioned dining table before anybody thought she was taking a long time answering the call of Nature. This whole wide-open, trusting, secure feel of the Lodge was great. Totally unsecure. She slipped into the room where Tuan and MeiMei resided in a Robinson Crusoe With Luxuries setup, everything rustic and Tarzan/Jane where it counted and the jungle loitering just outside doing its damnedest to come on in and get homey. Her tracking gizmo was in her hand, blinking and twittering to itself as she panned the room and oops, there it was, over there in the dresser. The little subdued signal that came from its own mini-battery meaning somebody had removed the camera's battery. And in a place like this, with scenery outside yelling for attention and every other guy you run into some famous movie type, that would mean they were hip to the camera doing a little multi-tasking. Smarter than your average slope, these two, and that was damned smart. But us corn-row niggahs come up with a few wiles, our ownselves.

She had her spare sender-cam ready, but under the circumstances took three seconds to open it and dump the batteries out into her pocket. The one she wanted turned out to actually be behind the dresser, but it's all good. She pocketed it, carefully taped the imposter back where it had been, shoved the dresser back to the wall, and headed back to the dining room. This place had to be good for some scrumptious kind of dessert.

Loris reached for the ceiling, staring straight up, stretching powerfully and rotating her fingers as Kenny and Gareth's voices dwindled down the walkway from the mediation room to the main lodge. Those poor saps needed more than she could give them in a weekend. She thought about oXo again, sitting on a dresser in their room. She could just walk in, pick him up, and walk out. But she knew that wasn't the right thing. Or not the right time.

She slowly brought her hands down, then lowered her head. And found herself looking right at Aphra Alisander, modest in a big white terrycloth robe. And saying, "So, you do women, too?"

"Massage is equal opportunity," Loris said, patting the padded yoga mat. Aphra flowed down into a prone position, the robe drifting off along the way. Loris arranged her arms and head, pulled her feet together, rubbed scented oil on her hands, and leaned into a long push up the black girl's spine.

After a minute she felt some of the muscles' residual guardedness start to unwind, but was waiting. And sure enough, Aphra said, "Believe I asked if you do women, too?"

Hands ringing her biceps, working in for the concreted fascia, Loris said, "My relationships with people are about who they are, not what sort of plumbing they have."

"You sound like my kind of girl," Aphra purred. After another minute she said, "Course you got that hunky boyfriend. Kind of a new one if I read the signs and scent correctly. Looks like he's plumbed pretty good."

"I haven't known him long, but I think it's something that's going to last and grow."

"So how'd you kids meet?"

"It was a business deal."

"Turned into a pleasure deal. I cotton to those myself. Hint, hint."

She turned over face up, sliding snake-like under the oil and light coat of sweat. She faced Loris, supine, and spread her legs a little. "I been liking you since we met, honey. And I'm wide open to getting to know you better, you see what I'm saying."

Loris adjusted her rub to her new position, working silently, but keeping her eyes on Aphra's.

"So listen," she went on, starting a slow and subtle movement under Loris' hands. "Turns out I'm the kind of person gets to know

311

things and find out shit beyond the average schlimizzle, gets his 411 from Google."

"That's what I hear."

"Ah, my reputation precedes me? We should talk about that sometime. But let me tell you about the studly Mr. Bannock there. At least his third surname, by the by."

"It suits him well enough."

"There's girls kind of cream over your bad boys, them rough-up scary types. But they're going for the image, not the real item, they got a brain left in they head. And your sweetie is the real thing. I'd even go so far as to classify his tight ass—and this is not a term I drop loosely—as a rather badass motherfucker."

"He's done pretty well so far."

"Not a guy to take crime lightly. Oh, no... quite serious is how the man takes his crime and punishment. Like Federal time, for instance. And would still be doing that time if they could've nailed down a couple of unfortunate in-the-pen fatalities that he was believed to have had guilty knowledge of. Heard anything about that?"

"Not until just now. But how about you? Have you ever been in prison?"

"Nah, there's still some of us sassy black folk ain't been rounded up yet."

"Because you seem a little dangerous yourself. And nosy. And maybe the type who doesn't pay much attention to laws and orders."

"No, I've not yet had the privilege of incarceration."

"Well if you did, do you think you'd do whatever it called for?"

"Oh, you just know it, sweetie."

"I appreciate the information. I know you mean it well. Well, more or less."

"Ah, 'More or less', ha ha. Pretty much my M.O."

"I mean, you're also hoping to weaken a relationship I'm growing increasingly content with, so you can get your hands on me for ten minutes."

"Ten *minutes*? Give me a little credit, Slim."

"Flattering, but also kind of, well... you know. You must run into that all the time. So let's try something different."

"Hey, something different..."

"No. I mean different thinking, also. Listen to me, okay?"

Aphra seemed to hit a deeper level of relaxation, subsiding on the mat and looking up without the arch manner she'd been showing since she walked in. "Might not be a bad idea."

"Why go to the trouble? Why not just relax?"

"Girl, I was any more relaxed, I wouldn't have any vital signs."

"No, you're on the prod. Playing angles." She wagged a finger in front of Aphra's mouth to stop the game. Then said, "I read people. No name on it or anything. I just have the gift to read people."

Aphra's legs edged wider apart. "Now me, I'm just an open book."

"More than you know. You think of yourself as a very sensual, sexual person. But I think you're playing yourself."

"I always thought if they make a movie of my adventures I could play myself."

"People use sex as an expression of love. They use it to get pleasure, to feel good and released at a deep level. But that's not what you do."

Aphra had a half-dozen quips to lay on that one, but instead was quiet under the seeking, calming hands.

"With you, it's all about power. You play a game you can win, you use your body to get things from people, get things on people. You seem selfish, and maybe you think you are. But actually, you aren't really getting any for yourself. You're just wasting it."

It took Aphra, her eyes closed and mouth soft, several long minutes to respond to that. Finally she said, "Okay, Dionne Warwick, what you think I should do? Long as it don't require no white clothes and coffee enemas."

"Don't just do something," Loris said, "Lie there. Try thinking about yourself instead of me. Try feeling instead of reacting."

Aphra spoke very softly at that point, no longer making the rhythmic movements. She said, "Just lay here? Think only of myself? I think I can swing that."

"You lay still, keep your awareness on yourself, what you're feeling. Not me. And I'll give you a very special massage."

"Oooo," Aphra murmured in a voice so low Loris could barely hear it. "I hope you're talking about the famous happy ending."

"I don't believe in endings," Loris said, shifting her weight forward onto her probing hands. "Just cycles."

313

LES FOLIES — TROIS

Bannock's head rested on his laced fingers, a straw hat low over his eyes. One leg dangled out of the huge cotton hammock, an occasional flick of his toe keeping him in a gentle rocking motion. He kept his eyes on the view down to Privassion Creek and the valley below, taking in all the delicate and charming graces of Blancaneaux lodge, but mostly the foreground view of Loris giving a very intense massage to Shane Black.

Not, rather pointedly, on Kenny and Gareth, who were leaning towards him in their cane chairs, positions and faces advertising supplication.

Or even on Curtsy, perched on a table over by the wall and moving her head back and forth to follow the conversation. She'd been tagging along with the "Melrose Mafia", as Loris called them, for three days, practically underfoot. Gareth actually saw possibilities for her in the film—apart from his more immediate schemes for her lush flesh—and had really nailed her when he mentioned they'd need a dolphin wrangler and that Hollywood was practically begging for people who could get cetaceans on their marks.

Continuing his abject crawling to Bannock, Gareth wheedled, "Listen, Big Guy, you did a fabulous job getting oXo for us and it was very small of us to quibble over the money. We felt shitty immediately and hope you'll accept..."

"But now you need something else," Bannock said quietly, his eyes half closed as he watched Loris' hands running over the writer's shoulders in an almost hypnotic sequence.

"Well not really *need*," Gareth said.

"And not so much *else*," Kenny stuck in.

"Look, Bannock," Gareth moved on with an urgency that indicated he might come to the point of their barging in on his siesta. "We've taken some meetings behind the skull, and now we're here. Here in the same house with Coppola and Cage and Shane Black and Marty Bregman and Pacino might even show up and..."

"But we're getting no love," Kenny pouted. "We need interface, *capische*? Input, liaison, face time."

"You want face time with a skull?"

"You know what he means," Gareth almost begging for sympathy and succor. "We've got access, the director of all time, building a cast... and we can't talk to oXo."

"Did you call his agent at Morris?"

"*What*?"

"Just fucking with you, man. So you need answers from oXo."

"Exactly. You nailed it."

"Well, you came to the right place."

Gareth turned to Kenny, gushing. "I told you. This man has a few rough spots on his diamond, but he delivers."

"I didn't say 'the right person'. I said the right place." When Gareth stared, puzzled, he nodded his head at Loris, now working on Black's fingers as he seemed to be liquefying.

"Of course. Didn't I tell you, Kenny..."

"You most certainly did not 'tell me, Kenny'. You said..."

"Okay, okay. But look, do you think she'd..."

"Ask her when she's done tenderizing Mr. Kissy Kissy Bang Bang, there. And you guys might consider a touch-up, too. You're both way too uptight."

Gareth looked at Loris, now kneading the soles of Shane's feet, and approved. Even Kenny seemed open to having a woman put her hands all over him. "So when will she be done?"

"A massage therapist's job is never done," Bannock said with mock gravity. "But I'd say that guy'll be medium well in about another twenty. Long as you're up, could you shag me a beer?"

Townsend flowed into the dark bedroom like a moonshadow. Moving silently but surely, he took a position in a dark corner to await alarms and gauge the breathing from the bed. He held his fist up to his face, reading his responder without releasing the tiniest amount of glow from the LED's which were all working overtime in the immediate presence of their obscure object of acquisition. It took two reads before he believed it was sitting in plain sight on the dresser. He ghosted over and scanned it, his stylish glasses giving him a "Terminator/Predator" view of it, all twisting, psychedelic color-maps with digits dancing at the sides of the projection. Just sitting there.

Just sitting there in the middle of a big, confused pile of silverware from the dining room, two glass windchimes from the pavilion, and various other odds and ends piled up in a gleaming game of Pick Up Stix. He bent as close as he could without his display feeding back too much to read, but knew there was no way to remove the teetering cage of noisy junk without toppling it onto the steel tray it rested on. Shit. Well, more ways than one to get a cat skin.

He crept to the door sticking close to the walls, opened the door six inches noiselessly, and exuded.

On the bed, Aphra watched the dim triangle of light on the ceiling narrow and disappear before relinquishing the butt of her Detonix, under the pillow. Man was a thief in the night, that's for sure. Could probably feel you up, knock you up, without waking you up.

Speaking of which. She slid her arm softly over Copper's ribcage and cupped her firm breast. With just the tip of a fingernail, she gave a tiny pluck at the end of her nipple. No response from the redhead, who must be pretty exhausted, all told. So she scissored two fingers around said nipple and started to move them slowly together and apart. It took about a dozen little squeezes like that before she felt a hand reach back, grab her pubic tangle, and slide down to cup her warmth and do a little finger-walking of their own.

Loris sat in a lotus position, regarding the producers with a neutral calm. Behind her, Shane Black was snoring lightly on the massage table. She thought out the two metrosexuals' dilemma, to the point where they were about ready to jump out of their skins from anticipation, and said, "Have you tried drugs?"

"Well, I've experimented a little," Kenny offered demurely.

"Tried them?" Gareth expostulated. "He's indicted them. Convicted them. He's like, rounded them up and exterminated them."

"She means on oXo, you twit." Bannock continued his slow rocking motion and languorous expression.

"How could we do that?" Kenny asked, genuinely stumped. "Maybe a sort of inverse bong-out? Second hand smoke?"

"Kenny," Loris said, "He doesn't breathe. He's a rock."

Gareth pointed two pistol fingers at her. "You are, baby."

"Oh, so now he's just a rock?" Kenny whined. "Before, he was some ascended soul brother."

"He's a great, transcended oversoul. He's a spirit, a mind. But then so am I. We all are. But here's the deal with him, and it's kind of sorry, really. He's been in shifty hands around L.A. for a long time and he's picked up, basically, a nagging drug habit. He's the ultimate monkey man. Likes to bring people around him and interact with them when they're stoned. He's right in your mind when you blow it and he likes the feeling."

Gareth stared at her. "So he surrounds himself with telepathically linked stoners and feeds off their energy?"

"If you want to put it like that."

"Not a problem. I've worked with directors like that before."

"And he's worked with weaselish Hollywood types before you two. That might help. But maybe not."

"What? Other producers and directors have had access to him? Why haven't we heard about this before? Part of the appeal here is novelty..."

"I only know a couple of names, but they're big names that I recognize."

"Name me one," Kenny challenged with his lip stuck out stubbornly.

"River Phoenix."

"Oh my God, don't even say that name." Kenny held his hands to his cheeks, stricken. "I could just sob every time I see that perfect face. And the hair to die for."

"Not the only bodily fluid you seep out at the very thought, I'm sure," Gareth observed waspishly. "But look, if he's such a great seer and fortune teller and all, it didn't seem to help River much did it?"

"Because he wasn't listening. Or asking the right questions."

Kenny shot a look at Gareth. "This is getting complicated."

"It always does," Loris admonished. "Because you turkeys always think he's a wild joker to cheat with or an ego medallion you can use like bling or a hood ornament. You have access to unlimited energy and use it to pull your puds, then go crash it into your own greed and silliness. You don't need to worry about him helping you, you need to worry about ending up worse off than when you started. Take my word for that. Or do whatever you want."

"Okay, what can I say?" Gareth saw no point in getting cute with Loris: she saw through everything he threw out. "You got me... I'm a weasel, I play angles. It's my nature. So kill me. But I have needs.... you know?"

"Maybe you can hire somebody else to ask questions for you," Kenny sniped bitchily. "Some slut who had a three month run on Jeopardy."

"Shut up, Kenny. No, wait, wait a second, you're right. I got it." He turned back to Loris, excited, "You know how to work him, don't you?"

"I definitely don't know 'how to work him'. Haven't you been listening to me? It's more like I'm learning how to let him work me. He's an influence."

"More like under the influence to hear you tell it."

"You paid a quarter million dollars for him, don't you think it's worth listening a little?"

That shut Kenny up but Gareth had seen the Route To Riches. "Yeah, yeah, that's what I'm saying. I'm seeing it now. We need you. On the picture."

"Look, if you're just going to play Hollywood games, I..."

"No, no, serious. We need somebody to liaise here. F2F peripheral. We'll put you on salary, you handle him for us."

Loris thought a minute and said, "I can handle that."

Gareth looked at Bannock, who had turned his head toward them as soon as he started talking about using Loris. "Full salary, above the line. No points, but hey, gimme a break. On the production payroll as of now. What I'm saying, she'd have a job and we'd treat her right."

In a low tone, almost a growl, Bannock said, "That's what I'd suggest."

"Sure, Biggie, no problemo. We'll list her as a scout."

"I was a scout once," Kenny mused idly.

"Really? Did you make Eagle?" Bannock asked him.

"Double bogie, I think they said."

"Look, she's on the film." Gareth scrambled to get back on track, nail it down. "You come along. No pay...hell we already paid you. We'll take care of her."

"If you know what's good for you."

"You bet, Bannock. Might even be a speaking part for you in this."

"You talk like you've seen a script," Loris said evenly.

"Nah, sorry," Gareth grinned apologetically. "Just reflex. It's my nature. See, that's why we need you."

"First thing we're going to do," Loris said with an understated forcefulness, "Is clean up his aura. Give him a nice bath."

RUB A DUB DUB

Francis Coppola emerged slowly from the hot pool and stood for a moment savoring the jungly scent of the night and the sounds of the waterfall into the pool. He was the last one out, the others slipping away to let him enjoy his soak. He didn't understand why these guys would get into hot water to relax, then get all stressed-out jabbering about projects and budgets and agents and residuals. Especially those two latecomers. God, they were insane: talking about directing a film by séance if he got their drift. What I need up here, he suddenly realized, is a steam room.

Definitely. Why hadn't he thought of it before? That was an offer to relax nobody could refuse. There was something really East Coast and borough about steam. Guys with Yawk accents sitting naked in the mist, walking around in rough Turkish towels. This whole hot tub thing was so California by comparison.

He rubbed down with a soft, fluffy towel and shook drops from his beard into the hot water. Thinking, kind of like me, maybe? Gone California? Or have I just disappeared into some global stratosphere, a tower in The Cloud?

Chuckling at himself, he turned to head for bed and almost walked into a half dozen truly lovely young women, also wearing only towels or shifts. His eyebrows raised as he smiled at them appreciatively and waved them towards the pool.

"*Aqua termal*," he said in his best Corleone rasp. "*Prego.*"

The girls laughed. All except the stone-faced little Maya girl, who was starting to fascinate him. What a face she had, really. He couldn't help framing her whenever he saw her.

"Mr. Coppola," the tall brunette said, "We really appreciate your hospitality here. It's such a beautiful, serene place."

"You're fairly beautiful and serene yourself, my dear," he told her. "You do massage, I understand?"

"I do. And I'd be honored to give you one any time you like."

"I'll take you up on that. Maybe tomorrow after breakfast."

"Any time. I just love your work. I saw Goodfellas six times."

He almost laughed his towel off. "Good one. Thanks for the laugh. You ladies are taking a really late soak tonight."

"We need to cleanse her skull," Copper offered as she shed her towel and slipped into the water.

He looked at Loris' hair a little differently, hoping it wasn't infested. "Please don't put any soap in the water."

Loris smiled, held up the towel-wrapped object she'd been carrying, and let the towel slide away from oXo, grinning at the director with eyes aflare from the mosquito torches on the deck. "He doesn't need soap, just running water," she said. "And love."

He fought the impulse to cross himself. "Okaaaay."

He backed away towards the lodge. As he walked off he heard the girls all giggling, a sound as bright and clean as windchimes. But he didn't even consider going back to bask in their beauty and youth. There were plenty of attractive young people who weren't nuts. Turning, he saw them all shedding their wraps and slipping into the hot water like sirens of many colors. He called back, "Just don't leave a ring."

Xchab was the last into the pool, even with the other girls teasing her and beckoning her in. She looked balefully at Aphra, timidly at Copper and Curtsy. But when MeiMei smiled and waved her in, she stepped down to the stone bench that ran around the perimeter of the pool, standing there thigh-deep in her cotton huipíl, frozen. Finally Loris walked the length of the pool and looked solemnly into her eyes, holding that spooky glass skull between her breasts. Slowly, gently, she reached up and rolled one shoulder strap down the Mayan girl's shoulder, then the other. Xchab didn't try to stop her shift from sliding down into the water and when Loris held up her free hand, she took it, stepped out of the floating garment, and lowered into the water. Loris beamed at her, turned and moved towards the other end of the pool.

She waded across to the waterfall that animated the pool's narrow end, the other girls watching as she marched towards it holding oXo in front of her like a sacrament. She extended her hands and the glassy skull slipped under the little cascade, water flowing around the smooth contours rather than splashing off. She stood motionless, head bent forward and eyes closed, as oXo luxuriated in the wash of moving water.

Aphra was playing a little submarine footsy with Copper, and wouldn't have minded sitting within hands-on range of the redhead, who it turned out contained a sexuality as wild and fiery as her own. But for whatever reason, the girls were all sitting a little too distant to touch, evenly spaced around the pool, heads leaning on the rim, watching Loris and oXo. So Aphra bided her time, and watched with them.

Curtsy lolled in the hot water, which seemed to be rhythmically palpitating her body. She played with the underwater sealed-beam floodlight beside her, trying to make shadow puppets in the water, her hands starting to move in time with the beat she felt in the water. The whole pool started to flicker in a slow, sure rhythm. She spread her thighs, then pushed them together. Her nipples tingled. She closed her eyes and suddenly had an image of Puch Pop, standing on top of the pyramid at Cobá, looking at her.

MeiMei was feeling the same insinuation in the water and "decided" to just lay back and like it. It figured that wealthy directors would have devices like this in their hot tubs. She wriggled her hips around on the smooth tier, watching Loris' careful laving of oXo, but caught movement from the corner of her eye and looked back towards the buildings. It was Tuan and Winston, strolling down the path, in quiet but intense conversation. She was glad to see OB, but wondered if he was crashing one of those "all-girl moments." Then she saw Townsend and Bannock behind them, also talking with interest. And behind them, that "Seagull" character chattering to Ganzo, who regarded him with a serious gaze. Tuan saw her and smiled and she giggled, "Company, girls."

Aphra opened her eyes and saw a group of males arriving, ringing the far side of the pool. They stood watching the women for a moment, probably impressed by the general tableau. Breaking the calm, she said, "Damn. There go the neighborhood."

Everybody but Xchab laughed: she was eyeing the men a little nervously. And suddenly the big *indio* that had come up with the blonde just stepped in the water right beside her, took off his wet towel, and tossed it back on the deck. Curtsy, on Ganzo's other side, smiled at him and reached out to stroke his hair as he settled down between them. Faced with the typical hot tub dilemma of what to do with his hands, he chose the usual approach and spread his arms along the rim of the pool. Curtsy leaned her head into his left hand, smiling contentedly. His other hand brushed the back of Xchab's torrent of black hair but she didn't shy away, for some reason. She looked sideways at him and he was looking back at her, his expression as blank and noble as a dog's. One thing she realized at that moment: whatever else there was about Ganzo, she knew she would never have to fear him. She sunk a little deeper in the water, also feeling the beguiling pulse and reluctantly starting to respond. A few minutes later she put her own arms on the pool rim, her left hand slipping behind Ganzo's head, the other laying on the nape of Winston, whose other hand was buried in Copper's cuprous curls.

Curtsy hadn't been the only mermaid getting an eyeful as Townsend and Bannock, standing side by side, peeled off their trunks and eased towards the pool. Couple of major swinging dudes, was the way she sized things up. Classic match-up: showy class versus brute power. It was hard not to linger on the sheer beauty of the slide of Town's abs and pecs, but the scars and welts made a tour of the big lug's torso rather interesting as well. She wondered what they'd look like out swimming. She watched Townsend move around and slip in beside Aphra, and the look she gave him. Something going on there, for sure. Didn't think that muff-mistress swung that way. He also laid his arms along the rim as he unwound and Aphra gave him a "Oh, please, whitebread" look, but didn't move away from his hand on her shoulder.

Bannock moved in between MeiMei and Loris, who smiled at him as she continued facilitating oXo's brain scrub. Mei felt his hand brush her left shoulder at the same time that Tuan slithered into the water like an otter, ducked his head, then shook it off before settling beside her and placing his left hand under her hair to caress the down on her slim neck. She extended her arm to give him a friendly Dutch rub, before resting it on his hard deltoid. His right hand moved behind Curtsy, who reached behind his neck to twine her fingers with MeiMei's.

Loris, who had been standing a few inches from oXo as she held him under the waterfall, had been exposed more heavily to the pulse that the skull was emanating. She moved slowly and dreamily as she turned around to face the circle of faces ringing the pool. Her nipples were tight, her aureoles puffy, her thighs tender, her face muscles slack and creamy. She moved to the center of the pool and bent forward to gently place oXo on the bottom. For a moment she appeared to everyone else as a sleek form on the surface, an hourglass of buttocks, fluted back and wide shoulders riding above the water like an island.

She straightened up and looked around, noticing the slackening and loosening going on around her. The Love, she thought, is the ultimate massage. Then she had another thought, which she knew she should share. "We are about to hear something," she said. "It's called the First Tone. There will be four Tones before this is over."

As she backed away from oXo, towards her place by Bannock, MeiMei asked, in a voice so relaxed she could barely articulate, "Tones? Like the Calendar? What does that mean?"

Loris smiled as she moved away from oXo, to the edge of the pool. "I guess we'll find out."

Nobody else asked why she had done what she did or said what she said, nobody spoke, nobody even really thought. oXo had begun to "broadcast" his pulse of live, whole, movement; stronger and at a slightly lower frequency. A frequency that those who give names to such things call "Alpha". She moved back to the edge and sat down. Immediately Bannock cupped the base of her skull. He extended the thumb and finger of his huge hand to rub behind her ears, like you'd do to a big dog. She closed her eyes in pleasure. Nobody ever thinks about massage people liking to be rubbed, too. But this guy did.

She put her hand behind his head, as well, idly ruffling his short, wiry crop. She extended her other hand behind Townsend, removed it to lift his hand behind her own head, then replaced it at the base of his skull. All twelve people were now touching, a dozen heads woven together by intertwined arms and hands. And in the water, an intimate pulsation was throbbing stronger and deeper, a righteous somatic dub that synchronized twelve heartbeats into a single chorus.

Kenny and Gareth discovered that somebody had walked off with their all-important director and spiritual leader and immediately spun into frantic, mostly ineffective motion. They blasted around the dark lodge, pushed into empty rooms—even Bannock and Loris' room, where it would have scared them green to intrude in less drastic circumstances. They burst out onto the side deck and looked down at the pool, where they could make out people lounging around in a gold mist created by the light from the pool. They tore along the porch until they hit the stairs, then stopped as if they'd run into an invisible fence. Kenny was at the point of tears, wailing, "It has to be down there. That bitch took it down there to play with in the fucking water."

"I guess," Gareth said, feeling extremely strange and out of place.

"Well, why don't we just march our perfect butts down there and seize it?" Kenny demanded.

"Nah," Gareth demurred. "You go ahead if you feel like it."

Kenny stared at the mist, which seemed to be vibrating in some way, his mouth working. "Well," he finally said, "As long as they bring it back."

"It's not like they can go anywhere," Gareth hastily added. He turned back and headed for bed. After a few tortured seconds staring down at the pool with fists clenched, Kenny followed.

CLIMATE OF CLIMAX

The vibration in the pool was no longer subtle, and had again shifted in frequency: to the slower, more evocative beat known as "Theta". Around the circle, legs were spreading open, nipples and erections were stiffening, membranes moistening, limbic systems reacting, anuses unclenching, breath slowing, muscles moving in a rolling rhythm, third eyes blinking.

A sound could be heard, but only to those in the pool: an inner sound like a thin, piping whistle or piccolo. Tuan automatically classified it as an artifact, a "beat" created by wave amplitude interference of the deeper frequencies. Which was more or less his last coherent thought on the subject. The pulse dropped lower and their bodies started rising, abdominals fluttering, inner visions seeing a long tunnel with a watery, golden light at the end.

Copper, veteran of hundreds of acid orgies, took it in her proprioceptive stride, opening herself to the beginnings of white waves of orgasmic release. Her lips grew cold and trembled, seemed to whistle a simple air like that of a piper.

Xchab, a virgin emotionally if not technically, had no vocabulary of stimulus or response to refer to. As wavelets of energy lapped at her mind she retreated into the stolid non-here of an Indian, then to the unreasoned purity of childhood. Her body floated upward, her mind sank into a vortex. She felt good. She felt. She............

Winston, another inveterate shocktrooper in the campaigns of sex and psychedelia, had long since hung a Gone Fishin' sign on his brain and surrendered serenely to what was happening. Which, judging by the storms and tsunamis his mind/body had weathered previously, was shaping up to one hell of a blow. He felt his legs spreading wider, his feet brushed the toes of Xchab and Charity on either side.

The vibration was slowing even more, and nobody involved would have, at that point, described what they were experiencing as due to pulsing water pressure. It was inside them, around them, all over and about them. They were strings being strummed, chants being hummed.

Bannock was on alien shores, but nothing in him resisted it. His spread feet touched MeiMei's, then Loris' and he was profoundly conscious of being in the right place, among the right people, at the right time, of the right stuff. He wasn't really aware of his body floating slowly up in the water, of the tip of his straining penis breaking the surface like a periscope seeking visions and orientation.

Beside him, MeiMei felt her left foot touch Bannock, and a second later her right foot contacting Tuan's. But she really had nothing to do with any of that. She was a disembodied point of view ascending a molten staircase of golden light, her arms spread wide to embrace the source of that light, which seemed to radiate from all around her, from an invisible bird calling above her head. The bird's song was as sweet as a gold flute. She no longer climbed, she drifted up like a bubble in a tall flute of champagne.

The beat of the night had slowed further, hovered at about one hertz. The frequency was fixed in each person in the tub, their hearts synchronized at sixty beats a minute, the blood in their arteries lub-dubbing in unison. Once a second: one hippopotamus, two hippopotamus, three hippopotamus, four. The inner circuitry of their brains was also firing as one, running subprograms that released treasured molecules into their brain fluid and blood. They vibrated like insistently plucked harps, shook like the throats of twelve-toned saxophones.

Ganzo was almost completely horizontal at this point, his dick poking out of the water like the other guys', one of a ring of standing members moving to inner fluctuations of blood pressure. He could feel Curtsy and Xchab touching him, could feel the music of inner tides and currents, the neaping and seeping that made him. He was alone in the dark except for that compelling, littoral music. Then a star shone above him. As he looked at it, it widened. A comet, a moon, a distant sun. He lay as limp as he had ever lain on a beach recovering from a deep dive. And the sun rotated, sucking his gaze into it, pressing down on him in a rhythmic massage. As he stared into that single light, something happened in him, as abrupt and definite as the flick of a switch. Ganzo woke up.

Seagull had felt like a third wheel when he first slipped into the water between Copper and Aphra, a useless membrane between them. But as his feet touched theirs, his fingers clutched around their necks, and he felt other twined fingers on his own, that changed. He felt as though he stood between them on a high platform, singing while they harmonized, cosmic backup singers stepping up to do a trio turn as the piping grew stronger and the vibration shook deeper down. It was a shell, like the Hollywood Bowl, or more like Red Rocks. And in the darkness in front of him, as he sang his cellular choir, little points of light were coming on. A dozen flames out there in the night, a hundred flares held overhead by an audience of everybody who'd ever lived; a million, million stars that claimed him as their own. His mouth came open and his teeth stopped chattering. He ran to the edge of the stage and dived out into the light.

Copper spun at the center of the sun. Surrounded by fire, warmed like soft wax in its radiation, buffed to metallic glory in its scarlet light, ignited with the proximity of all she had ever sought, she gave herself to the fire that moved upon her. It exploded into her eyes and she burst into flame like a bird bursts into song, like a rocket bursts into a hot white flower of final flame. She was burning, smoke coming off her in twisting, Sanskrit patterns, Tibetan flames layering out of her darkening skin. Her pubic hair rose above the surface of the pool, her nipples shed water like an emerging helldiver... she burned up and was gone. Finally rid of that. All gone.

The piping sound grew faster, louder, more piercing. It was an icepick now, a sixty hertz buzz drawn out into a white lance that ran them all through.

Townsend had fought against what he lacked the reason or wherewithall to fight off. And had seen his defenses flattened, his inhibitions blown to smithereens. He was taken and squeezed flat, kneaded like a tube of toothpaste, forced into a constricted passage of darkness. He was massaged through that black tunnel for centuries, knowing no time or space but the eternal, prodding pressure toward something he couldn't imagine or anticipate. He felt himself longing to be there, to emerge from this bowl of blackness into something open and light. And finally a time came when he could see it, somewhere in the distance or future. He squirmed toward it in vain, but was pumped on towards that light by the constrictions around him. He stopped fighting to be born and let himself flow out into the world. He slipped into blinding light, light that burned him clean and dry, polished him like ivory. He looked up at the lights above and realized he was held by hands. And the hands lifted him upwards and the light became a face. This was where he came from, he realized in exultation. This is my source! And he felt the love of it. It was not familiar to him, so it came over him like twilight, but it was The Love. He loved his parents for giving him life, he loved the children to whom he would some day return it. He loved the world for coming into existence, and for going back to nothing. For the first time since he was born, Townsend felt the motes of rock-deep, unbound, star-high love. His tears blew back out of his eyes, fell to the ground and sprang up as small beings of light.

Aphra, head lolling back on Townsend and Seagull's laced hands, legs spread open to receive the subtle but insistent pulse in the water, thought she saw something forming in the steam cloud the hot water generated in the moist night air above it. There was a swirling in the mist, then a bunching and compounding, then it was as though a shaft of mist—or light, or impulse or hallucination, or something—flared up into the sky; a column of quivering vapor that lanced as far up as she could see. Damn, she thought before she moved past thoughts, ET calling home for real. Hope he's not on roaming rates. Then her eyes dropped shut under the onslaught of internal sensation, the rhythm in the water deepening and spreading up through her body, down through her nervous system, out through her mind. Her head flopped back into cradling, shuddering hands, her long flat stomach muscles fluttered, then convulsed into a running throb. Her head filled with colors, with boomings, with sparkles and spangles and the wide pounding of oblivion.

Loris stood on top of a hill, looking up at the Milky Way, which extended from the center of her eye to the end of the universe. She raised her hand towards the glow of it and her hair was blown back by an almond-scented breeze. The rising wind plucked the pure white cotton robes off her, blew them away behind her. The wind was caused by her own motion: she moved steadily up the causeway of stardust, led by the light of the center of All. The rising wind blew off her hair, then teased away her skin, which rippled back and away from her. The rest of her flesh was also blown away by the rising sirocco of her own acceleration. She was lying horizontal now, flying like a harpoon into the center of the center of the center. Her bones turned to dust, more dross to curl away into her wake, fuel the long, flaming tail she streamed across the beckoning sky. She elongated as her velocity approached that of light, she was expanding, becoming the only object in the universe, streaking forward pulling an infinite cone of change towards the point of her death and birth. She was a beam, a ray just one point wide and infinite points long, motion no longer meaningful. As she pierced the eye of the cosmos... she bloomed.

All six men in the pool ejaculated at once, a tiny Vegas fountain in the glowing water. All six women orgasmed as they had never before, blasted into that sweet death as though lashed onto big rockets. They all shook and spasmed, arching up out of the water as though it had been electrified.

Then they went limp and subsided, slowing sinking back down, their feet touching the bottom, their butts drifting down onto the benches. But they continued to embrace each other, their eyes still closed. Their lips parted. Their throats loosened. In some cases, their balls descended.

From the window of his bedroom in the Lodge's highest room, Francis Ford Coppola looked down at his jungle hot pool. It looked like a carnation, like a fractal star, one of those Esther Williams musical numbers. Twelve people he didn't know from Adam, naked and arranged around the pool with their legs forming a Moravian star in the center. They seemed to be doing some sort of dance or exercise, kind of throbbing. He opened the mosquito screen for a better view through the dome of glowing mist over the pool... just in time to see it spring upward as though somebody had turned on one of those opening night searchlights under the pool. The shaft of golden light, the same diameter as the pool, leaped up, shone into the night sky, didn't diminish as it shined out of sight, had no end.

Then it went out and the whole pool plunged into darkness. Great, Coppola thought, now we'll have to drain the pool to change the bulb.

THE MORNING AFTER SHILL

Breakfast at Blancaneaux was delicious as ever, and the feeling on the open deck as delightful. But the big table surrounded by the twelve "interlopers", as they'd been dubbed by the conference staff and paid attendees, wasn't awash in taste or sensation. They huddled together trying to both come to grips with and avoid examining what had happened to them the night before.

"I wish you'd just tell us the whole works," Copper pouted behind her freckles. "I'd say we're all pretty involved in this by now."

"And if it's the end of the world you're talking about, I'd like to cancel some engagements and break a few dates," Aphra added, only halfway smiling.

"My guess, anybody you date or are engaged to is already broken," Townsend said, but without any real spite.

MeiMei was more on beam. "When you talked about that... whatever it was... being the First Tone," she asked, "Do you mean 'tones' like the date glyphs on the Mayan calendar? Because if so..."

"I'm telling you everything I know," Loris said. "As it comes in. I don't know what's happening, but I'm not questioning it."

"Hard to question getting your ashes hauled that thoroughly," Winston tossed out, pausing to burp. "Best safe sex I ever had."

That was the first time any of them had made a direct reference to the most spectacular part of their evening soak in such terms. The general, unspoken, feeling in the group was that nobody had ever had such a sweeping, explosive, wringing, pyrotechnic, obliterating orgasm before, and maybe nobody would ever again. There was a pause, nobody making eye contact, then Loris spoke again.

"Oh, sorry. There's also this. The four 'tones' are also known as 'calls'. What we heard was the First Call, and each of the future ones will be stronger and felt by more people, until the final one—which will be of universal scope."

That produced another silence until Aphra piped up. "Well, if they're going to be stronger than that, I'll definitely keep them on Call Forwarding."

"Just a call girl at heart," Copper chuckled, tapping her thigh to Aphra's under the table.

"Each one of us has been changed. Or more like... oriented. I get the impression of something like a magnet with a field around it. And each of us will in some way help to bring about the Second Call."

"Ah, a Second Coming," Tuan said, straight-faced. "I assume there are no dates and venues announced?"

Loris shook her head as if embarrassed not to have the press kit ready to hand out, then they all looked up because Francis Coppola was approaching the table.

He walked up, nodded around the circle of expectant faces, said, "About last night..." and gave it the beat any straight line needs to breathe.

"Mr. Coppola," MeiMei said with mock severity, "By your age you must have learned never to utter those words to a woman over breakfast."

He laughed with the rest, but obviously retained curiosity, which Loris nipped in the bud. "I hope you're ready for your massage, Mr. Coppola?"

He smiled back, "Is anybody ever not ready for a massage?"

"You'd be surprised."

And if there are surprises to be had, I'm sure you and your little bunch will be the ones to provide them, he thought. "You know," he said in an avuncular manner, as if veering off into some old-timer's reminiscence, "You shoot all these miles of film, and most of it gets left in the cutting room. Not really on the floor, I'm sure you understand. I've often thought it would be interesting to take all those cuts and splice together a picture. The same cast, same setting, most of the same scenes, but a very different film from what everybody gets to see."

"Sort of a 'defector's cut'?" Tuan ventured.

Coppola nodded absently then said, "I just look at you people, try to get a sense of you, and that comes to my mind. Some other picture than the one that we're seeing."

Nobody had a quip for that so he stepped back and made a courtly, old world gesture. "There will be transportation at the parking lot at one. If anybody wants to arrange something more spectacular than a bus or house van..." he looked at Townsend, "...there's a satellite phone at the concierge. Thank you for coming. I have to say, you've made this one of the more memorable conferences."

"Thank you Mr. Coppola," Loris said. "I know we're party crashers, but your hospitality has been wonderful and your place here is simply magnificent."

He turned and gave her a deprecating gesture of his fingers, straight out of Brando, and said, "It's been my pleasure to be your host. You've entertained me, as well. And an old maxim of entertainment is, 'Give 'em what they want, then beat it for the wings'."

He made an exit worthy of any stage trouper, leaving a dozen people charmed, but still totally unsure what to make of what had happened at the Lodge or why they were even there in the first place.

But there was no doubt of the "why" in the minds of Gareth and Kenny as they waited until Coppola had left the building then jumped up and buzzed over to the twelve-top burning with guarded outrage. "Where is it?" Gareth snapped without warm-up or intro. "It's not in the pool and not in your room."

"And definitely not in our room, where our property belongs," Kenny snipped.

Everybody just looked at them except Loris and Bannock, who knew exactly what they meant. "He," Loris emphasized, "Is in a safe place."

"Well then would it be safe to say..." Kenny started up, but Gareth continued.

"...that since he is ours and we paid you a large sum of money..."

"...plus expenses..."

"...that you're going to be honorable..."

"...not sneak thieves..."

"...and return him to us?"

Bannock looked up from the English muffin he'd been spreading with black Mayan honey and said, "No."

The simple finality stopped the two harried producer-hyphenates, as it was meant to.

Gareth immediately dropped into a whining competition with Kenny, no easy contest. "But listen, you guys... We can work something out."

"Maybe. Some time," Loris said. "But for now, oXo wants to go home so that's where he's going."

"Listen, you two." Kenny actually managed to snivel and bluster at the same time. "There are laws, even in this God-forsaken place..."

Almost everybody at the table turned their heads, taking in the simple grace of the dining deck and teeming green beauty of the morning rain forest, but Kenny plunged on.

"We paid for that thing, it's part of our film, and we are going to have it back."

"No," Bannock said. "You're not."

"Well you make your tactics pretty obvious," Kenny sniffed. "Mr. Incredible Hulk sitting there threatening to turn us into brunch. But things don't work like that in the real world."

"Sure they do." Bannock munched calmly on the honeyed bread.

"Okay, they do," Gareth practically sobbed. "But couldn't you just talk about this?"

"We'll talk." Loris' calm statement astonished the rest of the table, who regarded talking to the Van Niseguys as being as much fun and utility as self-administered dentistry. "Back in L.A. We'll call Curtsy when the time comes. She's on your picture, right?"

"What picture?" Gareth practically shrieked. "You stole our picture, remember?"

"Director-nappers!" Kenny snarled.

"Roasting Flesh," Loris said. "The festival brochure said you start shooting next month."

"Is it a cooking show?" Aphra asked. "Or one of those celebrity roast things gone horribly wrong?"

"It's a teen-aged grindhouse fucking flasher/slasher!" Gareth moaned. "We can do better. But you stole our director."

"And our buzz," Kenny glared accusingly. "You snatched Entertainment Tonight right out of our jaws."

"So it's 'ET meets Jaws'?" Copper asked with feigned innocence.

"I think Curtsy would be practically type-casting for a co-ed getting naked before some fugly freak takes a jackhammer to her," Aphra announced, drawing a scowl from Curtsy.

"Cut the shit, you crooks," Kenny spluttered. "We're going to..."

"You're going to shut up and get lost," Bannock said without inflection, but it was enough to stop Kenny in mid-spittle-spray. Bannock raised a battered hand and made a shooing gesture and the two producers started backing away, glaring as they bumped into waiters and chairs.

"You haven't seen the last of us, Chuckie," Gareth shot back as the two wheeled and fled the room.

"Now that's a dire warning," Aphra said. "I'd just as soon see Hannibal Lector for being overweight"

"You know what really sucks?" Loris said. "He's right."

TRANSPORTED FROM PARADISE

The parking lot was a bustle of people, luggage and conflicting itineraries. Tuan noticed an inverse proportion of luggage: the nobodies who'd paid to come touch the hem of Hollywood's garment looked like they'd packed for a safari, luminaries like Cage and Black had single carry-ons. He and Mei, of course, had the clothes on their backs and two small packs of gizmos and necessories.

No lack of ground transport, as it's called in the trade. A couple of cabs, driven by evil-looking RastaNefarious villains who broke into a lyrical Creole and engaging smiles when spoken to, a shuttle bus from Mayan Island Airlines, the Lodge's own combat Range Rover for those heading for Belize City, connections to the border, the Cayes, or points outward.

"No helicopters, though," Aphra condescendingly observed to Copper.

Copper squinted up through the rainforest canopy and said, "Yet."

The various guests and staff were sorting out into vehicles, most heading for the airport, a few to Caye Caulker to unwind after three days in paradise.

Winston and Cage had vanished, presumably "bowling" at the 420 Lanes. Shane Black was showing some odd arm and shoulder movements to Loris, telling her how she'd eliminated the whole carpal/zygoid glitch he called "writer's wrist", and asking if he could make an appointment with her back in California.

Warm farewells and promises to exchange emails were being made with all the assurance of people who believed they would actually continue to correspond. The "interloper" cadre stood somewhat apart, marked by general lack of luggage and the somewhat preoccupied expressions they'd worn all day. They spoke softly among themselves, both avoiding the subject and wanting to sort it all out.

"It's... I don't know. Like a ship hits a hurricane and things shift around down in the hold." Copper nodded blankly, but Aphra kept after it. "You know it's different, but might not find out until you start unloading. But definitely some differences."

Definitely. Some differences Copper would never really notice. And it would be almost three months before it suddenly dawned on her that she had no further interest in renewing her explorations of the non-world of Ketamine. Pharmaceuticals in general seemed uninteresting, like artificial lures. And it would be almost a year before she realized that she hadn't dumped her lover and started scouting around: an all-time record.

"I don't really notice anything different," Tuan said, looking down as if he'd spot some change in his posture. "I mean, it blew my mind like never before. But I'm still me."

"Probably because you're so normal anyway," MeiMei teased. Like she should talk about people being normal.

"Salvia and mescaline are like that," Copper volunteered. "The more fucked-up you are, the more you notice it."

"In that case," Curtsy said, "How are you doing, there, Aphra?"

Aphra shot her an eye, but tossed her hands up and gushed, "I'm queer no mo'! Bless gracious and praise the Lawd, I'se free at last. All I can think about anymore is big old dicks. And I'm going to donate my time and money to working with Retarded Unwed Manatees."

Loris looked up and caught her eye and Aphra toned it down a little. "Yeah, there's something happening. But nothing I want to talk about. Don't want to jinx the mojo."

Much of what shifted below decks in Aphra had to do with what Loris had noted in her, the conquest obsession with sex. The mighty orgasmablitz had shaken a lot loose inside her, and she felt a lingering effect every time she came, clutching Copper to her in a torrent of sensation with no thought of anything but feeling it more and passing it on. She was also, though it would have alarmed her to know it, developing a rudimentary conscience.

But she looked back at Curtsy and pointed with her chin to where Ganzo was sitting in front of Xchab, talking to her non-stop. "Now right there's a change you might take note of, Barbie. Looks like you might wind up short one boyfriend."

"He's not my boyfriend."

"I'd say it be like that ."

Everybody looked at the Mayan pair. You could spot something different about Xchab right away; there was no longer the shadow of subservience or abnegation in her pose or manner. She sat up, looked sharply, took account. And as for Ganzo...

"It's like he just came to or something," Curtsy said. "Snapped out of some kind of coma. I could never figure him out before. He wasn't stupid or gorked out: he just wasn't really around. And now..."

At that particular "now", Ganzo was telling Xchab, "So you see. You are who you are, you have your place to be."

"I see that," she said. "I just wanted... But who am I, then? Where do I belong? Do you have answers to that?"

Ganzo's steady gaze never wavered. "You're like me. You belong with me. We'll leave here and go find the place where we should be."

Xchab stared at him. This was one different guy than the one she'd seen around before. And he seemed to know exactly what he was saying. She looked at him and tried to weigh him against Winston, against the tantalizing promise of the glittery world she'd been moping around the edges of. She said, "Those men want to put me in a movie."

"Good. Maybe that will happen. Here's what I think. You should come with me. I feel that very strongly. I want you to come with me. Stay with me."

There was plenty of room for a girl to be thinking, Come where? Stay where? But Xchab looked at this sturdy, open young man of her own people and mold and slowly nodded her head.

"Tell you what," Bannock said, when people seemed done with gawking the young Indian couple, "I've had more remodels and refits in my head the last couple weeks than I can really deal with. Right now I just sorta feel the way I did after eating those mushrooms. Except maybe more so. I'm just... up for it. That's it, I guess: I'm all for it.

"That's it!" Curtsy blurted. "That's it, right there. Bring it on."

"When I was a little girl," MeiMei said softly, getting everybody's attention with her soft tone of voice, "My mother would always say, 'When you get old enough you'll know better.' Right now, I feel like I know better."

"That's what I would say about it," Loris said. "I feel like I'm charged, informed."

"Back in my 'hood," Aphra told her, "When peeps informed it worked out bad for 'em."

MeiMei and Bannock laughed and Loris smiled wide, but went on, "I have knowledge. Knowledge isn't just information, it has its own intelligence."

Aphra and Townsend both nodded at that, caught each other and looked away.

"There's only a certain amount of knowledge in the world and nobody can have all of it," Loris continued. "But it wants to flow out and know everyone. That's what the Call is: to know with total certainty who we are and what the world is, what we mean."

"And now you on top of all that? Got the inside skinny?" Aphra wasn't adverse, just wanted to hear her answer.

"It's coming to everybody and everything in the world," she said. "We have each been called to a task and our task is to prepare the next call, which will come in one year."

"Fine with me," Aphra grinned. "I'm still shakin' like a jellyroll from the last one."

"And the purpose of the Second Call will be to bring people together to amplify the next Call, each one affecting more people, more meaningfully, than the one before."

"Is the final one in 2012? What's its purpose?"

Loris stopped, looking at her—or through her—for a long moment, then she said, "The Final Call is its own purpose. Which is the purpose for everything alive, everything that exists."

"Hey, I heard last calls before," Aphra cracked. "Means you don't gotta go home, but you gotta move your action out the door."

There were smiles. but it fell a little flat. Then Townsend spoke quietly and simply. "All I notice is, I feel more like me. Trouble is, I don't really recognize myself."

"But you will," Loris told him, looking at him intently. "We all will. That's why this is happening. Why everything happened in the first place."

"Wow, cool." Winston muttered. Then straightened up and looked right at her. "But nothing you said makes any sense."

"It will," Loris said. "It's what sense is for in the first place."

"Tell you what I'm wondering here," Aphra said, and everybody turned towards her as she said, "What is the sound of one hand pulling your leg?"

Everybody laughed, including Loris. But she said, "You already know the sound. You just heard it. The First Tone."

As more revelations of inner alterations trickled out of the waiting passengers, testimonials Aphra thought of as "Change You Can't Help But Believe In", Copper suddenly started laughing and motioned her closer. She leaned over and the redhead said. "God, you know what this sounds like?"

"What, child? What?"

"The obligatory character arc."

Both of them clutched their cheeks and screamed, "Oh, noooooooooo!"

"First Tomb Raider, then Crystal Skulls," Aphra said, pursing her long-suffering lips. "Now we're Raiders of the Lost Arc."

THE ROAD AGAIN

Bannock, wary of untoward developments and never relinquishing the backpack in which oXo was hammocked, kept an eye on the two Valley Vultures, who were shooting him poison glares while being pestered by a bouncy, Hollywood-hyped Curtsy. But also took in his pool-mates standing there in shabby clothes with no belongings. Finally, uncomfortably, he spoke quietly to them, "It's been great meeting you... well... freaks. I'll miss you all. But listen, is everybody going to be okay, here?"

He was pleased, and a little surprised, to get nods all around. Winston made a "smooth sailing" gesture with a flat palm. "I'm stoned, I'm possession-free, and just got rid of a woman I had to take care of. How okay can I get?"

MeiMei and Tuan nodded, impressed by his implied gesture, but about as okay as a professor and millionaire newly in love can be. Copper and Aphra unconsciously inclined their heads toward each other, Aphra wearing the buddhistic calm of somebody in possession of an extremely high-ticket secret soon to become a government secret. Quasi government, anyway. Real government, probably. Seagull was evidently going to third-wheel the two "lebanese" girls for awhile, token different drummer.

Curtsy was in however good hands you would consider Gareth and Kenny to represent and anyway stacked blondes are seldom refugees in this world.

He gave a lingering look at Ganzo, making sure he was understood. The beachcomber slowly nodded and Xchab seemed to drift a little closer to him.

"So we're all heading to town?" Nods all around, except for Aphra and Copper, who pointed to the airport jitney. Even Curtsy, and less comfortably, the producers, were on the Belize City run. So he decided he wasn't needed. Which was just fine.

The shuttle motor fired up and Copper was moving towards the door, but Aphra turned and looked at Townsend, who stood apart and stared at her steadily, without expression. (Unlike Gareth and Kenny, who regarded Loris and Bannock with undisguised loathing.)

She stepped away from the shuttle door and motioned him closer. He paused for a long moment, then walked to within a pace of her. She waited for him in a natural stance, no posing, and looked at him in a very unaffected way that made him immediately suspicious. "Hey, Bigtime," she said. "No hard feelings?"

Townsend stared at her a beat, then turned away.

"Hey, wait," she called out and he stopped but didn't turn. She said, "We suck, huh?"

That got him to turn and look at her, so she blurted. "I mean, you know, as human beings. We're rotten and pull fucked-up shit."

He nodded non-committally so she went on. "Ever think about changing that? Be somebody, you know... good and decent and not like deceitful and all that?"

"Lately it's crossed my mind."

Now she stopped and regard him thoughtfully. "Well, maybe me too," she said dubiously. "Almost. But listen, MeiMei Chiang? She's good, you know? Not all sappy sweet new-age good like that Loris, but she's a straight-shooter and doesn't hurt people, you know?"

He just stood, watching her.

"And I fucked her over. Too. Just like you would've, if you'd been a little quicker. But maybe you could help her out."

"If you're so concerned, why not give her camera back?"

She smiled, but wiped if off and hurried on. "Look, I don't know quite which alphabet frat you work for. But whoever they are, they get shit done, I been noticing. So you got that guy on the yacht. Ronchel, on the Nahual. Heading south out of Cozumel like three weeks ago. So maybe somebody you know might be up to sorting his ass out?"

He started to give her a quick, shitty answer, but just didn't feel like it. "Yeah, sure," he said. "Consider it under advisement."

Then he stepped away and she moved to the door of the shuttle and stepped up inside. Townsend made no move to board either vehicle. He'd made his arrangements. He stood watching the shuttle pull out, enduring Aphra's smirk and fingertip wave through the window. Copper leaned over and kissed her palm, then high-fived it against the glass and they were gone.

Alone on the lot except for two Mayan groundskeepers hauling out a barrow and brooms to restore the immaculate grooming, he pulled out a pocket widget and checked the battery and display. Very tricky lady, that one. But basically, like many private spooks, living in a two-dimensional world. Like bugs crawling around on the floor, hiding behind bottlecaps and cigar butts, not realizing they could be apprehended from the mystic third dimension known as "up".

Curtsy sat in the very back of the bus with the Melrose Metrosex duo, who were as removed as possible from the rest. She chattered about wrangling dolphins, working in pictures. But she was a girl whose idle chatter wasn't that unpleasant to take in, especially for Gareth, so they weren't loath to have her along.

"Remember, I gotta do that thing first. In Belize City. Okay?"

"Sure," Gareth said indulgently. "Meanwhile we can talk to that little termite in the government film office about their program. Now that he's had time to come down from his coke blitz at the festival."

Curtsy grinned happily, her hot-weather ponytail bobbing. Then a shadow flitted across her expression and she got all earnest. "Listen, I know you guys paid like a quarter million for oXo, then lost him."

"Lost him?" Kenny asked shrilly. "Is that what you call it when somebody takes your property out of your room at night? Maybe you and your little pals, for that matter?"

"Hey, not me. Okay? But where does that leave you guys? How can you take a hit like that and still make a picture?"

"Thanks for caring, Curtsy." Gareth laying out his nicest manners. "It's complicated. Money's funny in The Wood. But okay, we don't have a director for that picture..."

"Or a script, or a treatment, or a concept, or a vaguest fucking idea." Kenny elaborated.

"All true. But we gotta whole lotta love at that seminar."

"And for once he's not bullshitting. We've got meetings at Zoetrope and Warners, exploring doing something down here. Maybe a real Maya picture. Maybe up there at the Lodge, down at the coast. Coppola loves it. He wants to see more of little Chabex, too."

"Xchab. That's great, guys. So are there dolphins in it?"

"Sure. You bet. I'm taking meetings with Flipper's people, seeing if we can use Willy free." He smiled to let her know he was more or less joking. "But how about Xchab? Is she going to be around? It might be almost a year before we do it, but we'd like to think..."

"Don't worry. She's going to be in a great place where they'll take good care of her."

"Great! Mind telling us where?"

"No problem. When the time comes. Now about your company for this film... where do you think I would fit in best?"

"Let's see," Kenny mused. "Blonde, built like a brickhouse, hot as a cell phone at Pico and Alvarado, full of mindless enthusiasm and dumb as a box of rocks... I'd say, executive producer?"

"I was thinking more like marketing," Gareth said. "Now all you need is a Best Boy."

"They're all best," Kenny said. "One way or another."

After carefully storing the pack with its crystal passenger, Bannock shifted to where he could keep the corner of his eye on Gareth and Kenny in the back. He knew they'd be back into a cell phone footprint before they reached Belize City and that the really dicey spot would be getting out at the bus station. Meanwhile, he turned his attention to Loris, asked her something that had been on his mind. "What I don't understand...you were so crushed to be parted from oXo, but now you're trying to lose him for keeps. So, what's the difference?

"Because he's going home. Don't you see? He has his spot in the scheme of things and now he's on his way. You said you were taking him home and you came through."

"Well I should confess, I didn't exactly..."

"Hey." She put a finger to his lips. "You did it. You can't sort out the reasons on things like this: you made it happen. And I'm never going to forget that."

"Well, you might, after a few years. So I figure I'll stick around and remind you."

She shot a sidelong look past the cascade of her hair. "Are you professional tough guys really allowed to say mushy stuff like that?"

"I'm considering retirement. Know any good beaches?"

"You're pretty young for that."

"Well, you know... I was looking at those movie people up there. And kept thinking, "Just how hard can this business be, anyway?""

"Oh, God. Are we going to jump off 'Get Biggie' here?"

"Actually, I think our next role should be 'Get Lost'."

"How else can anybody ever get found?"

HOMECOMING QUEENS

Bannock had dropped them off in the rented, dented van, as far up the rutted trail as he could navigate. And would wait for them there as long as it took. He sat on the ground, leaning back on a tire and just listening to the rain forest breathe and twitter. Funny how you didn't hear the world making its little sounds until you decided to listen. He inhaled the scent of pine and primordial rot and decided he was better off here than back in that motel with Tuan and Ganzo. That had to be a fairly one-way conversation. He gazed out into the forest and starting hearing it.

It had been a long hike and some of the girls offered to spell Curtsy, carrying the duffel of gear Tuan had hastily rented from that shady tour operator in Placencia. But now, as they trod carefully in the shadows of what seemed like a totally different world, that seemed meaningless. They were here in this egg-shaped cavern with a floor of blue water and tiny ceiling of sunlit leaves.

Curtsy, with the pack slung across her back, was the last one down the rope and even though she was no stranger to *cenotes,* she was subdued by the cathedral air of this one. She moved quietly up beside the other girls and looked down into water as clean and clear as the air up above.

There hadn't been any discussion when Loris told them about it. Aphra was hot to get back to the States, but Copper was dying to come with them and each of the six girls who had been in the hot tub that night had deeply felt that they should be here. MeiMei had realized, though not mentioned, that having everybody present meant six people who would know about the place, could come back and seek out the power, or just money. But she had a feeling nobody would do that. Just a feeling.

Curtsy was sizing up the cave and the water at the bottom, definitely impressed. She asked Loris, "How did you know this was here?"

Loris laughed and said, "How do you think?"

She reached into her backpack, pulled out the bundle of soft cotton, and unveiled oXo. The skull seemed almost matte in the cavern's filtered light, a primal green dancing with a sphere of gold light from the sinkhole overhead.

Aphra stepped over to stroke the gleaming occipital. "Way I hear it, those two dorks paid you a good chunk of change for that thing. Now you playing Indian giver?" Just to fuck with Miss Bettysue PerfectCenter. She nodded towards Xchab and mimed embarrassment, "Scuse me there, honey."

Xchab regarded her impassively as Loris buffed oXo with the shroud cloths then looked at Aphra and said, "You heard wrong then. They paid Bannock. Who took him from me, and now he stole him back from those guys. But that's meaningless, really. There's no ownership where something like this is concerned. We've all done our part to bring oXo home. Including those film guys financing it."

"Fine with me. Information wants to be free, and all that," Aphra shrugged. "Long as it don't get too free and there's no market for it."

Curtsy opened the duffel bag and started passing around masks and fins. No snorkles needed since they weren't going to be cruising the surface. She pulled her mask on and started pulling off her work shirt.

"Okay, everybody gotta get totally nekkid for this one," Aphra said in the same tone of finality they associated with Loris.

MeiMei, unbuttoning her blouse, looked at her suspiciously and asked, "Why?"

"Because we look so fine that way!" Aphra whooped and was almost instantly nude. Copper stripped down just as quick, and pulled the mask over her unruly red mop. The other girls all laughed and started following suit. Except Xchab, who merely undressed and stood naked and flatfooted to await the next move. Aphra looked around and gave a whistle, but something in the way the high pitch echoed in the cave silenced them again. Curtsy knelt at the edge of the pool, closely examining the bottom in the green/gold twilight, then smiled at the others and pitched forward into the water. She was at the bottom, peering further back into the subterranean lake, as five other splashes sounded around her.

She surfaced and looked around at the other girls. "I see some light back there," she said, "But it's a long damn ways."

"I think I heard that light at the end of the tunnel jive before," Aphra sneered.

"If there's light, there's air," Curtsy returned flatly, and once again Aphra had that awareness of being in a new element where she wasn't the prime player. Loris glided over to Curtsy and held oXo out, half of his dome above the water. "You take him. You're the one who can make it all the way."

Curtsy nodded and told them all about how to relax and rebreathe to get a maximum lungful of air. Then she dropped out of sight and kicked off powerfully into the long tunnel that ran through the bedrock. She held oXo in both hands, stretched out in front of her, zooming through the water with a crystal figurehead out front.

The other girls were behind her, each of them moving as well as they could. And each of them reached a point they knew was as far as they could push it. They would each stop, hover in the water, look down the tunnel to the faintly lit chamber at the end, and turn back. The last one to rein up was Loris, who stared ahead at what she knew she would see, a hemispherical dome in the rock, illuminated in yellow glow from above. And in the center of it, a broken-off stalagmite rose, creating a low plinth. She turned back, pulling her way along the roof of the grotto, but looked over her shoulder to see Curtsy flash into the chamber, gold/white body fluorescing in the filtered sunlight, and place oXo gently on the little pedestal before kicking the bottom once to rise up and breathe.

Five girls paddled in place in the deep end of the pool by the entrance to the tunnel, not looking at each other, just waiting for Curtsy to break the surface. Then she was there, bounding out of the water like an orca, whipping water out of her hair, laughing like a little girl at recess.

All six of them were quiet then, a circle of heads in the water. Without conscious thought, they extended their arms and found their hands on each other's napes.

Copper broke the calm, almost reverential, silence. "Think we could get oXo to spring for one more metagasm?"

"If he won't, it's on me," Aphra purred and the other girls laughed.

They broke the circle and climbed out of the water. MeiMei looked around, wondering when was the last time people were here. Had the Mayans placed oXo there? Or had he been there for millennia awaiting them? And somebody must have come to take him out and put him into circulation. She'd buy about anything at that point.

They dressed without much chatter, Curtsy quietly collecting the masks and fins and tossing them back in the bag. On the way out, Loris stopped at the bottom of the rope and looked back. She called out, "See you, oXo. I love you," and nobody even thought it was silly. In fact each one of them had a sudden thought in the same moment. One of those little mental jingles that makes no sense at all. "The Love loves to love you all."

FINAL PAPERWORK

Aphra saw the knife blade—a raptor claw of some gray matte spaceage metal—come through between the warped door and the frame, then flick upwards to toss the latch, but there wasn't much she could do about it. Caught flat-footed, about the only way you get caught when you're sitting on a toilet and the stall door blows open on you. And who else but Townsend Hardley, once again barging in on her private participles?

Her eyebrow arched delicately as she regarded him over the fist he stuck in her face. The fist that came wrapped around another dull-metal object that reminded her of one of those rubber hand-exercisers with finger grooves, but had this thing like a cigarette filter sticking out between two fingers and pointing right between her eyes.

Never saw one of those little tricks before, but got no doubt it would blow somebody's head off or poison their whole family or whatever nasty shit it was supposed to do. So she said, "Could you be a little dear and grab me some toilet paper from the next stall?"

Townsend didn't smile or blink, just kept the drop on her, held his hand out, and snapped his fingers. She'd thought she was home free, somehow getting off the airport jitney and slipping down here to the bus station in Belize City. Cute 2-D scrambling, unaware of hawkeyes from Up. So here he was with compulsion in his fist, and there she was with her slinky little undies around her ankles, a day late and a roll of TP short. He didn't want to speak to her and didn't feel like he really had to.

"Can see you're no gentleman, Town," she said archly. "You didn't hurt Copper on your way in here, did you?"

"No need. I know you have it on you. Give."

With a world-weary sigh, she reached up to where she'd hung her traveling purse to keep it off the decidedly unsanitary floor. Slowly, carefully bringing it down to where she could reach inside.

And he quickly, carefully took it from her. Held the straps in his teeth and plunged around inside it.

"You find that poisoned wolftrap I left in there?" she asked innocently. "Starting to feel sleepy from the Micky I put on the strap?"

He came out with the camera, quickly flipped the little door open and felt for the memory card without taking his eyes off hers. Then boom, he was gone.

She sat motionless without a sound, waiting to hear the restroom door close before she moved. Then the stall door popped open again and he tossed her a roll of the local toilet sandpaper and hit her with his rodeo smile. "No hard feelings."

Outside the nasty ladies' room, he moved through the grimy, echoing terminal, heading for the chartered car waiting in one of the bays. He saw Copper buying bottles of water for the trip to the border, showed her the bag, dumped it on a bench and got in the car.

As he pulled away from the apron, Copper moved over to pick up the purse, looking nervously at the restroom door. But Aphra walked out, cool and collected, to reach for the purse, sling it over her bare shoulder, and give her a grin. "Whiteboy just don't get up early enough in the morning to nab lil orphan Aphra," she said. Copper laughed her fool head off.

LATENT IMAGES

Denny "Stonecold" Mercer slipped out of his trenchcoat, damp from the showers of some little-known tropical capital, and hung it neatly over a bamboo chair. He removed his battered, "if this hat could talk, the stories it could tell" fedora and tossed it on the rack in the corner. All without taking his eyes off the woman on the bed: dark-skinned, exotic, of primordial, pre-whiteman breeding.

He'd completed his mission, against improbable odds, and brought home the bacon; squeal and all. He brushed the pleats on the front of his khakis, then undid the tricky knife/camera/buckle and let them fall to the floor. She was looking at him, ancient eyes staring out from the hard young body. He moved across to her, sat on the bed, checking around for snares, eye-holes, or listening devices. He reached to touch her soft, mounded breast and she sighed and rose towards him. "Aren't you going to turn off the television?" Lluvia moaned softly.

So he turned off the television and tossed a yellow towel over the lamp. And once again sat down beside Lluvia, old eyes in a young body in an obscure tropical capital. Slowly, shyly, she reached up to him. And in the moment her soft hands touched his face he felt a shift inside himself; a deep, tectonic meshing of two psychic worlds grinding into accommodation. Here he was. He eased down beside her, drinking in her touch and diving deep into a world where there was just no need to be anybody other than himself.

MeiMei didn't much like the look on Tuan's face as he viewed the screen of a "VIP" computer cabled to her camera in the Presidents' Lounge of the Houston airport. He glanced at her, blank, and said, "There's only one file here, Mei."

"There should be at least six shots. Things got a little confused there, but..."

"It's a video."

That set her back. How could that be? Well, one thing to do. "Let's have a look."

He started to shuffle his chair to one side, but she perched on his knee with an arm around his neck and peered at the screen as he clicked the file. There was the usual bevy of idiot Windows questions and kvetching, then Media Player opened and she saw a very close-up shot of the face of Aphra Alisander.

"Uh-oh."

Tuan turned up the volume. Aphra, looking into the camera in a mixture of faux embarrassment and possibly semi-valid sincerity, said "Hey, Chinatown. Hope you're not in Mexico watching this in a holding cell. Yeah, I took your camera. Beat Townsend to it by a nanometer. Sorry, kiddo. But I really need this stuff and I'm not into chasing down that yacht asshole. Thanks for everything and maybe I can return the favor some day. Give me about a six month lead with this shit, okay? Then some day you'll get an email from "Black Adder". Respond and I'll send you your stuff, is that cool? I figure you're not going to be back up to speed in academia before then, anyway. And I'm going to see if I can make some of your troubles in Mexico go away. Good luck. Hope it works out with the little Flip. I thought he was pretty cute, actually. I mean, you know, considering. I'd nab him myself, but I don't do short. Or smart. Or male. *Hasta la vista*, baby."

They both stared at the screen until Tuan moved to shut it down before it repeated. They both sat, MeiMei leaning her head on his.

"I gotta admit, she's kind of cool," she said. "For a back-stabbing, amoral bitch."

Tuan nodded absently, obviously lost in thought. Finally he said, "Do you think she can really sort out Mexico for you?"

"I really doubt it. You made it clear who that asshole is."

"Then there's the Old Assholes Network, Mexico Chapter."

"I don't know. I really want to know what's on that thing. Think maybe hypnosis might help? Recovered memories?"

"Aren't those always about sex abuse by parents and satanic cults?"

"You know what? I'm actually not too keen to get back to work right away. I've always been a workaholic but..." she turned to kiss his brow. "I never had any reason to goof off before."

"An excuse for procrastination and laziness. Few men could aspire to a higher calling."

"So what's this O.B. place like?"

"Ocean Beach? You'll love it. It's got a special beach for dogs."

"You'd enjoy Seattle, too. Until it starts raining."

Tuan reached into his carry-on and pulled out two boarding passes. "Two first class to SeaTac," he said. "I figured you'd want to touch base with your family."

MeiMei turned in his lap to hug his neck. And whisper in his ear. "I agree with that bitch on one thing: I hope this works out, too."

"It has to," he said. "We already did the honeymoon."

She was a hundred yards outside the reef, and pushing deeper with every dive. She felt slow and awkward with the strap-back SCUBA fins, but was getting some serious depth. Between recovery spells, lying still on the surface with her hands and legs pointing downward, she slowed her mind and oxygen metabolism with the meditation Royal had taught her years ago on Roatan. She started to ramp up another cycle of hyperventilation and breath packs and there they were, like she'd known they would be. Knew they would be. That's the way it was now, for some reason: she knew things.

Bruto was there first, rocketing past her in his coarse way, shouldering her roughly aside. Her heart jumped. They'd come for her then, and they came to her now!

She felt Pinoccio bump her feet, two other bodies slide along her legs, then Caruso made a pass at her waist as she shifted to an upright position, her head up as she laughed and whooped. When Bruto barged back through she caught his muzzle with cupped hands and he dragged her ten yards before diving and shaking her off. By the time she was back to the surface, Chido and Xochil had both nosed by, spinning her around.

Caruso nuzzled his beak into her crotch and she reached down to lean her hands over it. He reacted with a powerful ripple of his frame, powering him into what would have been a surface-clearing leap if she hadn't been leaning on his nose. She shot up out of the water, balancing on him like the cross stroke of a "T", then sailed off to splash down with a happy yelp.

Okay, fellahs, she thought to them, let's get down and get rowdy.

It wouldn't hit her right away, not until she was back on shore meeting Gareth and Kenny at the Paraiso, but she felt nothing sexual with the streaking black beasts. Not even a tingle. It had all been like rough-housing with her brothers, or playing co-ed basketball at college. One of the guys. And her guys came through, had her back.

Meanwhile she lay on her back in the water, with her head lolling back, looking up at the sky. Waiting for one of those scamps to bump by her butt with a fin. And suddenly, out of nowhere, she remembered lying like that on top of an ancient pyramid. And feeling the body, seeing the face, of a man who wanted to offer her heart to the Gods.

REVOLTING DEVELOPMENTS

"Got four shots off that memory card," Weistler said with a big butt-smacking grin.

Townsend nodded. He'd pulled and switched the card from MeiMei's camera in case Aphra somehow managed to re-acquire. Hadn't peeked until he handed it over to Monsoon. Now the whole thing was done and he could get rid of these clowns. "And they all came out all right?"

"Weeell," Weistler drawled. "Yes and no."

Well good, Town thought. Or not. He said, "So 'Yes' sounds good."

He glanced across the featureless White House basement lounge they'd grabbed to debrief him, hoping for a hint from the Monsoon. But the big Irish was ignoring him, watching that stupid POTUS show on a microwave-sized TV set. No clues there and The Weaseler was being a dick about it. But now he had a manila folder and was pulling out some eight by ten color glossies. He handed three to Town, holding the other one up and adjusting his glasses for a good look. "They're all damn good, but I like this one best."

Townsend casually picked up the glossies and fanned them for a look. And plunged into a personal interior abyss.

The first one showed Aphra, naked, giving him the finger. In the second one she was bent over, looking back over her shoulder with a feral grin as she shot him the dark side of the moon. The third one was her and that redhead fire freak, also nude, wrapped all around each other and obviously taking their own portrait in a full length mirror. He sat and stared. thinking what we always end up thinking about reversals of that magnitude: No way. No motherfucking way.

Weistler held up the fourth print, which depicted the two women in a much spicier embrace on a bed, Aphra holding the camera up for a shot at the mirror. "I want a couple of blow-ups of that one and a dozen wallet-sized of the squat shot," he said.

Townsend just sat, staring, his mind racing. How many camera/bugs had the bitch had down there? He was wracking his brain for a way to turn this around and couldn't come up with jack.

Weistler leaned forward and laid on a confidential tone, "So what's it like porking a dyke, anyway?"

Townsend stood and moved up to where his thighs touched the desk, leaned forward with his fists on the top and stared at The Weaseler with an impersonal kind of write-off that imparted a faint, chilly hint of the real fears and menace of The Field. When he recoiled with a sickly smile, Townsend said, "Pretty much like your mama, except she won't swallow after it's been in her ass."

Monsoon turned from his fascinated/appalled view of the POTUS show and roared with laughter. "That's telling him, Townie." He was breaking the tension between the other two guys, and moving to defuse what he knew must be starting to eat Townsend up. "Look, you think you got problems? Check out the guy I have to re-elect. Mugging with George Clooney like he's Bill fuckin' Cosby or something."

Sure enough, on the little screen Barak Obama lolled at ease in his host chair, inviting intimacy and confidence from his guest. Clooney nodded appreciation for the applause following his last mot, then asked the host of the POTUS Show, "So what did you spend your stimulus package on?"

"Stimulants." When the laughter died down Obama added, "What, didn't you read my book, George?"

"Holy Motherhumpin' Macree," Monsoon moaned as he switched off the set and threw the remote across the room. "I keep thinking he's crossed the line, then I start thinking there's no such thing as a line anymore."

He stood up and heaved around the room for awhile, puffing about the hated show his boss was drawing top ratings with. Townsend watched as he shook it off and turned back to the matter at hand. He lumbered across the floor, pulled up a leather-like ottoman to dump his ruddy bulk right in front of the faux Morris chair where Townsend sat, and leaned in like the Dutchest of uncles. "Look, whatever sort of emo framistan you were stupid enough to jam into this thing..."

"And, honest injun here, I can't blame you much," Weistler stuck in from where he lounged with his weejuns on the pristine upholstery of a GS-12 class sofa. "She's the five alarm hot sauce, no two ways about it."

"Not so much that..."

Monsoon guffawed. "Well, apart from *that*."

Townsend slogged on into it. He'd committed himself, for some reason he didn't completely understand, to playing this completely straight: total debrief, no cover, no chaser. The only one who'd had anything to tell him about Life After Megagasms had stressed that: truth brings truth, lies bring lies. Take the chance and you'll reap the harvest. Not the best career advice for a professional spy, but he didn't sense even an ounce of bullshit around that Loris babe. So here goes:

"She was like... like a colleague. A peer. Nobody else really understands what I'm doing. There's nobody to talk to about it. She's like... I don't know... like somebody I played with in college but now I'm a Yankee and she's a Red Sock, but we can talk in a place all the fans and leg humpers don't know about. That make sense?"

Weistler gave Monsoon a searching look, drawing a shrug, then a rueful grin. Then, "That makes a lot of sense to both of us, actually. What are we going to do, tell our wives what we did at the office?"

"If you could rent a hall big enough for all your wives."

"I'd have to look around for one big enough for just Erin these days."

"Somewhere inside that mound of lard there's still the sylphlike lingerie model, trying to eat her way out."

Townsend was still on the edge of his chair, leaning forward in a dark tension, but realized that the vaudeville was for his benefit. And was surprised to realize that he appreciated it.

"Look, kid," Monsoon rumbled. "There's no shame in getting faced by Beyonce, there. Aside from the obvious, you're a rookie, she's an old timer."

"Same age as me."

"Yeah but..."

"But she was grifting intel in her teens, Town," Weistler cut in. "Working top-level exec parties, clubs. Doing vice callouts to get next to top CEO's and mid-managers. Guys who run conglomerates. Are they stupider than you?"

"And what were you doing in your teens?" Monsoon asked.

"Dunking forty-three points in the Tri-State final," Weistler answered the rhetorical question. "Pitching three games in the College World Series. Playing bass with The Fugknuckles, I believe they were called. Laying waste to sorority row."

"Then you get almost like, tapped in to the Agency." Monsoon scowled. "After college. We should probably be recruiting little gamesters out of grade school. Running Spy Scouts camps like the gooks."

"Instead of getting the job because of my old man's network of admirers and envious loathers? Find out I'm not the right timber from some lez bimbo?"

"Who also has a bit of a parental shadow behind her, it might interest you to know. Difference was, her mom taught her Trade, wanted her in The Life."

"Just on some other side," Weistler snickered. "She probably runs into people all the time, old Panthers with their berets turning grey telling her what a great organizer her mama was."

"Not to mention what a come-to-Jesus great fuck."

"And she probably runs into them as little as she can."

"Like I said," Townsend said quietly, "Overlook a few obvious differences and we're the same thing. Karmic teammates or something."

"For one thing," Weistler said straight-faced, "You're both wild about pussy."

Monsoon saw Townsend about to stand up and walk out and spoke quickly but with an authoritative warmth. "Hang on, kid. Gimme a minute more, okay? You shut up, Jerry."

Weistler shrugged and leaned back to see what riff his colleague would roll out this time. He was actually surprised for a change.

Monsoon paused, looked Townsend back into his chair, then hiked a little closer and spoke right into his face. Talking like a man who'd taken off his official hat for a minute. Townsend slumped back and listened.

"Let me ask you a question, Townie. Why the screaming, shitting, wall-kicking, paddywacking fuck did we start a war in the Middle East?"

Townsend warped out on that one a few seconds, then shifted into Dudley Dooright. "So the terrorists wouldn't win? To make the world safe for Monday Night Football? To preserve our way of landing on aircraft carriers?"

"I'm being real here."

"Okay. I guess I'd say what anybody not stupid enough to repeat what we told them would say: Oil."

"So show me the oil," Weistler chuckled. "Show me why we're paying billions to rebuild Shithole On Sandgrit over there while they're pulling bejillions in petroprofits."

"I thought we agreed one of us would shut up," Monsoon growled, then returned to Townsend. "You're not that dumb. You probably figure it's all about some wheels within wheels hidden behind gears and guts down in the Beast. Nothing to worry your pretty head about because you're an action figure. The Jimmy Bond ninety percent of the agency really want to be but can't cut the mustard."

"Junior Grade."

"I'm getting to that. Let me tell you from a pretty damn unique insider perspective why we jumped off our personal jihad against Islam. Let's take a closer look at George W. Bush."

Great, Townsend thought. First I get the "thinking with your johnson" smirks, now I'm getting some old nutcutter's history lesson.

On the other hand, maybe that's what it calls for.

"One thing pretty unique about Dubya," Monsoon went on in his armchair lecturer mode, "How many presidents had fathers who were presidents? You're looking at a guy who made it to the most powerful position in the world and was still falling short of his old man's accomplishments. And Senior made it pretty clear he thought Junior was Howdy Doody. How could he possibly top the Pop?"

Townsend was jolted out of any lull in his attention at that point; staring at Munson as though he'd just morphed into a guru channeling Dr. Phil and Dr. Ruth.

"He didn't make his Dad's marks at Yale, was the joke of Skull and Bones, zippo military record, screwing around baseball instead of the Company. Second rate blowby right down the line. But there was one thing his father failed to accomplish."

Townsend almost whispered. "Take out Saddam."

"You got it," Monsoon nodded as if to a dull student finally picking up on the picture. "You talk to anybody who was around the Oval back then. Anybody who'll give a straight answer—and lotsa luck finding that—and they all know it: Georgie came into office already committed to going after Hussein. He'd been dreaming about it through the whole Clinton Scare and he hit the ground running."

"Shit, that almost makes some scary kind of sense."

"The only mystery is how he sold the sane, grownup world that such a reckless action was necessary to take care of a guy who didn't even make the Top Ten Dangerous Asshole Dictators list. But if there's one thing I've learned after blowing my life working in top-level politics is that it really comes down to personalities. You just can't go back and examine the political parameters and components of the times and explain a Bonaparte or Alexander or Hitler or Bolivar. They're pretending to now, of course, revisionizing history to get rid of bronze Paul Bunyans and Elvises that make them feel inadequate, but I'm telling you: things happen in this world because of diseased personalities, not graphs and flowcharts."

"And you get down to it," Weistler said, almost to himself as he examined Monsoon's thesis, "It's generally over something stupid and petty."

"Napoleon too short," Monsoon nodded. "Hitler too scrawny and Jewish-looking and gay. Duke's fucking the French king's wife. Chancellor snubbed the Premier at a state dinner. Chief of Secret

Police is impotent. The professor's parents tossed out his teddy bear. All explanations that bear no explanation. Most times nobody's even got a clue what's going on. And as little as we understand politics and economics, Christ knows, it's the lore of the savants compared to what we know about psychology."

Townsend took a slow pan of these power players, Monsoon regarding him like a kindly uncle—which would have creeped him out except there was that gnawing feeling of gratitude again—and Weistler highly impressed but curious as to how he'd take it. He licked his lips, looked over their heads for a moment. Then said, "It's been frustrating."

Monsoon nodded, pleased with the outcome. "I can see how it would be. And now this. And just maybe your old man's lingering fingers had something to do with you sucking a goose egg down there? Look. You're too young to be frustrated. That's one of the privileges of age and experience."

Weistler laughed, but kept that curious eye on him.

"I think things are different now."

"Know what?" Monsoon leaned back, regaining distance. "I was sort of picking up on that. God knows what went on down there, but I'm hoping it does you some good. Here's what I'm suggesting: don't let your hard-on for your old man make you burn down the world."

He didn't squirm or flare behind that. He'd already figured out what the older man was saying and was filing it away in places that seemed to have been recently prepared to accept it. What he said was, "Thank you very much. For everything. Next time I'll do better."

Weistler laughed and Monsoon filled in the bassline with his own jolly rumbling. "Next time is the New This Time," he said.

"You hear a fat lady singing?" Monsoon asked him.

"If so, I hope it's not Erin," Weistler tossed in. "She could shatter the plate in Yankee Stadium."

"You said this thing ties into this whole Maya bullshit? And the little chink is still after some way to make sense of it? And that splib rugmuncher is still after it? Well then..."

This time the gratitude threatened to break out in a tremor, so Townsend was very careful when he nodded gravely to the corrupt old machinators and said, "Thanks, you guys. I won't let you down."

"Good. See if you can tape the dirty parts this time out."

SHE DON'T STOOP TO CONCUR

Aphra sat up with her back straight as any finishing school girl, a Pollini-encased toe markedly not tapping the floor in impatience, while The Right Honorable Elijah Weatherwax scanned an eleven by fourteen high-contrast print on Oriental Seagull paper with a slight touch of selenium toner to render it about as black and white as any photograph ever gets. He grunted a few times as he scanned what he had already seen, already read a stack of reports on, already bounced around various think tanks and academic lairs. Finally he cut his pinkish eyes toward her and said, "That's one beauty of a picture, honeysuckle."

"Thanks, Mr. Chairman. A retired Navy darkroom tech I've been using for years. A real artisan."

"And if nobody else has said it, I'll say it now: it was a bang-up job. If I believe half of your report, it was one hell of a grab."

"Thanks again. So it sounds like payday for lil ol Aphra."

"Weeeeeell," he drew it out and chewed on it until she expected him to hawk a chaw into a spittoon for emphasis. "Yes and no."

Well, thanks and no thanks, you satchel-ass cracker, Aphra thought. But played a deuce on it. "I'm afraid I don't understand."

"Well, now," he leaned over the desk and flicked the print to her, "Just read that thing to me."

Uh, oh. She slipped the print back towards him and said, "Sorry, I snuck out smoking the day they had the Maya cartoon spelling bee. But that's not really my job description here, is it?"

"It's not? Did you contract to bring us an artisan-quality picture of Sammy Skull spouting little high-roglyphics? Or intelligence regarding proceedings on the dates in question?"

Shit. Shit, fuck, piss in your granny's ears. Try for the high hand, only way she could see to play it. Either that or see if they've got some kind of Berlitz course in MayaToon. "So you're sitting here at this desk, Senate Office Building, ready to go chair one of the heaviest committees in the galaxy, and you can't get some egghead, tell you what that shit's trying to say?"

"Couldn'ta put it better myself. Seems this is some very old version of a very regional kinda, you know, whatever it is. Only a couple people could translate it. Only one we got a line on."

Oh double fuck-shit-piss, Aphra almost wailed. Just let me guess. About five five, cute as a baby duck, of the Buddha-head persuasion? All she said was, "Let me guess."

"You got it, sweets. Any idea where the good Doctor Chiang is these days? Because we can't find her. And apparently it wouldn't be a good idea for her to go back to Mexico, where she was working. Seattle University said she called in sick for a couple of months."

"Doesn't matter. She wouldn't give me the time, not even the finger. She's sure to be pissed off solid from about the time she powered up that camera and found out it was empty."

"Ironic, ain't it? But there's an original out there, right? Or did you get that shot up?"

Aphra stared at him silently. So I can either find and win over a disappeared Chinagirl in company of a guy who got her out of that dragnet in Mexico and is probably ready to brain me and the horse I rode in. Or I can take on Señor Kingpin wherever the hell his wandering yacht has got to. Let me get back to you on that one. I shoulda just sold this shit to Popular Archeologist and got shet of it.

She stood up and gave a cool look at Sen. Weatherwax, who knew exactly her dilemma and watched wolfishly for her reaction.

"I'm all over it, Senator. You'll be hearing from me."

Weatherwax turned his full-candlepower rum-flushed beam on her. "Damn! I like your style, woman. No whining, just get back out there and kick ass. Tell you what, I'm gonna cut you a partial because like I said, you done it up real fine. Not so big an advance you don't wanna go get me that translation, though. You ever thought of going into politics your own self?"

"Senator," Aphra said, rising elegantly and gripping her Vuitton clutch chastely in front of her. "I have been a liar and thief, a spy with no allegiance or scruples, a traitor, and a whore."

She walked to the door, opened it and turned to face Weatherwax, who was waiting for it. "But there's still a few depths of scumbucketry I just can't stoop to."

She closed the door on his fervent applause and started hatching a new batch of plans.

LADY BEE GOOD

Mama Pop wasn't that impressed by the boy: a dreamy beach bum, was her take. But the girl? ¡*Que horror*! The slut skirt, those Nazi boots, the stubborn look... one of those little renegades who wanted to throw over centuries of tribe for the latest gringo fad or perversion, is what it all looked like. She let Puch deal with it, pretending not to listen from the porch while using an old corncob to scrub the kernels off maize for tortillas.

Puch couldn't figure it out either: these two just show up and seem to expect the Pops to put them up, take them in to what they were doing. He stood talking to this Ganzo under the workers' *palapa* while his little *ponkita* girlfriend wandered around the edge of the sinkhole, peering down at The Works.

"So Curtsy told you to come see me. Did she say why?"

"No. She said she didn't know why, but it seemed like the right thing."

Puch eyed Ganzo closely, his scan mixed with a little male territoriality. "So how long have you known Curtsy?"

"Only weeks. Since she came to live at my house."

Great. Well...

"She said we should talk to your mother."

"She said what?" Puch was flabbergasted and didn't mind it showing. "My mother never liked her, said I was crazy to be involved with her, and since she left me, she really doesn't like her."

"It's what she said."

Puch looked around, then motioned him over to the lip of the pit. Ganzo stood on the drop and solemnly surveyed the construction site below, which had become a ball court almost indistinguishable from the ancient ones at the ruin sites. He pointed to the growing pile of stone at the far end, where it rose to the level ground in tapering tiers, and said, "It's a pyramid that leads up to the head of a queen. A god, you know?"

Puch stared at him, then back at the stone breaks. He could almost see it himself. "What makes you say that?"

"I just see it," Ganzo said. "I look at things and see the shape that wants to come out."

Well, that sounded possibly useful. "So you make things? Masonry? What?"

To answer, Ganzo pulled a rolled towel out of the blanket purse he had slung over his shoulder. He held his forearm parallel to the ground and let the towel unroll over it, the way he always displayed his wares. Puch stared at dangling necklaces and bracelets, earrings clipped on to the towel: treasures crafted from the leavings of the sea. He bent to examine them more closely, touched one that really caught his eye; a classically stylized bee Ganzo had scraped out of a pork bone using broken files and old drill bits.

"They're beautiful," he said. "This one looks like it should be in a gallery."

"I made it for Xchab," Ganzo said. "I'm saving it to give to her when..."

Puch looked up at him but that was apparently all he had to say. Suddenly he was aware of his mother standing right behind him. She also reached to touch the little bee, made of bone scorched golden brown with a hot machete blade. She also looked up at Ganzo, and said, "What's her name?"

"Xchab Cab."

"We keep bees," she told Ganzo and Puch knew it was somehow part of her questionnaire for these two.

And the Pops did have beehives. For generations they had husbanded the rare, stingless Yucatan bees as the Maya always had, harvested the treasured black honey.

Puch nodded and motioned towards the back of the property, where the hives were set among the blossoms of the jungle. But his gesture stopped in mid-air as he stared at Xchab, now standing directly above the tapering ridge where Ganzo had seen a headdressed goddess head, looking down at their constructions and moving in a slow, silent dance.

And behind her, like a moving black shroud, a living version of the mantle of the Virgin, was a swarm of bees. She moved like a swimmer in thick syrup, her movements stately and composed for such a young girl. And each time she swung an arm out from her side, it was the lead edge of glistening black wing. When she clapped her hands over her head, two columns of bees clashed behind her, splashing upwards into the sun. She twisted and trotted and windmilled her arms, all shadowed by that teeming cloud of wings.

Mama Pop watched her for over a minute, then turned to Puch, not looking at Ganzo. "Find the boy a place in the shed with your workers and ball-players," she said, turning away towards the house. Over her shoulder she added, "The girl can have Yoli's old room."

Puch looked at Ganzo, regarding him blankly, and grinned. He stuck out his hand and Ganzo grasped it. "So we stay here?"

"No doubt of it, amigo. Dinner is in an hour."

"Then I have another message for you." He rolled the towel carefully, stuck it back in his shoulder bag, pulled out a piece of creamy stationery with the Blancaneaux logo across the top, and handed it to Puch.

Yo, Pooch,
I thought you'd find it in you to take care of this pair.
You're a sweetheart.
Kurtz
P.S. I don't think I'm done with you yet. So watch your ass.

He read it twice then looked at Ganzo, keeping his face impassive. Ganzo said, "She said only give you the letter if you invited us."

Puch shook his head with a smile that wasn't really amused, but not quite sad. "She doesn't really know me. Yet."

CALL WAITING

It was dusky in the green-filtered light of the *cenote*. A slight, steady drip from the surface swept a regular moiré of rippled light across the gleaming quartz dome that was oXo. At about an hour before noon, and an hour afterward, the water in a triangular area around his little "throne" would brighten for about ten minutes as a golden ray of direct sunlight penetrated the bush, threaded into the hole, and glanced off the reflective white sand and silt at the bottom. And for those twenty minutes each day the transparent eyes would transmit a gold-toned glow throughout his entire glassy form.

If a piece of rock could have thoughts, oXo's would often turn to what he was bringing to bear, midwifing into existence.

And if a stone shape could have awareness, he would be aware of a web of humans with whom he was connected by The Love, his central essence and message. Aware of what they were doing, without having any awareness of it themselves, to bring about his next great Call, the next ringing Tone of his countdown to timeless oblivion.

And if a solid chunk of quartz could have feelings, oXo would feel like he was dying to get high.

THE END OF THE BEGINNING

Yaxche was right there every second, of course. That's the way it works when you've lost your mooring in time.

And, as so often, focused on a young woman kiting on the winds of Big Change. Winds that were gathering around her, were blowing stronger and stronger the closer these people sailed to The End.

Yaxche lost herself in regarding a young body in timeless, placeless motion, a dark nimbus of winged creatures outlining her every movement.

One more girl on this stretch of temporary land, one more young woman who is somehow actually her. Another one living and dying under her unflinching gaze of cycles that never end, just cycle into greater cycles.

The life and tears and release and vitality of each girl creating a moment... and every given moment is an end unto itself.

FOOTNOTES

1   The Nohoc Mul is the tallest pyramid in the Yucatan at 130 feet, 30 feet higher than the Wonder of the World at Chichen Itza. Its name, somewhat anti-climatically, means "Big Mound".

2   An ancient Mayan city inland from Tulum, the Cobá site lacks the fame—or traffic—of Chichen Itza or even tiny Tulum, although it is close to the beaches and tourist zones and is an extremely large and impressive site, including one of the highest pyramids in the entire Maya zone. It also has a lovely setting with scattered ponds (the probable source of the name, meaning "Ruffled Waters"), and a network of mysterious stone-paved roads to nowhere in particular.

3   A *Chilango* is a person from Mexico City; in Mexico worse than being a New Yorker. So *"Chilangoware"* indicates the "Native Curios" she's selling are from factories upcountry.

4   A *huipil* is the classic *"ropa tipica"* dress, or native Mexican garment. A simple cotton shift, it is elaborately embroidered.

5   *Hennequen* is a natural fiber, similar to yucca, indigenous to the Yucatan. Won't degrade from sun like nylon or rot like cotton: one of the most desirable fibers in the world and perfect for hammocks. It was *hennequen* that built the plantations and mansions of Merida, but the introduction of synthetic fibers wiped out the industry and today it's very hard to find an *hennequen* hammock, even in the Yucatan.

6   A *caracol* is what we would call a "conch". (*"Conchas"* are flat shells like clam shells in Spanish.) The word literally means "Face-Butt", the anatomy of such creatures being such as it is. They lend their name to any spiral object, such as a circular stairway: *El Caracol* is the name for the ancient observatory at Chichen Itza.

7   *Coralcaturas* is a word of Ganzo's own invention. From "coral" and *caricaturas*, Spanish for "cartoons".

8   Ernst Forstemann, a royal librarian at Dresden, was the first to decipher the design of the Mayan calendar.

9   The Dresden "codex", an accordion-folded book painted on pounded fig bark, dates to Chichen Itza in the late eleventh century, generally thought to be the oldest written work from the Americas.

10   Sir John Eric Sidney Thompson's A Catalog of Maya Hieroglyphs in 1962 became the standard reference for study of the meaning of Mayan glyphs.

11   Dr. Victoria Bricker, one of the foremost Mayanologists alive, was the first person to comment on the relation of the Mayan Great Cycle end date with the winter solstice in December 2012.

12   Jose Arguelles, a Mexican-American writer and artist, is one of the people most associated with the whole 2012 concept, though scholars dismiss his melange of I Ching, New Age, cosmic paintings, and psycho-babble as parasitism, rather than scholarship.

13   Terence McKenna, another new-ager extremely associated with the Calendar and 2012, is harder to dismiss than Arguelles, and his early writings on hallucinogenic mushrooms and meditation are fascinating. His "Timewave" theories are also interesting, but basically their attachment to the Mayan Calendar in order to cement the end point of time or "novelty" have no validity except his own considerable charisma.

14   An old port and logging town, Chetumal is an unpreposing place to be capitol of a state that contains Tulum, Cancun, Cozumel, Xel-Ha, Isla Mujeres, Cobá, the "Riviera Maya", and a large collection of *cenotes*. Other than the usual political glitz, it's seen mostly as a gateway to the Belize duty-free zone

15   The Museum of Mayan Culture in Chetumal, capital of Quintana Roo, Mexico, is an attempt to elucidate and commemorate the culture of Mayan people throughout Mexico, Guatemala, and Belize. It's a beautiful museum with eye-catching displays and exhibits. It tends to show replicas, rather than actual artifacts—a fact that finds favor with many who don't like seeing sites looted—and to explain rather than just showcase antiquity.

16   INAH, the National Institute of Anthropology and History, is a sprawling bureau in charge of all ancient sites and ruins in Mexico, and even oversight of development and use of declared urban historical zones.

17   The PRI, "Institutional Revolutionary Party" for all you oxymoron fans, was the "Evil Empire" that ruled Mexico for eighty years, until 2000. The longest running incumbency on Earth, it was termed the "perfect dictatorship" and "the ultimate machine", ruling through tentacles of leftist/realpolitik power incorporating unions, family clans, and virtually every aspect of Mexican life. They are often depicted as dinosaurs —outmoded but still huge and scary.

18   The "Caste Wars" illustrate an interesting contradiction: that the Maya, while noted as one of the most pacifist Native American groups when left to themselves, have also been among the fiercest warriors in the hemisphere when pushed to fight. They were the last Amerind group subjugated by Europeans (if, indeed, they are actually subjugated today). The Caste Wars, as they were called by the Spanish settlers who the Mayan rose up against, were a bloody revolt over the last half of the nineteenth century. They will be further dealt with in future volumes of Mayan Calendar Girls.

19   The "Diving God" is a deity depicted only in Tulum, the only Mayan city on the beach, and so called because of the upside down posture.

20   Though not as large as Tikal and other Mayan sites, Palenque is noted for it's superb quality of architecture and art. It is a major star on the hippie/backpacker map of Mexico. Maybe you can see why.

21 Temple of Inscriptions, This "temple", located in the Palenque archaeology zone, is one of the most significant Mayan edifices. It is unique in several ways: the only Mesoamerican pyramid built strictly as a funerary monument, the rich tomb of Pacal the Great, the "King Tut of Mesoamerica" and for it's wealth of sculptured panels with extensive hieroglyphic text.

22 The Sun Stone, originally found in Mexico City, is the most famous image of the pre-Hispanic calendar, and though not "Mayan" is inspiration to all the "Mayan Calendar" art—including the logos of this book. However, it's not that far-fetched since the Mayan astronomy and hagiography influenced the calendar concept of the entire region, just as the Julian and Gregorian calendars did in Europe.

23 It is important to realize that the "Tzolkin calendar" did not exist as a physical entity, any more than a "billing cycle" or "teen age years" are physical things. However, the interpretation of the calendar as rotating gears is so intriguing there are many such physical models available today, including a huge working model in the Museum at Chetumal. This permutator of twenty named days and "*trecena*" of thirteen "tones" to produce a 260 day holy year is the "Tzolk'in calendar". Later a huge Great Year "wheel" was added, meshing with the Tzolk'in to produce the 5000 year "*baktun*" that will end in 2012.

24 "Time Wave Zero", a series of papers, talks and finally book by McKenna was a major origin of "2012ology", tying together his ongoing theories that the I Ching showed a progressive decline in "novelty" culminating in a sort of "null history" in 2012, feeding the weirdness leading to things like the disaster film. And, need we say, this book.

25 Xibalba is the Mayan underworld: the name means "place of fear". It is ruled by twelve Lords of disease, paranoia and death. They are evil conniving spirits against which the Mayan heroes struggle. Some ugly customers.

26 *Junior* has a very specific meaning as a Spanish word in Mexico. It refers to a highly despised class of people: sons of rich, powerful politicians, drug lords and business kingpins (there is little distinction among those categories), especially in Mexico City. These are spoiled, reckless kids protected by their family position. They abuse their total impunity from the elastic and wholly-owned Mexican legal system to do whatever they want without consequences.

27 Mexico City is surrounded by a zone under direct Federal jurisdiction, similar to the District of Columbia surrounding the American capitol city. All power in Mexico is centralized there and it is one of the largest urban areas in the world. Mexicans sometimes refer to it using the Spanish pronunciation of D.F. as *El Defectuoso.*

28 *Santa Muerte.* The Catholic/occult veneration of "Holy Death" in Mexico could take a book to explain and there are *many* cool images available. Some feature chains/rosaries, and white raiment, which help Copper's interest: beginning with a two day *salvia* trip, since which she has always felt the presence of Death just behind her right shoulder.

29 *La Anima Perdida.* "The Lost Soul" is practically the totem of Copper's personal "religion" of fire, dance and oblivion. Generally shown in art resembling a Tarot or *Loteria* card: a young woman hip-deep in a lake of fire, raising hands from which chains dangle.

31 *Lucha Libre* is Mexican pro rasslin' and it makes the WWF look serious in comparison. These wrestlers are folk heroes, sometimes shown in low class movies as crusading against crime in capes and masks... yet it's reported on the sports pages.

33 The Federally-enforced minimum wage in Mexico, for 10-12 hour days, pays the average *peon* around five U.S. dollars. Per day.

34 The Olmecs were Mexico's earliest civilization, and produced art that echos Egypt's finest sculptures and are some of the most famous images in Meso-american art.

35 The Mayer Center at the Denver Art Museum is dedicated to increasing awareness and promoting scholarship in the fields of Pre-Columbian and Spanish Colonial, based on the Museum's excellent collection.

36 Dumbarton Oaks is an important American museum associated with Harvard University. Named for an 1800 Georgian mansion in the Georgetown area of Washington D.C.—once the home of V.P. John C. Calhoun and subject of a Stravinsky concerto—the museum houses an extremely significant collection of Pre-Columbian artifacts.

GLOSSARY

Chilangoware, Chilango	People from Mexico City—or more properly, the surrounding D.F. or *Distrito Federal*. They run the country and are cordially despised by Mexicans, even more than New Yorkers in the United States. "Chilangoware" would indicate that the authentic Mayan artifacts were manufactured in the Big City.
Huipil	The classic *ropa tipica*, or "native garment" for women: a simple cotton shift, often elaborately embroidered.
Indio	The word for "Indian" or "native Amerian" in Mexico is *indigena*. *Indio* is a racial slur, signifying genetic stupidity, not too far off the American "nigger" in connotation.
Ponk, Ponikita	"Punk" in Mexico, often applied to *El Ponk* music (by Shaka Ponk, for instance) and the whole dress style that goes with it. *Ponkita* is the feminine diminutive, "lil punk girl".
Pendejo	A classic Mexican insult: "asshole", "dumbass" and anything in between. The literal meaning is "a piece of pubic hair".
Me'ex káak	Mayan. Literally "beard turtle", but in some senses could be equivalent to "crazy codger'.
Mota	Pot. 420. Chronic. Hell you expect a hippy to be smoking?
Hongos	Literally "fungus", but Mexican for "shrooms". Stay tuned for more on that.
Perico	Literally a parrot, but a very common Latin American slang for *coca*—cocaine.
Obras, obritas	*Obra* is the Spanish version of the Italian "*opera*", and refers to an artistic work: *obritas* is the diminutive.
Santeria	The Latino voodoo, a Catholic/pagan spin-off based on spirit possession.
Milpas	Small subsistence corn fields. The word has a resonance of agrarian reform in Mexican culture.
Nopal	*Nopales* are like small trees with prickly pear cactus instead of leaves. The pads are peeled and eaten, and rural homes often have *nopal* hedges around them. They have a highly country connotation (*nopalero* is slang for a hick) and a highly national significance: the Mexican seal and flag feature an eagle sitting on a *nopal*, eating a snake.
Chicle	Chewing gum was at one time made exclusively from this material, a tree sap harvested like rubber and found only in the Yucatan. A *chiclero* is (or was) a harvester of the sap.

Cenote	The Yucatan is a limestone slab riddled with holes like Swiss cheese. Many of these holes open to the air above. Some are caverns with stalactites, some are entirely underwater and connect to others. The main mythos of *cenotes* however, is their use in the Mayan's human sacrifice: large collections of treasure and bones have been found in sacred *cenotes*. They are often the local water supply.
Jipi	Spanish phonetic spelling of "hippie".
Pedo Viejo	Direct transliteration of "old fart". Mexicans do not use this expression, but it's heard from American expatriates.
Puta	As in, Italian, means "whore".
Colegio	Not a college, but a private high school, or K-12, in a country where the public schools are virtually useless. The main subject is generally English. The way to think of *collegio* students is the term "preppie", which is close to the Mexican term, *fresa*.
Cuate, compa	Pals, buddies, *amigos*
Baboso	*Baba* means saliva or drool, so a *baboso* is basically, a drooling idiot.
Eso	Literally, "that", but meaning, "That's it", "you said it", "attaway".
No hay pedo	Literally, "There's no fart", but means "no big deal", "don't sweat it".
Pinga, verga	Slang for penis or "dick"
Chingón	A highly Mexican word, very *macho*. It means "cool", but has the weight of "the person or thing who can fuck everything else."
Tremendo	Not "huge", but rather, "awful".
Chidísimo	*Chido* means "cool" or "hip" and the superlative ending is characteristic of the Snot Class
Güera	Literally, "fair", a blond or fair-skinned person.
Coralcaturas	This is Ganzo's invented word. From coral and *caricaturas*—meaning "cartoons" in Spanish. Therefore describing the coral-created "drawings" as he sees them.
Guapa	Means pretty, good looking—*guapo* means "handsome"—but is often used as a noun to address women, like saying, "Hey, Babe" or "Hello, cutie."
Mana	Short for *hermana*—"sister"—this and *mano* are almost identical to the Black American "bro" or "sis".

Provecho	Though coming from a word meaning "take advantage of", this means "dig in" or perhaps the best equivalent of *bon appetit*.
Pura carne	"Just meat". The Spanish draw no distinction between "meat" and "flesh". So really, refers to the carnal appetites.
Gabacho	Same as "*gringo*", but less of a slur. "*Gabacho*" used to mean "Frenchman", but now refers to "*Yanquis*", which were once only N.E. Americans, while "*gringo*" came from "Greek". Go figure.
Mulatas	Mulatto women, cross of Negro and White or Hispanic bloodlines. Commemorated in the Santana song, "*Oye como va, mulata.*"
Periodistas	Spanish for "journalists": *periodico* meaning a newspaper. Side note: in Mexico journalists are seen much as Americans see lawyers, rotten and corrupt. Spawning jokes about knocking them off as civic improvement.
Frijolero	A rare instance of Spanish slang derived directly from an American expression: literal translation of "beaner". The satiric song "Frijolero" was a monster smash hit for Mexican pop stars Molotov
Guayabera	Also called "Mexican Wedding Shirt", a staple item throughout Mexico, but particularly in the south. Often embroidered, frequently with pockets at the lower hems, the loose, cool guayabera is acceptable male attire ranging from beach wear to fairly formal gatherings. It's extremely popular with Mexican cops and hired assassains (usually the same thing) because it makes it so easy to conceal a handgun. Guayabera, RayBan sunglasses, and a badge tucked away just in case is the standard uniform for a Mexican mob killer or bodyguard.
Tipica	*Ropa tipica* is "folk garb", traditional native Mexican wear.
Mestizaje	Means "mixing", the elemental blend of European conquest and Indian natives to produce the typical Mexican *mestizo*, the majority of the population.
Peon	Has come to mean the common laborer. Also, tellingly, refers to a chess pawn.
Fresa	Literally means "strawberry", but is used to describe preppies, social butterflies, plastic airheads.
Pinche	This odd word is essentially the "bad adjective" in Mexico. Equivalent to "damned", "shitty", "fucking", depending on usage.

Peliroja	Redhead.
Matón	From *matar*, meaning "to kill", but actually applied more to any bully, tough guy, or thug than to actual killers.
Triciclo	A three wheeled bicycle/barrow that is many people's first transportation on Isla, carrying their luggage through the vehicle-free downtown streets.
Sindicato	In Mexico, means a labor union, not The Mob. Though sometimes the distinctions get very blurred.
Foclorico, foclor	Folklore, most often applied to traditional Mexican dancing.
Naco	A hick, rube, low-class and uncultured mouth-breather.
Buena onda	Means on the order of "good vibes": a great guy, good people, etc.
Riquisimo	*Rico*, or "rich", is the way Mexicans describe delicious food, physical beauty, wonderful sensations. The "*isimo*" suffix makes it superlative.
Padrino	Godfather, in both the church and crime sense.
Malecón	In Latin America, any boardwalk or promenade by the waterfront. All copying the name of the ocean-side street in Havana, in the same way such walkways in America are called "Boardwalks" after the original in Atlantic City..